ONE

MAN'S

JOURNEY

Theresa A. Bandaccari

2013 I Street Press All Rights Reserved
828 I Street Sacramento, California 95814

Published In United States by I Street Press in Sacramento, California.

ISBN: 978-0.9898209-6-7

Library of Congress Control Number: 2013920097

Printed in the United States of America

Cover shot taken by the author of the California Coast @ sunset.

ABOUT THE AUTHOR

Bandaccari lives with her Mom and their two cats in California. She graduated from California State University, Sacramento in the early 1990's but prior to that she graduated from Consumnes River College in 1987. It was while she attended CSUS that she published in two poetry anthology books.

However, she has been writing for a number of years; those poems were the start of her publishing career. She worked a variety of different jobs which she brings into her stories. Writing has and will be her first love along with her family, her animals and her friends.

People need to be aware that they might appear in one of her stories as a character or experience. But she writes about places she knows firsthand since she's been there. The writing stems from issues that come to her, and she builds a story on a central idea.

DEDICATION

To Scruffy and all Vietnam Veterans this is for you. You served your country proudly and honorably, and people didn't understand what you were fighting for. They still don't understand what you witnessed and experienced over there unless we took the time and effort to talk to you about it.

Tom Jones-thank you for your input on Vietnam protesters and other background that I didn't know before.

I hope I've given you all a voice in this story of Joshua Hernando.

Theresa A. Bandaccari

1

Journey of one's life is unique because the individual is unique. It's our signature of who, what, where, why and how we are all that shape our lives since its one's very own blueprint or fingerprint of who we will become. Yes, it's a journey we embark on all our own despite the people we meet along the way. But how fortunate or unfortunate, we are to have these experiences come down to us and the decisions we make along the way. But we are the masters of our own destiny, and no one else can change it. But they might alter it to some degree. But this is one man's journey life.

Joshua leaned against the railing to watch yet another sunset over the California Coast before his deep, raspy cough consumed his slow, frail body again. He was in his mid-sixties or sixty-four to be exact, but his forged birth certificate listed him two years older than he actually was. But it got him into a war no one fully understood why, yet Joshua wanted to be a part of it all.

Working class roots had gone back several generations in Joshua's family. However, he was second generation of US citizen here since his grandfather had come from another country at seventeen. But his father had been born in the USA. But it wasn't clear when or how his grandparents met and married because they hadn't discussed it with Joshua's Dad, Martin. But Joshua knew how his parents met at a dance and knew instantly they were meant to be together forever.

Martin was a baseball player and a son of a farmer.

Sara was a retail store clerk and a daughter of a plumber who worked for the Southern Pacific Railroad when they met. Together, they would raise Joshua with his siblings Andrew, Caroline and Elizabeth based on Martin's salary. But Joshua didn't realize his true worth since he was born dead last. However, Martin was drafted about middle of the war that was considered a war to end of all wars. His job allowed him to check on his family during the war due what he did by working on vehicles and airplanes for war effort. While Sara took care of their four children until Joshua was seven.

She would re-enter the job force, and she would excel in the insurance industry. Meanwhile Martin had landed a job with the Federal Government before and after his time in the service because of his skills as mechanic and able to learn new things quickly.

He wanted a change by the late forties briefly, so he worked on the early computers which took up most of the room and was cold most of the time. It was around the time Joshua's birth 1946. Then he decided leave this job in 1953. Thus, Sara headed back to work to support the family now. She left their children with Martin as she worked. No one really knew what he did after the government job since it was only a short time after the end of the War? It was the early fifties now and plenty of work to be had.

Martin and Sara had been children who survived and lived through the Crash of 1929 and the recovery of the great Depression. Then the soldiers who came home from another war that nobody would understand in the mid-fifties and talk of another war that might come in the near future. But Sara and Martin didn't want to see Andrew much lose Joshua to war. Andrew was only twelve at the start of the Korean War, but Martin didn't want to lose his boys to any war despite they were too young for the Korean War. He saw first-hand how war shattered families in his war, but he never talked about it.

Martin's war was considered a war to end a war of all wars, however, it didn't happen. It has been doomed to repeat over ever since then. He sheltered them from horrors of the war. He knew he could be called to serve again. But he wanted his boys to ride bikes, play baseball and be quote "normal boys". His girls were into boys and other girlie things that Martin didn't fully understand. He was an only child and worked on his father's farm when he didn't play ball or go to school. So when he met Sara at a dance, it was a break from his ordinary life. They were married two weeks after the dance and started a family right away. He could hardly wait to marry her.

So by the end of World War Two, Sara had Joshua who would be their last child. Martin didn't want any more children after his war. Then Korean War made him believe he and Sara had made the right decision of not having any more children. Now in the early sixties after the Bay of Pigs another war was beginning to surface, and Andrew might be called to serve since he was the oldest child and son.

But Joshua got someone to forge a false birth certificate and went off to the Vietnam War instead. Before Martin and Sara could stop him; he was off to basic training then to the war.

They could only hope he would come back to them

alive and in one piece if they cared at all. But it kept Andrew out of the conflict and deeper into law school like their parents hoped.

Caroline and Elizabeth would be free to go to college or start a family. Joshua wasn't expected to do anything spectator with his life. But he found he was good in hand to hand combat and keen eye for the firearms. But his family never knew how well he did since he cut himself off from them the day he enlisted.

"Dad, please come inside," a woman said, as she stood next to Joshua at the open deck. "The cold air isn't good for your lungs."

"I don't want to, Rita," he snapped back. "I like being out here."

"I've got hot clam chowder and fresh cracked crab for you, Dad. So please come inside," pleaded Rita.

His cough started up again, as she eased him back into his wheelchair. It was more aggressive, as they headed inside. She wheeled him up to the Oak table where he could still gaze outside. She rubbed his shoulders and mid-back, as the cough went silent once again. Then she headed into his kitchen to return with a tray of two bowls of piping hot clam chowder. She placed one in front of him and handed him a spoon before she placed hers next to him. Then she headed back into the kitchen.

"Where's the damn crab, woman?" he asked, as he reached for the fresh black pepper on the table.

"I'm coming with it now, Dad," she answered, as she returned with two plates of stacked high of shelled crab and bowl of sauce on the side. "Here you go, Dad. Enjoy."

"Thank you, Rita. I'm sorry."

"It's, okay, Dad," Rita said calmly. "I know it bothers you to cough like that. The kids will be here in a couple days."

"Why?" he asked in anger.

"It's Christmas, Dad. They want to be with their Grandpa on Christmas."

"But I don't know why. I was hardly ever there for you and your brothers and sisters growing up."

"It wasn't your fault, Dad. Mom was the one who was unfaithful and took us away from you. You tried to find us for what, or how many years," Rita said thoughtfully with a small smile.

"Twelve long, hard years so by then you had two stepfathers," Joshua replied back. "I worked long hours to hire those PI's to find you."

"I know, Dad. You've told me countless times. Now enjoy your chowder while it's still hot," she said, as she touched his hand.

"I love you, Rita and Patrick, James, Luke, Susan and Joan very much," he replied with tears in his eyes.

"I know, and they know, Dad, too, deep inside."

"I see so much of your grandma in you. She understood me better than I knew myself. Grandma Sara had a sweet and loving nature just like you. She would have loved you best. It's not say she wouldn't have loved them because she loved deeply for your Grandpa Martin and her other children except for me."

"Oh, she loved you, Dad."

"I'm not sure about that, Rita. I wasn't as smart as your uncle and aunts were and are. That's why I went into the service," explained Joshua.

"Dad, eat, please."

He nodded. Rita ate her fresh crab and clam chowder in silence. He stared at her in between bites of his crab and saw a little girl of five all grown up before him.

She and Joan were twins just like Susan and Luke. He had only been back in their lives for the last thirteen years.

They weren't sure so of him at first, but Rita was the first one to really reach out to him. She held a special place in his heart for that reason. The others held back at a safe distance maybe it was something their Mom said about him.

He or Joshua didn't know or much care because the day Rita showed up on his front doorstep there was hope in his life again. He remembered it was a cold and wet Christmas 1997. Rita's hair was wet and messy much like his in his youth. She stood there in a red raincoat with a plastic bag held tight to her chest, as she held onto it for dear life.

"Daddy, can I come in?" Rita asked, as her teeth chattered from the cold.

She was seventeen and had seen him two days earlier on her Mom's front porch. Her Mom stared at him then yelled at him to leave her and their children alone. They didn't want him in their lives, so he left the porch. But he left a postcard of where he was now. It was of the California Coast, and Rita had seen him place the card into the mailbox from the front window.

"Come in, baby girl," Joshua answered, as Rita walked in. "You go shower while I run your clothes through the dryer. There's a robe on the back of the bathroom door. Help yourself."

She nodded and found her way to his bathroom. There she turned on the hot water and slipped out of her wet clothes and the red coat that clung to her. It was worn out and didn't give much warmth or protection from the weather. She also left the plastic package on the floor, too.

However, Joshua was curious of what it was, but he respected his daughter's privacy. So he only gathered up her wet clothes and socks. He left her one of his flannel shirts, a pair of socks and sweatpants to put on under the robe. He dumped her clothes in his dyer and added another log onto his already blazing, warm fire. Then he warmed some piping hot clam chowder for her along with a cup of hot green tea.

He angled his chair to face partly the fire, and the other towards the couch. He placed the tea and chowder beside his favorite easy chair and waited for her return on his couch which was distance from the fire. He stared into the fire and didn't have to wait too long. She emerged dry and wore what he had left her.

"Thank you, Daddy," she said politely, as she sat in his chair.

"That's for you, baby girl. I hope you like clam chowder and green tea. It's all I have right now."

"It's, fine, Daddy. Thank you," she said, as she took the bowl into her warm hands.

Joshua got up and placed a blanket over her legs and brushed back her long, brown hair from her egg-shaped face.

"Warm enough?" he asked her calmly, despite how

happy he was to see her.

"Fine, Daddy. And thank you."

He walked back up to the fire to toss yet another log on before he returned to the couch. He stared at the fire again but also caught her out of the corner of his right eye.

Joshua couldn't believe one of his six children was in his house and back in his life. He found it difficult to believe but said nothing.

"Dad, are you all right?" Rita asked him, as he stared at the darkness outside.

"Fine, Rita, and thank you," he answered politely back, "Just remembering back..."

"To... or of what?"

"Our first meeting after twelve long, hard years being apart from you all those years and not knowing what kind of life you had without me, do you remember it?" he asked thoughtfully. "I remember the worn out red coat."

"And I remember the clam chowder and the warmth of that fire. I didn't want to leave the fire or you that day."

"But I had no legal right to you, Rita. Your Mom was right again."

"But I had come to you under my own free will."

"I know, but you were still a minor back then."

"I wanted to know everything about your life but didn't know how or where to start," Rita said calmly.

"I was so nervous and excited, too because I was looking at a grown child not a five-year old I left behind. I didn't know what to say or do either."

"So you gave me hot green tea, clam chowder and

warm clothes to wear while my clothes dried. You were off to a great start," stated Rita.

"I suppose, by the time your Mom found you and a couple hours of silence between us," replied Joshua. "You changed and left the package on my bathroom floor. I didn't realize it was for me until later. I saw the name tag on it."

"I guessed at your size when I brought it," she said with a small smile. "Do you want a fire?"

Joshua nodded, as he wheeled himself into the living room. Rita struck a match and lit the paper in the fireplace. He climbed onto the couch and laid down to watch the fire roar to life.

"Your Grandpa Martin was good at building fires in doors and out. I was learning by watching him do it as a small boy. He showed your Uncle Andrew but never me. I learned in the service and watching him those early years. We didn't have many fires in the war I fought in. You do pretty good job for lady. Who taught you? I know, you have watched me the last thirteen years, but you had someone to teach you before me."

"Luke was one to figure things out after you left, so Mom turned to him a lot when it came to fixing and doing things like that. Why didn't Grandpa Martin teach you things, Dad?"

"Andrew was his favorite because he was smart and looked a lot like him," Joshua answered thoughtfully and painfully. "I got myself drafted or enlisted, so Andrew wouldn't have to go. They or your grandparents didn't stop me, so I don't think they really cared of what would become of me or so I think, anyways."

He fought off a cough. She stared at him briefly.

"Hush, Dad, now you need save your strength for the kids. They'll be here soon with their Dad," Rita said, as she tucked another blanket around him. "I love you, Dad."

Joshua nodded, as he closed his eyes. She always knew the right things to say or do that made he feel okay with whatever she wanted him to do. She had her Grandma way about her he thought to himself and grinned, as he breathed lightly and steadily.

Rita knew he loved to sleep by the fire instead of his bed. But she never asked him why, and he never explained it either. He drifted off to sleep within minutes of feeling the warmth of the fire reach his sun-exposed face. He smiled, as he drifted off to a hopeful, restful sleep.

2

Joshua woke up to a dying fire, so he got up and walked over to the fireplace to add a couple more logs to the dying coals. He sat in his favorite easy chair and watched it roar to life once again. He smiled and leaned deeper into the chair.

"Do you think Santa will come this year?" Joshua asked, as he looked back at Andrew on the stairs above him.

"Of course he will," Andrew answered confidently. "He comes every year. What did you ask for this year?"

"A train to go around the tree," Joshua answered with excitement. "Mom has always wanted one of those."

"Always toys, never nothing to stimulate the mind," Andrew said back. "Books are what will last not toys, Joshua."

"We're kids, and kids get toys," Joshua replied back. "Geez, you're not much older than me, yet you act like an adult lately."

"Mom and Dad want me to go to law school someday, so I have to prepare myself for it," Andrew said confidently. "You should try harder, little brother."

"Don't tell me what to do, Andrew. You're not my Dad," he snapped back.

"No, I'm not, but I'm smarter than you by far. I don't waste my days and nights like you do."

"I'm going to bed and hope Santa will bring me lots of toys," Joshua replied; as he headed for their room they shared.

"Dad, are you okay?" Rita asked, as she brought him back to the present.

"Fine, Rita," he answered with a big smile. "We need more wood for the fire."

"I'll get it, Dad."

"I can get it. I don't need the damn wheelchair either. I'm not that old," he snapped back sharply, as he got to his feet.

"But your cough..."

"Comes and goes. Now you'll excuse me while I get more wood for my fire," he replied, as he stared at her.

"Okay but be careful, Dad. Please."

He nodded and touched her face. "I see so much of your Grandma Sara in you. I feel like I'm back with her again. I love you as much as I loved her."

"Dad stop, you're going to make me cry again," said Rita.

"I'll fix us breakfast after I bring in some more wood. You sit and enjoy the fire," he replied, as he kissed her on the cheek.

Rita nodded, as he headed for the side of the deck. He had wood in a box to keep it dry. He smiled, as he loaded arms with several logs. He made his way back in, as he noticed her in his easy chair.

"Do you need any help, Dad?" she asked, as she stared at him now.

"No, I got it. Thank you," he answered, as he walked closer to her and the fireplace.

He unloaded his arms and headed back out for more. But he stopped and looked out at the coast.

"You're home, man," a man said in an army jacket like his stood next to him. "We survived Vietnam."

"Yes, we're home Roger and for the most part in one piece," he replied back. "I didn't think I would ever see this ocean again. We saw a lot of water over there. Didn't we, Roger?"

"Yeah, we did and have come home to be called baby killers and no hero's welcome," said Roger. "But I owe you my life, man."

"My Dad came home to a hero's welcome to some extent," Joshua replied, as his eyes scanned the vast ocean view. "This is so beautiful."

"I know, you told me, man. You kept me awake after I lost my leg, and that's one thing you did tell me was about your father. You talked about him non-stop of all the things he could do. Didn't you feel the scapula in your shoulder ever?"

"No not really. If I had to do it all over again, I would do it the exact same way because you're my friend and comrade," Joshua answered back. "It's so beautiful and peaceful here. I'm going live here for the rest of my life."

Joshua begun to cough slow and steady before it picked up speed. Roger rubbed his back.

"Easy, man, take small bites of air like they told you at the hospital," Roger said calmly. "I don't think I could have gone back in as many times as you did and being exposed to what they had in that jungle like you did, man."

Joshua's cough was calmer now. "Someone had to go back and get Lt. Grahams out of there."

"But you already got the rest of us out. He said he

was right behind you, as you took the bullet in the shoulder before swinging me over your other shoulder," said Roger.

"I did what I had to do. I have no regrets, Roger."

"But what about what you were exposed to?" Roger asked painfully and with a degree of concern in his voice.

"A small price to pay for saving lives," he answered back. "Look at this view Roger. Isn't it something?"

"You got a bronze star, a purple heart and star of bravery along with a promotion to sergeant, yet you act like it was no big deal, man," Roger said, as he stepped into Joshua's view. "You're a hero, man. I don't know who told you that your life didn't matter or isn't worth anything. He or she was wrong because you were there when it counted. Our CO and platoon owe you our very lives, man. Do you hear me? You do matter. You're smart and have worth, man."

"Dad...Dad, can you hear me?" Rita asked, as she stood before him now.

"Rita."

"Yes, Dad, Roger is in the hospital. He's asking for you. Maria is on the phone," Rita rambled on. "Talk to her."

Joshua reached for the phone, as he dropped the wood at their feet. He bent down to help her.

"I got it talk to her, Dad. She sounds upset. They need you."

He nodded and put the phone to his left ear. "Hello, Maria."

"Thank God, Josh. Dad needs you. When can you get here?"

"A couple hours if I leave now, so tell Roger that

I'm on my way now," he answered calmly.

"Thank you, Josh," said Maria. "You're his best friend, you know."

"I'll be there soon," he replied back. "Rita, I've got to go. But I'll call you when I get there. I love you, baby girl."

"Dad, I know, you do. You don't have to say it."

"Yes, I do, baby girl. Yes, I do," he replied back, as he touched her cheek again. "I've got twelve long years to make up for."

"Dad."

"Let me," he replied, as he gazed deep into her eyes.

Rita nodded. Joshua made his way to the front door and grabbed his Blazer keys. She followed him and straightened out his army jacket and collar. There she wrapped a scarf snuggly around his neck and smiled.

"Drive carefully, Dad. We want you around for this and many more Christmases," she whispered to him.

"I will, baby girl," he replied, before he headed out to his green Blazer. "I love you."

"Do you have your cell?"

"In the car, I'll plug it in, as I head to Palo Alto. I'll call you as soon as I hit the parking lot but not before," he answered back.

She nodded, as she stood in the doorway of his house. They never got around to having breakfast, but he knew she would fend for herself. She was a fighter very much like him and her Grandma Sara she never knew.

His Mom suffered a stroke after Kennedy was killed in Dallas. The rest of the family blamed him for it since he enlisted without telling them. He knew differently because he knew his Mom followed Senator Kennedy then President Kennedy's career.

So she took the murder of Kennedy by Lee Harvey Oswald that November hard in '63. The service men heard the news of his death just prior to the attack. It made him think of her when he got the news. However, he was glad that he had gotten the little girl out in August earlier that same year.

But Joshua had been in an army hospital when he heard the news about his Mom. Someone told a chaplain to notify him wherever he was about her, so he didn't know who that was to this day. So he cried in his pillow because he didn't want the other enlisted men see or hear him cry. They had sent him home because of it. He hadn't arrived State side until a month and half later.

It was too late because she had died two days before he got there. His Dad and siblings were bitter and angry, so he had to find out from a neighbor of her final resting place was. El Cerrito he knew it well. Her parents were buried there, too. Roger was from the Bay area originally.

The cell rang on the console. Joshua looked at it before he answered it. It brought him out of his own thoughts.

"Hello, baby girl," he replied on his end. "I just pulled in."

"Thank God, Dad!" exclaimed Rita.

"What's wrong?"

"I heard about the shooting. I got scared, Dad," Rita answered quickly.

"Slow down, baby girl. Talk to me slowly," he replied calmly.

"They say a Vet is on the roof. He shot a guard in the leg already; oh my god!"

"What?"

"They're showing the roof top. Dad, it looks a lot like Uncle Roger."

"Damn," he replied back. "Not again."

He flipped his cell closed and ignition off, and he bolted to the front entrance of the hospital. He pushed his way through law enforcement and the media and could see Maria now. He gulped down some air quickly.

"Maria," he called out.

She turned to face his direction with tears in her eyes. "Josh, please let him through. He knows my Dad. They were in Nam together. He knows how to talk to him. Please."

"Let him through," a man ordered to the man next to her.

"Maria, what happened?"

"Oh Josh! He thinks he's back there before he lost his leg again. You need to talk to him. You can get through to him. Please."

Joshua stared at the man beside her. He nodded. So he headed for the elevator which only took him to four floors. The rest he would have take the stairs to the roof.

He had done it on and off since February of '64. Joshua knew this hospital and others back in Sacramento through the last forty-six years plus.

Roger had been in and out of hospitals a lot since they had come home. It wasn't just his leg that bothered him but his head. No one seemed to know what triggered his flashbacks to Vietnam prior to losing his leg. But Joshua had been there and brought peace to Roger's mind always.

"Roger, it's me, Josh," he replied, as he stood on the roof top now. "Roger, do you hear me?" He noticed two men in white lab coats. "You two go away, now!"

He continued to stare at them, as one held a straight jacket. They started to back up when he walked up closer to the ledge and Roger. Yes, he had a handgun in his hands. Roger looked worse this time somehow. He wore a hospital gown and socks on.

"I won't give up without a fight, man," Roger snapped back at him.

"Easy, now, buddy. It's me, Josh," he replied calmly, as he walked towards him. "Come on over here and away from there. Maria is worried about you. She loves her Daddy so very much."

He moistened his lips and walked slowly towards Roger. Roger backed up more to the ledge now.

"Who's Maria?" Roger asked, as he shook from the cold.

"As I said before, your daughter and only child, she's downstairs waiting for us," Joshua answered, as he stepped even closer. "She loves you."

"They're going to have to kill me this time," Roger snapped back.

"What do you mean, buddy?"

"They took my leg. Now they want to finish me," Roger answered back.

"Come inside with me. I got your back. You called me a hero in '64. Well, I don't feel like one right now. I can't get you away from there," Joshua replied, as he felt sweat pour out of him. "Please come over and talk to me. Tell me what's going on, buddy?"

Roger stood very close to the ledge now more than ever before. It made him and the others very uneasy. A helicopter drew in closer on Roger's position, but his footing was slipping. Joshua lunged for him, but he was too late. Roger headed down off the roof with a scream that echoed in Joshua's ears. His once silent right ear knew what had just happened.

He knelt at the ledge now and cried. He didn't look down but up at the helicopter. It was a news station logo on the side. He stared at it and shook his closed, tight fist at it.

"Damn you, bastards," he yelled at the top of his lungs.

He felt the rain on him now, as he cried. The pilot pulled away. Joshua failed Roger this time. Why did it happen this time? He had been so successful in reaching Roger in the past. But then it came clear to him. Roger wasn't thinking of before he lost his leg but after. Joshua got up and headed downstairs to Maria.

He held Maria in his arms, as she cried. They exchanged no words when he stepped out of the elevator.

Roger was three years older than him but looked five. Joshua didn't know what to say to Maria, so he held her like he did every time when he got him away from danger at yet another hospital. This time he and Roger couldn't talk about ice cream and vanilla lattes that sounded so good to them since his daughter wouldn't let him have them.

24

Roger had become a diabetic in the last ten years, so Maria monitored his glucose levels. She was a nurse and his nurse. Joshua, on the other hand, had Rita who worked in the DA's office. She walked the streets of Sacramento and dealt with a lot of veterans of Vietnam and other wars. They didn't think she understood them until she showed them a young man with another one in a combat uniform.

Yes, it was of her Dad and Roger before the attack. Someone snapped a picture and gave it to Roger who in return gave it to Rita on her eighteenth birthday. They didn't know what they were going to face that following month in the jungle. They didn't know the layout the land like the enemy did, so they didn't know much including whom their enemy was.

Maria tucked her head into Joshua's chest, as they exited the hospital the final time. She didn't want to face the media. He pushed them aside, as he found her car. He blocked their cameras and mics, as they tried to get a statement from her. The police cleared the path for Maria to get a chance to drive away. Now Joshua was faced with the media alone.

"Leave her alone. She just lost her father, and I lost my best friend," Joshua replied, as he glared at the media. "Let us all have peace especially my friend and comrade."

"What's his name?" asked a reporter. "We'll find out from the hospital if you don't tell us."

He gulped down some air before he spoke again. "He was a hero of the Vietnam War. He lost his leg fighting for his country he loved so much. When you look up the definition of hero in the dictionary, you will find Private First Class Roger Daniel Clemens beside the word because that's who he was. Now leave us alone to mourn our fallen hero. Please."

He walked by them to his Blazer. He started his car up and headed home. He turned on the radio which he never did while he was alone.

"This song is dedicated to our fallen hero Roger Clemens who fell to his death this mid-morning at a Palo Alto hospital in the rain," the announcer said calmly. "We'll miss you, man. You're a hero as your best friend said. We all salute you today."

Music played now. Joshua felt wetness on his cheeks again, as he pulled to the side of the freeway. His vision was blurred by his tears and grief. His cell rang to life once again.

"Hello, Dad," Rita said on the other end. "I'm sorry, Dad."

"Hi, baby girl," he replied, as he wiped away the wetness from his face. "I almost had him, baby."

"I know, Dad. I saw the footage on TV. Come home, Dad. Please."

"I'm halfway there, baby girl," he replied back. "I love you Rita Sara Hernando."

"I know, Dad. I love you, too."

"Okay," he replied, as he flipped his cell closed again. "Goodbye, Roger, my dear old friend. I miss you and love you."

Joshua merged into traffic and headed home. It didn't take long before he pulled into his driveway. He got out of his Blazer to find Rita stood at the front doorway much like when he left her. Their eyes met, as he walked closer to her. She grabbed him when he got close enough to embrace him. He took it in but didn't cry. He cried on the roof top for his friend and on the side of the freeway.

Rita cried in their embrace. So Joshua had comforted her. He felt numb now, as they stood in the rain. But Rita felt Roger's death because she knew him before and after her parents divorced. She had memories of him when his mind was clear. Roger knew how to laugh and enjoy life.

She led him into his warm house again. She headed the bathroom while he closed the front door and proceeded to take off his army jacket and scarf. She re-emerged with a towel for him and her. But he refused it, as he walked silently over to his easy chair.

She followed him, as he sat down and glanced at the blazing fire she had built. Rita knelt beside him and gazed up. He glanced down at her and touched her face. Her round-chocolate eyes stared back at him from the thick framed glasses she wore. She was legally blind without them.

"Was it like all the past times?" she asked finally in a low voice.

Joshua cleared his throat, as water trickled down his face, neck and shoulders from his wet, sandy brown hair. "No. It was different this time, baby girl. He knew his leg was gone and wanted to die fighting."

"That's why you called him a hero to the media," she said back.

He nodded then he stared back into the fire.

"Dad, tell me what you're thinking right now. You haven't said a whole lot about your life except I look like Grandma Sara. Uncle Roger knew you in the army, and you spent twelve long years looking for us. Yet, you haven't said much more of that these in the last thirteen years. Was your life that bad you can't even talk about it?" Rita asked him honestly.

"I suppose, it would help you understand the man before you," he answered, as he still gazed into the fire. "But not now maybe later. I would like to be alone now. Please. I don't want to talk or see anyone right now."

"What about, Maria?"

"I'll think about it."

"Okay, Dad. I've got plenty of wood inside, and I cracked more fresh crab. It's in the fridge with the sauce on the side when you're hungry. I need to make sure Jenny and Jordan are okay."

"Go, baby girl," he replied with a small smile. "They need their Mommy now. I'll be fine."

"I'll see you in a little while. We have a tree to pick up and maybe the rain will let up by then."

Joshua lifted up an eyebrow. She smiled back at him.

"You forgot, didn't you? That's okay. I'll be back at five," she said, as she kissed him when she got to her feet.

He nodded and heard her step outside into the rain. Joshua was alone again. He closed his and felt his chest rise and fall as the fire snapped, crackled and popped.

"Just like in Nam, buddy," he replied out loud. "Just like back in Vietnam."

3

Joshua called Maria and asked if there was anything she needed him to do. She said, no, but then changed her mind. So he spent the next couple hours on the phone trying to reconnect with their old platoon. Scott, Jerrod, Henry, Steve and Matt had watched it all unfold on TV, so he didn't have to explain it. No one knew for sure how to get a hold of Lt. Grahams, but Scott would try for Joshua. He would do anything for the man who saved his life.

Rita walked into the house, as Joshua stood out on his deck to look at the ocean. He heard her walk in but didn't look back. She walked up closer to him. The rain had stopped, and fog was rolling in now.

"Dad," she whispered in not very low voice to him. "Are you..."

"Roger and I saw the ocean this ocean when we came home in '64. Your Grandma Sara passed away two days before I got back. He couldn't take in the beauty of this at first. He kept on going on about how I was a hero," Joshua replied, as he glanced over at her now. "I was no hero, baby girl. Let's make this perfectly clear, so there are no misunderstandings here. I was far from it. I did what I had to do since I was the only one able. I know any of them would have done the same."

"I understand, Dad. Have you eaten anything since I left?"

"A little, Scott is helping with the search for Lt.

Grahams. Trev died last year. I still have to call Robert, James and Luke," he answered back calmly. "I know, you don't remember them, baby girl. They moved on after the war with their half shattered lives. Roger was the only one who remained close."

"He always considered you a hero, Dad. How did you know, how to reach the others?"

"Maria. She has addresses and phone numbers but didn't feel up to calling them, after all. She went to work for Veterans of Foreign Wars after high school before going into nursing," he replied thoughtfully. "I think she wanted to be close to people who could possibly help her Dad. You're a year younger than her."

"No, she's older than me by about ten years," she corrected him. "Let's go get your tree. Alex is with the kids, and they're fine."

He nodded and headed back inside. Rita closed the sliding glass door behind them and locked it. He grabbed his army jacket and put it on. He readjusted it and felt something in his pocket. He pulled it out.

"What's that, Dad?" she asked with interest.

"A photograph of me and Roger before we were shipped out to Vietnam," he answered back sadly. "Here you keep it for the kids."

"Dad!" exclaimed Rita.

"No, I don't plan on leaving this life anytime soon, I hope. Now your Uncle Andrew and Aunts Caroline and Elizabeth probably still think differently just like your siblings and your Mom," Joshua replied calmly. "It's hard to believe it has been nearly fifty years since I enlisted and fought in that damn war. A war that isn't over yet just like in Korea."

"You look younger than the other one you gave me, Dad."

"I was sixteen in that one. I was seventeen when the other one was taken over there. I would become a man in the service," he replied, as he shook his head, "My Blazer or what?"

"Alex gave me the truck keys," she answered back.

"We'll need the fog lights. It was nice of him," Joshua replied, as he held out his hand out for the keys.

"You know, how Alex feels about his truck," she warned him.

"I'll be careful with it, baby girl."

"I know, you will, Dad. Let's go get a Christmas tree," she said, as she started to hum Silent Night.

Joshua loved Rita's voice when she sang tenor in the church choir. She had her Mom's voice. Carly and Joshua met in mid-64 and were married later in '68 year. Carly sang 'Ava Maria' in church and calmed all his emotions and memories of the war. She had brown eyes and brown hair with a purple streak on the edge of her right side of her face but that wasn't there the first time they met. She wore a large flower print dress and colorful beads and symbol of peace around her neck under her choir black robe. The flip flops were a sign of rebellion against her Dad and her brother.

Rita wasn't like that as a child or the first five years of her life. She was born in 1980, and the hippie era was far gone by the time she came along. Joshua barely remembered his other children's lives now as children. Maybe he spent too much time with Roger. Carly had an affair and finally divorced him in '85.

Carly took their children out of State without telling him. So for the next twelve years Joshua tried to find them again. Yes, he worked and almost spent all his earnings to find his children again. PI's didn't care about what they did to him financially or did without. They took his money and left he only empty handed each time until he caught a break in his search.

"Dad, we're here," Rita said, as she brought him back into the present.

He didn't realize his mind had wandered off or drifted away from her. He tried hard not to do it to her. He didn't tell her and her siblings much about his life before his oldest son was born.

"Let's get the tree, baby girl," he replied with a big smile.

"Sounds good, Dad," she said with a big smile back. Joshua breathed in the scent of fresh pine into his nostrils. The fog didn't seem to bother him. Children chased each other through the various sizes and shapes of trees on the lot. Parents and couples examined the trees with more care than the kids. Rita started to talk to him, as he stared at people.

"What if you don't find Lt. Grahams in time for Uncle Roger's funeral?" Rita asked him. "What are you going to do then?"

"I don't know," he answered back honestly. "I haven't given it much thought really. I need to find Tim. Please, excuse me."

"Taunt hut, soldier," bellowed a voice said beside Joshua.

He stood at attention and faced the voice before he saluted. There was a man who stood before him in his late seventies and wore an army jacket like his. It had two trips on the sleeve. Joshua couldn't believe his eyes of the man who stood before him now.

"At ease, soldier," the man said, as he stared back at Joshua, "Sergeant Hernando."

"Dad," Rita said a little confused.

He glanced quickly her way then back at the man, as he stepped down. He cleared his throat.

"No one has heard from you in years, Sir," Joshua replied in a clear but calm voice.

"I wanted it that way, Sergeant Hernando," said the man. "I was in a bad way for a long time. I lost what made me that day in the jungle."

"I didn't know, Sir."

"No, you grabbed me like everyone else and got me to safety. Then we were all sent to different hospitals to recover. I never had a chance to thank you for that day. But Private Clemens told me what you had done for all of us. I didn't remember with the head and body injuries. As I begun to heal was when I was told what you did. The only thing I could do is recommend you receive the Bronze Star and promotion since I couldn't locate you back then and say a proper thank you. They were already awarding you a Purple Heart."

"How did you meet up with Private Clemens, Sir?" he asked with interest.

"Walter Reid Hospital, as he headed out to go home. I think it was couple days before because I left before he did. He was being fitted for a new leg."

"He never said anything, Sir. I would like you to meet my youngest daughter, Rita, Sir," Joshua replied politely.

Rita walked up closer to him and the man. She stared at him.

"Tim's Dad," she said, as her jaw dropped in surprise.

"This is Lt. Grahams, baby girl," Joshua replied back.

"I've been coming to this lot for twelve years, and I had no idea you knew my Dad," said Rita in amazement. "Tim and I always said our Dads should meet since they both served in the same war."

"Rita," said a red haired man. "I see you finally met my Dad. Sorry, Mr. Hernando, but your tree is at the back of the lot."

"Tim, this is Sergeant Hernando. He saved my life back in late '63," Grahams said, as he placed his good hand on Joshua's shoulder.

"He's a true hero like the one who just died at Palo Alto hospital earlier today," Tim said with a smile.

"Sir, about that soldier," interrupted Joshua.

"Do you know something about him, Sergeant?"

"Yes, Sir, it was Private Clemens, Sir."

"Oh damn! I need to sit down."

"Dad," Tim said, as he rushed to his side.

Joshua was at the other, and together they led him to a chair. By the green house, he had gone pale quickly. Tim rushed to a jug and returned quickly to his Dad's side.

"Take a sip of it, Dad," Tim said, as he offered it to him.

"I'll be fine, Tim. Go take care of business. Sergeant Hernando, can you stay here and talk to me. Please."

Joshua nodded. Rita and Tim left them alone. He stood beside him now and waited.

"Pull up a chair, Sergeant. I mean, what's your first name anyways?"

"Joshua or Josh, I answer to both, Sir. You used to call me Sniper."

"Drop the sir and call me Allen. We're civilians now. Tell me about Clemens."

"Roger had been in and out of hospitals since February of '64. He had flashbacks of Nam before his leg was gone," he explained carefully. "I had always been there for him and to talk to him away from any ledge he stood at. But..."

"This time it was different," Allen interrupted him.

"Yes. It wasn't just the draft from the helicopter like I thought briefly at first. It was different in the sense; he was dealing with after his leg was gone. It was a first time we ever dealt with it," explained Joshua. "They could never figure out what triggered the flashbacks all these years."

"But yet you managed to reach his mind," Allen said calmly. "It surprises you since you had no formal training or schooling to do such a thing."

"Yes," he replied in surprise.

"You were the youngest in the platoon and made your shots count," Allen explained calmly. "I know you're going to tell me that you were eighteen. I know, differently, Josh. You see, I had a little brother who0 would have been your age. He died in my arms after a car accident. I was angry, so my parents sent me to boot camp. I took my anger out on the training then the war came. Roger knew you had a past and struggled with it. He didn't know how to help you, and I was in no condition to help either. I lost a leg and an arm and was trying to deal with it and very angry again. However, I did have a spot of clarity when I did what I did for you. Then I went back to a terrible place from March of '64 to '77 when I met Tim's Mom. She didn't put up with my stuff, and it turned me around."

"Sir, I mean Allen. What gave me away?" he asked him.

"You soaked up the attention on your hand to hand combat and marksmanship ability. I admired your marksmanship, Josh. Did you ever handle a rifle before the service?"

"No. My Dad served in World War Two, and my parents feared Andrew would be drafted for Korea in '50. He wasn't eligible so they feared he would be drafted for Vietnam. He was about to enter or in law school when I enlisted," Joshua answered Allen. "He is smart and so are my sisters. I never did well in school, so it was best that I go."

"You are smart, Josh," said Allen.

"No, I'm not."

"Yes, you are. Look how you were able to read Roger all these years. You understand people and have a way about you that you don't seem to understand about yourself," pointed out Allen. "You may not grasp book learning but excel with hands on things easily. Anyone can pull a trigger but not have the accuracy one hundred percent all the time without working at it. You took to it like it was born for your hands. Have there been other things like that in your life? Before you answer it, I want you to really think hard on it then answer me in a few days, deal?"

Joshua nodded. They sat there in silence for awhile. Allen sipped the contents of the cup slowly. Joshua stared at his hands which were rough and had calluses from hard work. He didn't count on himself to do anything dealing his brain because of his lack of schooling. He didn't have a high school diploma from a known high school like his siblings and children, but a GED he didn't admit to anyone he had. So he did a lot of odd jobs with his body like his arms, hands, legs and such.

"Dad, are you okay?" Rita asked, as she stared down at him.

"Uh...sure, baby girl," he answered back, as he got to his feet. "I'll see you after Christmas uh...Sir."

"Allen just Allen," Allen repeated back, as he stared at Joshua now. "I live over there. Stop by anytime day or night."

"Merry Christmas," Joshua replied back. "I'll be in touch about Roger's funeral. It will probably be in El Cerrito or somewhere in the Bay area since that's where he was from originally."

"I would appreciate it, Josh. Thank you, Merry Christmas to you and your family."

Joshua nodded and followed Rita back to the front of the lot. He noticed a six foot Douglas fir tied down in the bed of the truck. Tim walked up with a big smile.

"How much?" he asked him.

"No charge. If you didn't save my Dad back in Nam, my Mom would never have me, so I owe you one for the rest of your life," Tim answered, as he held out his hand. "It has been a real pleasure to meet you after all these years. He told Mom and me how you saved his life and the rest of the platoon back then. But he also how good you were as marksman. He used to say it can't be taught. It has to come from within one's self. Rita, take care and Merry Christmas."

"Same to you, Tim," Rita said with a smile back.

"Rita."

"Okay Dad. I'm coming."

They got into the truck. Joshua slipped the truck into gear and headed home. Rita hummed another Christmas Carol, as the miles few by. He thought of what Allen asked him, as he drove and later; as they unloaded the tree. Rita started to decorate it when he stretched out on the couch.

He realized how tired he was, as he felt the warmth of the fire on his face. He didn't want to think of anything. It had been another long day for him. He didn't want to think of Roger either, and he felt guilty about it briefly.

"Dad, what do you think?"

"It's nice, baby girl. Thank you," he mumbled, as he drifted off to sleep.

"Dad."

He was out for the night. He woke up briefly to notice more wood on the fire and a blanket covered him now. Rita must have done it before she went home to be with her family. Joshua snuggled deeper into the blanket for the warmth along with the blazing fire. He went back to sleep again in no time.

4

"I understand, Maria. They'll be there including Lt. Grahams," Joshua replied on his end.

"How did find him after all these years?" she asked a little surprised. "Scott came up empty. I thought I would have been looking through piles of files to find him."

"He found me. He or his son owns a Christmas tree lot up the hill from The Tides motel," he answered calmly. "Rita has been going there for the last now twelve years for my tree. She knows his son Tim."

"That's great. Does he know what happened to Dad?" she asked sadly.

"Yeah, so they concluded with the autopsy that it was an accident then," he answered, as he stared out at the ocean. "When and where's the funeral?"

"Day after tomorrow, Mom's coming in with Jake. Thank God, he wasn't here when it all went down. I always hated explaining to him why his grandfather was in the hospital again."

"He's old enough now to understand, Maria," pointed out Joshua. "He's not much older than Jenny. She's five almost six now."

"Don't remind me, Josh, Merry Christmas."

"Merry Christmas, Maria."

"Grandpa...Grandpa," Jenny called out from inside the house.

He turned to see Jenny coming towards him. Jordan was three and still struggled to walk much less run to him. He waited for them on the deck. He left the phone on the railing to hug them both. Jenny looked like Rita, and Jordan looked like his dad Alex. His blonde hair and blue oval-shaped eyes along mixed portioned body. The broad shoulders, narrow chest and wide hips made him stand out in the coward, but Joshua loved him all the same.

"Grand pappy," he said, as he reached Joshua finally.

He held them both close to his chest. Rita stepped onto the deck with a big smile.

"Hold it right there, Josh," Alex said with a camera.

Jenny and Jordan smiled back at their Dad. Joshua hardly smiled for him because Alex still unnerved him. He couldn't understand why Alex who was clearly in his early or late thirties had taken interest in Rita. She starting working for the DA's office a week, and he asked her out. Then two days later he proposed to her.

"Has Santa brought us lots of toys?" Jordan asked him.

"Yeah, and the best for my two best grandchildren in the world," he replied cheerfully.

"Did you always love Christmas, Grandpa?" asked Jenny.

"Sure did despite Uncle Andrew...oh never mind. Your Great-Grandma Sara loved Christmas," he answered with excitement. "She made homemade gingerbread men and women cookies, freshly made breads and dinner enough for all. No one went to bed hungry at our house. Have you ever had eggnog and fresh made crab cakes?"

"No, Grandpa, but they sound good," answered Jenny.

"Well, I'll warm up the eggnog and put cinnamon

sticks in it while I bake us up some fresh crab cakes."

"Crab cakes, Grand pappy."

"Yes, Jordan, crab cakes just like your Great-Grandma Sara used to make," Joshua replied, as he led them into the kitchen.

"I'll be outside. I saw something to photograph," said Alex.

"Don't you want...oh never mind," Rita said to him, before she joined her Dad and the children. "Dad, can I help you?"

"No, baby girl, do you want some eggnog, too?"

"Sounds good, Dad."

Jenny and Jordan sat on the stools at the breakfast bar. Joshua poured another portion into the plastic pitcher before it went into the microwave. He started it then he arranged the fresh crab cakes onto a tray. He smiled at her. Rita smiled back.

"Grandpa," Jenny said, as she watched him.

"Yes, Jenny doll."

"Have I ever had these before?"

"Nope, but I decided you two were old enough to try your Great-Grandma's famous crab cakes."

"When did you first try them?"

"Jordan's age maybe earlier," he answered back thoughtfully. "Three each to start with, kids. Okay?"

"Sure, Dad," Rita answered a little surprised. "Did you make them when I was little?"

"Afraid not, your Mom didn't like fish that much, so I had to buy it on Friday and other times," he explained thoughtfully. "You and I would have a bowl of clam chowder every Friday from the time you were a year-old until..."

"I was five."

He nodded. "Here you go guys. It will be hot, so blow on it and sip it."

He focused on his grandchildren now with the eggnog.

"I'm sorry, Dad," she said sadly.

He held out a cup to her. "It's okay, baby girl. I need to put them in now. Enjoy."

"Grandpa, I love it!" Jenny exclaimed with delight.

He noticed an egg nog mustache on Jenny's face, so he laughed. Rita laughed, too. Jordan did the same. Alex re-entered the house and took some candid shots of his kids. Joshua placed three crab cakes on holiday plate with a gingerbread man in front of Jordan.

"Gingerbread men, Grand pappy?"

"Yes, Jordan, but try the crab cake," he replied, as he stood beside him now.

"Um....these are good, Grandpa," Jenny said with a big smile.

"You made them from scratch," stated Alex. "No one does that anymore not since..."

"During the depression and war time," added a male voice said by the doorway.

Joshua looked up to see his father tall, lean and auburn hair with white at the temples. He shook his head before he spoke.

"It's been too long, Josh," the man said in a soft voice.

"That it has bro, that it has," he replied finally. "How..."

"I had been in touch with Carly and Rita for years after the divorce. Yes, I or we all knew you got married back in '68," Andrew filled in. "We were wrong back in 's64. You were hurting too. You loved Mom, too, and now you never had a chance to say goodbye to either one."

"Dad's gone!" Joshua exclaimed, as he placed his hand on Jordan's small shoulder.

"Ten years ago. That's when your daughter here knocked some sense into us. She should have come into my practice back then," Andrew explained calmly. "I'm sorry about your friend. Were you two, close?"

"Like brothers," he answered back coldly. "He's having a military funeral the day after tomorrow."

"Elizabeth, Caroline and I would like to be there."

"Why?"

"For moral and emotional support for you, Josh, so now before you say, no, and anything more hear me out. Please."

Joshua nodded more for the sake of his daughter and grandchildren. He loved them with his whole heart and soul and didn't want to create a scene in front of them.

"We treated you badly after Mom died. You spent years without us in your life. I met up with Carly early in your marriage. I think she was pregnant with James. She had Patrick at her side. I started up the conservation how he looked like someone in my family." Andrew paused for a few minutes before he continued. "So I asked him his name which he refused to say anything. Then Carly told me since Patrick wouldn't talk to me. You and her raised him to not to talk to strangers, and he kept it, too. But I was hooked. Then she would drop me a line to tell me the status of you and the kids then just the kids. Unfortunately, my bitterness and anger I felt for you would be passed down to your kids. I made no effort in helping you find them, and I convinced them how you didn't care and love them. I know I was wrong to do that to you, Josh."

Andrew had tears in his eyes now. Joshua continued to stare at him.

"You enlisted so I didn't have to go. I could stay in law school like they planned for me. They waited for me to be called then Dad discovered you were already in. So they weren't going to call me in. The military had learned from World War Two about having more than one son in the service. I was sent to continue school and not look back," Andrew continued on. "I was so relieved at first then we saw and heard reports of soldiers over there. Mom didn't believe you were a baby killer or anything negative that would come out of there."

"The enemy used women and children as shields," Joshua replied calmly. "The jungle was the worst because you felt the slap of the plants on your aching body. But most of all you had to be aware of deadly traps they set up in those jungles. We were fighting the unknown enemy and their tricks had lost many lives on both sides. We bombed the jungles after we got clear from in hopes to stop the war. But Johnson wanted to victory, and it couldn't be had. Agent Orange and other things screwed up both sides up. Men lost not just limbs, exposure to other things and their minds, and they would come home effected by what happened over there. Innocence and trust were lost by some, and it's only the beginning. So you don't know how hard some of us tried to have a quote normal life of wife and children. The public doesn't know the whole picture and truth of what we experienced over there. If you want, I'll tell you what Trevor went through and even Roger, but it won't be easy on the stomach. But I won't go into it today."

"Grand pappy, more please," Jordan pleaded with him.

"Sure, Jordan," he replied with a small smile. "Andrew, would you like some?"

"Yes," he answered with excitement in his voice.

Joshua returned to the microwave, and Andrew joined him there. Andrew stood next to him and held out his hand. When Joshua hugged his big brother Andrew embraced him back, and Joshua knew he was crying.

"Thank you isn't enough, Josh. Welcome home and I love you, little brother."

"We'll talk later. Jordan. How many?" he asked, as he looked at his grandson.

"Same as before please," answered Jordan.

"Same for me," said Andrew.

Joshua nodded and went back to work. He made a dozen and half more before the kids opened their presents. Andrew watched Joshua at a distance. He felt his brother's gaze but focused on his grandchildren.

"Dad, how did..." Rita said then stopped in mid-thought.

"Santa knows everything, baby girl," he replied with a big smile. "Boys love trucks and trains. Girls love dolls and pretty dresses. Ladies love jewelry and other expansive trinkets. It was your Grandma Sara's locket. It was all I had of the family when I went to Vietnam. I think, your uncle and aunts would agree that you have it now. Plus this box and before you say anything, Roger gave it to me a month ago. I don't know what it is."

Andrew nodded at Joshua. Alex snuggled up closer to Rita with the camera.

"Enough, Alexander," she snapped back. "The locket is gorgeous, Dad."

"I think the photo is of Grandpa Martin when he was younger. I added hers when I left home. I was determined to come home to them. I wanted them to be proud of me."

"And maybe see you differently," Andrew added, as he stared at him. "You're not the same person I thought you were growing up. You only wanted toys for Christmas and your birthdays, but you did know the world far better than I have or ever will."

"Dad, look," Rita said loudly.

He focused her now. There was a bracelet made of shells and precious stones with a few pearls. It was truly stunning, but he had seen one similar to it before but couldn't recall where at first then it came to him.

"Maria has one like it," he replied thoughtfully. "He must have made one for you at the same time, baby girl. You were special to him, and he did try to help me find you, guys, during those long years we were apart."

"Uncle Andrew, where's Aunts Caroline and Elizabeth?" she asked him.

"Snowed in up at Tahoe with your cousins Russell, Morgan and Christina," he answered back. "But they promised to be here tomorrow. Yes, Josh, your uncle to two nephews and one niece. They're in their late thirties.

Russell and Christina are Elizabeth's kids. Then Morgan is Caroline's kid. She suffered several miscarriages, and Kevin left her. Elizabeth never married their father. I never married unless you want to say I've been married to my work and myself."

"You said my baby girl knocked some sense into you. What did you mean by that?"

"It's Christmas, and we can discuss it another time. I would like to hear about Roger and Trevor, too but not today."

"Fair enough."

"Dad, they need to take a nap. It looks like you could use one, too," she said calmly.

"You know, where the spare room is. Jordan, its nap time, little man," he replied, as Jordan walked over.

"Thanks, Dad. Jenny, nap time," Rita said with a smile. "Your cell is ringing in my purse, Alex."

Joshua picked up Jordan and carried him into the spare room. There was full size bed, chest and his old army footlocker in the room. He stretched Jordan out on the bed, and his sister joined him. Rita hugged her Dad and looked up at him.

"My brothers and sisters are coming for dinner," she whispered to him. "I love you."

He nodded and kissed her on the forehead. They looked over at her children.

"I missed so much your life and your siblings. I dropped everything for Roger. I guess, that's why your Mom..."

"Dad, don't go there, not today. Let's just enjoy this moment or time in our lives now.

"But you need to know the man who is standing before you."

"We have time, Dad but not today. We've worked at the last thirteen years but please not today."

Reluctantly, Joshua nodded and hugged her back. Then he headed for his room. It was dark, but he liked it that way. He knew where everything was, so he didn't have any lights on. He could feel the blades of the tall grass and brushes from the jungle in his mind as he briefly thought of Nam. He didn't struggle with what he saw and experienced over there like most soldiers did.

"Get your grades up before the term is over. You're not focused like Andrew, Caroline and Elizabeth. I wonder why I even bother with you.

"You're hopeless," Martin yelled at him.

"Martin, stop," Sara said calmly, "don't compare him to the other children. It's not fair, Martin."

"He won't amount to anything in life. He'll have a string of odd jobs here and there if we're lucky. Otherwise, he's worthless."

"Martin, don't say that. Joshua is your son."

"Sometimes I wonder if he is. I think, about it a lot," Martin said in anger. "Look at the year he was born."

"Martin, don't go there. I have never been unfaithful to you all the years we've been married," Sara said, as tears streamed down her face. "How could you accuse me of such a thing?"

"You work in a male dominated profession, my dear."

"Get out!" Sara exclaimed back. "Get out now!"

"Fine, I don't want to be here with a worthless and

stupid boy. I'm taking Andrew to the science fair," snapped Martin.

He walked away, and Sara focused on Joshua now. He stood with his history book in his hands.

"Mom, I do try, but I don't seem to get it all," he replied back.

"I know, you do, Honey," she said, as she knelt before him. "You are only nine."

"Mom."

"What, Joshua?"

"Will you ever give up on me?"

"No, Honey."

Joshua sat up in his bed and wiped away the tears from his face. He believed her that day and up two years after. She would turn on him after that, so he was on his own for the next five years. He managed a C average but knew what the family thought of that.

When Vietnam was coming, Joshua saw and heard his parents fear of Andrew being drafted, so he had to act quickly to save his big brother from being drafted. It was the only option he had now.

"Dad, are you awake?" Rita asked through the closed door.

"Yes, baby girl. I'll be right out."

"Okay. Everyone is here," Rita said, as she walked away.

He opened his door to come face to face with James and Susan. They smiled then hugged him. He wrapped his arms around them both.

"Merry Christmas, Daddy," they said in unison.

"Merry Christmas, James, Susan. Where's..."

"Patrick is telling Rita how to braise the turkey. Joan and Luke are playing with Jenny and Jordan. Alex had an important call then left. He hasn't come back yet. Uh....I guess, our Uncle Andrew is watching us all," interrupted James, "Sorry, Daddy."

"He's creepy at times," commented Susan.

Joshua laughed out loud, as they entered the living room. All turned to stare at them including Andrew. He had Alex's camera in his hands now.

"Susan here thinks you're creepy, Andrew. She needs to get to know you better," Joshua replied with a warm smile towards his big brother.

"She's had me in and out of her life before and after you found them again," Andrew pointed out with a small smile back.

"You seem so different than Daddy. You're brothers that I know. But you're still stuffed shirts, and Daddy is casual and relaxed," explained Susan.

"Are you saying I don't know how to have fun?"

"Yes."

He flashed a goofy smashed up face look at her and tossed the camera on the couch. He limped and slumps his back over, as he swaged towards them.

"I'm going to get you my pretty and take you up to my bell tower," Andrew said in an unrecognizable of voice.

Susan clung to Joshua with big eyes. Joshua chuckled and soon everyone did, as Andrew stood before them now. Andrew smiled.

"I never..."

"Seen this side of me because I used to tease your aunts with that when your Dad was real little," Andrew interrupted her. "You probably don't remember it, Josh. I had to entertain them while Mom changed your diaper or bathed you."

"Then you did a few times later and stopped," added Joshua. "I remember it vaguely. Caroline and Elizabeth used to scream, and Dad didn't like it at all."

"It's there I became serious and never looked back. I was hard on you at Christmas for wanting toys all the time. You must have wanted to play with me back then. I neglected you like our parents and sisters did. You must have felt alone back then. I'm sorry, Joshua."

"It's in the past, Andrew."

"But it is part of what has made you the man you are today, Dad," Rita said, as she stood in the kitchen doorway next to Patrick.

"You tried to make time for each of us, Dad," Patrick said in a confident voice. "Sure you left us when Roger needed you. But you did get down on the floor to play with us and talk."

"You would hug us and told us how much you loved us," filled in James.

"You would tell us to do our very best in school and life. You would always be proud of us. That's why it was so hard to believe what Mom said about you," said Joan.

"It was twelve years on the run with Mom and two failed marriages later you were back in our lives," Rita said, as she smiled at him.

"She didn't want me back in your lives."

"We know, Dad. But I showed up on that very doorstep Christmas morning in the pouring rain with a present from all of us," Rita said, as she continued to smile at him wiping away the tears. "I had to find out why you didn't want us anymore."

"Carly or your Mom may have lied to you, all, but I have forgiven her. It must been hard on her to see me drop everything for Roger so don't judge her, kids. She loves you, all, so very much," replied Joshua. "We've discussed this before. Now let's all move on."

"How..." Susan started to ask but then stopped.

"I loved your Mom as much as I could give, and she gave me, you guys. I love her for that, and I can forgive her, too. I wasn't perfect and wasn't there for her. Love can hurt like hell, but you begin to heal in time. You can't shut love off because it's what your heart is meant to do," replied Joshua.

"That's why you could forgive me," Andrew said with tears in his eyes now.

"Yes, and anyone else who crossed paths with me including, Mom."

"I don't understand," Andrew said a little confused.

"Mom gave up on me at eleven, and it would send me into a war that they feared you would be in. But it was me, who went, and I'll never know what she felt about that, nor do I want to know now. I need my kids and grandkids and even my niece and nephews know I believe in them always. They are my focus now, as I reveal the man standing before them today."

"How do I fit into it all?" a woman asked, as she stood at the front door with Alex. "I heard Roger is gone. I didn't know if you wanted me to be there."

"Carly."

"Mom."

"Grandma."

Joshua stepped around Susan and Andrew. He held out his arms to her. She wasn't sure what to do, so he stepped closer to hug her. She cried in his arms.

"That was important call," said Rita.

Alex nodded. Rita rushed to his open arms. She was beside her parents now.

"Everybody now in front of the tree," Patrick said with a big smile. "I thought I saw a tripod around here somewhere. There by Dad's easy chair."

"We'll set it on continuous and one minute timer," said Alex.

"Sounds good," Patrick said with a smile. "We'll have to take some more when the others come."

"It can be arranged," commented Alex. "You kneel beside the kids, go. Here, we go everyone."

Three times the flash flashed, and Alex walked over to the camera. He examined the images, as everyone looked on and waited. He smiled back.

"One more time folks," he said, as he hit the timer again before he returned to Rita's side.

Again three times the flash fired off, and Alex smiled, as he put the camera and tripod aside. Patrick and Rita walked back into the kitchen. Everyone had gone back to what they were doing before Joshua walked over to the fireplace to add more wood to it.

"You could always build a warm fire," Carly whispered to him. "Not just in a fireplace but in my heart as well."

He faced her with a big smile. "I was angry at first when you took off with the kids. But…"

"What?" she asked with interest.

"I was mostly to blame of our failed marriage. I put Roger first and you and the children second. It hit me hard after I got Roger off yet another roof top. He went home to Christine and Maria. I sat in a motel room and cried like a baby. I hadn't done it since I heard the news of my Mom's stroke."

"But I knew you helped Roger before we met, and it would continue throughout our marriage. I knew it going in when I married you, Josh. It wasn't just Roger but your past."

"What do you mean?"

"It wasn't just Vietnam, but your family or them not being fully in your life," Carly whispered to him. "You talked in your sleep, so I couldn't tell you. So when Andrew and I met up before James was born. I didn't know how to open up just like you."

"We were some kind of pair. Did you ever love those two other men?"

"Not like the way I love you," Carly answered honestly. "I heard what you told our kids. You're not the same man I fell in love with and married back in '68. I would like to know this man standing before me, too, if that's okay with you, Josh?"

He nodded and kissed her on the forehead. She smiled at him and touched his weather worn, tanned face. Everyone slowly walked into the kitchen to a buffet style dinner. Then they sat at various places in the living room to eat. Time seemed to pass quickly.

Joshua hugged and kissed his children and grandchildren, as they left. It was the best Christmas he had in a very long time. Joshua slept on the couch, as the fire died peacefully much like Joshua's mind. Whatever he thought of Alex in the past was a distant memory now. He had done something nice for Rita and him.

5

A couple days later, Joshua walked the beach. He watched the sunrise over the calm ocean now. It always appealed to him all his life and found a deeper calmness within outside Carly's voice of an angel. The ocean was calm despite the lateness of the year. It had been untamed the last few months.

He saw the remains of a sand castle, as he walked alone. It made him smile, as the chilly air swept across his sun-exposed, tanned face. He breathed in deeply.

"Betty, come make a castle with me," Joshua replied from the sand below at her feet.

"I don't think so, Josher," Elizabeth said, as she watched the boy up the beach. "Maybe you can get, Caroline or Andrew to help you. Excuse me, little brother."

Joshua shook his head and carried on making his sand castle. When his Mom appeared before him, he looked up at her and smiled, but she didn't smile back. It meant one thing and one thing only trouble.

"Joshua Matthew Adam Hernando, how could you do this to me, your father and the family?" she asked in a very loud voice. "I believed in you, young man. You are a very big disappointment after all I've done for you."

"But, Mommy," he replied back.

"You are not trying hard enough. Your Dad is right about that. You would rather dream your life away and play all the time," she snapped before she walked away from him.

"Mommy," he called out with tears in his eyes.

"Dad, are you all right?" Rita asked him.

Rita stood before him dressed in black and looked cold.

"Just a memory of your Grandma Sara, but I'm fine," he answered, as he stared at her now.

"I don't think I've ever seen you in army dress before not even in a photograph," she said with a smile. "You look handsome in uniform, and I'm impressed with the merits, medals and rank."

She examined them and his sergeant strips on his shoulders of his uniform. He tucked his finger under his collar to loosen it some.

"Is it too tight?"

"No, just don't like things super close to my neck. The uniform is a little loose since I last wore it," he answered honestly.

"When was that?"

"They awarded me the medals of bravery, Bronze Star, Purple Heart and promotion. I did what I had to do. I'm no hero, baby girl."

"Whatever, Dad, we've got to go in order to be there on time."

"Yes, I'll drive us," he replied, as Rita took his hand.

They walked back to his Blazer and headed for El Cerrito. Rita glanced over at him a few times, as they drove. Something was on her mind.

"What do you want to know, baby girl?"

"Uh..." she answered in hesitation. "You were crying on the beach, and I..."

"Wondering why," Joshua filled in, "I saw remains of a sandcastle and thought of your Aunt Betty and your

Grandma Sara. Your aunt was more interest in the boys then making a sand castle with me. Then your grandma walked up. I was eleven when I disappointed her. She gave up on me from that day on. I would struggle with my school work for the next five years alone."

"What kind of grades did you get?" Rita asked him.

"C's mostly when everyone else got A's and B's, I couldn't understand the books sometimes, but the tests were the worst," he explained thoughtfully.

"What do you mean?"

"I knew it backwards and forwards in my head, but then it escaped me, as the test was placed in front of me. It had been like a foreign language, as I struggled to answer the questions. I couldn't explain my answers completely or to the teacher's satisfaction. Here we are. I'll see what Maria needs me to do. Excuse me, Rita."

Joshua walked up to Maria. She was dressed in black except for the pink scarf around her neck. She had dark circles under those chocolate brown eyes of hers. She looked like her Dad, Roger. He gave her a quick hug then stepped back.

"Is there anything I can do?" he asked back.

"Just help with his casket. The Army will play TAPS at the cemetery. Thank you for contacting them. He loved you, Josh," answered Maria. "You were a great friend to him through the years."

"Sergeant Hernando," a male voice said from behind him.

"Sir," Joshua replied, as he turned in a saluted position to face the voice. "Sergeant Hernando, Sir."

"It's, okay, Josh. It's nice to know you still

remember it all. Who is this beauty?" asked Allen.

"This is Maria, Roger's daughter and only child. Maria, this is Lt. Grahams our commanding officer back in Nam."

"Your father was a fine soldier and was proud to serve his country," Allen said, as he held out his good hand. "We were lucky to have him with us, and he made us laugh at times."

"What do you mean?" asked Maria.

"Wasn't he the joker guy?" Allen asked Joshua.

"Yes, Sir, we never knew what he did until it happened," Joshua answered with a small smile. "But it all changed that day in the jungle."

"It changed all of us, but you were the hero that day, Josh. You saved us all."

"I need to see if Louie needs me now. Please excuse me," he replied politely.

Joshua headed for Louie. He noticed some other men dressed in uniform. He knew them Scott, Jerrod, Henry, Steve, Matt, Luke, James and Robert. They were all older than him. Trevor was the only one besides Roger now gone from this unit. They had their CO back with them again.

It was Steve, Scott, Henry, Trevor, Matt, Jerrod, Robert, Luke, James and Roger who were in the order Joshua hauled out of the jungle that day outside of Allen out of the jungle. Allen was behind Joshua, as he carried Roger over his shoulders. But Joshua was forced back in and got Allen out since another attack made it impossible for him to get out on his own. Joshua still remembered the mist before the fires and explosions. It was the explosions all around them that damaged his right ear. He never complained, as it popped then fell silent two years later.

"Josh, man," Steve said with a small smile. "Who's with Maria?"

"Lt. Grahams," he answered calmly. "Didn't you tell them how he found me, Scott?"

"No, Maria left it to you, man," Scott answered, as he looked at him. "I would be interested to know what he has been doing since '63."

"Uh..., Louie, I was on my way over," Joshua replied; as he spotted him approach them.

"Yes, I'll need you guys after we close the casket the final time," said Louie. "Maria wants to see him one more time before closing it. It was hard for her view him last night because damage to his face from the fall. Last night we had a closed casket."

"I'll talk to her," Joshua replied calmly.

"The beauty artist did her best as she could," said Louie.

"I understand," Joshua replied, as Maria approached them. "Maria listens to me. I know, you want wouldn't want you to since he loved you ever so much."

"Josh, I know, he loved us, but I have something to put in there," Maria said with tears in her eyes. "It's from his grandson. Please, Josh."

"Okay, but I'm going with you," he replied calmly. He pulled her closer to him, as they walked inside. "Let's go."

Louie nodded, and the others followed behind them. Joshua stared ahead, as they walked to the casket. Briefly, he flashed back to Roger's face on the hospital roof top. He shook his head, as Louie stepped back. He noticed a water color of Maria and Jake on her hands.

"He's becoming quite an artist now," Joshua whispered to her.

"Yes. He doesn't want his grandfather to forget us in heaven," she whispered back. "He worked on it all day yesterday. It had to be perfect."

"Your Dad drew pictures, too, besides his joking around," Joshua replied thoughtfully.

"I did know he drew over there, but he never shared them with me or that I can recall right now. Yes, I didn't know a lot about Nam. He only talked about it when he went through...."

"It's, okay, Maria," he replied, as he helped her place the watercolor on Roger's chest.

He didn't look at his face. The others walked up and each placed a hand on Maria's shoulder with his. She managed a small smile now.

"Strength in numbers," said Scott. "We're here night or day for you and Jake all of us."

Then they all stepped back to let Louie close the casket one final time. With an American flag draped over the casket, the men filed beside it and walked out the side door, and Rita stood with Maria and Jake now. Joshua touched the casket, as it entered the Hurst. He didn't remember to and from the church or even the cemetery.

But he and others stood at attention and saluted, as TAPS played for their friend and fellow soldier. Maria held Jake's hand in hers while Rita held her other. Joshua caught a glimpse of his siblings, children, grandchildren, niece, nephews and even his ex-wife. They were all here after all these years. He never met his niece and nephews in last recent years, so this was going to be awkward for them all. They studied abroad and very seldom came home when he had time to meet them. Roger's moods would come between them.

Joshua didn't blame or hold a grunge against his best friend Roger. No one could figure out Roger's flashbacks to Nam, so Joshua stayed closer to Maria than the others. They were the only two men who ever married despite they ended up in divorce. Now Allen was back in their lives, and they don't know much about his life State side.

"Baby killers," called out a young boy's voice after TAPS stopped.

"Yeah, baby killers. Killing innocent babies, children and women," chimed in another young voice said in the distance.

"Drop outs on society," said a third voice at a distance.

"You don't know what you're talking about, boys," Tim snapped back at them. "So get the hell out of here."

"What do you know, about these guys?" a tall, auburn haired boy asked him.

"My Dad lost an arm and a leg fighting for this country you so proudly stand on. You don't know what all these men experienced and seen over there. You don't know what kind of war that was since their only given a couple paragraphs in your history books if they're lucky," Tim answered in anger.

Joshua stepped up proudly next to him now. He watched the others join them. Then he felt hands on his shoulders. He didn't have to look back because he knew it was his family. He stayed focused on the young boys in the distance. He held his emotions in from them all. The boys bolted, so Joshua cracked a small smile now.

"Strength in numbers," repeated Scott.

"Indeed, Private Kemper," said Allen.

"Ms, on behave of the President of the United States and America with the United States Army, we're so proud serve; we're proud Roger Daniel Clemens served his country, too," a soldier said, as he stood before Maria now.

She nodded, as she took his American flag that was draped on his casket folded up in a triangle. Jake reached for it then she started to hand it to him. Jake turned back to the casket and saluted it. Then he took the flag from his Mom. The soldiers walked away, and everyone started to walk to their cars. But Joshua looked around when Andrew walked up to him.

"They are buried in the old part," he said to him. "Over there in the building in the family crypt with her family."

Joshua nodded and walked that direction. He heard someone running after him. Jenny took his hand into hers. He glanced back to see how they all were following him. He felt the wetness on his cheeks, as his whole family made this journey with him.

"Grandpa, where are we going?" she asked him.

"To visit your Great-Grandparents Sara and Martin Hernando," he answered, as he tried to smile back.

"But you're crying, Grandpa."

"I never saw them alive again. It was about forty-six plus years ago, and we weren't on good terms back then," he replied honesty and thoughtfully. "Your Mom looks a lot like your Great-Grandma Sara."

He had begun to cough, as he took the steps and turned down the hallway to the family crypt. He didn't want to stop now. He had come this far, and he didn't want to turn back. He had come here a few times with his Mom as small boy, so he knew where the family crypt was. Jenny stopped and pointed, so Joshua looked where her little finger pointed inside a room; they were about to enter. He nodded, as they resumed their journey. His cough picked up speed, but he had to press on harder. Jenny had come back to him.

"Lean on me, Josh," Andrew said, as he grabbed Joshua's arm and grabbed his waist close to his own body. "Easy, Josh, just breathe in and out slowly. Relax."

Joshua felt lighter now despite holding Jenny's hand, and Andrew supported him on the other side. They reached the wall of the room when he dropped to his knees before their nameplates.

"Martin A. Hernando loving husband, father and grandfather," Joshua read out loud, "Sara M. Myshrall-Hernando loving wife, mother and best friend."

He glanced up at Andrew who stood before him now. Joshua managed to stop his cough on his own. Jenny was at his side still. So he turned to her, as Jordan walked up next to her.

"These are your Great-Grandparents, Jenny and Jordan," he replied, as he suppressed a cough and tears. "Why doesn't hers say grandma?" Jenny asked with interest.

"She died before I came home from Vietnam, and

she didn't have any grandkids by then. I don't think. She didn't know about your Mom, your aunts, uncles and cousins, but she would have loved all of you. She had a big heart. A heart of gold much like your Mom's," he answered honestly.

"Dad, we didn't..." Rita started to say.

"I don't need the damn wheelchair," he snapped back. "It's under control, Rita."

"Sorry, Dad, I was only..."

"I know, I'm sorry, too," he replied, as he turned back to touch the letters on his Mom's nameplate. Then back to the gathering of people in the crowded room. "Why, best friend?"

"I'll explain it later," Andrew answered calmly.

"Why, not now?"

"You need to rest, Josh. You looked tired," Andrew answered again, "For once in your life listen to me as your big brother since I care and love you very much. Please."

He nodded and worked his way up to his feet. He stood with his back to everyone. He felt someone touch his leg then he turned to see Jordan smile at him. He smiled back.

"He smiles like you when we were kids," Caroline said, as she broke the silence. "I see a lot of you in both of them but also Mom, too."

"I think, Jenny looks like Rita or her Mom," replied Joshua.

"Don't talk, Dad. You can crash at my house. I'll drive us there."

"Fine," Joshua replied, as he held out his keys.

She grabbed them quickly. Andrew walked up to

him and helped him. The others had parted a path for them. He felt their hands on his shoulders and back. He stopped at Allen who stood in the hallway away from the opening of the room.

"Sorry, Sir," he replied, as he struggled to fight off another cough.

"You did great, Josh. Now rest and we can all talk later," Allen said with a big smile. "You're a great soldier and man. It's time for them to know."

Joshua nodded then walked with Andrew towards his Blazer. His cough returned and took its toll on his sixty-six year old body now. He coughed for most of the journey back to Rita's place. Alex and Andrew helped him to the spare room and the bed there. They stepped back, as Rita placed a warm blanket on him. He stared at her, as she brought it closer to his neck. He reached up and tried to touch her face.

"I know, Dad. I love you, too. Rest now," she whispered to him.

He closed his eyes and let his body relax. He saw an image of his Mom then his Dad then of Trevor then Roger and back to his Mom. He felt wetness on his face, as he rolled on his side before he fell into a deep sleep. He didn't remember anything else not even his dreams. Joshua always had dreams of his childhood, Nam and pieces of his life with Carly and after. But he had none today which was unusual for him.

He woke up three hours later and still lying on his side. This disturbed him, but he didn't know who was out there beyond the closed door. It could be all who were there for Roger's funeral. His family and his extended family all could be out there. He heard the door open.

"Daddy, are you awake?" Susan asked, as she walked near his legs.

She combed back her blonde hair with her fingers. She looked a lot like Caroline his older sister with the fair skin. She had a beautiful smile but was cautious around people she knew and didn't know at all.

"What's up, Honey?" he asked her calmly.

"I got worried, Daddy. You had attacks all the way here. It's not..."

"I'll be okay. I'm rested now," he replied, as he reached for her hands. "I guess stress of the last few days finally caught up with me. I'm fine, Honey. Now how does it feel to have an uncle, two aunts and three cousins in your life?"

"Okay, I guess," she said sadly.

"Now I know something besides me is bothering you. What's wrong, Honey? Talk to me," he replied, as he edged him closer to her.

"I'm a disappointment to you," she blurted out, as she stared at their hands.

"Now look at me right now, Susan Mae Hernando," he replied sharply, as he lifted her head towards his. "I will not I repeat I will not ever be disappointed in you or your brothers and sisters. Do you hear me?"

"But, Daddy..."

"No, buts Honey. I love you very much, and you'll never disappointment to me. If that's one lesson I learned in this life of mine, I don't want you running away like I did because I was disappointment to your Grandma Sara."

"Is that why you joined the army?" Caroline asked,

as she stood in the doorway.

He glanced over at her, but she wasn't alone. Yes his siblings were all there waiting for his answer, too. He drew in a big breath and exhaled slowly.

"Partly, but Andrew, Mom and Dad had big plans for you. Remember law school. You, all, were so much smarter than me."

"Yes, but you risked your life for all of us in that jungle, Sergeant Hernando," Allen said, as he made his way through. "We may be broken in some ways, but we all came home because of your bravery back then. You left no one behind, soldier. Now don't tell me how you're not smart. Who does a thing like that and still not let it all go to his head like most men would have?"

"You're a modest hero but a hero no less," Elizabeth answered with a small smile. "I'm proud of you, my little brother. I hope you will tell us your side of your time in the army. We only know what these guys started to tell us about saving their lives. But you told Rita that you wanted her to know the man who is not just her Dad."

"Ouch! Now my words bite me in the ass," he replied with a small grin. "I'll talk to you all later, but now I have to deal with Susan here."

"That's our clue to give them privacy," Caroline said with a bright smile. "Just like Mom. You're more like her than you will ever realize little brother."

"He's also like Dad, too," commented Andrew.

They said no more and walked away from the door. Rita closed it, so they were alone. Joshua loosened his collar of his shirt and took off his jacket. Susan got up and stood by the dresser now and couldn't look at him. So he walked over to her and put his hand on her shoulder. "Oh, Daddy," she cried out, as she buried her head into his chest now.

He held her close and didn't say a word. She sobbed, as he rubbed her back. She clung to him tighter. Joshua couldn't remember how long they stood there, but Susan looked up at him when she was cried out. Her eyes were puffy along with her red cheeks. She stood five foot two in height compared to her Dad's height of six foot two. She had blonde hair and oval-shaped brown eyes.

"Oh, Daddy," she cried out again.

"Before you start, let me tell you something. I said I disappointed your Grandma Sara. Let me tell you why."

She nodded. So they sat down on the edge of the bed.

"I was eleven-years-old when she turned her back on me forever," he started to explain.

"You need to study harder, Joshua. You need to focus more on school then playing all the time," Sara said to him, "Sometimes I think, you don't even try."

"I do try, Mommy," Joshua replied back. "I do try."

"You can't prove it by me, Joshua Matthew Adam Hernando. Your teacher wants to hold you back," said Sara. "Do you know, what your father will say about this?"

"No camping trip for me this summer," he answered back.

"No camping trip. Is that all? What about your future?"

"I just don't get the books, Mommy," he started to explain.

"Oh, forget it, Joshua. You are a big

disappointment to this family," Sara said, as she walked out of the room.

"But Mommy, I want to explain," he replied, as tears weld up in his eyes.

"Did you ever get the chance?" Susan asked him.

"No, I didn't, Honey. She didn't help me with my studies ever again."

"Were you held back?"

"No, I asked my teacher to give me oral exams from there on since I struggled with the books."

"Did she help?"

"Yes. My grades came up to at least a C average, so she had no other choice but to pass me. I did it for the next five years, but I still struggled with my studies. So what's wrong, Honey? I'll never turn my back on you, so talk to me. I promise."

Susan stared at him then down at her hands. He took them into his and stared at her.

"I love you, Susan," he replied calmly. "Always will no matter what."

"Daddy, I'm pregnant," she blurted out, as she turned her head away.

He bit his lower lip then he turned her head towards him. "Okay, so I'm going to be a grandfather again or unless you don't want to keep it."

"I'm no better than, Mom," Susan said with tears in her eyes.

"I don't follow you, Honey. What do you mean?"

"Mom cheated on you. That's why she divorced you. We had gone through two divorces besides yours when you found us again," Susan answered with tears again in her eyes.

"You're not married, Honey," he replied calmly. "Oh, I get it now. The baby's Daddy is."

She nodded. He wiped away her tears from her face with his thumb.

"Daddy, your hands are so rough."

"I know it's called hard work working with your hands and body for most of your life instead of your brain. Does he know about the baby?"

"Yes. I texted him a little while ago after I took the home pregnancy test," Susan answered calmly.

"Well first, we'll confirm it with a doctor."

"But Daddy, I took a test..."

"Don't worry, Honey."

"He wants me to have an abortion."

"Listen to me, please," he begged her.

"Maybe he's right for all concern, Daddy," she said sadly and honestly.

"What are you saying? I know, you admitted that he is married."

"Yes, and you know, him, too."

"I do."

She nodded, as she got to her feet to block the door. "You have to promise not to beat the crap out of him, Daddy. Promise me."

Joshua drew in a shallow then exhaled. "Against my better judgment, I promise. I've been in too many fights in my life. Do you hear me? I promise."

"Alex is the baby's father. We didn't plan it, Daddy."

"Rita's Alex," he replied, as he tried to process it,

"When? How? Why?"

"Rita was so wrapped up in taking care of you or so Alex said. About three months ago, he showed up on my doorstep and one thing led to another; as I comforted him. He peeled off my robe and took me on my couch then again in my bed. Then he followed me into the shower," Susan explained in detail. "I told him to go and pushed him towards the front door. He shoved me down on the hardwood floor and slapped me hard. It dazed me because the next thing I knew he was on me and in me. I felt his release, as his mouth covered mine. He had my hands pinned to the floor."

"That's why your face was bruised," Joshua replied calmly. "Was it the only time that day or other days?"

"Just that day Daddy, I swear. When his mouth came off mine, he warned me about screaming or telling anyone about it because it would be my word against his. He said he would be the one people would believe since he's an honorable, respected and married man," she answered honestly. "He did it two more times then left."

"Okay," Joshua replied, as his heart vibrated in his ears lightly despite not having hearing in the right but picked up speed. "You still need to confirm it."

"His last words were 'That's the best sex I've had in a very long time, bitch. I'll be back for more if you tell anyone, and I will fuck you so many times that you won't be able to count, bitch. Daddy, I know, he meant it."

"It's, okay, Honey. We need confirm it with a doctor. I have a friend. She owes me one. Now step away from the door. Please."

"But you promised, Daddy."

"I did that I did," Joshua replied with a smile. "I have to use the little boy's room. Please."

"Oh, sorry," she said, as she stepped out of his way.

Joshua walked out and into the bathroom. He ran cold water on his face then he joined everyone in the living room. He noticed Alex with Jenny, so he marched over to them.

"Hi, Josh," Alex said, as he looked up at him with a big self-confident smile.

"We need to talk privately," Joshua replied, as he tried to remain calm.

"Sure. Let's go outside."

"Sounds good," Joshua replied with a glance a brief glance over to Susan.

He winked at her then followed Alex out the front door. He shoved Alex towards his Blazer hard.

"Easy, Josh," said Alex. "What's on your mind?"

"I promised I wouldn't beat the crap out of you for her sake. You're lucky that I keep my promises," he answered as calmly as he could. "You had sex with Susan six times and threatened to come back for more. Did you plan on making her pregnant with your bastard child? Or was it rape?"

Alex's smile faded quickly. His face turned pale, and he had fear in his eyes now.

"Which one is it, Alex?" he asked him directly. "I'm waiting for your answer."

"You have to understand," Alex answered finally. "Rita..."

"Don't lie to me. You may have entered Susan's

place with that stupid story, but you had another reason for going there. Now again I'll ask you, and you better answer me honestly this time. Which one is it?"

Alex stood up straighter. "She was easy to screw since she never saw it coming. Six times only made me want to have more of her small body under mine. He knows his business when it comes to the Hernando women."

"What are you saying?" Joshua asked, as he tried to control his anger.

"Susan and Rita aren't the only ones he met inside," Alex answered with a confident smile.

"Are you saying what I ..."

"Yes Joan and your ex as well. She's a real dish your ex. We did it on Christmas day before we came to your house. I'm looking forward to having more of them with him in the New Year," Alex interrupted him.

"Why you," Joshua replied back, as he glanced down. "You're a sick, bastard. You better release but not into anyone I love or you'll be suffering a pain you will never forget."

Joshua stepped closed to Alex. Alex backed into the Blazer. Joshua unzipped Alex's zipper and grabbed his erect penis with one hand. He made sure no one saw what he was about to do to the man. He knew the position of the front window and door, so he stopped in their view. He squeezed hard on the penis, as he aimed it inside Alex's pants.

"Too bad you had to wet your pants. He's not to ever enter any woman I love ever again. Do I make myself clear? I'm waiting," he replied, as he squeezed harder.

"Yes, Sir," Alex answered, as wetness streamed down his pale face now. "Can you let go?"

"Why?"

"It hurts like..."

"Crap. Good then you'll remember how or where he belongs. Won't you?"

Alex nodded. Joshua let it go and smiled.

"Good day. Excuse me. I need to wash up," Joshua replied, as he lightly touched Alex's right cheek. "You can count your blessings for the promise."

Joshua walked back into the house. Susan walked up to him, but everyone else didn't seem to notice that they stepped outside.

"Daddy," she whispered back.

"He won't be coming back after you, Honey. Excuse me."

"But..."

"I kept my promise, Honey."

6

It was a couple days later, and Joshua picked up Susan at her place. He drove them to a tall medical building to be exact. He didn't speak to her all the way there. Susan sat in his Blazer with her hands on her lap and didn't try to engage him into any meaningless conservation. He took her hand into his, as they headed inside and to the elevators. Joshua tried to control his temper, so he decided not talk to her right away.

"I'm not angry with you, Honey," he replied finally, as they headed up to the fourth floor. "It's not your fault. Know now you're not like your Mom. Do you hear me?"

"Yes, Daddy, what happened outside after Uncle Roger funeral?"

"Let's just say he won't be coming after you ever again. Ah, here we are," he answered, as he opened the door. "I'll handle everything. Trust me."

She nodded. He smiled and walked up to the counter. A male nurse sat at a computer looked up at him.

"Yes, Sir, how can I help you?" he asked him.

"Josh, come in," a female said on the other side. "Carl, I got it. Thank you."

"Come on, Honey," Joshua replied back to Susan.

She got up and walked through an open door. She turned back to her Dad. He hugged the woman dressed in a white lab coat.

"Thank you," replied Joshua.

"I owed you one," she said with small smile.

"Susan, go straight ahead into that waiting

examining room. Please."

Susan nodded, walked in the room and stood there. She turned quickly at her Dad. He took her and guided her to a couple of chairs on side of wall of the room. She sat down, and the woman sat on a stool near them.

"Relax, Susan. My name is Robyn. I'm a GP doctor, and I would like to do an ultrasound," Robyn said calmly. "But first I need to know a few things. Now if you don't want your Dad..."

"He stays," Susan interrupted her.

"Okay," Robyn continued on. "Are you sexually active?"

"This was my first time," Susan answered, as she stared.

Joshua pounded his free hand into the arm of his chair.

"Easy, buddy," Robyn said, as she glanced over at him. "This isn't going to be easy for either of you."

"She can't get it back," Joshua snapped back.

"I'm aware of that fact," Robyn said sharply. "Now your Dad said he forced you to have sex with him six times. Is that correct?"

"Yes," Susan said, as she started to cry again.

"Did he have any protection at all?"

"Not to my knowledge."

"Did he intend to make you pregnant?"

"That's what I wanted to know, too. I was ready to rip his head off, but I remembered my promise to you, Susan. He said she wasn't the only Hernando woman he screwed," answered Joshua.

"He's Rita's husband," said Susan.

"Not just Rita, Honey," Joshua replied honestly.

"Josh, what are you saying here?" Robyn asked, as she stared at him again.

"I think, you should check Joan, Carly and Rita for any transmittal diseases, too," he answered, as he stared back at her.

"No, Daddy," Susan cried out.

"You wonder what I did to him. His penis became erect, as he talked about screwing you, Joan and your Mom."

"What did you do, Josh?" asked Robyn. "You didn't...."

"Yes, I did. He had it coming to him just like that other veteran who started to go after you. I grabbed Alex's friend and squeezed it hard, too," he answered, as he felt a cough start to build within him.

"Oh my..." Robyn started to say.

Joshua's cough was deep and husky like it always did. He let go of Susan's hand and reached for his chest. It was stronger than before, but Robyn was in front of him now.

"Calm down, Josh," she said calmly. "Easy, buddy, we need to calm down. This isn't going to help Susan. Susan, slip that gown on but keep your bottom half clothed. Hop onto the table. Please. Josh, focus on the waves crashing against the rocks."

Joshua closed his eyes and pictured the view of the ocean from his deck. The coughing was slowly down now. When he opened his eyes again, Robyn had his hands in hers, and he stared at her. She smiled back at him.

"Okay, buddy."

He nodded, so she tended to Susan. She did another test before she did the ultrasound, and Joshua stood beside Susan. He held her hand. He watched Robyn while Susan watched the monitor. Robyn looked worried. He could see her frown lines on her face.

"What?" he asked her; as he tried to stay calm himself.

"She's about six weeks along. It's up to you what you want to do, Susan. It's your body. We'll draw some blood for any transmittal diseases," Robyn answered with a sigh.

"There's more. Isn't there?" asked Joshua.

"I'm afraid so," Robyn answered sadly. "It might be the only child Susan will ever have."

"What? Why?" Susan asked in her confusion.

"He forced his way in all six times. Correct?"

Susan nodded.

"Your body wasn't ready for his entry," Robyn started to explain carefully. "He might have done some internal damage. It won't be able to be repaired. Now Josh, stay calm. Let me finish."

Reluctantly, he nodded back.

"We can't asset it while you're pregnant. So the choice is yours, Susan. You can have the baby then we'll see the damage afterwards. Or you can terminate it, and we check out the damage and try to see if anything can be done. But it could be ending a life you will only carry this once but never again. So the choice is yours alone, Susan. Your Dad and I can't make it for you not even Alex. It's your body and life," explained Robyn.

"Damn, bastard!"

"Daddy, I have to ask you…"

"I'll support whatever you decide, Honey. I love you, Susan."

"Whatever happened to the veteran?" Susan asked Robyn.

"He has never been able to get an erection after your Dad did that to him. So children weren't in the cards for him," Robyn answered honestly. "He tries, but it won't produce."

"So you knew what you were doing then," Susan said, as she stared at him.

"Clifford was a sex addict," said Robyn. "He was molested at five by his own mother. So it's his only way to be with a woman. I was his doctor after the fist fight."

"The woman said no, but he pushed it," Joshua explained calmly. "So I shoved him away. Well, he didn't walk away like I suggested him to do."

"That's how you got into the fight. But that's why you grabbed him there?" Robyn asked thoughtfully.

"He threw the first punch then all hell broke loose after that. The woman fled from the bar. Thank God," Joshua continued honestly. "You didn't notice it since you were reading his chart. He would have grabbed you if I hadn't stepped in."

"You mean it was…" Robyn said a little stunned.

"Why else would I have shoved him against that damn wall? You think I enjoyed fighting that I wanted to continue the fight," replied Joshua. "Remember he cut me with that beer bottle on the head and arm."

"You needed stitches for both as I recall and shot," said Robyn.

"Yep," Joshua replied back. "They're faint now."

"When did this happen?" Susan asked with interest.

"Mid-eighties, I think," Robyn answered thoughtfully.

"Late eighties I was looking for the kids and Carly back then. I had a temper back then, too. That's why I didn't like Clifford in how he was acting. He was drunk."

"Weren't you?" asked Robyn.

"No, I only started to drink my drink. I had about half in me when he acted like a jerk. But that's enough about the past. What are you going to do, Honey? I'll stand by you on whatever you decide. I love you."

"I don't like how it was conceived, Daddy. However, it might be the only child I'll ever have. You know, I'm pro-life," Susan answered calmly.

"So you're keeping it," replied Joshua. "It's fine with me, Honey. Now we need to discuss your health mainly the damage he caused."

"I must tell you that you could lose the baby, too due to what he did. We'll watch you carefully, and you won't be able to go through natural childbirth. It could cause more damage. But we'll take it one step at a time," Robyn explained to them.

"I don't have any insurance at my job," said Susan.

"Daddy, what am I going to do?"

"You're covered under your Dad's medical just like he has a GI bill to go to college. I wish you had taken it when you were younger. But it's still not too late, Josh."

"I told you then and again now. I'm not smart enough to go to college," he snapped back.

"Did you ever look at your grades before you entered the army?" asked Robyn.

"No, and I don't care to either. I'm stupid and did exactly what Dad told me about my life would be like. He was smart and knew his kids," he answered back.

"People make mistakes, Josh. You know, it firsthand. What makes your Dad any different then all of us struggling to survive in this world?"

"Are we done here?" he asked back sharply.

"Yes, but I have some things to discuss with Susan privately," answered Robyn.

"Fine, I'll wait outside."

"Thank you, Josh."

He nodded and walked out. But he paced the waiting room, as other patients stared at him. He had readjusted his army jacket for the fourth time when Susan emerged from the door.

"I'll see you in a month unless you need to see me sooner," Robyn said with a small smile.

"Thank you again, Robyn," Susan said calmly.

"Is it good between us, Josh?" Robyn asked him.

"Yeah, we're good," he answered with a small grin. "Thank you, Robyn."

She smiled back at him. He and Susan headed out. Susan took her Dad's hand, as they reached the elevator again. He felt her clammy hand in his.

"It's going to be okay, Honey," he replied back. "We'll figure out how to explain it to the family. But leave it to me."

"But, Daddy..." she started to protest.

"Let me be your Dad, please. We've struggled to

get this far in our relationship. I'm not walking away. I never wanted to walk away the first time," Joshua replied with a deep sigh. "I need time to iron out some details in my head first. Can you give me that?"

"Yes, Daddy, I love you."

"You know, I love you and don't worry; I'll keep my promise when it comes to Alex. That's what I have to iron out in my head, and how I'll tell the family."

"Daddy," she said, as she stared at him now.

He turned to face her. "Yes, Honey."

"Thank you."

"You're welcome, Honey," he replied, as they stepped out of the elevator and stood at his Blazer. "Are you hungry?"

She nodded, as she slipped in. So he got in and drove them to a local restaurant. They didn't speak on the way over or except to the waitress who gave them menus. Joshua took a pen out and wrote on his napkin check J&C.

"Daddy, I know, you're thinking. But what's that mean?" she asked, as she pointed to his napkin. "You mentioned Mom and Joan back at the office about being tested, too."

"He admitted to having sex with them, too. Your Mom on Christmas day, but no details when with Joan, I have to find out when and where," he answered, as he took a bite of his salad. "Eat please."

She nodded and begun to eat her salad, too.

"It's going to be all right, Honey. I need to figure out how to approach them with it," he replied, as he touched her left hand. "Those tests can be unsettling to most people."

"Did you have them done after Mom?" she asked with some uncertainty in her voice.

"Yes. It all came up negative, and I said to myself no more women. I didn't want to be exposed anything. They might have passed onto me or me exposing them to anything like AIDS. I came home to peace and free love which included drugs or hard drugs. Your Mom was the only woman for me in that way. I like women, but I didn't have much time for them."

"Looking for us was a full time job," added Susan.

"Partly and working odd jobs to hire people to locate you, guys. But I never gave up on you, all. I love you, guys that much."

"I'm beginning to see that these last thirteen years. We haven't made it easy."

"You needed time, and you came to me about this. Thank you."

"What for?"

"Letting me be your Dad."

"Rita has always said all along we didn't know the real you, and we should try and see it like she has."

"She's only beginning to see the real me."

"But she must have seen glimpse of the real you since you came back into our lives," Susan pointed out.

"She may have, I don't know or don't remember."

"But you're mentally stable, right?"

"Sound as they come, however, unlike some of us vets who came home from that war."

"Like Uncle Roger and Uncle James?"

"Uncle Roger wasn't insane. He dealt with flashbacks of prior to having a piece of metal in his leg that they would have to amputate below the knee. Now Uncle James or Jim keeps hearing that ringing in his ears since the bombing which he doesn't talk about. I think he suffered something to the inner ear."

"You don't have hearing in one ear. Why don't you get a hearing-aid?"

"The ear is silent now, yet I could swear heard Uncle Roger's scream, as he fell to his death," he answered, as he shook his head thoughtfully.

"Oh my, I'm so sorry, Daddy," Susan said honestly.

"It's okay. I know, he took me away from your Mom and you, kids, for years. I don't think he ever realized how it affected the people around him or himself for that matter. He tried to help me locate you, guys, too, and he offered what little money he could spare to help with the search."

"I didn't know that."

"There's a lot about my life you, kids, and Mom don't know."

"Like your schooling and Clifford."

"Susan, don't go there," he warned her. "I don't need you on my case like Robyn is."

"But you told me how Grandma Sara gave up on you, and what you did afterwards."

"I was making a point, remember? You said I would be disappointed in you."

"Daddy," she said with a frown.

"It's the truth. I know that look so don't remind me. It's your Mom's look when she thought I wasn't paying attention to what she was saying."

"Never mind, Daddy."

They ate the rest of their late-lunch, and Joshua walked Susan back to her front door. Alex stood there.

"Easy, Daddy," she whispered back to him.

"If he throws the first punch, all promises are off because I won't stand by and let him hit me," he whispered back, "Do you understand, Honey?"

"Yes, I do, Daddy."

"Susan, we need to talk privately," said Alex.

"Whatever you have to say to her, you'll have to say in front of me," Joshua replied in anger, "Her Dad."

"Uh..., it still hurts down there especially when I pee," Alex informed him. "I can't seem to get an erection either, so I'm going to a doctor to see..."

"Hate to see you waste money on it," Joshua interrupted him. "The last man I did it too hasn't become a father since and has the same problem. Save your money because you'll need it for alimony and child support for three children at least."

"You're keeping the baby!" Alex exclaimed in shock.

"I'm pro-life," said Susan.

"And I'll stand by her, her sisters and my ex, as they go through a series of tests any and all transmittal diseases you might have passed on," Joshua replied back calmly.

"I..."

"I don't believe you now or ever again. I'll be expecting you to take full responsibility for your actions. I suspect this isn't the first time since you told me about Joan and my ex. One tends to have done it before. You seem too pleased with him, and how he performs."

"Are you suggesting I divorce Rita?" Alex asked him.

"She'll divorce you after I tell her what you've done to her sisters and Mom," Joshua answered honestly. "Plus Susan here being pregnant with your child my grandchild."

"That's it. Isn't it? I produce two grandchildren with Rita, and you want more. So you convinced her to keep the baby," Alex snapped back.

"It was her choice after weighing the possibilities. So I respect and will honor it. Now move away from the door and leave her alone."

"You're not my father, and you don't own me," shouted Alex.

He threw a fist at Joshua's face. He drew blood on Joshua's lower lip. Joshua placed his hand in front of Susan now.

"It's off, Honey," he replied, as he glanced quickly at her. "I'm sorry."

"Come on, old man," Alex said in a fighting position now.

"You're going to regret it," warned Joshua.

They went to blows, as Susan stepped away. Alex bite Joshua's hand and ear as they fought. But Joshua managed an upper cut Alex's right eye. He knew it would turn black and blue since he had done it in a previous fight with someone else.

"Damn you, old man," yelled Alex. "I need this eye for my career."

"You should have thought of it before you threw the first punch."

They were fighting now on the ground. Alex tried

for Joshua's face, but he blocked the punch. Alex had no real form in his fighting. But Joshua had the military training as a soldier and knew hand to hand combat. He did exceptionally well back in basics. It had come in handy through the years.

"Dad!" exclaimed Rita.

Alex hit Joshua in the chest, and Joshua had begun to cough. He clenched his chest, as it got more aggressive. The girls were at his sides now. Rita rubbed his back gently, as Susan looked on with worry.

"Easy, Dad," Rita said calmly.

"You're on your deck and see the ocean in the distance. Hear the seagulls and fog horns on the boats, as they approach the docks," Susan whispered to him.

Joshua closed his eyes and listened to what Susan said. It calmed him and his cough. He could see and hear it all. His smile had begun to form now, as he breathed easier. He opened his eyes and looked at his girls. Then he looked up at Alex. He had a black eye, a bloody nose and split lip, but he clung to his rib cage, too. Joshua got him good, as he spit out some blood.

"What's going on here?" Rita asked in anger. "Dad? Alex? I damn an explanation."

"Your choice me or you, either way it's going to be the truth," Joshua answered back.

"You got to be kidding, old man," Alex snapped back. "You attacked me for no damn reason."

"No damn reason," he replied back, as he got to his feet. "Own up to the truth, you coward."

"Dad, stop!" exclaimed Rita.

"You tell her or I will," yelled Joshua.

"Rita, take me to the hospital. My ribs hurt like hell," Alex whined at her.

"No not until you tell her in front of me and her sister," he replied, as he blocked Rita. "Tell her now, bastard!"

He shook his head, no, as he stared at Joshua. Joshua used his other hand to keep him away from Susan.

"I don't care who tells me about what's going on. Just I can't…"

"I'm pregnant with Alex's child. He raped me after telling me lies about you, Rita," Susan blurted out.

"What!" Rita exclaimed in disbelief.

"He can't keep his friend in his pants. He had relations with Joan and your Mom, too. I recommend you all get tested for various diseases including AIDS. It's not the first time he has strayed from you. I'm sure of it," explained Joshua. "Don't blame your sister because he knew full well what he was doing. Now this might be or will be the only child she'll ever have."

"What are you saying, old man?" asked Alex.

"You forced your friend inside her before she was ready six times and caused possible internal damage. Damage they can't assess right now due to her condition," Joshua explained in anger.

"Oh My Gosh!" exclaimed Rita. "Is that why…"

"He hasn't had sex with you in a few days. No, baby girl, I squeezed his friend so hard that it caused pain to pee and probably can't get an erection either. I'm sorry. I recommend you divorce this bastard and get child support and anything else you can from this horny bastard."

"Dad, no," Rita said with tears in her eyes now.

"Divorce isn't in the cards, old man. I know, Rita, and she won't divorce me," Alex said with a big smile.

"We'll see about it, bastard," Joshua snapped back.

"I'll be back for my car after I take Alex to the hospital," Rita said calmly.

"What? After what Dad just told you, Sis," Susan said surprised by it. "You can't..."

"Believe I'm doing this. I owe it to my children to take care of their Dad. I won't let them grow up without their Dad in their own home."

"Rita, don't do it," replied Joshua. "Please."

"Sorry, Dad, I'm all grown up now," Rita said, as she walked over to Alex. "Let's get you to a hospital."

Alex grinned back at them, as he leaned on her.

They headed down the walkway. Joshua wanted to beat him up more, but he felt Susan's hand on his shoulders now. He stared at her. She was crying, so he hugged her. Joshua couldn't remember how long they stood there. But he did manage to get her inside and into her warm bed.

Susan let him be her Dad. He cleaned himself up and stretched out in her lazy-boy chair. He stared at the floor and the couch, as he shook his head. He noticed some magazines next to the chair, so he picked one up. He glanced at the pictures and stopped at one in particular.

"Mommy, what's this?" Joshua asked, as he held out the page to her.

"Read it, Joshua," Sara answered, as she continued to place cookie dough on the cookie sheet. "You're old enough now."

"But, Mommy."

"You can do it."

"San Fran...cisco's...Cliffff house," he replied with difficulty.

"Now repeat it again."

"San Francisco's Cliff house," he repeated back, "Have we ever been there?"

"Good," she said with a small smile. "No, it's a bit pricing to eat there and take you, kids, there."

"That's why we go to the wharf," he replied with a big smile, "Besides we can see all those seagulls."

"Exactly."

"Someday I'll take the whole family there. Do you think we'll see the ocean?"

"Yes because of where it's located on a cliff. It's the first of three on that location," Sara explained to him. "You don't need to take us to a place like that."

"But I want to."

"Stop, you're hurting me," Susan yelled, as she brought him back into the present.

He rushed into the room and straight to her bed. He took her into his arms and held her. She shook violently. Joshua stroked her back and rocked her gently. Susan clung to him with all her strength.

"I'm here, Honey," he whispered calmly. "I'm not leaving you."

"Daddy, I'm scared," she said sadly. "What if he comes back?"

"I'm here as long as you need me, Honey. He hurt you once and once was too much," he answered back.

"Daddy, lie down next to me," Susan said, as she

now looked into his blue-gray eyes. "Please."

He nodded. She moved over, as he stretched out beside her. She snuggled close to him, as he wrapped one arm around her.

"Thank you, Daddy. I love you."

"I love you, too, Susan. Now let's get some sleep."

She rested her head on his chest. She drifted off to sleep, as he hummed "Puff the Magic dragon" to her. Soon he felt his own eyelids had heavier and soon fell asleep, too.

7

Joshua stirred, as he thought he dreamed of loud voices. But then it hit him. It was Carly's voice coming from the living room, and Susan wasn't beside him anymore. She had gotten up and now faced her Mom alone. He sprung off the bed and felt a sharp pain in his chest.

He tried to ignore it, as he reached for the door. He opened it to see his ex and their daughter face to face. Susan was crying again. He could tell from her puffy pink cheeks. She stood there bravely, as she could before her Mom.

"Enough!" he exclaimed, as he stood in the doorway.

"Daddy," Susan said, as she rushed to him. "Are you okay?"

"The pain will pass," he answered back. "What's going on here?"

"Our daughter here is pregnant," Carly answered in anger. "I was telling her how irresponsible she is."

"More like yelling, Carly," he pointed out calmly.

"Now sit down and calm down," he turned to Susan. "I need a glass of water, Honey."

She nodded and left. He backed Carly to the couch, yet she stared at him. He still had a hand on his chest.

"You look like hell," commented Carly.

"Yeah like a train wreck, I know. I'm not as young as I used to be, but I didn't want Alex get the best of me."

"Our son-in-law, why were you fighting him?" she

asked puzzled by it.

"He raped our daughter here, and now she's pregnant with his child. He told me about you and him on Christmas day. He gloated about having sex with our other daughter Joan, too," Joshua answered back. "He raped Susan six times in this very apartment. The first time right where you're sitting, then her bed, shower and three more times on the floor over by the front door. So you and Joan should be tested as well as Rita. A guy like him tends to have a string of relationships when he's stuck on his friend."

"Daddy," Susan shouted, as she walked into the room.

He moved closer to her and took the glass from her. Carly moved closer to them, too. She touched Susan's hand. Susan stared at her Mom.

"He took advantage of her," Joshua replied calmly. "He charmed her into believing all Rita cared was me. We have to convince her to divorce him. He may or should say will be a father again."

"What did you do?" Carly asked, as she turned quickly at him.

"He squeezed it hard and has done it before the man can't get an erection to this day," Susan explained in a low voice.

"He was a fellow vet, and it wasn't one of my proudest moments. You had the kids, and I was trying to find you. I still love you after all these years. I haven't been with any woman but you, Carly. I wanted my family back. I know, I made my mistakes along the way," he replied honestly. "Roger came first then you and the kids. It wasn't fair to you, all. I'm sorry."

"I look into those blue-gray eyes and see pain. I saw it when we first met. I know, Roger was a big part of your life before I married you," Carly whispered back. "I hoped it would change, as we started our family; but he demanded more of your attention. I didn't know you had family until Patrick was little and was carrying James. Later Rita was born, and I discovered more. You never talked about them. But you rocked her to sleep one night shortly after she came home. You said something about her eyes."

"Mom's eyes," Joshua replied with tears in his eyes. "Susan is a lot like Caroline. Joan is a lot like Elizabeth. And the boys are a mixture of your Dad, my Dad and my brother and yours."

"And you," Carly added. "But Luke is more like you in a lot of ways. He keeps to himself and doesn't let people know him. You were like that when we met at the diner."

"That seems like a lifetime ago," Joshua added with a small grin. "Now you have to listen carefully to what I'm about to say."

Carly nodded.

"Susan decided to keep the baby. We have to accept it if she carries the baby full term or shorter," Joshua replied cautiously.

"What do you mean?"

"He may have caused damage that's irreversible. This might be the only child I'll ever have," Susan explained, as she bit her lower lip. "I've been pro-life all my life. So..."

"Abortion is out of the question," Carly filled in. "I understand, Susan. I'll have the tests done."

"Get a test for AIDS, too," added Joshua.

"Do you think...oh never mind," Carly said in mid-thought. "I'll get Joan tested, too. Susan, remember I love you. Okay."

Susan nodded then they hugged. Joshua drank the water, as he walked over to the lazy-boy chair. He felt he was being watched.

"He's no fighter just a scraper," he replied, as he stared at them.

"Does it hurt, bad?" asked Carly.

"Not much, it'll pass. He has strong teeth, but my jacket is stronger. I guess that's why he had to go for the other places. Are you, ladies, a little hungry?"

"Some, Dad, but I can order combo pizza. We don't need to go out."

"You have nothing to be ashamed of, Honey."

"I know, but I see you are sore, and I want to be with you and Mom alone."

He nodded and smiled back. Carly nodded, too. So Susan walked into the kitchen to order the pizza. He sat down and stared at Carly. She walked over to him. She combed back his hair and noticed the cut on his upper lip.

"I cheated on you, yet you still love me."

"Yep," he replied back.

"And no other woman since me," she whispered back.

"Yep, you spoiled me," he replied back honestly. "No other woman held or will hold a candle to your beauty."

"Stop," she said, as she was blushed a bright pink.

He pulled her face closer to his and kissed her lips

gently. It tasted as sweet as honey, just like the first time they kissed. He remembered it all too well now. It seemed only like it was on yesterday when they shared that first kiss on their wedding day.

"Stop," she said, as she pulled away.

"It'll be here in a half hour. I'll make a salad. I got only water and milk for beverages," said Susan.

"Milk sounds great, Susan," Carly said, as she smiled. "We love milk. Don't we?"

"Yes we do," Joshua answered with a warm smile. "Yes we do."

Carly joined Susan, and together they walked back into the kitchen. Joshua closed his eyes and smiled.

"Who drinks milk?" Roger asked, as they sat in the diner. "They have wine and beer here."

"Milk is just fine for me, buddy," Joshua answered with a smile. "But you order whatever. I'm driving. Remember?"

"Yeah, I know, I can't believe I didn't ace that test," Roger said a little pissed off.

"What will you gentleman have to drink today?" Carly asked, as she stood at their table now.

"Large milk, please," Joshua answered, as he made eye contact with her.

She smiled back.

"Budweiser and keep them coming," Roger answered, as he stared at the menu.

"I'm driving," Joshua informed her.

"I'll have a New York steak medium well with the works. Plus chili and chili cheese fries," Roger said to her. "Do you have all that, baby doll?"

"Yes," Carly answered back, "And for you?"

"Clam chowder with fisherman's platter," Joshua answered politely. "Could I get a side order of the vegetable of the day instead of coleslaw?"

She nodded.

"Are you still here?" Roger asked her. "I want my beer, baby doll."

"I'll be right back with your drinks," Carly answered before she rushed off.

"Thank you," replied Joshua.

She nodded again. Joshua watched her walk away.

"Man, you keep looking at her like that you'll have to fuck her or marry her," Roger said with a small grin.

"I wouldn't mind being married to her for the rest of my life," he replied back with big smile. "She's beautiful."

"You act like you've never dated a girl before. You're twenty-one, man."

Joshua glanced back at Roger. Roger stared at him briefly.

"Oh, crap," Roger snapped back.

Joshua only nodded. Carly returned with their drinks, chili and chili cheese fries. Roger drank half of his beer before she finished putting it all down.

"I'll bring you another," she said to Roger.

He ate his chili fast along with his fries. Carly walked away with a smile for Joshua. He drank his milk and ate his clam chowder in silence.

"I'm going to marry her," he replied, as he finished his dinner.

"You're crazy, man," stated Roger. "We're not

heroes but baby killers. Or have you forgotten that fact? Oh, you're a hero to all who you saved but not to the outside world."

"I'm going to marry her," Joshua repeated. "I'm going to win her heart."

"Didn't you notice huge rock on her hand?" asked Roger. "She belongs to someone else."

"Things can change, buddy."

"You're crazy, man."

"Dad, pizza is ready," Susan said, as she leaned into his face.

"Uh...thank you," he replied with hesitation.

"You had a big smile on your face, Dad," Susan said, as she stepped back. "It must have been a good dream. You haven't had many of those. Have you?"

"No," he answered, as he headed for the table. "I was only remembering our first meeting at the diner." He stared at Carly who had already sat down. "I knew I wanted to spend the rest of my life with you. Roger thought I was crazy."

Carly blushed, as she stumbled to hand him the bowl of salad. He took it and grazed her hand with his.

"I was engaged to Robert back then," Carly explained, as she found her voice again. "He was my high school sweetheart and he came from wealth. He was called to serve, too, like your Dad."

"How did Dad win your heart?" Susan asked with some excitement in her voice now.

"A single red rose everyday for two weeks with a note attached to it," Carly answered thoughtfully with a big, warm smile.

"What did it say, Mom?"

"One word each week," Carly answered, as she stared at Joshua now.

"I don't understand."

"'**Will**' was the first word," Joshua answered back.

"'**You**' were the second."

"**Will you**..." Susan said, as she tried to put it together.

"I was spelling out will you marry me when I ran out of money," Joshua replied quickly. "I was forced to leave her hanging because of Uncle Roger needed me, too. It would cause her and me to be apart for the next three years."

"When I saw your Dad again, I couldn't believe how much he had aged," commented Carly.

"I was surprised to see her again, too. Roger was in the Palo Alto hospital for some tests for new leg, so I stopped at Spangers in Berkeley to get a bite to eat. There was your Mom waitressing again or still but in a different location," Joshua replied with a small smile. "I was working construction by then, and Roger had several bouts with the war and pre-loss of his leg. I looked like hell."

"Like you did a little while ago," added Carly. "I couldn't believe I was seeing him again."

"She waited on me and acted like she didn't know me at all."

"I didn't at first then you ordered the large milk."

"I noticed no ring on her finger like Roger pointed out three years before. I knew I could stand a chance again. I wasn't going to leave this time."

"We had milk after my shift that day and days to

follow. I told him how I kept what he sent me and asked him why he stopped."

"Because of Roger or Uncle Roger," added Susan.

"Yeah, but not completely, but I asked her about the rock she had on her finger at our first meeting."

"Robert had come back six months after your Dad disappeared. He wasn't the same man I knew and loved. War changed him, so I gave him his ring back. Then I moved on with my life alone or until I met your Dad again," explained Carly. "Your Dad asked if I knew what he was asking before. I said I think so. Then...."

"I asked, what would be her answer," interrupted Joshua, "I didn't want to spend anymore than I had to away from her again. You see, I thought of her a lot, as I was working and helping Roger. She was my reason to face another day by putting one foot in front of the other."

"But you married in '68," pointed out Susan.

"I had to prove myself to your grandfather and Uncle Henry that I was a sane soldier from the war. But it wasn't easy."

"What do you mean, Daddy?"

"I had to prove I was worthy to take care of your Mom."

"So you won them over."

"But the only one I wanted to win over was your Mom, but I did win them, too, in the end."

"We were happy. Weren't we, Josh?"

"Happiest I had ever been my whole life," he answered said, as he turned to Susan. "When your Grandma turned her back on me, I was very lost and realized I hadn't been really happy as a boy growing up, but

I could see things clearly with your Mom. I thought the toys meant happiness but like Andrew said they didn't last. I saw it how true that was. Then I was shocked by the affair, but I wanted my family back."

"I thought you hated me," Carly said painfully.

"I know, I yelled and said things in anger because of the initial shock. Then time passed, and you were all gone. It's why I wanted to find you, all. I reacted in haste. In the past I had always thought things through, but I was out of control. This felt different somehow," he replied, as he stared at her now.

"Why?"

"I felt love and secure, and I hadn't had them in a very, long time. You understood me when no one else did. Do you remember our long walks on the beach?"

"Yes. You were a man of few words except for telling me how you longed for a family of your own. You never discussed the war, or what it was like over there," Carly answered thoughtfully. "You mostly listened to me, and what I dreamed about as a little girl."

"You told me about Robert, too. What he was like before and after the war. I said...."

"War changes people like him and Roger," she interrupted him. "That's the last he said about the war. When Roger went through his flashbacks, your Dad here only said he had to go, but he would be back soon. I felt like a time traveler's wife."

"But he was strung out on meds, as he stood next to me on our wedding day, and you looked as beautiful the day when we first met," replied Joshua. "You glowed during your pregnancies."

"I didn't think you noticed me that much."

"I did. It was hard to leave you with kids alone, as I headed out to help Roger," he replied back. "I wanted to stay so many times, but you would say go and wave your hand at me. You struggled with our kids while I dealt with the war over and over again with Roger. I was stuck in the past, and you and the kids were living in the present and future. Then I came back and ...."

"I was with another man," Carly interrupted again. "You yelled and screamed things I didn't understand."

"I was angry. How could you? I didn't understand betrayal before. You were my first and only love, Carly. I know, I said in anger to get out of my house. I didn't want to live with a whore. You don't know how many times I regretted saying those things to you. Then I was served with the divorce papers, and I realized you didn't want me back. You couldn't forgive me. You turned your back on me like Mom did years before."

"But you signed the papers," pointed out Carly.

"Because of the note attached to them," Joshua replied honestly.

"What note?"

Joshua reached into his wallet and unfolded a piece of worn out white piece of paper. He held it out.

"What does it say, Mom?"

"It's over," Carly answered back. "But you spent time and money looking for us."

"I hit rock bottom, as I got into a lot I mean a lot of fights with Roger and Steve starting them. I barely got healed from one then we were in another one. I thought of when I was most happy," he replied back. "It was with you and the kids. I started looking for you then Roger chipped in some money, too. I think, he realized how unhappy I was, but he couldn't stop his flashbacks. So he gave me money out of guilt. He wanted to settle down, too. He also noticed you knew where to find me, but I had no clue about your whereabouts. Plus I hadn't taken off my wedding band even after the divorce was finalized."

"You're not wearing it now," Carly pointed out.

"It's here with my dogs tags," he replied, as he pulled out the chain around his neck. "I didn't want to confuse the kids and grandchildren about us being still married."

"That was nice of you," Carly said, as she looked into his eyes. "I don't know where my rings are now?"

"In a small brown box under your wedding dress in your hope chest," said Susan.

"How do you know that?" Carly asked with interest.

"Rita and I found them, as we played dress up," Susan answered with a little pink in her cheeks now.

"So you still have them after all these years," Joshua replied with a small grin.

"I guess, I do," she said with small smile back. "Leave it to our daughters."

"You didn't want me back in your lives. Remember?"

"But Rita did. She wanted her Daddy," commented Carly.

"And the rest of us stood on the sidelines and waited for you, Mom. We heard a lot about Dad through Rita and wanted to go to him. But..."

"You thought I wouldn't approve," Carly filled in. "It's because I thought he hated me."

"I guess, I should have said I was sorry that day I stood on your doorstep maybe things could have been different," Joshua replied sadly and thoughtfully.

"It didn't help when I yelled at you. I didn't let you speak because I was afraid of the past. I didn't want you to bring it up again not in front of the children again."

"I said it all in front of the kids," Joshua replied a little shocked.

Carly nodded. "They thought it was you in our bed, so they didn't enter the room unless it was an emergency."

"You were gone a couple days later, as Mom packed our all belongings with hers," Susan said in a low voice. "The man helped us. We moved into his house."

"I shouldn't have done it," Carly said sadly. "But I had nowhere else to go. By the time Rita was five, I had lost Mom and Dad, and I didn't know where Harry was. Manuel said I shouldn't be married to a man with a temper like that. So I filed for divorce despite I still loved you."

"I signed the papers because of that note," replied Joshua.

"I didn't attach it to the papers," Carly said with tears in her eyes. "I kept moving with the kids because I didn't want you to hurt them. They needed a father figure in their lives who was there for them and kind and loving."

"Manuel wasn't that, Mom. He controlled you like he tried to control us. We fought back. That's why he left and never looked back. Patrick made sure of it," said Susan.

"But..."

"You were really screwed up after you and Dad

divorced. You entered relationships for us, not for your own happiness, so they were doomed from the start."

"How..."

"Rita was the youngest and held us together. She would remind us of Dad and you. You were truly happy with him when he wasn't off helping Uncle Roger. She told us the day she met Uncle Andrew. We waited for you to tell us more."

"I didn't know about him or your aunts."

"I didn't talk about my family. They didn't like me very much after your Grandma Sara died. So I shut them away just like the war. It was part of my past I didn't discuss."

"But you saw grandma's eyes in Rita as a baby," Susan pointed out.

"I thought I was alone, and no one knew until now. You had never pressed it, Carly. Why?"

"I waited on those long walks at the beach. I knew you had parents and maybe siblings, but I loved you enough to not push it," answered Carly. "I knew the man I was so deeply in love with had his secrets, and I had to wait patiently for you to reveal them. I shared everything with you in hopes you would share it all with me. But it never came."

"Until now," replied Joshua.

"You seemed to have this so far away look, as you looked out at the ocean, but now I see a different man before me. He is open about his past and willing to let people see him for what he has done in his life..."

"Including mistakes. I'm sorry, Carly. I can't stress it enough."

"What's changed, Dad?"

"I guess time alone and more recent events since I found you, all, again," he replied, as he stared at her, "And Uncle Roger being on that roof top and you."

"I understand me but not Uncle Roger."

"In the past flashbacks, he freaked out before his leg was gone."

"And it was different this time," said Carly.

"Yes, I didn't have time up on that roof to process what happened. But it became clearer with my CO that Roger was living with was after it was gone. We had rehashed the events leading up to it that I knew what to say and do to get him off that ledge. But I couldn't get him off because it was different. It was new situation. One we hadn't worked through before, so the old things didn't work."

"So he died," Susan said sadly.

"I think, he lost his balance and the helicopter spooked him. I couldn't get to him fast enough," Joshua replied, as he cried openly now. "I miss him so damn much like Mom and Dad."

Carly grabbed him close to her chest now. "Cry Joshua for them now. You're not alone. You haven't disappointed any of us. We love you, Joshua Matthew Adam Hernando."

"Why?"

"Because that's what family does," Carly answered calmly.

"Daddy, I'm sorry about keeping you at a distance until now," Susan said sadly.

"It's okay, Honey. I'm just glad you came to me on

your own just like Rita did. It had to be that way, Honey. If you came by force, it wouldn't be good for either of us because there would be tension between us. I knew it firsthand."

"I don't understand," she said confused.

"Your Grandma Sara had to be the peacemaker between me and your Grandpa Martin. I guess she felt she had to do it. So she got tired of it as years went on. That's why she turned her back on me that last and final time. It was too much."

"But you're not sure about that, are you?" Susan asked him.

"No, I'm not. But it makes sense to me, as I had time to think about my life twelve long years."

"But you never talked to Uncle Andrew or Aunts Caroline and Elizabeth our whole lives."

"I think you should talk to them. They have things to say to you, too," commented Susan.

"They do?" he asked with some interest now.

Susan nodded. He glanced into Carly's face. She nodded, too.

"Not now but soon. We have another matter to face first," he replied back. "Our daughter here needs us, Carly. Are we ready for it?"

"Our children need us, Josh," she answered with a bright smile.

"That's the smile that captured my heart back in '64 and couldn't get out of my mind while we were apart."

"Silly, old man," Carly said, as she nudged him.

"Who's old?"

They all laughed and finished their dinner. Carly

headed back to her place while Joshua stayed with Susan. He didn't trust Alex. So he was going to protect his daughter with his life. He was and is her Dad again. She wanted him back in her life. He thought after he walked back into Susan's place after walking Carly to her car.

"Good night, Daddy," she said, as she headed off to her room. "Are you sure you will be comfortable on the couch?"

"I'll be fine, Honey. You call me if you need me for anything," he answered back.

"It was nice to hear how you and Mom got together corny as it sounds," she said with a small grin.

"I'm glad you shared, too."

I'm glad you both are in my life now. Get some sleep, Honey," he replied back with a small grin. "Maybe you can tell your siblings how corny we were."

"You know, I was right when I told you about Mom not being happy with those other men," said Susan.

"Give it a rest. Will you? Now go to bed, Honey. We can talk more another time. We're both tired."

She nodded and closed her door. He checked the front door again before he stretched out on her couch. He was a little angry that Alex took advantage of her on there and the floor by the front door. So he decided to be use the lazy-boy. It was easier to accept. Plus it helped his aching back now. He closed his eyes and saw Carly's face there. It made him smile.

8

It was more than once Joshua relived coming in and out of the jungle. He felt the mist on his body, as he carried another comrade to safety. Then the explosions followed it and damaged his right ear forever. It was four days into the New Year, and Carly and Joan had the tests done. They waited for the results which was pure agony for all involved.

Rita hadn't returned his calls since his fight with Alex. She shut him off from her and his grandchildren which he had a right to see under grandparent law. Carly said she would try talking to her. So all he could do is wait for the outcome.

However, their other children were brought together on New Year's Eve over to Susan's apartment to explain what was going on. It had been four days since Roger was laid to rest and three days after Susan seen Robyn the first time and his fight with Alex. Carly volunteered to be the one who field their questions and answers instead of Joshua.

Joshua stared at their faces and tired to read them in how they were taking it all in. But he couldn't since he didn't know them well enough yet. All he saw was the faces of them back in the mid-eighties just before Rita's fifth birthday. None of them spoke to him when Carly finished, but they offered love and support for Susan.

It was clear how they held back, but Alex had said something to them. It made Joshua angry because he didn't know what he was up against, and no one was giving him any clue to help understand. He's only hope could be is time to figure it all out. He didn't like their distance which hurt him deeply.

A knock on his front door made him jerk towards it quickly. So he marched over to open it. A man stood before him who was mirror image of himself only younger.

"Can I come in, Sir?" he asked politely.

"Yes, please," Joshua answered, as he nodded his head. "I know, we don't know each other, but you can call me, Dad."

"I'll have to think about it, Sir," he said sharply. "I'll decide if and when I call you that, Sir."

"Fair enough, I understand," Joshua replied, as he headed to the deck. "Please close the door behind you."

He listened for it to close with his good ear and smiled. Yes, his son did listen after all these years. He leaned on the railing and gazed out at the ocean.

"What brings you here, Luke?" he asked, as he made eye contact with him.

Luke stood straight and proud of the man who he was, and he was confident, too. He wore an Air Force jacket, cords and work boots. Joshua remembered what Carly told him about how Luke was like him.

"Do you want to walk on the beach?" he asked him.

"If you're up to it, Sir," Luke answered finally.

"I love the beach and looking out at the ocean anytime of the day. It calms me like your Mom used to years ago."

"But..." Luke started to say something then decided not to.

"I've got steps leading to the beach," he replied, as he headed that direction. "Don't worry no one will break in. If they do, I don't have much worth stealing except my memories."

Luke followed him in silence. They walked to the beach, and he flipped his army jacket collar around his neck. Luke tucked his hands into his pockets and said nothing. Joshua breathed in the fresh air and felt refreshed by it.

"This is the life outside of warm clam chowder, fresh crab cakes and a freshly made crab cocktail."

"And an extra large glass of cold milk to wash it all down," added Luke.

"Exactly," Joshua replied with a warm smile. "You and I are a lot like, so your Mom tells me. Tell me about yourself, son."

"I don't think so, Sir," Luke said sharply.

"So what brought you here then?"

"This," he answered back. "It's a restraining order. I had friends pull some strings, so she wouldn't have to face you in court," Luke said coldly.

"Who?"

"Rita, Alex and the kids, I'll be there for Susan as her twin brother, but I'll also be there for Rita, too. Don't ask me to choose a side. They're my sisters after all. I've got to go now. Will you need help back?"

"I'll be fine," Joshua answered, as he took the papers.

"Goodbye, Sir," Luke said, as he turned sharply and headed back to the house.

"He has it in him. The military training is still

there," he whispered to himself. "He served in the Air Force. Maybe I need to talk to Carly more."

He stopped and watched Luke ahead of him. It was hard to see his youngest son walk away, but he had to give them time and distance. He trudged up the steps a little later and leaned on the railing again.

"Buddy, are you okay?" a male voice asked him.

Joshua glanced up to see two other men in army jackets like his and found their faces. Steve and Scott stood in their army combat clothes. He nodded, as he walked by them. He could hear their boots hit the deck with deep thuds. They had their own battle scars of their war in Vietnam.

"How about some hot clam chowder, buddies?" he asked, as he headed inside.

"Okay," answered Scott.

"Sounds warm," Steve added. "Do you have any beer?"

"Nope only milk, green tea and instant coffee," Joshua replied, as he poured clam chowder into a deep pot. He used two storage containers to make sure there was enough. "So what will be, buddies?"

"Instant coffee then," Steve said, as he leaned against the sink.

He nodded and grabbed a cup out of the cupboard. Scott had the milk carton in his hand and was a man of few words since the war like some of the Vietnam vets. Joshua understood it because he didn't talk about it either. The chowder was hot enough to serve now, so he divided it into three bowls.

"Hot water from the tap makes semi-warm

coffee," said Steve. "It'll have to do since I don't know how to use a microwave. Plus, you and Scott are milk drinkers of all things."

Scott sat down with two glasses of milk while Joshua walked to the table with three bowls on a tray. Steve had his coffee and sat down, too. Joshua handed them each a bowl before he joined them.

"Thank you," Scott said in a low voice.

"You're welcome, buddy," he replied with a small smile.

"So you took a walk on the beach alone," stated Steve.

"No, my youngest son Luke of few words stopped by," he answered, as he blew on his chowder.

"Why?" asked Steve.

"To serve me these," he answered, as he put his spoon down and took out the papers from his pocket.

Steve reached for them and scanned the pages. "Crap. Why?"

"A family matter."

"But you and Rita are close," Steve pointed out the obvious.

"Were close but now this has divided us," he replied sadly.

"It can't be that bad," protested Steve.

"Steven, let it go. Can't you see it hurts him to even mention it," Scott said in a calm voice.

"Don't call me, Steven," snapped Steve. "We survived a war together not heroes war, but we all came home alive as so many wish we hadn't."

"Ours was due to this man, here. He saved our

butts in that jungle over there. He's entitled to some privacy," Scott said back.

Joshua ate his chowder in silence. He felt Steve's anger start to build inside him. It was coming soon since he wasn't a man to let things go easily.

"Tell us why you and Rita are estranged," Steve yelled at him. "Or I'll find out from her myself."

"Stop it!" Joshua exclaimed, as he got to his feet. "This is a family matter, and I'll deal with it on my own. It's my family not yours, Steven, so butt out of it. It's none of your damn business."

He had begun to cough which attacked his body now. He slumped back into his chair. Scott was at his side and rubbed his back.

"Easy, buddy," he whispered in Joshua's good ear. "Calm down. Someone needs to take a walk and leave the truck keys on the table."

"Fine," Steve snapped, as he slammed the keys on the Oak table. "I'll take a walk out there on the beach."

"Thank you," Scott said politely.

Steve stormed outside. Joshua calmed down enough now. But Scott remained at his side and looked concerned.

"Thanks, Scott," he replied back.

"I owe you my life," said Scott. "We all do."

"I know."

"We don't have to talk about it, you know."

"But I want to. I may have lost my baby girl because of her husband. I can't tell Steve because he's always been the hottest head of all of us. Matt is mild compared to him."

"That's true. Go slow then and take your time."

"Alex raped Susan six times in her place nearly four months ago. She is pregnant with his child," he explained, as he bit his lower lip. "He caused irreversible damage that can't be asset until after the baby is born. Yes, she's keeping it since it's probably the only child she will ever have. We don't know if it will be full term or not at this point." He paused for a moment to gather his thoughts again.

"There's more. Isn't there?"

Joshua nodded. "Yes, I'm afraid so."

"I know, and understand if you already said too much, Josh. You're right about it being a family issue. You don't have to explain anymore."

"But I need to tell someone outside the family. I didn't open up to Carly and anyone else about my life years ago. It cost me a lot," he replied painfully. "Alex had sex with Carly and Joan, too. He was proud of his damn friend. I haven't asked Carly and Joan about their encounter with him in detail. Susan told me in detail about hers. It was hard for her to come to me since I hadn't been part of her life for twelve long years. Then I was back, and Rita who came to me first. I had to give them time and space despite how I wanted so desperately to be a part of it all by being in their lives again. I let my family down, Scott."

"Stop, man, Susan came to you, and you were there," Scott said back. "You didn't walk away or blame her, right?"

"He's scamper. He doesn't know how to fight like a real man. He bites," he replied thoughtfully. "I'm not walking away from any of my family that includes Rita."

"Good. She'll come around. She came to you before. She'll do it again," pointed out Scott.

"Thanks, buddy, I don't think I could have told Steve."

"He has a real bad temper all right, but so did you for awhile."

"Yes believe it or not, I was meaner than he is back when I was trying to find my family."

"But you're not like that way anymore, Josh. You always knew when to choose your battles and when to back off. Steve doesn't show that restraint."

"I didn't back then."

"Who hurt Susan?" Steve asked, as he stood in the doorway of sliding glass door. "Who made her pregnant?"

"Steve, let it go," Joshua answered, as he stared at him. "I'll deal with it, not you."

"We all became a family back in Nam, buddy, so your children and grandchildren are part of the family, too. We take care of our own. That's what Grahams told us years ago. Do you remember or have you forgotten?"

"I guess I have forgotten that part, Steve. But I need to handle this one alone since it's a sensitive matter," answered Joshua. "Please. I saved you in that jungle back in December of '63. You owe me, buddy."

"Damn!" exclaimed Steve. "You've never pulled this on me before, so how could I not but back off, man. You saved all our damn lives that day. Damn you, man! Why now bring it up after all these years?"

Steve turned his back on them and faced the ocean. He was angry as hell but also upset, too. He was right about Joshua never used rescuing card on them before.

This was the first time and hopefully the only time. It made Joshua uneasy now, but he knew how they all were indebted to him for it. He shook his head and finished his soup which had gone cold and his milk was room temperature in silence.

It was two days later when Joan called him. She said everything was fine, so he didn't have to worry about her anymore. But she wanted to come up and see him if it was all right with him. So he leaned on the railing of the deck to look out at the ocean. He had seen another sunrise couple hours ago.

"Dad, I am here," Joan said from behind him.

He turned to face her. She wore a Navy blue business suit because she was a legal secretary in a well-known law firm with other duties, too, in Sacramento. She had gone to night school and worked as a waitress by day for two years. He was proud of her.

"I can see that, baby," he replied, as he smiled at her.

She walked up closer and hugged him. He felt her stiffness in her body, as she pulled back. He stared into her eyes, as she turned towards the ocean.

"It's so peaceful here, Dad," she said calmly.

"Baby, what's wrong?"

"Nothing," she answered back.

"Baby, look at me," he replied, as he stared at her. "I know, I haven't been a part of your life, but I'm...."

"It's not you, Dad. You're fine so is Mom. Hell with the rest of the family except Mom and Susan," she snapped back.

"All right," he replied, as he turned her. "What gives, Joan? I can't read you like your Mom can but know something is wrong. I'm your Dad. I want to help if I can. I've been around for twelve almost thirteen years now. Your Mom took you, guys, out of State and tried to disappear. I went looking for you, guys, remember. But I never gave up. I can't take credit for the woman you've become or your career which I'm very proud of you in all aspects of your life."

Joan had begun to cry. He brushed away her tears aside with his thumbs. Her arms went limp now. He pulled her towards him, and the tears flowed harder now. He rubbed her back gently. After a time, she pulled away from him, and he slipped inside to make some hot green tea. He poured hot water into two cups when she joined him.

"Dad," she started to say.

"Yes, baby," he replied, as he handed her a cup.

"Thank you," she said politely. "This isn't easy. Can we sit?"

"Sure," he answered, as he sipped his cup. "Where do you want to sit the table or the living room?"

"The table is fine," she answered calmly now.

She sat down and her cup as well. He joined her there. He took her hands into his. She didn't resist him. She drew in a big breath and exhaled slowly. So he waited.

"Six months ago, Alex walked into my law firm," Joan explained slowly. "I was surprised to see him. I guess it has been almost seven months. Things aren't still clear in my mind, so please bear with me."

Joshua nodded.

"He wanted to talk to Howard. I informed him that

he had to have an appointment. He said he did, and it was true. It was right there in Howard's appointment book, so I had to tell Howard that Alex was here to see him despite he was two days early. Howard told me to have Alex come back when he was scheduled to meet. Howard deals with corporate law," she continued on. "So Alex came back two days later. Howard asked me to escort Alex into one of the conference room since he was with another client, and Alex was early again. So I did." She looked down at their hands now. "I don't remember passing out, Dad. I offered Alex water then I found him over me. He said I passed out and helped me to my feet. I felt strange and excused myself."

Joshua slowly tilted her head to face him. "Where did you go, baby?"

"The ladies' room and found my underwear drenched in blood, Dad. I must have started my period and didn't know it. It was two weeks early," she answered panic sound in her voice.

"Go on. You're safe. I'm here," he replied back calmly. "What happened next?"

"I cleaned up and showered at my lunch hour. I waited for my cycle to continue, but it didn't. This was different somehow. But I stopped thinking about it because of the stress I was under. Later I realized it hadn't resumed for a couple months now," she answered back. "Then I felt a sharp pain down there, so I called my doctor. He told me to come in right away. That's when he told me that I lost the baby. Dad, I was shocked. I hadn't been with any man. I was a virgin."

"What happened next?" Joshua asked, as he felt a

deep tightness within himself.

"He said unless you're like the blessed virgin then you've had sex with a man. Dad, I have never been with man," she explained, as she begun to cry again. "Honest, but I had the tests you asked Mom and me to have. I haven't told her about this because it got me thinking back. It's still not fully clear to me. Do you think he..."

"Raped you, too. Yes, but it sounds like he used something to control you unlike he did with Susan," he interrupted her painfully, as he wanted to admit it. "We need talk to your Mom right away."

"Mom thinks it happened like Susan's. I couldn't tell her differently. What she's going to say or do when I or we tell her the truth?"

"I don't know. Alex said his friend took your Mom on Christmas Day. So we have to see her version of what happened to her that day then go from there," he answered thoughtfully.

"Dad, I am scared really scared," she said, as fear consumed her eyes and face.

"It's okay," he replied calmly. "Let's go see your Mom then I'll figure out our next move. We can't waste anymore time. Do you need to be back at work?"

"I took the rest of the day off because I had to tell someone about it. I guess, I blocked it out since the tests came in negative," she answered sadly.

"I'll drive. Where's your Mom at this time of day?"

"Volunteers at McKinley library," Joan answered back quickly.

He got his keys and quickly headed for the front door. Joan stopped to close the sliding glass door and joined him. He waited for her there.

"Thank you, Daddy," she said without a smile.

"It's not your fault just like it wasn't Susan's. Alex is a sick bastard. Do you hear and understand me, baby?"

She nodded. They got into his Blazer and headed back to Sacramento. Joshua clung tightly to the steering wheel, as he drove. He blocked out Alex's face from his mind.

"I should have done worse to, the bastard," he replied sharply in a loud voice.

"Dad, Mom said you had a fight with him. Was it over this?" she asked cautiously.

"He threw the first punch. He's scrappy fighter," he answered, as he tried to stay calm for two reasons. He was on the road and his feelings towards Alex.

"He said you did, so the boys sided with Rita. She believes him when he said didn't rape Susan," Joan continued on. "So we're divided now. I think they wanted to believe Mom about what happened to..."

"I know, Luke served me with a restraining order a day or two ago. Was he in the military?"

"Air Force for about two years, he was shot down in Desert Storm. He doesn't talk about it. Why?"

"I remember the training. I still do them and salute. It's drilled in you for life," he answered back.

"I noticed it at Uncle Roger's funeral."

"Here we are," he replied, as he turned the engine off.

"I'll get her. You wait by the duck pond," Joan said, as she got out.

He nodded and headed that way. He smiled at the

small children who fed the ducks with their adult who were with.

"You need to read more," Caroline said to him. "Joshua, do you hear me?"

"Yes, I hear you, Sis," he answered, as he threw another piece of bread out to the ducks. "Reading gives me headaches sometimes especially when there's a lot of reading involved."

"You have to try harder like Mom and Dad said these last five years."

"Mom gave up on me five years ago, so your information is incorrect. I've been on my own ever since I was eleven. Now I ask my big sister to help me on a history paper and get a lecture of not trying hard enough. I may not be as smart as you, Elizabeth and Andrew, but I do try my best. I don't need your help after all. So forget it!"

"Dad... Dad, are you okay?" Joan asked, as she stood in front of him now.

"What? Oh memories," he answered quickly.

"You seemed miles away," Carly said, as she sat down next to him.

"It was before I went into the army, and I asked Caroline to help me with a history paper. I got lecture instead."

"She grew up to be a school teacher then principal. She has been tough in a lot of ways or so I hear," said Carly.

"Like Dad," commented Joshua.

"Joan says you want to know about Christmas day. Why?"

"Alex admitted having sex with you, too. I want to know what you remember of the encounter," he answered thoughtfully and calmly.

"Well not much really. I invited him in, as I finished dressing to join you, all, at your place. I was nervous, so he offered to get me a glass of water," Carly said thoughtfully. "The next thing I remember I was on my bed, and I was naked from the waist down. Alex had his back to me, as I focused on the room." She paused for a time then her eyes went wild. "He asked if I loved his friend in there. He had crazed look on his face then he asked if his friend could do it again. I snapped back, no, and reminded him that he was married to Rita, my daughter. He laughed and said it hasn't stopped him before."

Carly had begun to shake. Joshua placed his arm around her and pulled her closer. Joan knelt before her now and hadn't said a word.

"He led me to believe I consented to it. I hadn't thought of that last part until now," Carly said to him.

"What does it mean?"

"I need you to see my doctor friend," he answered thoughtfully.

"Dad, what are you thinking?"

"I need to confirm it first," Joshua answered. "Tell your Mom the whole truth, and I'll be back soon. Trust me."

Joshua rushed to his Blazer and reached for his cell. He scanned the directory then pressed the green button. He tapped the roof of his car as it rang.

"Hello," a female voice said on the other end.

"Robyn, it's me, Josh. I have a question for you," he replied quickly.

"Go ahead," she said back calmly.

"If a woman blackouts or don't remember having sex with a man and things are unclear afterwards. Could a drug be given without her knowing about it?" he asked her.

"Yes. It's known as the Date Rape drug. Why?" she asked him. "Josh, tell me what you're thinking and talking about?"

"Damn, Bastard! I should have killed him when I had the chance," he answered, as he pounded his fist onto the roof. "The damn bastard slipped it into her glass of water, and Joan is foggy about her encounter with him at her office still."

"Calm down, Josh. I discovered something when I examined all three women. I've been waiting for the results now," Robyn said calmly.

"What did you find?" he asked with interest now.

"An oily substance at the base of virginal canal, some of it was washed away but, not all of it. It clung to the hairs down there, and unless women wash thoroughly and completely down there then it stays there. It's not uncommon for women to miss some places down there because they are uncomfortable or comfortable with their bodies. It's easy to overlook it."

"Did you tell them?"

"No, I wanted to get the results first."

"Then I won't say anything until then. Do you think it could tie him to raping them?"

"I don't know for sure. Do you want me to contact the police?"

"Yes, so this Date Rape drug," he answered thoughtfully, as he noticed Carly and Joan headed towards him now. "Oh crap!"

"What?" asked Robyn.

"Joan told her Mom. They'll want answers to what I'm thinking."

"Do you want me to tell them? I'm a medical professional, you know."

"I know, and I appreciate it, Robyn, a lot. This is something I must do myself. Thanks for the information, and let me know about the results. Bye."

He flipped his cell shut. They reached him at same moment.

"What are you thinking Joshua Matthew Adam Hernando?" Carly asked seriously.

"Have you two ever heard of the Date Rape drug?" he asked back.

Carly's eyes widened, and Joan fell to her knees. Joshua rushed to her and gradually brought her back to her feet. He moved her to sit in the passenger side of his Blazer. He glanced back at Carly.

"I take it you both have heard of it then," he replied back calmly.

"I didn't think it existed. I just thought it was to keep us girls aware around boys," Joan stated, as the initial shock wore off.

Joshua gulped hard. "That's why it's unclear to you, baby."

"Did he offer you anything?" asked Carly.

"I don't remember, but what I told you and Dad," Joan answered, as she cried hard now. "I'm so very sorry."

"It's okay," Joshua replied, as he tried to remain in control. "We're going get your little sister and kids away from the bastard. Do you hear me?"

"What about our brothers?" she asked him painfully.

"I have to make Rita see Alex for who he really is first. Then your brothers will come around. They'll have to know about you and your Mom in detail," he answered back.

"But you have a restraining order. How are you going to talk to her?"

"That's where I come in, Joan. She'll bring the kids to see their grandma. Leave it to me. I'll let you know, when to come over. It won't be easy to do," Carly warned them both.

"She's like my Mom, and Mom wasn't easy either. Try hot clam chowder and freshly made crab cakes," he suggested with a small grin.

"She would know you're involved then and won't come," Carly said back with a grin, too.

"Hey, it worked for me."

"Yeah, that's you, not me."

"She loves cheesecake with blueberries, Mom," Joan said thoughtfully. "Remember she always has a supply of it in her fridge all the time."

Joshua laughed out loud. Carly and Joan stared at him now confused.

"She has touch of both of my parents in her," he replied with another grin but bigger than before. "Mom loved cheesecake, and Dad loved blueberries on pretty much everything he ate. I hadn't thought about it in years."

They nodded then could laugh with him. Joshua saw his Dad in a different way that day. He loved blueberries, too and by sharing it with Carly and Joan eased some of his pain he once felt about his Dad. It felt good in some ways now.

9

Joshua sat in his Blazer up the street from Carly's condo. He tapped the steering wheel, as he waited for Rita's car. Carly called him two days ago and informed him Rita had agreed to let her see her grandchildren. Carly was on edge ever since.

By then he had Robyn's report in a large envelope next to him and knew the results of the oily substance. He shook his head then focused on the road. Joshua saw Rita's gray minivan approach then pass him. He gulped down some air hard.

"Sorry, baby girl," he replied to himself. His cell rung to life, so he picked it up, "Hi, Carly."

"She just got here with the kids," Carly said a little nervous sound in her voice now. "Give us some time to get them settled in before you arrive."

"Okay," he replied, as he flipped it closed again. He glanced at his Swiss army watch. "Ten fifteen so ten thirty our lives are going to change again. Here's another turn in the road of life, Josh. You didn't plan on this one late in your life. Dad, how would you handle it? Please not in anger. I've been there and done that already. I paid the price once already."

Silence filled the interior of the Blazer. Joshua leaned back his head against his bucket seat and closed his eyes. He couldn't recall at first what his Dad looked like then he remembered how Andrew was Dad's twin. He opened his eyes again and glanced down at his watch. Ten thirty-two.

"Here we go," he replied, as he started the engine.

He pulled up behind Rita's minivan and got out with the envelope in hand. He walked up to Carly's door. He knocked firmly.

"I'll get it, Mom," Rita called out, as she opened the door.

"Hi, baby girl," he replied calmly.

"Dad, you're not supposed to be within one hundred feet of us," she snapped back. "Go before Alex finds out."

"Grandpa," Jenny called out.

"Jenny, come back here," Carly called out to her.

Joshua knelt down, as Jenny rushed to his open arms despite the envelope in his left hand. He hugged her close to his chest and kissed her on the cheek like he always did.

"Go back to Grandma, Jenny. Your Mom and I need to talk," he whispered in her ear before he put her down. "You and I need to talk, Rita. Now I don't want this to be a shouting match either, so let's sit down and talk like the adults we are."

"Dad, I can't do this," she said in protest, as she stared at him.

"Rita, listen to your Dad, please. You need to hear him out," said Carly.

"But..." she started to say.

"Read this, and I'll sit out in my car if you want to talk about it," Joshua replied, as he placed the envelope in her open hand. "Remember I love you and so does your

Mom and sisters."

He walked back to his Blazer and climbed in. Joshua felt his heart race deep within his chest and tried to calm it. He closed his eyes and pictured the ocean in his mind.

"Thank you," he whispered to himself.

"Dad, we need to talk," Rita said, as she stood at his door.

He opened his eyes and motioned for her to join him inside. So she climbed in and held out the results.

"What does it mean?" she asked him.

He drew in a deep breath then exhaled. "Well, the doctor who examined Susan, your Mom and Joan found an oily substance in the virginal canal. So she sent a sample of all three to the lab and see what it was. It's the results of their finding s you have there," he answered thoughtfully and slowly.

"It lists chemical break downs, I don't understand," Rita snapped back.

"Vaseline jelly and olive oil more applied on your Mom and Joan then Susan. He seemed in a great hurry with Susan that he damaged her internally. She..."

"Dad, stop!" Rita exclaimed with tears in her eyes.

"I'm sorry, baby girl," he replied, as he touched her hand on the console between them. "I'm only telling you the truth."

"You don't understand, Dad," she said, as she looked down at their hands.

"What, baby girl?"

"Alex uses it on me since it hurts when he puts his friend in there. I don't know about the olive oil though," she explained to him. "He says it's his own lubricate."

"Baby girl," Joshua replied not realizing they had gotten out of the car. "Come here to your Dad."

She rushed into his open arms. She cried hard in his embrace. Joshua didn't know how long they stood out by his car, as she cried. He rubbed her back and let her cry. Then she stopped and looked up in his face. They headed up to the front door.

"Dad, I believed him over my sister and you. How can you two ever forgive me?" she asked painfully.

"Easy. We're family," he answered back.

"Mommy's crying, Grandpa," Jenny said at the front door.

"Oh, my kids," Rita said in horror. "How do I tell them about their Dad?"

"Relax. Let's go inside," Joshua replied calmly.

They walked up to the door. Rita and Jenny exchanged glances before Rita picked her up. Then they proceeded to walk deeper into Carly's condo and put her daughter down. Then Rita walked over and knelt then sat beside Jordan who was near the couch. He was building something out of blocks.

Rita sat down, as Jenny climbed into her lap. Jenny looked deep into her Mom's face and was puzzled by it. Then she looked around the room and spotted her grandfather. He stared back at her now.

"Yes, Jenny, Mommy's upset," he replied back.

"Why?"

"She's heard some bad news, Honey," Carly answered back. "She needs think it over and decide her next move."

Rita touched Jenny's brown hair, as silent tears fell down her cheeks now. She stared at Carly then Joshua. She only shook her head.

"Do you want them to stay here for a few days?" asked Carly.

"Uh…, I don't know, Mom," she answered in hesitation. "I don't think I should go back there alone."

"That's wise, baby girl. Let's get your brothers over here and explain everything."

"He'll think how we're ganging up on him, Daddy."

"We are, baby girl. What he has done is wrong and has to pay for it."

"Jail," Rita said, as she gulped hard.

"Who's going to jail, Mommy?" asked Jenny.

"How about some milk and cookies, kids," Carly suggested to them.

"Crab cakes," said Jordan.

"Only at Grandpa's. Now Jordan, come on with me," Carly said calmly.

Jenny walked over to him then they joined Carly in the kitchen. Rita stared at them then back at Joshua. Clearly, she was lost. She jumped when her cell rang. She reached for it, as Joshua sat down beside her now.

"Hello," she said calmly. "Yes, I know, Alex, but the kids need to be with their grandmother."

She pulled it from her ear and pressed the speaker.

"Are you still there, Rita?" Alex asked in a loud voice.

"Yes. I'm not hard of hearing," she answered, as Joshua held her hand now. "I think what has happened between my Dad and you shouldn't deprive my Mom seeing her grandchildren."

"I know your Dad is there, Rita. He is violating a restraining order. I'm calling the police," yelled Alex.

"Good. Then they can haul you off to jail for three counts of rape," Joshua replied, as he took the phone from her. "I look forward to their arrival and you, too, jerk."

He flipped it closed then stared at Rita. She was shaken by it all.

"He has to be nearby. Stay strong for the kids, Rita. They'll need you, and you won't be alone," he replied back.

The doorbell rang, and Rita walked over to answer it. Alex pushed her aside and spotted Joshua. Joshua got to his feet, as two uniform officers followed Alex in.

"That's him," Alex said, as he pointed to Joshua.

"I wouldn't do that, officers. He's my guest, and the man next to you is a rapist. I'm pressing charges and will get my other two daughters to come down to file charges as well," Carly said calmly, as she stood in the doorway of her kitchen.

"When did this rape occur, ma'am?" asked one officer.

"Christmas day of this last year and it happened here. There are some lab results by a respectable doctor who performed. I believe the papers are there on the coffee table," Carly answered calmly.

"Sir, please step outside," said the second officer. "I don't want to upset the children."

"I'm innocent," said Alex. "Rita, you can't believe him."

She stepped back farther from him. "The truth is out, Alex. I read the results. I'm divorcing you and don't want any part of you in my life or theirs. Take him away, officer."

"No!" exclaimed Alex.

The second officer moved Alex near the open door. He had his handcuffs out which Alex resisted him. So the officer shoved him against the doorframe and proceeded to cuff him there.

"Sorry, kids," he said, as he walked Alex out.

"Come down to the station, ma'am, and bring your documents," said the first officer.

"I'm innocent, Rita. I've been framed by your family. Can't you see that," Alex yelled, as he entered the squad car. "Rita."

"Mommy, where are they taking Daddy?" asked Jenny.

"Jail," answered Jordan. "No more pain, Jenny."

Jenny stared at her little brother. She looked scared now. Joshua rushed to kneel before them. He stared into their faces.

"Jordan, what are you saying?" he asked him.

"We won't hurt down here anymore," Jordan answered, as he pointed below his waist.

"No not his own children!" Rita exclaimed out loud.

Joshua turned back to Rita. He dove for her, as she clasped into his waiting arms. He carried her to the couch. Carly held out a damp towel and glass of water. Rita's eyes flittered as they opened again. Joshua placed the damp towel on her forehead.

"Grandpa did Jordan say something wrong?" asked Jenny.

"Dad, Mom, where are my kids?" Rita asked, as she

tried to sit up on her own.

"They're here, baby girl," he answered calmly. "Drink the water slowly. It'll help."

She drank the water and glanced over at Jenny and Jordan. Joshua motioned them to come closer, so she could see them. She smiled a weak smile.

"I love you, Jenny and Jordan, so very much," she said to them.

"We know," they said in unison.

"I won't let anyone hurt you ever again," she continued to talk calmly to them. "But you have to tell me if someone does. Do you understand?"

"So Daddy's, finger doesn't belong down here," Jenny said, as she pointed below her waist now.

"He hurt Jenny. She screamed real loud," said Jordan. "She begged him to stop it. It was hurting her too much."

"When?" Joshua asked, as he stared at Jordan.

"Last week on their bed," Jordan answered back.

"I had him touch Jordan down there, too. Daddy said all fathers do it to their children," explained Jenny.

Joshua got to his feet and paced the room. Then his cough started up, and Rita was at his side to rub his back and shoulders. He shoved her away and headed into the kitchen. Carly joined him there.

"Joshua, you're scaring us. Let us help you," she snapped at him.

He breathed in deeply and slowly exhaled. He tried to think of the ocean, and how it calmed him while he stared at her.

"I never and neither did my Dad do that to me and

ours," he shouted back. "I said he was sick. He is, big time. Let's put this bastard away before I kill him with my own two hands. Do you hear me, Carly?"

"Yes, but you're in no condition to drive and neither is Rita," she explained calmly. "So I need one of you to fork over your keys. I'm driving us, all, to the station."

"Fine, take Rita's. Her minivan can hold all of us."

They returned to the living room. Rita had the kids ready and held the envelope. She stood up straighter now and smiled at them.

"I'm driving us in," declared Rita. "Kids, get into the van. Dad, do you think the doctor who examined Mom and my sisters could check us out, too?"

"I could ask, baby girl," he answered surprised. "I'll call her at the station."

"Sounds great, let's go now," Rita said firmly. "I'll need a good attorney. I want him to stay there for a very long time, and I want to be able to testify against him. I know, the law states a spouse doesn't have to, but I want to for the sake of my kids. He hurt them, and that's unforgivable. I don't like what he did to you, Mom and my sisters either now. I love you very much. Again, let's go."

"That's our girl," Carly said with a little stunned but also proud.

"Just like her Grandma Sara. Family was everything to my Mom until she gave up on me. But that's beside the point now Rita has her fire within her. We'll, all, survive this," Joshua replied with a big smile. "Let's head out."

The kids climbed into their car seats, so Carly snapped them in. She rode in the back with them while Joshua rode up front with Rita. He watched her eyes fixed on the road ahead and smiled. He flipped open his cell and pressed Robyn's number.

"Hello," she said on the second ring.

"Hi, Robyn," he replied, as he stared out the window. "Can you perform a test on minors to see if they were sexually molested?"

"Not her children," Robyn answered in horror.

"Possible since they indicated pain below the waist," he replied calmly. "He has been arrested. They are pressing charges."

"Tell Shay Harkins that I'll do the required tests," Robyn said calmly.

"You know someone in the department," he replied a little surprised.

"I told you that. I'll be there in twenty. Bye."

The line had gone silent. So he searched and pressed another number.

"Hi, Daddy," Susan said on her end. "How did it go with Rita?"

"Your Mom's going to file charges. Rita is driving us there as I speak."

"I'll be there, Daddy. I'll get Joan, too. Meet you, guys, down there. Bye, Daddy."

He shut his cell off and continued to stare out the side window. He shook his head.

"You want a piece of me then come on. Bring it on, man," Joshua yelled at the man who had a broken beer bottle in his hand. "I said bring it on, man. You started it, and I'll finish it."

"I must tell you, buddy. He was the best in our platoon in hand to hand combat," Steve informed the man with a big smile.

"You better be a great fighter. Otherwise, you lose, bubby, big time," Roger chimed in with a big grin, too.

"He doesn't stand a chance," added Matt.

The man stared at them then back to Joshua who was ready to attack. The man lunged at him and drew blood on Joshua's forehead. Joshua disarmed him of the bottle then soon after that he got the best of his attacker. Matt, Roger and Steve decided the man had enough, so they hauled Joshua off him.

"He's not the enemy, buddy," informed Roger. "That's enough. Let him go now."

The man struggled to his feet and stumbled out of the bar. They, all, walked back to their barstools and sat down.

"Three beers and a milk, and thanks for not busting up the joint," the bartender said with a return big smile. "They're on the house. You should have that cut checked out."

"It'll stop soon. Thank you," Joshua replied, as he drank his milk.

The bartender placed a wet cloth next to Joshua's coaster and another cold glass of milk. Then he walked down to the other end of the bar to help another customer who just walked in.

"You need a whiskey, buddy," Steve commented, as he held up his glass. "This is real man's drink."

"Leave him alone. He's driving us home again. Remember, Steve," pointed out Roger.

"Oh that's right. Hey, I need another," he said, as he held up his glass. "Make it another round for all of us, my treat."

The bartender nodded. But he delivered the man at the other end of the bar first he did theirs again. Joshua drank his milk and used the cloth to dab the blood off his face. The guys started to get loud for his good ear, so he knew they would be asked to leave soon.

"Dad, we're here," Rita said, as she brought him back into the present.

He nodded and followed her in. There he saw a female officer take Carly aside. Another officer approached with Susan to Rita and the kids.

"I'm here for them," Robyn said, as she stood beside him now.

"Robyn, over here," the officer called out.

"I'll introduce you," she whispered. "I'll be careful, Josh."

"I know you will," he replied back.

"Shay, this is my friend, Josh," Robyn said calmly. "Josh, this is Shay."

"Nice to meet you and thank you for protecting my Mom years ago," Shay said, as he offered out his hand.

Joshua turned quickly to Robyn. She smiled back.

"Honey," Robyn warned him.

"What? I know you're not my biological Mom, but you have been there more than I can count when Kelly wasn't."

"Stop," she said, as her face turned a bright pink now.

"You'll explain later," replied Joshua.

"Let's get this done first," said Robyn. "And maybe I'll explain."

"The usual room," said Shay. "Tammy is already back there waiting."

"Baby girl, you and the kids go with Robyn," Joshua replied, as he turned back to them.

"I'll come, too," Susan said calmly. "They don't understand."

"That's fine," said Robyn.

Jordan walked up and tugged on Joshua's jacket. So he glanced down then knelt down to his level. "Yes, little man."

"I'm scared."

"It's okay. Robyn won't hurt you like Daddy did. She has to do a test of some kind then we'll go for some ice cream," he replied calmly.

"Crab cakes, Grand pappy," Jordan said with a small smile.

"Okay crab cakes at my place," he replied back.

"Jordan," Susan said, as she offered her hand.

She led him behind his Mom and sister. Robyn led them to the room. Joshua wiped away the tears from his face and found a seat.

"It's never easy," said Shay, "especially when it's family."

"They're his children, their aunts and grandmother for Pete's sake," Joshua snapped back.

"I'll admit that this is the first of this kind in my ten years on the force," Shay said thoughtfully.

"So tell me, why you call Robyn, 'Mom'," Joshua replied thoughtfully. "I need to think of something else before I want to beat the crap out of Alex."

"Easy, Josh, I know what you can do besides your

training for Vietnam."

"She told you!" Joshua exclaimed in shock.

"Uh...we talk about everything. The woman who brought me into this world was a drug and sex addict. She would leave me in our apartment for hours on end," Shay said calmly. "She didn't care if the guy screwed her in the room next to mine. Sex got her money for drugs. Sometimes, he would supply them just to screw her two or more times. It depended on her drug demand."

"Wow!"

"Yeah, she did it until I was three. That's when Robyn moved in next door. The landlady told her how my...the woman who gave birth to me treated me up to that point," Shay said sadly. "I cried because I was hungry. Robyn fed me milk and cheerios for a couple weeks. She washed my clothes and got me new ones, too. She did everything a mother should do for their child."

"Then what happened, Shay? I mean with your biological mother."

"Well, Kelly found out and wasn't very happy. They got into a shouting match then I went to live with Robyn from that day on. She gave everything I owned to Robyn and left."

"Did she ever come back?"

"Nope, I heard on the streets a few months later how a woman overdosed. I didn't know what it meant at the time. Robyn explained it when I got older. But I also heard the woman loved lots of sex and didn't care who she hooked up with for her drug habit," Shay answered, as he glanced down at his shoes. "She never told me that she loved me my whole life. But Robyn did and still does."

"Then you're lucky to have her in your life."

"Yeah, I drifted for awhile maybe hoping to find my Dad. But I never did, and Robyn was very supportive and loving. I call her Mom because of all she has done for me."

"Why?"

"Why what...oh a police officer, she taught me how to help people at very early age. I didn't have money for medical school despite her offer. She had done so much already. I had to do something on my own. She has been proud of me with my high school honors and police academy top honors for a cadet."

"Do you still want to find your Dad?"

"No not really. I thought about it, but now he left me with her and never looked back. So I can let them both go now. Robyn is Mom now, always and forever," Shay answered with a big smile.

"So you told him," Robyn said, as she walked up.

Shay nodded. She kissed him on his cheek and smiled.

"I love you, Mom."

"I love you, too, Shay," Robyn said back. "Tammy took them to the lab."

"Yeah, we have a rush on it," Shay whispered back. "We can only hold him basically on your previous victim's report and maybe their statements, but the case will be stronger with what he did to his own kids. Was there evidence there?"

Robyn nodded. Joshua was on his feet again.

"Easy, Josh," Shay said, as he held out his hand against his chest.

"Grandpa," Jenny said, as she ran up to him.

"It's okay. I got you, Honey," he replied, as he stared into her eyes.

"Crab cakes?" asked Jordan.

"Crab cakes at my place. I'll drive us, all, this time," Joshua replied to everyone.

Shay nodded so did Robyn. Together Joshua walked out of the station with his grandchildren, daughters and ex-wife. They rode in silence. He picked up some hot clam chowder and fresh crab meat, as he headed home. He noticed his girls sleeping against each other while Jenny and Jordan slept in their car seats. Carly was up front with him now.

"Does that remind you of another time in our lives?" he asked in a low voice.

She glanced back then at him. "Yes, our trip to the Grand Canyon when Rita was only two." She smiled back.

"We got up so early to watch the sunrise over the canyon. It was breathe taking back then. We planned to go back when she was older," he added with a small smile.

"But we never did," she said thoughtfully. "Our lives changed drastically after that. Roger was deeper out of control. And we saw less of you."

"Let's not dwell on it now, not today. They need us, and I'll call their brothers when we get settled. You need them and me, too."

"Sounds like a plan."

Joshua pulled into his driveway then carried Jordan and Jenny one by one in. Carly carried the chowder and fresh crab meat to the kitchen. They woke up Rita and Susan, so they could head inside, too. In the kitchen was where, he fixed crab cakes and hot clam chowder, as they, all ate in silence.

Patrick, James, Joan and Luke joined them shortly after. When the kids needed another nap, Joshua offered his room, so Rita and Susan cuddled with Jenny and Jordan between them while they slept. Now Luke laid by the door as if standing guard over his sisters and niece and nephew.

Joshua stared out at the ocean from his deck. Patrick and James played checkers while Joan slept alone in the spare room. Carly stood beside him now. He could smell a sweet, light fragrance which was truly Carly.

"You've always loved the ocean in all the time I've know you," she whispered to him.

"You should rest," he replied back. "It has been a long day."

"I know Joan was the first to file charges of rape against Alex. She's so strong. That's why she wasn't down there at the station earlier. Our girls are all so strong. Did I ever tell you what happened to my brother?" Carly asked him.

"No, I hadn't given it much thought really," he answered honestly. "I'm sorry."

"I lost him in Desert Storm. Mom and Dad were never the same after that. Luke served in the Air Force but doesn't talk about it. All I really know is that he was shot down over enemy lines and struggled to get back on our side before they captured him again. He looked up to you, and my brother as a kid. Then he came home changed. He goes off on his own sometimes days on end. I worry about him, Josh. I want to help, but I don't know how. Nobody knows how to reach him, not even Susan his twin. It's like they've been disconnected somehow. I can't read him anymore."

"I'll try in talking to him. Go get some rest now. You're all safe here," he replied with a small grin.

"Thanks," Carly said, as she kissed him on the cheek. "You still listen to me after all these years."

"You listened to me years ago about wanting a wife and family on that very beach. Oh, have you forgotten?"

She glanced out at the view then back at him with a small smile, "I guess I did for time."

She walked back inside the house. Joshua stared back at the ocean and smiled.

10

Shay and his fellow officers gathered up evidence of rape and incest against Alex for the DA's office. Rita knew what they had to do since she worked there. Joshua watched his ex-wife and girls rally to each other's side while Patrick and James stood at safe distance. Luke, on the other hand, was nearby if any man approached them. Joshua never had the nerve to do that for his own his sisters but was proud of Luke because he did.

"Dad," Patrick said sharply.

Joshua looked at his oldest son. He was no longer that little red face, blue-eyed baby crying his lungs out, as Joshua held him in his arms. They, meaning Patrick and James, were slowly coming to him in light of recent events. He knew Patrick and James sided with Rita and Alex against Susan. But they didn't know everything. How could he, their father, hold it against them?

"Yes, Patrick," Joshua replied calmly. "What's wrong?"

"They set his bail at a million dollars. He wants to use their home as collateral. Rita refuses to do it," he answered with a big smile.

"She's got Grandma Sara spirit running through those veins," Joshua replied with an even bigger smile back.

"I wait for her to fall apart like…"

"Go on, I'm listening, Patrick."

"The divorce and Mom kept moving for the longest time. Men drifted in and out our lives then Mom said she couldn't do it anymore. We were back where we started then you found us. Rita was seventeen, and she told us how you treated her that very doorstep." He pointed back at his front door. "You've never forced us to accept you as part of our lives again but stood on the sidelines watching and listening to all you could. We weren't fair to you despite how much Rita begged all of us to give you a chance these almost thirteen years. Time wasted on what. Nothing! We don't know what you did during those twelve years and since then. Time isn't a luxury, yet you waited for us to come around."

"Easy, Patrick, if you want to know about my life, I'll gladly tell you it all, but I must warn you that I wasn't always as open as I am now. I took directions in my life that I didn't plan on taking," explained Joshua. "I wasted a whole six months before I marched up to your Mom's front doorstep."

"Why?" Patrick asked a little surprised.

"Fear... fears of all your rejection. It's worse than my coming home from Vietnam. Your Grandpa Martin, Uncle Andrew, Aunt Caroline and Aunt Elizabeth were so filled with hate. I wasn't there when Grandma Sara died. It didn't matter how I was working my way back. It would be another direction I didn't plan on," Joshua explained painfully.

"But you took shrapnel in the shoulder," pointed out Patrick. "Do you remember your first direction change?"

"Oh, that's easy one when your Grandma Sara turned her back on me at 11-years-old. It would lead me to the army and war. War changes people, Patrick. You stare to face to face with life and death daily."

"I don't understand, Dad. I wish I could, but it would be lie. I have never been in a war like Grandpa Martin, Uncle Harry, Luke and you. I know each one had a different perspective on the war than the one before," Patrick said thoughtfully. "But I want to and so does James. We had more memories of you dropping everything for Uncle Roger and tried to explain it to the younger ones but lacked the knowledge of what was happening. Mom wasn't much help."

"So you didn't understand the effects of Agent Orange and other things soldiers faced over there. A war we couldn't claim no real victory despite what President Johnson wanted it so badly," Joshua replied thoughtfully. "Did you know Kennedy planned to pull us out? He had signed the paper to that effect before he left for Dallas. If he wasn't killed a lot less lives wouldn't have been killed, but Johnson decided to fight for a victory. It couldn't be had. It cost too many lives, and it was a war we should have never entered. I can tell you of what my experience was over there, but it wouldn't be complete, son."

"But you know Uncle Roger's, don't you?"

"Some but not all; no one knew what triggered his irrational behavior to relive prior to losing his leg. And no one realized until it was too late how Roger was dealing with after his leg was gone that last time on the roof. I had gone down that road too many times in the past but didn't notice the change until later. I failed him when he needed me the most. I can only tell you what I know. Maybe my comrades can tell you of their experiences and help you and James, start to understand it all."

"Thanks, Dad. I won't press you today since I have to get back to Rita. She wanted me to tell you the latest. She knows how you feel about Alex. We, meaning her brothers, didn't protect them very well. Did we?"

"It's not my place to judge, Patrick. I know I've been judged pretty much all my life, but no, I won't judge anyone, not even you, son. Life is a growing process. I've learned it with each direction I headed in. I'm reminded of a poem called "The Road Not Taken" by Robert Frost. Your Grandma Sara read it to me as a small boy. I haven't thought of it in years until now," Joshua replied thoughtfully. "That's life, son."

"I remember Mom reading it to us as kids. One road was well-traveled, and the other remained untouched or less traveled by travelers," Patrick said thoughtfully.

"Yes. It's true to life as I said. You can stay with what is considered safe or take leap of faith and go the unsafe route. I guess I took that road less traveled because I was a disappointment to all who ever loved me. So I kept getting these changes in the road or direction to help me find my own way in life the road less traveled and uncertain. Wow!" Joshua exclaimed thoughtfully.

"What?"

"This is a first for me. I didn't see this one coming. Well, you better check on Rita and the kids. Give them my love."

"I will. Dad, uh...I love you."

"I love you, too, Patrick, and you trusted Alex. He's

a charmer and stuck on his friend that will put him away for a long while now."

Joshua watched Patrick head for the front door and leave. He smiled and looked back at the ocean. He felt the light sea breeze across his tanned face. Joshua could see the seagulls in the distance, as he drew in a deep satisfying breath of fresh, clean air.

"Well Mom, I remembered your favorite poem after all these years. I know I disappointed you, and we hadn't talked in years," he replied out loud.

"Dad, who are you talking to?" a female voice asked from behind him.

He glanced back at Joan. She looked her Mom in a lot of ways except her long, braided brunette hair. He smiled at her.

"Your Grandma Sara," he answered back. "She's probably ignoring me like she did in life. What's wrong?"

"Can we go for a walk?" she asked him politely.

"Sure. How does the beach sound to you?"

She nodded and followed him. He shoved his hands into his Army jacket and walked next to her, not knowing what to say.

"I had to promise Luke that I was coming straight here. No stops in between. He watches us like a hawk," Joan said, as they stood on the beach now. "He manages to keep track of all of us. I can turn around or to the side, and there he is standing not too far from me. I think he's with Mom or Rita or even Susan right now."

"He cares and loves you, Joan, so much."

"I know he does. I've never doubted it, Dad, even after he came home from Desert Storm. A war he doesn't talk about. It changed him somehow."

"I'm sure you didn't come all this way to talk about your sister's twin and being a twin yourself."

"Do you still love, Mom?"

"I never stopped. Why?"

"I thought so," Joan answered, as she continued to walk the beach.

"Hey, Joan, explain yourself," he demanded, as he caught up with her. "She knows I never stopped. We've talked about it."

Joan stopped and stared at him. He moved closer.

"If you're holding onto an idea, we'll get back together and live happily ever after. I can't say that for sure, Joan. Years and a lot of things have happened since 1968. We're not the same two people we were back then."

"But you had seventeen years of marriage, and no man stayed that long in Mom's life since," Joan snapped back. "She never got over you. You have her heart still after all these years. It doesn't matter if it's 1968 or 2011. You two still love each other and deserve to be happy with each other."

"Now you sound like your Aunt Caroline because she is the hopeless romantic in my family. Now you're in your family."

"Dad, it isn't relevant your family or our family. Love is love. It's the purest thing or emotion in the world."

"You're so much like her," he replied, as he touched her cheek.

"Stop, Dad! Listen to me, please. Mom may not tell you how much she loves and needs you. But I remember how she cried those nights into her pillow after it was finalized. It tore her up deep inside, and every man was shallow and empty because they weren't you, her one true and great love."

"Joan, I love you very much, but you can't say things like that."

"So you're saying you're happy with the direction your life is going," she snapped back with her hands on her hips now.

"Yes, for the time being. I'm not ready for a new fork in the road. I want to enjoy this way while it lasts."

"What you say makes no sense, Dad. Neither one of you have someone in your life. You still love each other. Why not hook up? I don't think there is a problem under the sheets."

"Okay that's enough, Joan. If that's why you come over to discuss only, I'll ask you to either change the subject or leave because I won't discuss this with you or anyone else for that matter."

"Not even, Mom."

"We've talked about things, but it's between us only, Joan. Do I make myself clear?"

She nodded and slowly walked a ways from him. Then he touched her arm gently. She looked at him now with tears in her eyes.

"I'm sorry, Honey," he replied softly, as he wiped away her tears. "I love you and your Mom, too. I know you are holding out hope we will get back together. I can't promise you that it will happen. We've said and done things we aren't proud of. Then even with it all worked out, it doesn't mean we will get back together. Life holds no guarantees, Joan. I learned it a long, very long time ago. So please, I don't want to hurt you more than I already have."

"What do you mean?"

"I divorced your Mom and never talked to you, kids, about it. I was angry and thought it was an adult matter. I realized my mistake in that, Joan. It was partly why I searched for you, guys, all, those twelve years."

"You said partly. What do you mean by that?"

"Yes, I was still in love with your Mom. But she signed the papers, and I went into a deep funk. Then I saw the light how much I still loved her and you, kids. If I couldn't be her husband, I could be a part of your lives because I didn't give up my parental rights to you, kids. Roger pointed it out to me, so I visited a lawyer. Roger was right, so I set out to find you, all."

"But you needed money and time," Joan pointed out.

"Yes, I didn't much of either one, but Roger didn't help much by his thing. I don't blame him and neither should you, kids, and your Mom. He chipped in money when he could in the search for you, guys. He had to take care of Maria and her Mom, too. Plus I'll tell you some people just take your money and give you nothing in return."

"Sorry, Dad, I didn't realize."

"It's, okay, Joan. I'm glad that we're talking. You, kids, are coming and talking to me. It's important."

"Did you ever think we wouldn't come to you?"

"Like I said before, fear crept into often, so I guess, yes. I didn't think you, kids, would come then Rita came. Then you, all, were around I know for her sake, not me. I understood it since I hadn't been a part of your lives for twelve years. I didn't know what to say or do."

"I wanted you come back to Mom during those twelve years and since then. You were and always will be my Dad," Joan said with a small smile.

"That's nice to hear. Now let's get some hot clam chowder," he replied with a bigger smile.

"You and clam chowder, what's up with that?"

"Hey, I learned to heat it on my own then make it from scratch. I watched your Grandma Sara make the crab cakes, so I've tried making them now."

"Yeah that's right. You made them at Christmas, I think," she said thoughtfully. "Let's go have a big bowl of chowder at The Tides, my treat. Do you think they'll have crab cakes and espresso there, too?"

"I'm sure they'll have fresh crab cakes but not sure about the coffee. You seem to enjoy different types of coffee."

"Uncle Roger and Jimmy got me to adventure or explore different kinds."

"Who's Jimmy?"

"A boy I dated as a teenager. He was in a band and used coffee to keep himself going. He and Uncle Roger drank a lot of different kinds of coffee and discussed them."

"Where was I during all this?"

"Not sure really, maybe that's when you were out of our lives but can't be sure about it. Some things are fuzzy about back then sometimes."

"Do you remember the camping trip to the Grand Canyon?"

"Yeah, but what I remember is going to Canada,"

she answered back with a small smile. "The big caution sign at the top of the hill on that big board."

"I don't recall."

"How can you forget? We were on top then purged straight down to this nearly empty camp ground," she started to explain.

"And we didn't know why until that night after the sun went down," he recalled now. "Bugs came out in droves."

"Blood thirsty bugs and we stayed in the tent most of the time."

"Except for when we dashed for the bathroom."

"But you know it was trips like that I missed after you and Mom divorced. The last trip I remember we took as a family was when Rita and I were two," Joan said sadly.

"Didn't you like being with your Mom and siblings?"

"It wasn't' the same without you, Dad. We being on the road every couple months were hard, but we pulled up stacks when Mom said to. We didn't understand why she was always looking over her shoulder. She broke down and told us. She didn't want to fight with you anymore, and now she had nowhere else to go. She hoped you wouldn't start to fight again."

"I behaved badly with the affair, and you, kids, were caught in the crossfire. So whatever happened to the man I caught her with?"

"Manuel. Mom married him a couple months after you two were divorced, but we left him in Portland, Oregon."

"Why?"

"He was cheating on, Mom. She found him in their bed with Beth. She was our babysitter and only fifteen," Joan answered coldly. "Mom mumbled something about Beth being pregnant with his child. We never pressed it. She also understood how you felt about her now."

"Two espressos, two orders of crab cakes and two large bowls of chowder," Joshua replied to the waitress who stood before them now. "Please."

She nodded and left. Joan folded her hands in front of her on the table, so he reached over to touch her hand with his.

"I'm okay, Dad, really. Mom never said anything negative about you all those years because you were hard act to follow for any man in Mom's life. But she had married two more times. I don't know why they divorced, but I don't think she ever got over you. They were rebounds."

"Two espressos, crab cakes and chowder. Anything else?" the waitress asked with a small smile.

"No, thank you," he answered with a big smile. "Dive in, Honey."

So Joan helped herself to her crab cakes and chowder. Joshua felt her gaze on him, as he put black pepper in his soup. She did it, too. It made him grin.

"What?"

"Just like when you were little, you always followed my lead. It's nice to know some things haven't changed, Honey."

"Silly, Dad."

"That's me, silly Dad," he replied with a big grin.

She shook her head back at him and smiled, too. So

they ate in silence, and she paid the bill like she said she would when the waitress returned with it.

Then they walked on the beach to his place because it was all within walking distance. He used his Blazer on important matters like grocery shopping and stuff like that. Then she hugged and kissed him before she got into her car to leave. She honked her horn as she left, and he waved back with a smile. She smiled, too. But he waited until she drove off before Joshua walked back into his house and sat down in his chair in front of the fireplace.

"This feels good, Mom. You were right about family and that saying is so true. You can pick your friends, but you can't pick your family. Family is family no matter what," he replied out loud before he closed his eyes.

11

"Josh, come quick. I need some back up," Roger called out for him.

Joshua emerged from his room to Roger's room. They were installing carpet in a house. The carpet was too heavy for Roger to maneuver on his own, so Joshua had to help him.

"Where's Bryan?" he asked, as they lowered the roll slowly to the floor.

"Hell, I don't know. He always ditches me when you turn your back," Roger answered, as he struggled to catch his breath.

"Crap," he replied, as he stood beside Roger now. "I thought, oh never mind. He's fired when he comes back. Lay it out smooth the best you can. I'll cut it and make everything tight in an about ten minutes. I got the other room almost done. Are you going to be okay?"

Roger nodded. So Joshua walked into the other room to finish his job. He sensed someone was in the room with him. He looked up and gulped hard.

"Yes, Jerry," he replied to the foreman. "Can I help you with something?"

"Everything okay?" he asked back.

"Fine."

"That kid you brought with you and Roger. Where is he?"

"I don't know. Why?"

"Some things are missing from the supply shed," answered Jerry.

"And you think Bryan took them," replied Joshua.

"Yeah, I do. He's the only one not on the site right now."

"Hey, guys," Bryan said, as he walked up cheerfully.

"Where have you been?" Jerry asked coldly.

"Outhouse," answered Bryan. "Why?"

"For two hours, I don't buy it, boy," Jerry snapped back. "Give me the truth or you walk today with no pay."

Bryan's lower lip quivered, as he quickly looked down at his hands. Joshua saw blood or something red on them.

"What happened to your hands, Bryan?" he asked him, as he tried to remain calm.

"I've never seen so much blood in my life," Bryan answered, as he had begun to cry.

Joshua sprung up and saw more blood on Bryan's clothes. He tilted his head up to face him. "What are you saying?"

"My girlfriend Lorraine paged me. I didn't want to leave Roger like that, but she really needed me. I had to go. I'm so sorry, Josh. Blood was down there, I had to rush her to the hospital. They said she had internal bleeding, and she lost our child at five months," explained Bryan.

"But you walked up very upbeat," Jerry pointed out.

"Shock does that to you," informed Joshua. "It's like men seeing something in the name of war. It's traumatic, so you try to wash it away or block it out of your mind."

"I don't need this on my site. Go be with your girlfriend with pay. Go before I regret it," said Jerry.

"How..." Bryan stumbled to say.

"Go, son. We got it."

"Go, little buddy. She needs you," Roger said with a small grin. "You need each other."

He nodded and headed out. Jerry walked away, too. So Roger and Joshua went back to work. A couple hours later workers stood outside the trailer. Roger looked beat and leaned on Joshua, as they walked out of the house.

"Did you hear?" another man asked them.

"What?" Roger asked back.

"A teenage girl was found in the far dumpster. She was killed with several stab wounds to her belly."

"Why didn't she scream?" asked Roger.

"Her hands were bound and mouth gagged. Jerry found the body. They're talking to him in there. I saw the coroner arrive, so I told everyone. I didn't know you, guys, were still in the house working."

"It took us longer than we planned, Jessie. We're down a man," Joshua replied back. "Bryan had an emergency."

"His girlfriend," Roger added, as he stared at Joshua.

Joshua shook his head, no. Jessie stared at him. Then the police emerged from the trailer, and Jerry look very pale.

"Gentleman, these officers want to speak to you individually. Please answer their questions honestly then you can go home. This site is a crime scene now, so I'll notify the proper people. So you will get paid. You have my word on that," Jerry said clearly. "Roger and Josh, can you come in here for a second?"

They nodded and walked up. They all walked deeper into the trailer. Roger sat down in the nearest chair while Joshua closed the door and stood near him. Jerry walked over to his desk and sat down.

"It wasn't' a pretty sight. The girl was four or five months along. Her neck was broken, so she knew her attacker. They said they found a chisel near the body. Do you think Bryan is capable of doing this?"

"I don't know," Joshua answered honestly.

"She was about his age or close to it," Jerry said calmly. "I have calls to make. Please excuse me."

"Let's go, buddy," Roger said, as he struggled to get up on his own. "I need a couple beers in me after a day like this."

Joshua nodded. The crowd was gone now, so Joshua went back into the house to collect his tools and lunch box. He started out when he saw something out of the corner of his right eye. He stopped and it stopped, too.

"Who's there?" he asked in a spiked voice.

Bryan emerged from the kitchen. He still had blood on his hands and clothes. He looked paler than before.

"I thought, you went to be with Lorraine," he replied calmly.

"She's dead and so is my baby girl," said Bryan.

"What are you saying? You said how you took her to the hospital."

"I lied. She kept paging me about the baby and her body changing. She demanded how I should come over when I would call her back. She said how she was in labor. I said to myself how it was too soon, but I went to her anyway." He paused and looked around. "I had been disappearing on you and Roger for awhile now. I told her enough was enough."

"Roger told me."

"Lorraine started on about her neck. She said it was too stiff, so I massaged it. She demanded harder, so I snapped her neck before I realized what was happened. So I tied her up and gagged her. Then I kept hearing her nagging voice and don't remember much after that. I found myself back here, and I was talking to you and Jerry," Bryan explained, as he stared at Joshua. "Did I kill her and my baby?"

"It seems so," an officer answered from behind him. "I'm afraid that you're under arrest for two counts of murder, son."

"No!" Bryan exclaimed, as he fell to his knees and cried. "Not my baby girl."

Joshua woke up from his memory. He got up and walked into the kitchen. He decided to warm some milk and heard a small meow. He glanced down and saw a black, small kitten stare up at him.

"Hey, kitty, do you want some milk, too?" he asked it. "It'll be a minute or two, but I have some fresh crab meat. All cats love fish."

He placed some fresh crab on a plate then put it down next to the kitten. He stroked it gently. It had begun to eat and purr. Then he stirred the milk until it was warm enough for both of them to drink. He poured his into a cup and bowl for the kitten.

"Good stuff," he replied, as he watched the kitten.

Then he walked out on the deck when the kitten

jumped up onto the railing. It rubbed against his hand, so he stroked it again. He offered his cup, and it drank more of the milk.

"We need to see a vet to find out if you're a boy or girl and belong to someone," he replied calmly to the kitten. "You drank my milk and yours, too. That's okay. Come on, baby."

He headed back inside, and the kitten followed him faithfully. It made him smile, as he grabbed his Blazer keys. He placed the kitten in the passenger's seat and saw it stare back at him.

"All right, my lap," he replied, as he tapped his leg.

The kitten crawled up, as he pulled out of the driveway. The kitten fell asleep quickly. Joshua smiled, as he drove to Rosemary's clinic. It was a short distance from his house.

"We're here," he replied, as he scooped up the kitten, Then he walked in the front door.

"New friend," Rosemary said, as he walked in.

"It found me," he replied back with a small smile.

"No tags and no collar," she said, as they walked into an open examining room.

"Nope, but I fed it warm milk and fresh crab."

Rosemary took it from him. It meowed back at him.

"It's okay, baby. She wants to check you out," he replied to it.

It meowed again. So Rosemary handed it back to Joshua's empty arms.

"I can examine it in your arms. It's about two months old, first of all," Rosemary said calmly. "I find no microchip in between his shoulder blades."

"You said his."

"Yes, it's a boy. He needs a name, Josh."

"I don't know what to name him. I never had a cat let alone any animal my whole life."

"How did he get your attention?"

"Just cried at me," Joshua answered thoughtfully. "Bryan."

"That's an odd name."

"How's Bryan sound, baby?" he asked the kitten.

He stood up in his arms and pawed his way to Joshua's face. There he rubbed his face into Joshua's. Joshua let out a hearty laugh, and Rosemary joined him.

"Bryan, it is then," Rosemary said with a smile. "No, charge for this visits, but let's get some shots in him though."

Joshua nodded. Bryan purred at Rosemary who left to get the shots. So Joshua petted him and allowed him to walk on the examining table now.

"Why can't we have a dog or cat, Dad?" Joshua asked his Dad again.

"Do you really need to ask me that kind of question, Joshua?" his Dad asked sharply.

"But you were a farm boy and was surrounded by animals all your life," Joshua answered thoughtfully and quickly.

"Times are different. But we won't have a dog or cat in this house until your grades are up with your brother and sisters. So go hit the books harder than you ever did before."

"But Dad, I'm doing my best," Joshua replied in his defense. "I got them up at C's now. Isn't it better than before?"

"No, I managed A's and B's despite being a farmer's son. I had dreams of going pro in baseball. You're being lazy, Joshua Matthew Adam."

"Why didn't you become a pro baseball player?"

"That's not the point. Now go hit those damn books, young man," his Dad yelled at him.

"Josh, are you okay?" Rosemary asked him, as she brought him back to the present.

"I'm fine. Are you done?"

She nodded, so he held Bryan closer in his arms. They all walked out of the room and out to his Blazer.

"If you notice anything out of the ordinary call or stop by anytime, but he needs a litter box and kitten food. He can't live on crab all his life," said Rosemary with a small smile. "See you, Bryan."

Joshua started the engine and slipped it into gear. He waved and headed home. There he placed some newspapers in a half cardboard box and placed sand in it. Bryan watched him and followed him back into the house.

"There a litter box," he replied, as he placed it in the kitchen. "It'll have to do until I go shopping. You can sleep anywhere in the house. This is your new home, Bryan."

He walked over to the couch and stretched out. Bryan jumped up onto his chest and begun to purr loud. Joshua stroked him gently, as he closed his eyes. He had begun to fall into a deep sleep.

He woke up to a chill in the air and noticed Bryan snuggled up in tight ball on his chest. The kitty reached out to him with his white-tipped front paws. He yawned, as he stared back at Joshua.

"Nice nap, little guy," he replied with a small smile. "Are you hungry again?"

Bryan jumped down and headed for the kitchen. So Joshua got to his feet and followed him. He closed the sliding glass door before he entered the kitchen. Bryan waited for him. So Joshua opened a tuna can and placed some on the plate from earlier for Bryan then he added more milk to his bowl.

He poured himself some milk, too and put some tuna on some crackers. Then Joshua walked back to the couch and noticed Bryan followed him. But then Bryan stopped to clean himself up before he rejoined Joshua on the couch.

"Dad, are you home?" James asked, as he opened the front door carefully.

"Yeah," he answered, as he sat up straighter.

"Come in, James."

"Cute kitten, but I didn't know you had a cat," James said, as he petted Bryan now.

"He found me actually a little while ago. His name is Bryan and a couple months old," he replied back. "So what brings you here, son?"

"I know, Patrick talked to you about your life," James answered, as he walked over to the couch.

Bryan led the way and jumped up next to Joshua. He ate his tuna and crackers while he petted him. James sat down and folded his hands on his lap.

"I was looking through some old photo albums Mom has," James said in a low voice. "I came across these."

He held out the photos with a shaky or nervous hand. Joshua reached for them and glanced at them.

"Your grandparents Martin and Sara, it was taken on their wedding day. Your Uncle Andrew and Aunts Caroline, Elizabeth and me when we were younger, I took them with me when I joined the army. Your Grandma Sara made sure we all had a copy," Joshua explained calmly. "Your Grandpa Martin loved baseball but was a farm boy. The one of your Aunts, Uncle and me were at his high school graduation. I carried them all with me in the jungle and open land, so I wouldn't forget who I was fighting for. I gave them to your Mom shortly after we were married. She never asked who they were. Why?"

"Uncle Andrew gave me this a few days ago," James answered, as he took something again out of his pocket.

Joshua took it and adjusted his eyes to it. "It's a bank passbook."

"It's yours. I noticed small amounts then they increased during your service time. Then a huge one that was about five years ago," James said calmly. "It was your share of their estates. Your net worth is close to two million dollars, Dad. Uncle Andrew explained it all to me. Turn to the back of the passbook. Is it you?"

Joshua flipped to the back and stared at a black and white of his self. He noticed something stuck to it, so he pulled it gently apart from the other photo. It was of another photo there, so he flipped it over.

"Your Grandma Sara at the same age, I didn't realize how much I looked like her until now."

James moved in closer to look at it, too. He didn't

say anything but stared at the new photo. Bryan stared at them both then meowed. It was what brought James back to look at his Dad.

"She must have really loved you."

"Maybe, before I disappointed her."

"I don't think she ever stopped by the entries in the passbook. She loved you right up to her end of her life or November of '63, but in July she seemed to double the amount."

"My birthday is July fourteenth. What do you remember before your Mom and I divorced?"

James sat back and petted Bryan. He seemed to be in deep thought now.

"I would have to say the time you tried to teach me how to fish. Do you remember it?" James asked with interest.

"Bowman Lake near Jackson meadow," Joshua recalled with a small smile now. "It was my first attempt at it. I watched your Grandpa Martin teach your Uncle Andrew. I thought I could do it, too."

"You never fished before," James said a little surprised. "But you seemed so confident in what you were doing and explained everything like you had done it for years."

"Until we caught the big tree next to us," Joshua pointed out. "My confidence was a little shaky after that. Didn't you notice?"

"I couldn't tell, Dad. We casted out again, and I reeled it in like you said slowly, but we got the seat of your pants this time," pointed out James "But you never yelled or screamed at us no matter what we did. You would sit down and talk to us."

"Your Grandma Sara was like that," he replied sadly.

"So Grandpa Martin was the one who yelled and screamed?"

"Afraid so, and I turned out like him years later. Do you think less of me now?"

"No. you found Mom in bed specifically the bed you two shared with another man. It had to hurt like hell. Mom left the bed behind. Did you know that?"

"No. You kids seem so..."

"Well adjusted. We had guidance counselors' check on us regularly since Mom picked up and moved so often. Mary, my guidance counselor, said I was old enough to understand things and needed to face you someday. I wasn't ready when you appeared on Mom's front door. Then time slipped by us quickly and ..."

"But you're here now. Your little sisters and your Mom need us. The men it's our duty to protect them."

"I think Luke has it covered."

"We all should be like him."

"You're right. I've never been able to reach him even as a kid. He's so different than the rest of us."

"Your Mom said he's a lot like me. Well, you're here with me now, and we're talking. That's what you have to do with Luke"

"I talk, but I don't think he hears me."

"Promise, you won't give up on him."

"I promise, Dad. I'm glad we're talking, too, Dad. I've got to go now, but I'll be in touch. Keep the photos and passbook. See you later, Bryan," James said, as he got to his feet. "Bye, Dad."

James was out the door and gone. So Joshua started lie down on the couch, as Bryan settled in, too. He closed his eyes and fell asleep.

12

Maria stood at Joshua's front door with a big brown box in her arms. She had been crying because her cheeks were puffy and red. Bryan stared up at her then back at Joshua.

"Let me take that," he replied, as he took it from her. "Come in, please."

"I can't have these in my house, not now," she said, as she followed him.

"What is it?"

"Dad's stuff from Nam, Josh, and I can't look at those drawings. He showed them to me when I was growing up. It was how he saw the war," she answered sadly. "I had forgotten about them after awhile until..."

"I remember him drawing a lot then he..."

"The attack had changed all of your lives," she interrupted him. "Why did he stop drawing?"

"I guess it was too painful. But I tried to encourage him to continue after we got back home but got nowhere."

"But you did. He would draw landscapes and of Mom and me. That's why I know about these. He captured you beautifully."

"What!" exclaimed Joshua, "Uh... sorry."

She stepped forward and dug through the box. Bryan peered in on his back white paws with spots of black at the ankles, too. Maria pulled out an artist sketch pad and flipped through it.

"Here," Maria said, as she held it out to him. "He captured your sad eyes and everything, but despite what a good looking man you were back then, too."

Joshua took the pad and sat down. He stared at the charcoal drawing of himself. His eyes looked far away from the war they were in. It was a reflection of his inner battle of war. The five o'clock shadow on his face had become visible and becoming a man. He must have been seventeen then. The dark circles under those blue-gray eyes indicated he hadn't slept much.

"You must have been twenty then," she commented with a sigh."It's dated 7/63 in the lower right hand corner."

"I suppose. Wasn't your Dad older than me when he got drafted?"

"Yeah, he was older than most at Columbia. But he never went back not even under the GI bill. I think he was about five years older than you."

"He definitely had talent," commented Joshua.

"That he did. His grandson is a lot like him in that sense," Maria said sadly. "I can't look at his drawings and not think of Dad's. I need you to hold onto them for a little while. Please, Josh. You were his best friend."

"I would gladly hold onto them for you. I still think of him and miss him, too. I was remembering a time at a jobsite," Joshua replied thoughtfully.

"What time was that?" she asked with interest now.

"We laid carpet there that would become a crime scene later," he answered back calmly.

"I think, Dad mentioned it briefly to Mom. I was real young at the time, so they were careful of what they said around me. What really happened?"

"A sixteen or seventeen old boy who worked with us killed his pregnant girlfriend and their unborn daughter."

"O, my God! Why? What became of him?"

"She bugged him about the changes in her body. I think, it was ruled as temporary insanity, but he got life prison anyway. I hadn't thought of Bryan in years. I was in my forties when I met him. The kitten is named after the kid."

"Was it before or after you and Mom divorced?" Rita asked, as she stood in the doorway with Tim.

"Not sure exactly, baby girl," he answered honestly and thoughtfully. "I know we worked in construction for a long time. I hadn't thought of him much in recent years until this little guy showed up. I named him, Bryan, after the boy."

Rita walked up closer and looked at the drawing. "That's you in the service. Who drew it?"

"My Dad," answered Maria.

"He was a joker and an artist," Joshua replied with small smile.

"You look tired, but I can see pain your eyes, too," Rita said to him. "Were you thinking of..."

"Yes, I thought of her a lot when I was over there. Fighting a war, we didn't belong in and should have pulled out sooner than we did," Joshua interrupted her. "I thought a lot about the family that I left behind and how they wouldn't have missed me. But I've discovered Andrew realized what I did for him."

"Uh...Mr. Hernando," Tim said in hesitation.

"Oh, Tim, call me, Josh. What's up?"

"I'm sure you heard that Alex wants to get out on bail," Rita answered calmly. "I've filed for divorce, Dad. I'm afraid for Jenny and Jordan. Luke wants to protect us, all, including Mom, Susan and Joan, but he has job to do. We're keeping him from it. I feel guilty about it. That's why I asked Tim to be with me sometimes, Dad. I'm worried about Luke."

"Take it easy, baby girl. What does Luke do for a living anyways?"

"Odd jobs mostly but has written poetry and songs here and there through the years. He's smart, Dad. He went to Top Gun school and was the top of his class," Rita explained thoughtfully. "He's a lot like you. Mom has said it more than once especially since he came back from Desert Storm. The limp isn't always so noticeable."

"He was shot down behind enemy lines, right?"

"Yeah, and that's all we know. He doesn't talk about it," said Rita.

"I told your Mom that I'll try to talk to him. Now tell me more about Alex."

"His bail is so high since his job takes him everywhere. He's an AP photographer and a good one at that. He's paid two thousand a shot," Rita said back, "Plus a salary with benefits."

"Wow! It should make him a flight risk and denied bail based on that. Shouldn't it?"

"That's what I thought, too," answered Tim. "But he has a good attorney from AP. They're standing by him."

"Don't go there, Tim," warned Joshua.

"I should have questioned his interest in me, Dad. I didn't know. He was the first guy to ever take an interest in me, and I fell in..." Rita said, as she begun to cry.

"It's okay, baby girl," he replied, as he hugged her. "I know and understand. Your Mom was my first, too."

Rita shot a glance up at his face. "Mom was..."

"Yep, it was love at sight," he replied with a big smile.

"Dad talks about you a lot, Josh," said Tim. "Steve and Matt were real hot heads and dogs in the war. Has it ever changed?"

"No not really. They liked to fight and fed on my anger at times after my divorce," Joshua answered honestly. "Does your Dad talk about Vietnam?"

"Pieces, Mom didn't like him talking about how bad it was over there. But I do know you guys were under attack in the jungle and grenades went off by him and Roger. He lost his arm and leg, and Roger lost his leg."

"Yes with pieces of debris was everywhere. It made some of us snap in the mind. Then the orange mist followed the explosions effected the rest of us," Joshua replied thoughtfully. "We, all, walked out of there changed."

"Dad said you hauled everyone out of the jungle. You're a hero."

"I did what I had to do. I had to stop some from wanting to chase the enemy in a blind rage. I couldn't let them run into another trap. We needed medical attention, so I forced the issue. I'm not a hero."

"But you are, Dad."

He shook his head, no, and then he petted Bryan. The kitty took it all in. Joshua didn't want to talk to anyone. Tim noticed the drawing.

"Is my Dad in that?" he asked Maria.

"I believe so. He drew the whole platoon then other things he saw," she answered back.

"It was time to be focused on something other than the war we were in," Joshua replied sadly.

Tim flipped through it then he stared at Joshua.

"There are a lot of you in here with the back drop of the war. But this one doesn't seem his style."

"Which one?" Maria asked with interest.

"This one," Tim answered back, as he showed her.

"Dad always said he didn't remember doing that one," she commented back.

Rita looked and shot a look over to Joshua.

"What?" he asked her.

"I've seen it before," she answered quickly.

He got up and followed her. She had his bedroom light on. She stood at his chest and had the top drawer open. Joshua noticed Bryan, Maria and Tim followed them, too.

"You drew it, Dad," she said, as she held out a slightly, worn small black book. "You drew it as a boy. I found it when I was little. Luke only stared at it and didn't say anything about the discovery."

"How..."

"How did we find it?" she asked back. "Easy when you're looking for paper. Luke and I liked to draw a lot. You expanded on it in the bigger book and more detail, but you drew it, Dad."

He nodded, as he sat on the edge of the bed. "It was one picture I could never get out of my head, until I moved here. Then it all made sense to me," he replied in a low voice.

"What, Dad?" she asked him.

"Rita, don't you recognize it?" Tim asked seriously.

She stared at him. He closed Roger's pad and took her hand into his. "Come with me. I think, I understand."

He led her to the deck. Joshua, Bryan and Maria followed them. Tim opened it again.

"There and here," he said, as he pointed outside then back at the drawing. "Am I right, Josh?"

"Yes, it was also at that very beach I told your Mom how I wanted a wife and a family of my own. It was the same beach we came to on vacation when I was boy. It was coming full circle finally," he answered sadly. "Roger and I saw the ocean when we came home from Nam. He couldn't seem to enjoy it like I did. You can let yourselves out. I'm tired."

Joshua walked back to his room. His hand was on the light switch.

"Dad, I'm sorry," said Rita.

"It's okay, baby girl. Your Grandma Sara was a gifted artist and had dreams nobody understood, or so she thought anyways. I think they call them visions now. Excuse me."

"I love you, Dad," Rita said, as she kissed him on the cheek.

"I know, I love you, too," he replied, as he kissed her back.

"I'll turn off the light for you."

He nodded and walked over to his bed. Bryan rushed up and purred at him, as he lay down. Rita turned off the light. Darkness filled the room now. Joshua could hear his breathing and Bryan's purr. He slowly drifted off to sleep and dreamed.

Joshua walked into a village with his gun in hand and finger near the trigger. Then he heard someone crying, so he approached a hut with a great deal of caution. He felt sweat at his neck and brow. His eyes adjusted to the darkness of the room. A figure rushed to his lower body.

It was a little girl about five. Her face was dirty and stained with tears. Her clothes were ragged and barefoot. He lowered his gun and knelt in front of her messed up dark hair.

"It's, okay, Honey. I won't hurt you," he whispered calmly to her. "I promise."

"Mommy dead," she said hoarse voice.

"Where's Mommy, Honey?" he asked calmly. "Take me to her."

She took his hand and led him to a corner of the hut. It was darker than the rest of the place. He knelt down and felt her very cold and lifeless body. She had a blanket around her body.

"Hey, man, what's going on?" Roger asked, as he stood in the doorway.

"We need to dig another hole," Joshua answered calmly. "We need to bury her Mom."

"Oh hell!" exclaimed Steve. "You do it. They aren't our people."

"Shut up," Roger snapped at him. "I'll tell Lt. Grahams our plans."

"Crap," said Steve.

"Come help me lift her," Joshua said to Steve. "We're going to bury your Mommy. Come with us, Honey."

Steve walked over and helped him. She lighter than most. They stepped out into the light. The girl stayed close to Joshua and stopped crying.

"Over here," Matt called out.

Roger and Scott were digging a hole. So he and Steve walked slowly with the body. Lt. Grahams, Jerrod, Henry, Trevor, James and Robert stood guard. He didn't see Luke anywhere. They lowered her body near the hole.

"Almost done," Roger said back. "When we get home, we should be professional grave diggers because of all the digging of so many in the last months we've been here."

Luke stumbled out of some bushes. Everyone held up a weapon to his pale face. He joined the platoon, so they finished the hole. Roger and Scott climbed out, and Steve and Joshua carefully lowered her body into the hole. The little girl had begun to cry again.

Luke had a board and chalk in his hands now. He walked closer to her and talked t her in a low voice. Then he had begun to write. She only nodded. Roger and Scott folded up their shovels and put them away. Luke planted the board into the freshly dug soil.

"Here lies Mommy. The best Mommy in the world," he said, as he cleared his throat.

"Rest in peace," Joshua replied in a low voice, too.

"Let's go me," Lt. Grahams said to them. "It's not safe to be out in the open like this."

"How many does this one make it now?" Steve asked with a tone of anger in his voice now.

"Too many," Trevor answered back.

Joshua took the little girl's hand into his and his

gun on the other side. He offered her a portion of his food and water. She only smiled at him as they walked.

"I called ahead to say we had an orphan with us," Matt said in a low voice back.

Joshua nodded, as they continued to walk. He sat up now in his bed. He felt a chill come over his body, as he sat in the darkness. He hadn't thought of her in over forty-eight years.

"Why now?" he asked himself. "She must be in her early fifties now. Did she come to this country to be adopted?"

He shook his head and heard Bryan's purr. Then he felt softness on his face. The kitty found Joshua's face and decided to rub against it. So he petted him and fell back on his pillow. Bryan had come with him.

A couple days later Joshua was walking on the beach with Bryan. It was cold, wet and windy, so he picked up Bryan and tucked him into his army jacket. He carried his cell in his pocket in case anyone wanted to reach him. He placed a call into Luke, his youngest son, but got only his voice mail.

"I can't recall it being like this before," he replied to Bryan.

Bryan poked his little head out, as they walked. The ocean was fast and furious, as everything picked up speed. He saw a figure run towards him. It was becoming clearer to him who it was, Carly. So he stopped in his tracks.

"What's wrong?" he asked her.

She tried to regain her breathe. She rested her hands on her knees and bent over. So he waited.

"Susan needs us. Tim and Rita rushed her to Mercy

Hospital. Robyn's meeting us all there. I've got Jenny and Jordan in the car," she answered finally. "Oh, hi, little one, I didn't know you had a cat."

"Bryan found me. What's wrong with our daughter?"

"Let's walk while I'll explain."

He nodded.

"She was almost run down by a car. She headed for her car when a car came out of nowhere. Tim grabbed her and the baby close to him, as it sped by. Rita and Tim had just lunch with her," she explained calmly. "It sent Susan's heart racing, so they rushed her to emergency at Mercy. She also complained about lower pain where Tim grabbed her."

"Did he hurt her or the baby?" he asked with concern now.

"I don't know. I came to get you since I was on my way here anyways," Carly answered, as they reached the car.

"Hi, kids, I have a little kitten," Joshua replied, as he showed Bryan to them.

"Kitty," Jordan said in delight.

"Can I hold him or her, Grandpa?" asked Jenny.

"Bryan would like that," he answered back, as he held him out to her little hands.

"He's so soft," she said, as she held him in her lap.

Bryan purred, as they headed down the road. Carly tapped the steering wheel, as she drove. Joshua looked over at her.

"They're going to be fine," he replied confidently.

"You're right. Tim is a good guy. He wouldn't hurt

them on purpose. He's good to our grandkids and Rita," she rambled on. "So his Dad was your CO back in the war. How many of you guys did actually married?"

"Two or three but not sure really," he answered thoughtfully. "Does our son Luke call back when you call his cell?"

"Usually, but why?"

"I've been waiting for his call back."

"He must be busy. I'm sure he'll get back to you when he has the time. He always gets in touch with me even if it's just to say hi and say he's alive. He's a lot like you when we first met."

"So you said before."

"Here we are," she said, as she pulled into a parking space. "I don't think they'll let him in."

Joshua glanced in the backseat. Bryan was asleep on the seat between the car seats.

"I think, if we all get out quietly that he may not wake up," he whispered to them.

They nodded and proceeded to get out. But Bryan's eyes popped open, so Joshua grabbed him quickly put him back inside his jacket.

"Let's go," he replied back.

"But..." Jenny started to protest.

They, all, headed inside. Joshua felt warmth on his face and chest, as he held Bryan in his jacket. Carly focused on Jenny and Jordan, and what was ahead of them. They noticed Tim and rushed up to him.

"They're admitting them," Tim said to Joshua. "I'm so very sorry, Josh."

"What happened?" he asked calmly.

"The car came out of nowhere extremely fast. I had to react quickly," Tim explained in rushed voice. "I pulled us up on the hood of her car."

"She'll be fine," Carly said calmly. "Where's Rita?"

"With her," Tim answered her. "She called everyone from the ambulance. She's a tough woman."

"Like her Grandma Sara," he answered with a small smile. "Take the kids to the cafeteria." He pulled Bryan out of his jacket. "They don't allow animals in here, so I have to be careful around here."

"I understand. I'll take him," said Tim. "Jenny and Jordan, come with me. Please."

"Mom, Dad," James said, as he walked by Tim and the kids.

"Mom," said Patrick.

Joan stepped around them and straight into Carly's open arms. Luke walked up with his hands in his Air Force jacket and stood in silence.

"We have to wait," Joshua replied back.

"Babe," Carly said to him. "There's Rita."

He smiled and nodded, so he walked up to her and a woman in a white lab coat that wasn't Robyn. They looked over at him.

"This is our Dad," said Rita. "Dad, this is Kim. She'll work with Robyn on Susan's case here."

"My pleasure," Kim said, as she held out her hand. "You're a vet."

"Yes," he replied, as he shook her hand. It felt familiar to him for some reason. "Have we met before?"

"I was about to say the same thing," Kim answered back.

"Kim, we need your key," said a nurse.

She released her hand from his and pulled out a key chain out of her lab coat. It had a frog on it. Joshua flashed up to Kim's eyes.

"Here," she said, as she held it out to the nurse. "Sorry, we keep the meds under lock and key. Doctors are the only ones with a key."

"Here lies Mommy. The best Mommy in the world," Joshua replied from his memory.

Kim stared at him with her mouth dropped open, as she stood there. "You saved me that day in August of '63. It was cold and dark in the hut, but you heard my cries. I had been there with her a day or two. I tried to find you when I came to the United States. I was adopted by an American couple in San Francisco. We had no luck in finding you for years. All I had was the key chain and a memory of your eyes."

"That's why you walked with me," he replied, as he gulped down some air. "I had just a dream of that day."

"We ate your jerky and drank water while we camped. You held my hand all the way and later in the night, as I drifted off to sleep," Kim said thoughtfully. "I realized I wanted to help people like you helped me. So I went into medicine like my adopted Dad, but I've thought a lot about you through the years. My daughter loves the frog, but I won't part from it. It was my link to you and my new life and freedom."

Luke walked up with everyone else behind him. He stared at Joshua then at Kim.

"So you're admitting my twin," Luke said calmly. "It's a pre-caution, right?"

"Yes, Luke," Kim answered with a small smile.

"Robyn will explain everything. Please excuse me."

"We need to talk, Kim," Joshua replied back.

"Yes, we do but not now," Kim said, as she walked away.

"You know her!" exclaimed Rita.

"Back in Nam, we buried her Mom," he replied calmly.

"You never told me about that," said Carly. "There's a lot about your life I don't know about, Babe."

"We didn't know either," said James. "But you talked about a little about Vietnam."

"I know but I'm sharing now unlike someone else," he replied, as he stared at Luke briefly. "Family can help if we let them in. You can choose your friends but not your family."

"Excuse me. I have a job to get back to. Let me know more in a text, Rita," Luke said with a nod.

She nodded back, and he walked away. They let him walk away without anything more to say. Robyn explained it was only pre-caution to keep Susan and the baby in the hospital overnight. So the family gathered at her bedside, after she was transferred to a room upstairs. Joshua didn't remember much after that. He and Bryan were in a chair in her room. Susan slept peacefully, as the monitors beeped for hers and the baby's heartbeats. They were both strong. It made him smile, as he drifted off to sleep, too.

13

Kim walked into Susan's room and checked the monitors then at Susan's body. Joshua watched her, as she went about her business. Tim had brought Bryan back to him since he didn't want to leave Susan's bedside. Now he heard Bryan's purr start to pick up speed. He begun to stretch and emerged out of Joshua's jacket. He jumped up onto the bed and stared at Kim.

"Well, hello there, fella," she said, as she petted him. "Where did you come from?"

"Inside my jacket," Joshua answered, as he cleared his throat. "I know it's against policy, but I didn't want him to be alone."

"He's cute. What's his name?" she asked in a low voice.

"Bryan. He found me."

"Just like when you found me in that hut back in Nam. You saved my life back then you know. I was all alone and scared, but you showed me true kindness."

"You were just a child without a Mom. We were in a war and that was no place for a little girl or any child to be."

"You were different than the rest of them. I know that's why I never forgot you all these years," Kim said thoughtfully.

"So you were adopted by Americans. Tell me about your life."

"Well, I was five when you found me. I had no family, so a nurse brought me here. They asked me questions like family and birthday. They got a dummy birth certificate to allow Rachael and Jeff to legally adopt me." She paused for a moment, as she glanced back Susan. "They tried to help me find you as I got older, but I didn't know your name. All I had was the key chain, but it wasn't much to go on despite you being an American soldier. I could only explain how sad your eyes were, but they also knew love and compassion."

"Were they, meaning Rachael and Jeff, good to you?"

"They were great and very supportive in everything I did or wanted to do. Jeff provided funding to find you without much luck. He loved me so did Rachael like I was their own," Kim explained sadly. "But they never got to know their granddaughter Brittney."

"What happened?"

"The driver was high on drugs and drunk when he ran the red light," she answered sadly. "They died at the scene."

"I'm sorry," he replied, as he walked up. "It's hard losing people you love."

"That's true but to lose them on the night of their granddaughter's birth is bitter sweet," Kim said sadly. "But I'm glad Luke was there."

"My son was there!" exclaimed Joshua.

"I should have known by looking in his eyes. Luke looks and acts a lot like you. Brittney adores him. He was in the delivery room with me."

"How did you two meet anyway?"

"During my residency at SP hospital in San Francisco, he was an EMT, I think or studying to be one. But he was a natural at what he did."

"My twin was interested in medicine?" Susan asked, as Bryan walked up to her now.

"Yes, my fiancé died in Desert Storm. The same war your twin brother fought in. Albert and Luke were close, but Luke and I dated before I was engaged to Albert. Luke stepped back when Albert took an interest in me. We dated a couple times before they were shipped out. I wasn't sure who Brittney's father was, but Albert still wanted to marry me," explained Kim. "Luke didn't get sent out right away, so he was there at Brittney's birth. I don't know why or how he was able to stay behind. But after she was born, he left and came back changed to some degree. But he does spend time with Brittney when he has time."

"Why didn't you get a test?" Susan asked, as she sat up in her bed.

"I didn't see the point," Kim answered, as she looked back at her. "I was planning to marry Albert when he got home. Then he died in the field. Luke was shot down since he was pilot over enemy lines. I think there's a degree of guilt Luke feels."

"What do you mean?" asked Joshua.

"He was the only one who survived the crash. I can't get him to talk about it and neither can Brittney. I know it must be bad since she couldn't get him to share. She has always been able to reach him on anything."

"He sounds like you, Dad," Rita said, as she walked in. "Until recently."

"Roger's death," added Joshua. "Did he ever draw you, Kim?"

"He was he vet back in December," Kim stated a

little shocked. "It was you and him on the hospital roof. Uh, I don't know about him drawing me. Why?"

"His daughter Maria brought his stuff from the war over to my Dad's place. He was pretty good at drawing," commented Rita.

"Well, Luke is pretty good at anything he sets his mind to including the guitar. There you hear the depth of his very soul. So that's what Brittney tells me, anyway. I've tried to get him back into medicine, but "no dice" as he would say."

"Do you think what happened in the war effected him somehow?"

"War. Nothing prepares you for what you'll encounter no matter what war you're in," Joshua answered thoughtfully.

"That's right, Dad. You said it before. Grandpa Martin's war was a hero's welcome. Yours and Korean weren't ones to proud of. I'm sorry, Dad," said Rita.

"Talk to some of the guys from the platoon, and you might understand some of what we faced. It might be some of what Luke's going through. But I told you before how your Mom wants me to talk to him. All I can do is try talk one veteran to another veteran."

"I guess, that's all we can ask," said Rita.

"When can we go home?" Susan asked Kim.

"A day or two since the police want to get your statement, and Robyn and I want to be sure you both are good to go home."

"Fine," Susan said, as she folded her arms across her upper body.

Meow. Bryan didn't like a quick stop of being

petted. He looked at them all then he nudged Susan's hand. She started to pet him again. He had begun to purr again. Joshua laughed while everyone looked on.

"What brought you back, baby girl?"

"Mom said she drove you here, so you had no way of getting home. So I came to take you," Rita answered calmly.

Tim walked in with Jenny and Jordan. They rushed to the bed to Bryan. He loved their attention, as he purred louder.

"You need to get him out of here," Kim whispered to Joshua.

"Your Mom and Joan are downstairs with Luke," Tim said finally to Rita. "Luke won't let any of you, ladies, out of his sight. He believes Alex is behind it."

"No!" exclaimed Rita. "He's in jail."

"But he's in contact with his lawyer, and he does have access to a cell phone that way," Tim said back.

"He wouldn't do that to my big sister and hurt his children this way. He's been trying to get out on bail," Rita rambled on.

"Let's step out in the hallway, baby girl."

She walked by Joshua, Kim and Tim. She stood in the hallway, as they followed her.

"Listen to me, baby girl," Joshua replied calmly. "He wasn't happy about her pressing charges then on top of everything else. A man unstable like he is would do anything. I know I dealt with Roger for years. He dealt with the loss of his leg, and they never figured out what triggered it."

Rita stared at him like his Mom did. It shot a deep

pain in his heart now. He gulped down some air and felt a deeper burn in his throat and chest now. He had begun to cough hard. Kim stepped up closer, as he backed away.

"Dad," Rita said, as she rushed up to rub his back.

His legs clasped out from under him. Kim and Rita were on either side of him now. He pushed himself up, as he coughed and walked over to the opposing wall but slid down. But they managed to stay with him despite how hard he tried to move away from them.

"Easy, Josh," Kim said in low but calm voice. "Does this happen often?"

"More frequent in recent months," Rita answered back, "Dad."

"Leave me alone," he managed in a loud voice now. "I'm going home alone."

"No, Joshua Matthew Adam Hernando, you're not going anywhere but to be checked out by a doctor," Carly snapped back sharply.

He looked up at her, as he got to his feet again. "Go to hell! You don't run my life, woman."

"Dad," protested Rita.

He shot her a quick glance, too. Then he saw fear in her eyes now. She backed up, but he walked by her, Carly, Joan and Luke. But Luke stood in his path.

"Sorry, Sir, I insist you stay," Luke said coldly. "If Mom and my little sister are concerned, I stand by them, and you taught me years ago."

Joshua's cough got worse, as he stood before his son. He felt lightheaded and felt that he was falling, too.

"I got him," Luke said, as he had Joshua in his arms.

Awhile later, Joshua woke up to a gurney beneath

him. He was hooked up to a monitor and could hear his own heartbeat on the machine. He saw Luke in a chair at the far end of the room. He had a guitar against his legs. He stared at the guitar and its strings. Luke begun to strum and closed his eyes, as words escaped his mouth in a low but controlled voice.

"In the darkest place of my mind you're there. I don't know what you believe in or what you stand for. But you're burning deep within me or of depths of my very soul. Then it comes all screaming back to me. It comes, all so clearly back to me now."

Joshua noticed Carly, Rita, Joan and Kim stood in the doorway. He placed his fingers to his lips. They, all, nodded. They, all, listened to Luke now.

"You're there for a reason and purpose. You're what I saw over there and can't seem to share with people who haven't been there. You're so cold and uninviting to the world. You're in the depths of my very being."

He drew in a breath and continued on. "It all comes back like a slash on my flesh. It slips out slowly then faster as I try to stop it. But you have a name that I am sure of. It's what I lost over there. How could you abandon me like that?"

Luke's voice was soft and sweet much like Rita's. Joshua couldn't call Luke ever singing as a child or when he lived with them. Luke seemed to repeat what seemed like was the refrain before going on. His eyes remained closed, but Joshua could see tears roll down his son's face. He kept the ladies at bay, as Luke continued on.

"We're fighting a war we don't understand. Yet State side they meaning the general public gave us unfair names. But the pubic didn't understand what we saw or experienced over there. Now how important we needed their support and understanding. We lost our innocence over there."

The ladies cried in silence with him, as he played on. Joshua could see it on their faces now. He was moved by the song, too.

"Can it be any clearer than that? It's, all, coming back k clearer to me now. We're reduced to a paragraph or two in the history books. But it doesn't tell our whole story. We're you so why can't you see that," Luke sang softly and tenderly.

He repeated the refrain then his voice fell silent. He played the final notes. The women looked to Joshua for guidance now. They wiped away their tears and put on some brave faces, as Luke slowly flirted open his eyes.

"So how long have you been playing the guitar?" Joshua asked him.

Luke glanced over at him and cleared his throat, "Long enough, Sir."

"What's the title of the song?"

"Battle in the night," Luke answered, as he continued to make eye contact with him. "It's in honor of you, and what you might have encountered in Vietnam. I can only guess what you felt, thought and experienced over there, Sir."

"You seem to give some real thought to your words as you played."

"With this I speak from the heart, it's the only way I know, how to express myself. Mom and the other don't get it. Do you?"

"Yes. Yes I do, Luke," Joshua answered with a big smile.

"Thanks," Luke said with a smile back. "I've got to check on Mom, Joan and Susan. I hope you'll be okay."

"I will. I'm an army man, remember."

"Who has a heart of gold?"

"I don't know about that, Luke."

"You aren't one to take praise. Are you?" asked Luke.

"You're a lot like him," Carly answered, as she walked deeper into the room. "You gave us quiet a scare there a couple days ago."

"What!" Joshua exclaimed shocked.

"You have been down for the count for two days. Kim and other medical personal have taken turns looking after us," Joan said calmly.

"Did you know you had an irregular heartbeat?" Kim asked him.

"No."

"That's why you passed out. Luke was there to catch you. Your heart is weak and will only get weaker in time," explained Kim.

"Who's with Susan now?" Luke asked no one in particular.

"Tim, Bryan, Jenny and Jordan," Rita answered calmly. "Plus she has a guard outside her door now. You have to have a password."

Luke glanced over at Carly, as he got to his feet. "At least someone listened. What's the password?"

"Twinkle," she answered with a small smile.

"She's not far from your memory. Is she, Mom?"

"She was a special cat. Yes, she had a short life, but I loved her," Carly answered with another smile.

"I know I got to go now. Bye everyone," Luke said, as he left the room.

"There goes our youngest son," Carly said, as she approached the bed, "Running away again. But I'm glad we heard the song. I never heard him play before."

"I have many times. You worked a lot of different jobs while we were on the run from Dad," said Rita. "He played someone else's work not his own back then."

"I never understood why you felt that you had to run away with the kids," Joshua replied thoughtfully.

"You were so angry in the beginning," she started to explain. "I thought..."

"What?"

"You might hurt me or the kids."

"Not all of us, vets are violent, Carly. I believe Steve and Matt suffer from effects from Agent Orange," he replied back. "So use caution when talking to them, baby girl. Promise me, baby girl."

"I will, Dad," said Rita. "I will, I promise."

"Dad, we come to see you. How do you feel?" Joan asked, as she at the foot of his bed.

"Tired, but otherwise I'm fine. When can I go home?" he asked Kim.

"After we check your diet," answered Kim.

"Fish, chicken, turkey and pork," he replied back with a big smile, "And plenty of fruits and vegetables, too."

"Skinless chicken and lean meats," added Carly.

"That sounds all good to me, but..." Kim said thoughtfully.

"Our platoon was exposed to Agent Orange despite the Government denying it ever happened. I remember the mist, as I went back into the jungle to get my comrades out," interrupted Joshua. "It's a pesticide. I do know that much about it."

"There's a website about it and symptoms," commented Joan. "I found it, as I was surfing the Internet the other day. It's new."

"That's right you have access to all that," he replied thoughtfully.

"It is part of my job to check out those websites," Joan said with a confident smile. "In the law firm I work in as an addition to my secretarial duties."

"I would never hurt you or the kids, Carly. I may yell and scream, but I don't hit people I love. I would like to know more about that website, Joan."

"Sure, Dad."

"Thank you," he replied, as he stared back at Kim who stood near his heart monitor. "What's wrong?"

"You never got treatment for the exposure," Kim answered thoughtfully.

"Nope like I said, the Government has denied it for years."

"I'll look into it then," Kim said, as she walked out of the room.

"But you hit and hurt Alex," Rita pointed out. "Didn't you care about him?"

"I often wondered why he pursued you like he did, baby girl," he answered honestly. "I'm sorry. It never felt..."

"To be honest, Dad, I wondered it, too, and I did fall in love with him," Rita said sadly. "I gave him two

beautiful children Jenny and Jordan and was faithful to
him, always."

"He knows that, Honey," Carly said, as she hugged
Rita now.

"You said you did love him," said Joan. "You don't
anymore."

Rita nodded, as she clung to her Mom. She stated
to cry again.

"Go to your Dad, Honey," Carly said calmly.

Rita rushed up and lay beside Joshua. He felt the
warmth of her body, so he allowed her to snuggle closer to
him.

"How can you say you don't love him anymore?"
asked Joan. "With everything he has done to this family."

"Joan, stop it! She needs our love and support, not
be grilled like this," snapped Carly.

"But he not only hurt her but you, me and Susan in
the worst way possible," Joan shot back at her. "Susan is
pregnant by him for Pete's sake, and it's a high risk at that.
He might be involved with the attempt on Susan and the
baby's life."

"Your mother said to stop, Joan!" Joshua exclaimed
in raised voice. "Listen to her. Don't you see what you and I
have done to Rita here?"

"What gives you the right to talk to me that way?"
she asked in anger.

"I'm your father," he replied, as his monitor
beeped louder. "This stops now, young lady."

"Fine, I'm taking a walk with one of the uniform
officers outside this door," Joan snapped back, as she
stormed out of the room.

"Daddy, settle down," Rita whispered to him calmly. "Please."

"I'm fine, baby girl," he replied calmly. "I'm fine."

Carly placed her hand on Rita's shoulder now. So Rita had her parents there for her and her kids. He smiled at Carly, as his heart returned to normal rhythm again. Then he closed his eyes and slowly drifted off to sleep.

14

"She's so beautiful," Joshua replied, as he looked down at the baby in his arms. "We didn't get just one but two."

"Yes, now we need to pick two girl names," said Carly, as she held the second baby in her arms.

"You name her, and I'll name this one."

"Joan after Joan Kennedy, it's a strong name. Right?" asked Carly.

"Yes it is, Babe. I'm going to name this one Rita," he answered back with a big smile.

"Why?" she asked a little surprised.

"Her cry sounds so musical maybe she'll have a professional singing career. Then she can support us into early retirement," he replied back with big grin. "But I'm only kidding."

"Oh, okay, I like the name. Joan is going to be one tough kid."

"Why do you say that?"

"Her tight grip on my finger right now, so she's a real fighter."

"But we will love her all the same."

"Yes, we do just like all the other children," Carly said, as she smiled back at him.

"Dad," Rita's voice brought him back out of his dream.

He opened his eyes, and Rita still lied beside him. She had her hand on his face, so he looked down at her.

"Yes, baby girl."

"Mom stepped out. You seemed happy. What were you remembering?"

"The day you and Joan were born. Your Mom named her after Joan Kennedy, and I named you. You both were so beautiful," he answered back. "I was kidding with your Mom that day."

"What about?" Rita asked him.

"Your cry was musical, so you were destined to have a professional singing career. Then you would support us into early retirement."

"Dad, you know I sing in the church choir and traveled with them, too, when we settled back here."

"I know, baby girl. I'm proud of all of you, kids, because who you are and followed your own journey of life."

"Even me, Dad?" Joan asked, as she stood in the doorway of his room again.

"Yes, Honey. Your Mom did a great job in rising you, kids, when we were married then divorced," he answered back.

Rita climbed off the bed and walked up to sister. "It's hard to believe we are twins but can be so different. But I do love you, Joan always and forever."

They hugged then Joan got a hug from her Dad. She cried, as he held her close. When she stepped back and sat on the bed, she stared at him because he wiped away her tears.

"I'm sorry. I was being disrespectful."

"It's okay. I love you, too, Joan."

"Do you love Mom?"

"Yes, I never stopped. She gave me three beautiful,

smart and independent daughters. Three strong men who are yes caring and loving who respect woman and life. She's a remarkable woman, too, in her own way."

"Joan, it's their business," Rita said in a low voice. "We already discussed it."

"But I haven't," Joan snapped back. "Did you know Mom still has an old photo of you, Dad? She has one in her wallet behind her license. It's one I'm sure, we kids, have never seen."

"How do you know that?" he asked with interest.

"I've seen her looking at it through the years and more so recently," she answered back with a big confident smile.

"Stop, Joan."

"But, Dad," Joan protested back.

"No, buts, Honey," he warned her again. "Let it go."

"Dad."

"I mean it, Joan. Now listen to me good if your Mom and I were meant to be together then we would have been a long time ago and maybe never divorced. So I ask you for my sake and your Mom's. Let it go. Do you hear me?"

"Yes," she said unhappily.

"Good. Now this subject is closed, ladies. Any status on who tried to run Susan down?"

"Maybe," admitted Rita. "Robyn's son, Shay is following up on a hunch, but it is hush, hush, right now. He's doing it by the book before you ask. He doesn't want it thrown out on a technicality. He's been a lot of help with the case against Alex."

"So has Tim. I think, he feels something for you, Sis," commented Joan.

"We're just friends. That's all. He's also great with Jenny and Jordan."

"You said you were going to divorce Alex. How's that going?" asked Joshua.

"Alex refuses to sign the papers."

"He knows it clears you to testify against him at his trial. It's going to trial. Isn't it?"

"Oh, yeah, my boss at the DA's office is going after him for three counts of adult rape. Then two counts of sexual abuse to two minor children. That's the hard part with Jenny and Jordan being under eighteen," Rita answered, as she begun to cry again. "I thought Alex loved me. I never thought...."

Joan rushed to back to the doorway to hold her twin. Rita cried in her sister's open then closed arms. Joshua ached to hold her, too then she rushed to him. She climbed on his bed and snuggled up to him again. Joan placed one hand on her twin's sister shoulder. The heart monitor peeped, and Rita's crying were what was heard in the room outside their breathing. No words were exchanged.

Carly walked in with Tim and the kids. He held Bryan in his arms. He wiggled out of his arms and rushed up to Joshua despite Rita being there, too. Bryan purred loud, as he sat on his stomach.

"Hi, Bryan," he replied to the kitty.

"Sorry," said Tim.

"Grand pappy," Jordan said, as he approached the bed.

Rita climbed off, and Joan stepped back. Rita wiped away her tears from her face. Jenny approached the bed, too. She stared briefly at her Mom then at Joshua.

"Crab cakes, Grand pappy," Jordan said to him.

"Later, Jordan, we have to get him home first," Rita said calmly.

"I'll fix crab cakes and clam chowder when I get home. I promise," Joshua replied with a big smile.

"Dad, don't make any promises you can't keep," warned Rita.

"I've always kept my promises, baby girl," he snapped back. "So have you guys enjoyed being with Bryan."

They nodded, as they climbed on the bed. He and kids petted Bryan. Then they all left his room. He asked a nurse to bring him a pen and paper. Now he played with the pen on the table tray, as it spins on its own.

He couldn't recall clearly why he asked for them, or how long ago the nurse came, left, returned and left again. He was alone with his own thoughts now. He knew it was dangerous. How dangerous he wasn't sure right now? He remembered briefly back to his bedroom that he shared with Andrew.

He held a fake birth certificate in his hands. Now he paid a man on the streets ten bucks for it. Joshua only needed it and pass the physical then off to basic training briefly then the war.

"Hey, Josh," a familiar voice said to him.

He stared back his big brother Andrew. Andrew walked up closer to the bed.

"What brings you here?"

"You, I heard you were in the hospital, too. I came to see my niece Susan down the hall," answered Andrew. "She's worried about you."

"It's nothing," replied Joshua.

"Being out or asleep a couple days," pointed out Andrew, "is something to be worried about. You're my little brother Joshua."

"Your only brother, so what's your point?"

"I could have lost you back in Vietnam but didn't by the grace of God. He heard Mom's prayers before and after her stroke."

"What's that supposed to mean?"

"Your short note to us all, it sent Mom to church daily and for hours in deep prayer in between her job," Andrew answered in anger. "Dad carried it in his wallet and before that Mom had it in the family bible. Then I...oh hell."

"How do you know it was in Dad's wallet?" Joshua asked in anger, too.

"I found it after he was admitted to the hospital. I had to get his medical and social security numbers to them. Mom knew all that not us. Remember?"

Andrew reached in his back pocket and tossed a piece of paper to him. It was old, worn and faded. Joshua unfolded it.

"War by Joshua," he read out loud.

"It's all they had from you. When Dad was able to locate your basic training location, it was too late because you were on your way to Vietnam. Caroline, Elizabeth and I watched them glued to any and all reports of that damn war. Fear consumed their lives not seeing their youngest son ever again. You put them through pure hell, Joshua. It was far worse than when you were here to screw up things. I'm out of here."

Andrew stormed out of the room. Silence except for his monitor that hit a high point now was back to normal again. He folded the paper back up and left it on his table tray. He picked up the pen that he played with earlier. He drew in a deep breath and exhaled slowly. He had begun to write the following letter:

Dear Family,

It's obvious how I affected all your lives badly. I tried at the time to write to you over there but struggled to read and write. Roger helped me in ways that you won't ever understand. I don't if I can help you, all, understand now.

I struggled in school before going over there. I was good at hand to hand combat and marksmanship, so I was told and have been told repeatedly. I received merits for those, too and was promoted to Corporal before going over there. I guess I had a survival insect in me. Now I discover Mom prayed to God daily for me. It makes me question a lot of things in my life.

Kim had who lost her Mom over there. I did think of Mom when I took Kim's little hand in mine. She needed someone after her Mommy died. But she was alone in that hut crying, as her Mommy's dead body lay next to her for a least a couple days. No one not even a child should go through a thing like that.

I've never talked about the war in much detail because of things or events change you like Kim. The war scared me for life I am not sure about. I know you don't fully understand all what happened over there. But you *need to know baby killers are words that will stick with the Vietnam War. Plus soldiers were using drugs, too. Did you ever think we might want to forget the horrors we experience over there?*

You draw your own conclusions. But think about talking to some Vietnam veterans who are willing to share their experience with you besides me. I know you may find some willing not all of us are drop outs of society as well know with me. I had a wife and children once a long time ago. I miss it. Thank you for listening to me.

Yours,

Joshua Matthew Andrew Hernando

Joshua folded the letter up and left it on the table next to the other one. He leaned back deep into his pillow and closed his eyes. He could see in his mind walking through those parts of the jungle. The vines slap against his face and body, as he held his rifle firmly in his hands. His eyes gazed across the untamed land.

"Boys, be alert at all times," Lt. Grahams whispered repeatedly to me. "We're not native to this land. They know it and can have all kinds of deadly traps set up for us. So be alert boys."

Joshua felt sweat throughout his body, as they walked cautiously through the jungle. Scott looked terrified more each day, as he walked ahead of him. He heard snapping of twigs and munching of ground cover behind Lt. Grahams. It was Roger. Both Grahams and Joshua brought their fingers to their lips, but Roger ignored them as usual.

"Sir, I see a camp ahead," Roger reported to Grahams.

Everyone stopped at his news and looked back at

him.

"How far up are they, Private Clemens?"

"Less than a hundred yards, Sir."

"Oh, crap," he said in a low voice. "Corporal Hernando, see if you can pick them off quickly as possible. Go now."

"Yes, Sir," Joshua replied, as he proceeded out carefully.

"Hey wait up," Roger said, as he trudged in behind him.

"Roger, watch…"

"Ah…." Roger yelled followed by a big boom.

Gunfire sprayed everything, and Roger was down. Joshua dragged him to a nearby tree then noticed a piece of metal in Roger's leg. He glanced around for the rest of the platoon. It went deadly quiet then he heard screams. So he turned to Roger, but he wasn't the one screaming.

"I'll be back," he replied, "Be still and above all, quiet."

He rushed to the rest of the platoon. They were pinned down behind him. They didn't know if the enemy was still out there ahead of them. He approached the first one in uniform. Scott looked paler then before.

"Can you walk? It's clear to move now."

He shook his head, 'no'. Bombs had begun to explode around them again. Scott clung to Joshua's arm now.

"Come on," he yelled at Scott.

But Scott didn't move, so he grabbed him and headed back where they came from. Bombs continued to explode, as he headed out in the clearing near the river they crossed earlier in day. He left Scott there and headed back for the platoon one by one. He felt the mist come over his body, as he grabbed each one. The bombs still exploded, too. His right ear had begun to pop, as he rushed back into the jungle.

Henry had the radio still attached to his side when he brought him out. Henry was unconscious now. So Joshua reached for it and yelled into the receiver.

"AFA tango Charlie, rush all but one injured badly so far."

He rushed back in to get Scott out and rest of the platoon he could find. He felt more mist hit his body again, as he headed back.

"Josh, slow down," a female voice said to him calmly.

Joshua opened his eyes and saw Kim's face in his. He felt the wetness on his face. His breathing was labored now but slowing down.

"Breath slowly small bites of air," she said to him. "When you're ready, I need to know what happened here because it's affecting your health."

He drew in some air and felt oxygen hit his lungs. He became calmer with each second that passed. Kim pulled back and stood near his bed now. He also noticed Carly, and Susan was in a wheelchair there, too.

"I'm fine," he replied finally to them.

"You seemed to be running by the way your heart was racing, Dad," Susan said with concern in her eyes.

"I hadn't thought about the day Roger lost his leg forever. It was about four months or so after we buried your Mom." He glanced over at Kim. "He hit a trip wire, as I headed out to pick off the enemy at their camp ahead of us."

"Dad, you never...." said Susan.

"I know I never talked about that day and or the war. I didn't want Roger to talk about it either to you, kids," he interrupted her. "I'm sorry."

"Rita said since Roger's death that you started to open up, Dad. You did know Roger didn't remember triggering the wire trap. He let it slip one day. But he always called you a hero that day."

"It's like his death caused some deep soul searching," Carly said with a small smile.

"He regretted coming into our marriage. He gave me some money he could spare to find you and the kids. I think he realized how much I really needed you all in my life."

"He was one of a kind just like you, Joshua."

A small smile formed on his face, as he stared at Carly. He felt his heart flitter a little but still remained calm.

"I'm trying to get someone from the VA's office to send over symptoms of Agent Orange and any other possible war related issues," Kim said, as she stared at him. "I'm concerned what you were exposed to. It could explain your heart..."

"Kim, please," he pleaded with her.

"Well, I've got to go anyway," Kim said to him. "Susan, you're lucky to have him as a Dad and Luke as a brother."

Kim left the room. Silence filled the room now except for his monitor. Carly walked over to the window and stared out.

"What are you thinking about, Mom?"

"My brother and my ex-fiancé," she answered sadly. "I lost your Uncle Harry in your brother's war. My first fiancé came from your Dad's war changed. Yet not, one of them talked about their war. I know, I lost my brother in his war but your brother and father don't say much except what has been revealed recently."

"Mom, you've hardly talk about my Uncle Harry since he died," Susan said, as she wheeled over to her.

"It's painful, Sweetie," Carly said, as her eyes moistened slightly. "He and your grandfather were so protective over me with your Dad. I was Daddy's little girl despite the purple streak I had in my hair. Plus I was your Uncle Harry's baby sister. He didn't think your Dad was good enough for me."

"Why?"

"Your Dad's past of lack of knowing it," she answered honestly. "When I had the affair, your uncle wasn't surprised by it, but he never judged me."

"Bu they came around before we got married. Didn't they?" asked Joshua.

"Some but I still think they had their doubts. But they didn't want to step in the way of my happiness," Carly answered with tears on her cheeks now. "Then your Uncle Harry said to me before he went off to war that I'll never forget."

"What's that, Mom?" Susan asked, as she reached for Carly's hand.

Carly looked up at the ceiling then Susan then Joshua then Susan again. She cleared her throat.

"Love is all we got. It stands the test of time, so

reach for it and hold onto it tight. For its one thing that will last forever," she answered thoughtfully. "He kissed me and told me how much he loved his 'little pokey'. Then he was gone forever."

"He called you, 'little pokey'," Joshua stated a little surprised.

"I was chubby until I turned ten," she said back. "What you thought I was born like this? No, Mom had me work it off. She was tough on me, but the ..."

"Results turned out amazing," Joshua replied with a big smile.

"Stop!" she exclaimed with a touch of pink to her face now.

"I held back my past, and you could never take a complaint. We were some strange pair."

"I know people did wonder how we hooked up. "Love, I...I need to go. I'll see you, Susan, later. Bye, Joshua," Carly said, as she rushed out of the room.

"Carly," he called out too late.

"Mom is very emotional since my pregnancy," explained Susan. "I try to get her to talk to me, but she takes off like that or closes down. I don't know how to reach her just like Luke. I need her, Dad."

"I know you do. I can see it, but I think she's scared."

"Scared of what?"

"The risk you're taking. She carried you and Luke for eight and half months. She only has you, kids, and me now. Give her time, Susan. I know this isn't how we wanted you to have a child."

"I know marriage. I wanted it, too," Susan said with

tears in her eyes now. "But things changed."

She wheeled over to the bed. He padded the bed next to him, so she climbed up. He wanted to hold her close.

"Hush, little girl, Daddy's here," he sang to her. "I love you, little baby."

"You haven't sung to me before," she said, as she looked up at his face.

"When you were a baby, I did," he replied back. "Your Mom sang 'Twinkle Little Star' to Luke, and you cried real loud. So I took you into another room sang to you privately."

"I didn't know that."

"I don't have much of a voice, but I tried for you."

"Thanks, Daddy."

She closed her eyes and snuggled closer to him despite her pregnancy. Joshua felt his eyelids getting heavier, so he drifted off to sleep, too.

15

The rape slash molestation trial had begun a week ago. Joshua barely had time to recover from his hospital stay. But it had to happen and both sides guarded their case close to their chests. Alex sat in jail until the trial. The State Prosecutor convinced Judge George Montgomery that Alex was a flight risk due to nature of his profession.

Alex was an Associate Press photographer who went all over there world to capture a story on film. So he was denied bail due to that reason. In his anger over it, Rita manager to slip him divorce papers which he signed, but he wasn't happy over this either. It allowed Rita to have a quick divorce from him, so she could testify against him if she had to for the sake of her children.

Joshua heard this all second hand from James later Rita. Rita and the children were in a disclosed location now for their own protection. Susan, Joan and Carly were there too, since them, meaning law enforcement, hadn't found the person or persons attempt on Susan and her baby's life. So he, Patrick, James and Luke had time on their hands now.

Luke still kept his distance. But Joshua was glad to have his brother Andrew and sisters Caroline and Elizabeth around with their kids. However, he never sent the letter the he wrote in the hospital. He thought maybe later after the trial. Yet, Joshua missed his girls and his grandchildren, but they, all, had to be safe. His army buddies rallied around him, too.

"How many beers must a man drink before he passes out?" Steve asked, as he sang really off key. "Tell me, man, for I don't know."

He stared face to face with Joshua on his deck. Bryan stayed in his room when he heard Steve stumble up to the front door. So Joshua put his food, milk and litter box in the room and closed the door.

"Go somewhere else and sleep this off, Steve," replied Joshua.

"You never hit the bottle in the whole time I've known you, buddy," Steve said, as he smelled of strong whiskey.

It turned Joshua's stomach just at the smell of it. He felt a few light taps on his cheeks.

"Here's a man who can fight but drinks milk," Steve continued on. "My hero, Roger always reminded us of this important fact. But you didn't want to take any bows or the glory that came from being our hero."

"There you are," Scott said, as he walked into the house. "They said he left The Tides, but his truck is still in the parking lot. Tim suggested he might come here."

"Hey, Josh, old buddy, got any beer?" Steve asked, as he still focused on him.

"Sit down," Joshua answered, as he shoved him into a nearby chair.

"I need more alcohol," yelled Steve, "Buddy."

"Stay put," Joshua snapped in anger.

"Yes, Sir," Steve said with an awkward salute before he went silent.

"Thank, God," said Scott, "He has us."

"Passed out as usual," Joshua replied back. "So

why is he drinking so heavy this time?"

"Julia left him again," Scott explained back. "He slapped her around one too many times now. I found her on the floor in real bad shape, so I took her to the hospital before looking for him. She's leaving him for good this time. She'll be pressing charges, too after she recovers from the miscarriage."

"She was pregnant again!" Joshua exclaimed a little shocked. "How many..."

"I think, six, but I don't think this one was Steve's."

"Why do you say that?"

"There was another man; Julia mentioned in passing last week," answered Scott.

"Crap, I should have known when he smelled of real strong whiskey that it was serious," he replied thoughtfully. "He can't stay here. I've got a kitten in my room, and I have to be at the trial."

"I forgot, man," said Scott. "It's a week already into it. How are the girls and kids holding up?"

"I was going to find out when he showed up."

"Go, I'll take care of him. I'll call Tim if I need more help," Scott said confidently. "I'll let your kitty out after I get him in my car. What's his name?"

"Bryan. I'll help you get him into your car. He'll have a big and ugly hang over."

"And throw up, too," Scott added. "Let's drag him to the backseat. I don't know how you were able to carry us, all, with our gear and shrapnel in your shoulder back in Nam."

"You do what got to do," he replied back, as he swung Steve over his left shoulder. "Lead the way."

"You can still do it after all these years," Scott said with a shake of his head.

Steve moaned.

"He's heavier now, so move."

"Gotcha, buddy."

Later Joshua paced the hallway of the courthouse. He couldn't sit and wait to be called in. It had been a surprise how the Defense wanted him on the stand. The Prosecution tried to figure out why. So they asked him to stay outside but that was a half hour ago. It was over two hours ago since he left Bryan alone in the house.

"Stop it. Stop it, now. He will be fine," he mumbled to himself.

"Joshua Hernando," the bailiff called out at the double doors.

"Yes," he replied, as he approached him.

"I need you to come in and take the stand. I'll swear you in there, Sir."

Joshua nodded and followed. He felt the tension in the room, as he took the stand. Then he turned around and faced everyone. The bailiff walked up.

"Raise your right hand, Sir. Do you solemnly swear to tell the whole truth and nothing the truth so help you, God?"

"I do," he answered calmly.

"Please state your full name and occupation for the record, Sir."

"Joshua Matthew Adam Hernando currently retired."

"Please, be seated, Sir."

He took his seat and clasped his hands in front of

him now.

"A pretty long name, Mr. Hernando, I am Lance Jones, the lead attorney for the Defense. Thank you for coming today," he said politely.

"You're welcome."

"So polite, too," Jones said, as he walked over the juror box and stood. "But you weren't the two times you attacked my client. Were you?"

"Once I attacked after he attacked me," Joshua answered honestly and calmly. "Yes, I admit to losing it temporary after I heard what he did to my daughter."

"What did you do to my client?"

"Which time, Mr. Jones?" he asked still calm

"The first time, Mr. Hernando, explain to the jury what you did outside by your car on Christmas day of last year."

"Susan, my daughter, had told me what Alex had done to her a couple months earlier. I'll admit it made me angry. I wanted him to know that I knew what he had done," Joshua explained, as he felt his throat dry. "Could I have a glass of water?"

"Of course," answered Judge Montgomery.

The bailiff approached with a glass. He took a sip before he continued.

"Thank you. As I was saying, I wanted Alex to know I knew. I wasn't proud of what I did to him next."

"And what was that, Mr. Hernando?"

"I think, I grabbed his penis and squeezed it hard," he answered, as he sipped more water. "I guess he wet his pants. I think, I warned him to leave Susan alone. I didn't know he attacked my ex-wife or Susan's Mom prior to coming to my place that day."

"Did you serve in the Vietnam War?"

"Yes."

"Weren't you the best shot of your platoon?"

"Yes."

"Weren't you the best one in hand to hand combat in your platoon as well?"

"I suppose, yes."

"So you had formal training in the kind of fighting prior combat. Correct?"

"No."

"No. Then where did you learn this?"

"I did it before when a fellow vet went after a doctor there at a hospital. It worked, so I did it on, Alex."

"Your honor, Mr. Hernando, isn't the one on trial here," the Prosecutor said, as he stood up.

"I'll allow it," Judge Montgomery said to the Prosecutor calmly back. "Mr. Jones, will you move this along?"

"Yes, your honor. So you're known to have a temper. Is that correct, Mr. Hernando?"

"Yes, in the past, but I've learned to control it through the years."

"But you showed no control when you attacked my client when he came to see if his sister-in-law was all right," Mr. Jones said, as he walked towards Joshua. "You attacked him for no reason."

"Alex attacked me first. He fights like a damn girl. He wasn't there to see if Susan was okay. I think, he wanted to know if he succeeded," Joshua snapped back, as his heart begun to race.

"Dad," a female voice shouted in the courtroom.

Rita and Joan rushed to up. Judge Montgomery slammed down his gavel, as whispers filled the courtroom.

Joshua felt tightness in his chest stronger than ever before and his cough soon followed.

"Please stop. He's got a heart condition," Rita pleaded with the judge.

"Daddy," Joan whispered to him.

"No one told me!" exclaimed Judge Montgomery. "Please escort him to my chambers and get a damn doctor here stat. This court is adjured for the day."

He slammed his gavel down for the last time. Joshua leaned on two women, as they followed the judge.

"We got you, Dad," Rita said calmly. "Mom and Susan are coming behind us. Take slow and small breathes. Please."

"In here, ladies," Judge Montgomery said, as he held the door open.

They walked him to the waiting couch, and Rita rubbed his shoulders now.

"Relax, Dad, please," Rita said, as she begged him.

"I'm here," Kim said, as she knelt down. "Josh, listen to me. I know it hurts like hell but stay with me. I'm going to give you a shot to slow down your heart and to ease the pain in the chest. So it'll help the cough, too. Do you understand?"

He nodded. He felt the needle in his leg. It acted rather quickly, as he started to feel some relief.

"Is he going to be all right?" Judge Montgomery asked Kim.

"Yes, your honor. He has an irregular heartbeat

and only left the hospital yesterday," answered Kim.

"Can he resume the stand tomorrow?" asked Mr. Jones.

"He almost had a heart attack, and you want to know if he can be back on the stand tomorrow," Judge Montgomery answered in anger. "Where's your concern for this witness?"

"That's my point, your honor. Mr. Jones is only concern is to get his client off no matter what it takes," answered the Prosecution.

"I see your point now. I'll make a note of it in the courtroom in front of the jury in the morning. I assure you that I didn't know this would happen, Mr. Hernando. I'm truly sorry. Stay as long as you like or your doctor sees you fit to move. Please excuse me and anyone not related to him out."

Joshua watched Jones and Prosecutor follow the Judge out of his chambers. Susan and Carly stood by the now closed door. Kim checked his pulse again.

"That's better," she said with a small smile.

"Daddy," Susan said, as she edged closer.

"I'm okay now, Honey," he replied, as he smiled at all.

"I don't know how it shifted from me to you, Daddy. But I had to be honest about it all," she said, as tears glided down her puffy cheeks. "I love you, Daddy."

"I know you, do, my Honey bear."

"You haven't called me that in a very long time," she said, as she knelt before him now.

"Not since Rita and Joan were born," he replied, as he took her shaky hands into his.

Kim allowed her to move closer. She knew he needed his girls to be near him now. He was grateful that Kim understood it without saying.

"I wasn't the baby anymore. Mom gave birth to Joan then Rita. Luke was before me. I thought you had forgotten after all these years."

"How could I forget my pet names for all of you? There are yours and yours alone," he replied back with a small smile.

"Ladies, it's time," a man said, as he stood in the open doorway now.

"Do we have to?" Joan asked in a deep whine.

"It's for your own protection, Ms. Hernando," answered the man.

"Joan, my little mouse," replied Joshua.

"Dad, I often wondered how I got that pet name," she said, as she stared at him closer now.

"You were so quiet at your baptism and any other time you were in church," said Carly. "Right, Joshua?"

He nodded. He hugged her then hugged Rita. Then he bent down in front of him to hug Susan. The man glanced at his watch.

"Do they have to be somewhere?" asked Joshua.

"Rita's kids will be at the safe house," he answered back.

"Bill, relax," said Carly.

"Uh..." he said in hesitation. "It's William."

"Mr. Stuffy Pants," Joan said in a low voice. "Is more like it..."

"I heard that."

"He's only doing his job," Joshua pointed out. "I'll

be fine. I'm sure Uncle Scott got Uncle Steve to sleep somewhere else after I loaded him in the car."

"You did that before you came here," stated Carly. "He was drunk again."

"Yes, Julia left him for good this time. She lost the baby, too, but Scott seems to believe it wasn't Steve's this time."

"Ladies," William said coldly.

"Fine," Joan and Rita said in unison.

"That's our twins," Carly said proudly.

Rita and Joan stared at each other then laughed. Then they gave Joshua a quick hug and helped Susan to her feet. She stood before him. She had an extended belly now.

"Three maybe four."

"I say four going onto five," Carly said with a small smile. "It's that or she's expecting twins."

"It could be possible," replied Joshua.

"No way," Susan snapped back.

"Well, you eat like a pig," said Joan.

"I'm nervous about this trial," she snapped back.

"I didn't know I was expecting twins with you and Luke. You overshadowed your brother right up to delivery."

"No way!"

"Afraid so," Joshua pointed out with a big smile.

"Crap, let's go," Susan said, as she headed for the door. "It's been a long day, and Dad and I need our rest. Bye, Daddy."

"We'll talk to her, Dad," Rita said, as she passed her Mom.

"Yeah," Joan said, as she rushed to join them.

"You take care of yourself," Carly warned him. "You're not as young as you used to be."

"I know," he replied, as he held out his arms.

He held her close and breathed in a sweet scent he knew so well. He grabbed her tighter to his chest when she wiggled free. She touched his cheek then headed for the door.

"Take good care of my ladies, William," he replied with a nod.

"I will, Mr. Hernando."

"Call me, Josh. I'm sure they prefer you call them by their first names, too" he replied with another smile.

"Yes...Josh," William said with some hesitation. "Have a great rest of the day, Sir."

"Thank you and same to you."

He nodded and walked out of the judge's chambers. Judge Montgomery walked back in. He changed out of his black robe now.

"Are you feeling better?" Judge Montgomery asked him.

"Yes, your honor. Thank you."

"Your girls are very pretty just like their mother. You're a lucky man, Mr. Hernando."

"Thank you, your honor."

"You know, the Defense tried to get today since you're a Vietnam veteran. I've seen a lot of veterans come through my court, but you were calmer longer than most. I can see how you've learned to control it," Judge Montgomery with a small smile. "Keep up the good work and take care of that heart of yours."

Joshua only smiled back and headed for the door.

"I read you were a hero," comment Judge Montgomery. "It was in the DA's report."

"I did what I had to do to get my comrades out of that jungle. I'm not a hero, Sir," he replied back, as he faced the judge.

"But you are risked your own life for the platoon with bombs and gunfire repeatedly."

"And don't forget the mist under a clear blue sky," added Joshua.

"You were exposed to Agent Orange," Judge Montgomery said a little surprised.

"I guess the possibility is there. My doctors are looking into it. Kim seems to think it has affected my heart and lungs, but she's trying to get some more info on it all."

"She seems to care for a Korean."

"She's from Vietnam. My platoon buried her Mom over there. She was adopted by Americans here. They gave her better life here then over there as an orphan. I hadn't seen her since she was a little girl and over there back in '63."

"Wow! That's amazing after all these years. But you're amazing, Mr. Hernando."

"Why do you say that, your honor?"

"The DA didn't have that important fact in his profile on you. He has profiles on all his clients, witnesses and anyone related to his cases. I'm impressed by it all. Well, have a good night, Mr. Hernando. I'll see you in the morning."

"Same to you, your honor."

Judge Montgomery nodded, so Joshua walked out. He felt stronger now, as he stepped out of the courthouse.

He readjusted his eyes to the different light source.

"I'm not a hero. I did what I had to do," he replied to himself again.

"Sergeant Hernando," a familiar voice said to him.

"Sir, Allen," he replied a little rattled by it. "What brings you to the courthouse?"

"Mr. Jones has summoned me to testify in your son-in-law's trial," answered Allen. "I don't know why. I don't even know the guy."

"But you know, me, Sir."

"What's that got to do with the case?"

"Jones had me on the stand today. He had me explain what I did to my ex-son-in-law. Maybe I shouldn't be telling you this, but I felt and so did the judge that Jones was putting me on trial instead of Alex."

"Hi, Dad," Tim said, as he walked up. "I'm parking in loading zone. Oh, hi, Josh."

"Hi, Tim," Joshua replied with a friendly smile.

"Dad and I were going to get a buffalo burger at Cookies. Would you like to join us?" Tim asked with a return friendly smile, "My treat."

"Never had one, but do they have any fish?"

"No clam chowder but fish and fries, shrimp and a salmon burger and tuna sandwiches."

"I'll try it. I'm parked in the lot. So are you parked out front?"

Tim nodded.

"I'll be meet you there and follow you out."

"It's best I come to you," said Tim.

"Okay," Joshua replied, as he headed for the parking lot.

It took him ten minutes to get his Blazer out of the lot and followed Tim to Cookies on 57th and H streets. They pulled into the parking lot, and Tim helped Allen into his wheelchair.

"Are the milkshakes good?" he asked Tim.

"Blueberry is the best," Tim answered back. "Do you want a small, medium and large?"

"Large if it's okay," he answered quickly.

"Okay. Dad, do you want your usual with zucchini sticks?" Tim asked, as they approached an outdoor table. "Did you want fish or…"

"I'll try the buffalo," he interrupted him. "Sorry. I realized I haven't eaten all day."

"Okay. Three buffalo burgers hold the mayo but add baroque sauce and cheddar cheese, three x- large blueberry shakes and an order of zucchini and two green salads, anything else, gentleman?"

"Zucchini and salad sounds good, too," answered Joshua.

"Another order of those, so is anything else?"

"Sounds good, son," answered Allen.

Tim nodded and headed off to order. Joshua sat down and clasped his hands in front of him. He focused on Allen.

"So I need to be on guard with this Jones guy," Allen said to him. "He likes to push people's buttons. I've dealt with his kind since Nam. Haven't you?"

"I suppose, I used to get into a lot of fights after my marriage fell apart. Then I knew I had to find them and have them back in my life."

"How long did it take to find them?" Allen asked

interest. "Who was the first to come to you?"

"Twelve long years and my youngest girl, Rita. It's her ex who's on trial right now, and she was seventeen. I missed twelve long years of my children's lives that I can never get back," Joshua answering sadly and thoughtfully.

"But you bounced in and out of their lives before that. Didn't you?" Tim asked, as he placed the shakes on the table. "Rita said Roger took you away from them a lot."

"Yes, he did. He regretted it, too. He gave me money or what he could to help in finding them."

"I think you rubbed off on him," said Allen

"How so?"

"You reminded us all of compassion in the middle of a war. We buried mothers, children and elderly because you felt everyone should be buried with some kind of dignity," answered Allen.

"Rita is lucky to have a Dad like you," said Tim. "She has fond memories of you when she was little. She got a little sad after you and Carly divorced. I sense it was a very lonely time in her life, but I didn't push it. I know when to back off, Dad. I know, you don't think I do but then I see her face light up when you found them again."

"How old was she when you divorced?" Allen asked with interest.

"Five," Joshua answered, as he took a bite of his burger. "This is good."

"We like them," said Tim. "We have every time we're here in Sacramento."

"We discovered buffalo meat the first time at Grand Tetons years ago," said Allen.

"Thank you for inviting me along," Joshua replied,

as he ate everything before him.

"You still look fit since the war. How did you provide for your big family?" asked Allen. "You never ate this much in military."

Joshua swallowed the last piece of his burger before he spoke again. Allen ate his burger and waited.

"Construction mostly which consisted of being a brick layer, carpenter and some electrical where the big money was, I also did house framing and fencing," Joshua answered honestly. "I did anything that I set my mind to pretty much. It was a way to keep Roger with me most of the time in case he flipped out."

"So your Dad taught you all this," said Tim.

"No. He focused on Andrew, my only brother."

"The lawyer?"

Joshua nodded.

"Tim, could you get me more napkins?"

"Sure, Dad," Tim answered, as he got to his feet.

"Andrew is older?" Allen asked after Tim left.

"Yes."

"They had big dreams for him, so you signed up. You sacrificed your own life for his, so they wouldn't see him go off to war."

Joshua nodded, as he ate his salad.

"I'm only beginning to understand your journey through life. Have you talked about your life with anyone?"

"Not really. I didn't tell my wife about my family before and during our marriage. I only recently had begun to talk about my life."

"Here you go, Dad."

"Thanks son. What about the rest of them?"

"Roger affected us, all, Sir. Steve is going to have a real hang over when he wakes up."

"Oh, he had a wild side to him over there, as I recall," Allen said thoughtfully.

"It's still that way, Sir. His girlfriend or now ex will probably file charges of physical abuse against him. The case of the baby she lost, too," Joshua rambled on. "That war seemed to mess us, all, up. Didn't it?"

"I guess," answered Allen.

"But you seem all right," Tim said, as he stared at Joshua.

"I guess," replied Joshua.

"Tim, don't push it," said Allen. "My son here wants to write a story on Vietnam or any eye-witness, accounts of the effects that war. My version is clouded because I'm his Dad."

"But facts are fact, Sir."

"That's what he told me, but it's easy to use family in articles. Moreover, it doesn't help with your investigating skills when writing and developing a story of interest," pointed out Tim.

"That's a valid point."

"Thank you, Josh. Do you think we can talk after the trial?"

"Uh...we'll see," he answered in hesitation.

"No problem. How was everything?"

"Great. Thank you ever so much."

"You're welcome, Josh."

Joshua didn't remember much after that since he drove back home. Bryan was glad to see him, and he felt the same about him. Scott had left the bedroom door open which gave Bryan full access to the house again. The kitten ate his dinner then cuddled up next to Joshua on the couch. They both seemed tired from the long day.

He ignored the blinking light on his answering machine. So he closed his eyes to only fall into a deep, dark sleep. Bryan stretched out on his chest. He felt light against his chest.

16

The next morning Joshua fed Bryan and played with him a little before he headed back to Sacramento and court. Bryan was asleep on the couch in a soft pink blanket that Joshua brought him sometime back. He smiled at the kitten and headed out.

BABY KILLER was sprayed in bold, bright red paint on his Blazer. He touched the paint, and it was dry. He shook his head and got in. It was four thirty when he left Bryan home alone. He pulled over and searched his phone directory on his cell and saw the name he wanted.

"He...l...lo," a female voice said on the other end.

"I'm sorry to wake you up so early, Rosemary," he apologized to her quickly.

"Josh, is that you? Is Bryan okay?" she asked, as she sprung awake now.

"He's fine or will be. Someone sprayed painted my Blazer. A hate crime, I think. But I don't like the idea of him being alone at..."

"I'll go get him now. The spare key is in the usual place."

"Yes."

"Go, be with your family. I'll get him and bring him back to my clinic."

"How do you..."

"It was all over the news yesterday. Go, now."

"Thank you."

The phone went silent now. So Joshua closed it and headed for Sacramento. He reached the courthouse in a sea of reporters and camera crews at the main doors.

"There he is," a reporter called out in his direction.

"Damn," he replied under his breath.

"Back away. Let him through," said a uniform officer. "Make way for him."

Another officer stood next to Joshua now. "We're here to escort you into the courtroom, Mr. Hernando. Judge Montgomery's orders, he issued them last night."

Joshua allowed them escort him into the courthouse and courtroom. He glanced up at the clock on the wall 7:45, as the bailiff approached him.

"Come with me, Mr. Hernando, quickly."

So Joshua followed him back to the judge's chambers again. He stepped into see his girls, Prosecutor and Defense lawyers and Judge Montgomery were all in the room.

"Daddy," Susan said, as she rushed up.

"Honey bear," he replied, as he held out his open arms.

"I see, you're okay," said Judge Montgomery. "Mr. Jones, you're lucky this time, but I'll warn you if anything happens to Mr. Hernando due to this trial..."

"Excuse me, your honor," Joshua interrupted him. "What's going on?"

"You need to tell him," Montgomery answered, as he gazed at Jones. "You started this mess."

"Yes, your honor," Mr. Jones said unhappily. "A death threat was sent to the judge since I put you on the stand yesterday. It made reference to your time in the service."

"About being a 'baby killer'," stated Joshua. "I

killed no babies in that damn war. I buried them with my comrades. But it explains everything now."

"What are you talking about?" Mr Jones asked.

"Baby killer was spray painted in red on my Blazer sometime last night," Joshua explained sharply back. "I'm sorry, your honor."

"That's understandable, Mr. Hernando," said Judge Montgomery. "I'll send an officer to take a picture of the damage. Mr. Jones, you'll pay for a new paint job out of your own pocket."

"But, your honor…," Mr. Jones started to protest then stopped.

"Now we have a case to continue today. Let's get this going. Do you want Mr. Hernando to return to the witness stand this morning?"

"Yes, your honor."

Susan released from Joshua's embrace. They all proceeded into the courtroom. Alex was in a jumpsuit, chains at his ankles and cuffs on his wrists at the defense table. He smiled at Joshua, as he stood at the witness stand. He felt a deep chill down his spine before he focused on the bailiff.

"I must remind you, Mr. Hernando, you're still under oath."

"I do."

"Before you start, Mr. Jones, I have something to instruct the jury," Judge Montgomery said quickly.

Mr. Jones nodded and held his hand out to Alex.

"Jurors, I must remind you that you're here for Alex Walters' trail not, Joshua Hernando. Mr. Jones, you may precede."

"Thank you, your honor," Mr. Jones said politely. "I'm sorry about yesterday, Mr. Hernando. Are you feeling better today?"

"Yes, thank you."

"Now you took your daughter Susan to your doctor. Why?"

"I trust my doctor and thought she could keep Susan calm since it was woman to woman," he answered honestly.

"Is that how you felt about your other daughter Joan and ex-wife Carly, too?"

"Yes."

"I see. But isn't it hard to find proof after it being my client who had relations with these woman? Was your doctor qualified to do this kind of exam?"

"She assisted law enforcement in the past. She knew what to do."

"How do you know this?"

"She told me after we rescheduled one of my appointments with her for my care."

"You have a female doctor. Why, not a man?"

"I feel more comfortable with a woman. I had a female doctor since I was seven until sixteen."

"Do they sexually arouse you?"

"What do you mean, Sir?"

"Have you ever wanted to fuck a female doctor?"

A gasp was heard in the courtroom followed by whispers.

"Um... no, Sir," Joshua answered calmly.

"But you admitted seeing a female doctor until you were sixteen. Boys begin sexual activity as early as thirteen, so you were with a female doctor for at least three years. Didn't you want to screw your doctor, as she felt your private parts?'

"Your honor," the Prosecution said, as he shot up from his table.

"Mr. Jones, we discussed this in my chambers. The jurors will disregard these personal questions, and they will be stricken from the record after he explained why he brought his daughter to her," Judge Montgomery said back. "Are there anymore questions?"

"No, your honor."

"Mr. Prosecutor, do you have any questions for this witness?"

"Yes, I do your honor."

"Then please proceed."

"Thank you, your honor," he said politely. "Mr. Hernando, what was your first impression of Alex Walters when he was involved with your daughter, Rita?"

"I didn't understand his interest in her," Joshua answered honestly. "She's pretty in her own right despite she doesn't think so."

"Why was that, Sir?"

"He is older than she and more experience about things than Rita. She was barely out of law school for one thing."

"What do you mean?"

"Sexually and probably more worldly as well since she didn't date anyone until she met him."

"I see. Did your first impression of him change?"

"I didn't feel right about him, but I kept my mouth shut. I didn't want to hurt Rita and possibly send her deeper into his arms."

"How did you feel when he married her?"

"Uneasy, but I asked her if she truly loves him."

"What did she say back?"

"She loved him, so I gave her my blessing and kept quiet. Her happiness is all I ever wanted. I wanted it for all my kids since they came from a broken home. My parents stayed with each other until death do us part. My marriage to their Mom didn't happen that way, so this is one thing I could give them."

"You don't care about family except destroy it," Alex commented bitterly. "You were a baby killer over there in Vietnam like all vets from that damn war were. Then you come back to the States and destroy families here."

"Mr. Jones, advise your client to hold his tongue in my courtroom until if and when he is put on the stand," Judge Montgomery said to the defense.

"Yes, your honor," Mr. Jones said, as he whispered to Alex.

"I won't be silenced. Do you hear me? He messed with my family years ago. He destroyed it when Bryan went to prison for life. Our mother was never the same after that," Alex yelled at Joshua.

"Mr. Jones, I advise your client to be quiet," Judge Montgomery said in unhappy tone in his voice now.

"Put me on the stand," Alex said to Mr. Jones. "Let me tell the court why I did what I did. I have nothing to hide not like that man sitting there right now."

"You can't go against your counsel," Mr. Jones said back to Alex.

"Yes, I can and I will. You're fired," Alex snapped back. "Do you hear me?"

"So Mr. Jones, you are dismissed from this case," Judge Montgomery said calmly now.

"But... your honor."

"I have to honor his wishes, Mr. Jones."

"Damn," Mr. Jones said, as he gathered up his briefcase and legal papers.

He hustled out of the courtroom. No one seemed to want to follow him.

"So you're acting as your own counsel, Mr. Walters?" asked Judge Montgomery.

"Yes, your honor," answered Alex.

"Please note it in the records that the defense attorney was removed by his client, and the client is defending himself in this case," the judge said to the clerk.

She nodded.

"Precede, Mr. Walters. Do you have any questions for this witness?"

"Yes, I do, your honor," Alex answered, as he stood up at his table. "But first I must ask for more moment in the courtroom to cross-exam this witness."

"Of course," the judge said with a nod to the officer.

He stepped closer to Alex and removed his ankle chains then stepped back.

"Precede, Sir."

"Thank you, your honor," Alex said, as he walked to the jury box then looked back Joshua with a serious look on his face. "Mr. Hernando, do you remember a seventeen or eighteen year working with you and Roger Clemens on a construction site named Bryan?"

"Yes."

"Tell us or the court what you remember about him."

"He helped Roger and I layout carpet since Roger had only one good leg. He lost one in Vietnam years earlier, and Bryan was looking for work. He said something about his girlfriend was pregnant." Joshua paused for moment then stared into Alex's eyes. "He disappeared part of a day then only to reappear with blood on his clothes and hands. Bryan had left the site to go see and killed her. He had disposed her body in the construction site's dumpster. We, all, got sent home for the rest of the day because of it being now a part of a crime scene."

"What became of Bryan?" Alex asked coldly.

"He was arrested. The last time I saw him when I was on the witness stand at his trial. I told the truth then and now."

"Did you know he had a mother and a little brother?"

"No, Bryan only talked about the girlfriend, and why he needed the money. I was helping him out. He was a good kid who needed a break."

"So you're saying that you didn't know he had a family besides the girlfriend," Alex said with anger in his voice now.

"Nope, he had only talked about was her girlfriend at the site."

Alex glared at him. Joshua stared back and remembered Bryan's eyes on that day. He sat back in the chair. He couldn't believe what he saw there now.

"Mr. Hernando, are you okay?" Judge Montgomery asked him quickly.

"Yes, your honor. Thank you. You're his little brother," Joshua answered thoughtfully. "You sat behind him with your mother, as I sat on the stand. I didn't know...."

"Save it. The damage is done. Bryan hung himself in prison, and I swore to get my revenge. I was ten then. I waited and plotted my revenge on you. Rita was easy to get back then," Alex interrupted him. "She was my first taste of revenge. I wanted more, so I went after your older girls and ex. Then I still wasn't satisfied with that, so I seized Jenny and Jordan. They were easy targets just like their dear, old Mom. I didn't think they would say anything to anyone, but they did. I'm not happy with that fact or the divorce either."

But he let out a wicked laugh that unnerved Joshua and probably others in the courtroom. Silence filled the courtroom now.

"So you planned revenge on this man's family because your older brother murdered his girlfriend and their unborn child," Judge Montgomery said after some time passed.

"Yep, I had the family divided like mine was. It was the ultimate revenge," Alex said with a confident smile.

"What became of your mother after your brother hung himself?" asked Judge Montgomery.

"Her mind snapped finally after three years passed. Then I was shipped into foster care since my father didn't want the responsibility of raising a thirteen year old. Dear, old Mom died last year in a crazy house," Alex explained rather cheerfully. "She hadn't recognized me in years. She thought I was Bryan. He could no wrong in her eyes."

"So you're admitting to raping three women and molesting two minor children under eighteen for the solo purpose of revenge. Is that correct?" asked Montgomery.

"Oh, don't forget I made one pregnant, your honor. That's a bonus since Susan has decided to keep my baby. She's was so very ripe more than the others and fertile, too. How lucky can a man get while plotting revenge on his enemy? You know at first I thought, I wanted them dead but sitting here in the courtroom and time to think. I rather like the idea of being a Dad again," he answered with a big smile on his face now. "I know, every time they look at him; they'll see me and my family and remember it all over again."

"YOU'RE BASTARD!" Rita exclaimed, as she got to her feet. "I loved you with all my heart and soul."

"I didn't love you, my dear. You were easy to screw. I wanted to keep you popping out babies as long as possible or until you cried out for mercy. I would then go in for the final time. But then I liked the idea of screwing your sisters and Mom then our children too more than you will ever realize, my dear."

"That's enough. I think this court has heard enough. I believe with the jury is in agreement with me that we find you guilty on all charges against you," Judge Montgomery said in anger. "Plus two counts of attempted murder."

The jurors, all, nodded at the judge. So he preceded forward.

"Therefore, I sentence you to life in prison without

the possibility of parole since you admitted in this court about wanting to kill Susan Hernando and her unborn child."

"I'll file for visitation right on my unborn child and my current children," Alex snapped back.

"And I'll assist these women in blocking that ever happening," Montgomery snapped back. "Verdict is ruled in favor of the Prosecution. Now guards get him out of my sight."

"You haven't gotten rid of me yet. Wait and see with my baby. It'll haunt you for the rest of your lives," Alex said, as the guards led him out of the courtroom.

Joshua left the stand and noticed Rita's hands over her face now. She muffled her tears. Her world was shattered, and he didn't know how to make it better for her and her kids. Carly escorted her out. Susan and Joan followed in behind them. He held back, as the press rushed outside after them. He shook his head, as he sat down in the empty courtroom.

"You need to take responsibility for your actions," Martin said to Joshua.

"But I didn't break the fence, Dad," he replied in his best defense. "Honestly, Dad."

"You're going to stand here and tell me it broke on its own. What do you think I am stupid? Well I'm not, Joshua. I maybe a farmer's son and had a dream once a long time ago. But I'm no liar, but I know a liar and stupid one at that when I meet them, too. Now remove the broken pieces and put up new ones. Make sure they match like the others. Do you hear me?"

"But, Dad, I didn't do it, and I'm not lying to you,"

protested Joshua.

"Joshua, don't argue with me. Now get cracking on it before I gave you additional punishment."

Joshua nodded and begun to work on the damaged fence from the frame. Martin walked back into the house, so Joshua was alone.

"I didn't do this," he mumbled to himself. "I didn't do this."

"You're right, little brother," Andrew said with a big smile.

"You did this!" he exclaimed, as he stared at Andrew now.

"Ceira dumped me for Stuart. I was pissed off, so I kicked the fence hard with my foot."

"Why didn't you tell, Dad?"

"He already blamed you for it and besides I'm going to law school," he answered confidently.

"What's that got to do with it?"

"Everything attorneys are always in control at all times. They're not to get angry."

"That doesn't make any sense."

"You're too stupid to know anything different. Have fun," Andrew said before he walked away.

"You need to tell the truth to Dad."

Andrew laughed, as he headed across the street. Joshua wiped the sweat off his face.

"Joshua, hey, little brother" Andrew said, as he brought him back to the present.

He looked up at Andrew and got to his feet.

"You seemed so far away there."

"Just remembered back when I fixed the fence you

broke. You never admitted it that you did it. Did you? Dad went to his grave believing I did it. Didn't he?"

"Wow! I hadn't thought about Ceira in years. She was so pretty back then. I wanted to marry her like most boys my age. But Dad said she wasn't good wife for the powerful attorney I was going to be," Andrew answered thoughtfully back. "I told him that I did it, not you."

"Are you the powerful attorney Dad wanted you to be?"

"No not really. I think he was happy that I was successful, but I also got a feeling something inside him was sad or maybe heartbroken. I could never figure it out."

"He loved baseball and was really good at it. He could have gone professional if Grandpa hadn't held him back."

"How do you know, that?" Andrew asked a little surprised.

"I struggled to read his yearbooks especially his senior year. People made reference to a career in baseball. Then one said she was sorry that his Dad didn't think he could have a career in baseball. So I looked back in previous yearbooks. Sure enough, Dad played at least all four years in high school."

"Man, I didn't know that, and I spent a lot more time with him than you did. I had no idea," said Andrew. "You said you struggled to read. What do you mean?"

"Never mind, what has brought you here?"

"You actually…"

"Oh. Why?"

Andrew stared at him. "Let's walk little brother."

"I don't like the sound of this," Joshua replied back.

"Just tell me, Andrew. You're a lawyer."

They stepped out of the courtroom and stood in the hallway.

"Mom had a minor stroke prior to you leaving. She bounced back from it so quickly that we didn't even know she had it in late '61," Andrew said calmly. "We thought she only had the one in late '63, but she had another one in late August of '62. It was minor, too. But the one we blamed you for was in early December of '63 which was her third and final one. It was the worst one of all them. It was that one where she slipped into the coma?"

"Will you get to the point?" Joshua asked knew his patience was running thin now.

"In light of this and this morning's developments, I knew I had to tell you all this."

"Damn it! Andrew, will you get to the point," he snapped, as he felt anger build inside him now.

"Someone sprayed painted our parents' home in red paint," Andrew said calmly.

"Baby killer," he snapped back.

"Lived here," added Andrew, "How did you know?"

"It was on my Blazer, too. But why bring up Mom's stroke?"

"The new owners found a lose floorboard in Mom and Dad's old room. They found a metal box with a book in it. Mom had a diary. We discovered a lot of them when she died. We thought she stopped doing them after the Bay of Pigs," Andrew explained, as he glanced down the hallway. "I realize how I that I didn't know neither of them very well."

"Didn't you tell me that Mom went to church to

pray?"

"I read it in her diaries. She didn't always say why she prayed so much. But she talked about her job and promotions. What was happening in Dad's and us kids' lives, but something was missing. A deep sadness despite how successful she was at her job or career."

"Could it have been the Bay of Pigs?"

"No, it seemed so personal then I begun to read her last diary," Andrew answered thoughtfully. "She was sad for you, and I don't know why fully."

"Just let it go, Andrew. I disappointed Mom the final time at eleven, and I've managed to go on without her. So the new owners want us to spring for new paint job on the old house."

"No. They wanted to know what it meant. I told them that you served in Vietnam."

"That explained it all then, right?"

He nodded. "Oh, I'm representing a friend of yours. I need to know what kind of man he is."

"Let me guess in one word. Steve. He has a temper. I think the war affected his brain."

"How so?" Andrew asked with interest.

"I remember the mist over the jungle, as I grabbed them out of there. Later I learned it might have been Agent Orange, but the government has denied it. But Kim is looking into it now."

"Interesting," Andrew said thoughtfully, "Now Kim is one of your doctors, right?"

"Yeah, I or comrades buried her Mom years ago or back in August of '63. It was four months prior to our attack in the jungle that changed all our lives," he answered thoughtfully. "I'm glad Kim got out of there when she did. She was the first child we found alive during our time over there. I decided early on after my run in the enemy that everyone including elderly, women and children deserved a proper burial. I had been there since August of '62 and seen a lot of bodies of innocent lives. I had to give Kim a chance to live. Does that make sense?"

Andrew nodded, as he faced him now. Joshua noticed tears in his eyes now.

"Are you okay?"

"I don't know if I could have survived over there," Andrew answered, as he cleared his throat. "I probably would have come home in a black body bag if Mom and Dad were lucky."

"I need to go home now. I need to be with Bryan. Was there anything else?"

"Uh...no. I'll be in touch."

"Fine."

He walked down the hallway alone and out of the courthouse. He headed for his Blazer and headed for the ocean and Bryan. Words echoed in his mind now.

"We're fighting a war we don't understand. Yet, State side they meaning the general public gave us unfair names. But the public didn't understand what we saw or experienced over there. Now how important we needed their support and understanding. We lost our innocence over there."

Joshua smiled now. They were Luke's words, and he wrote the song for him and other Vietnam Veterans. He never told his family of that war. But his youngest son captured what he and men like him lost over there.

17

Luke stood out on the deck with a young woman. She had long, waist length brunette hair in a braid that showed her slender figure. Her hands were petite and lightly tanned like most of her body that was exposed to the sun. She was soft spoken when she did speak. She had sparkling blue-gray, oval-shaped eyes like Luke's, but her head was round like Kim's. Joshua noticed these things about her.

"Britt, you came," Kim said, as she walked through the front door.

Maria, Tim and Rita weren't too far behind her. Joshua held two cups of green tea. Luke and Brittney turned to face the voice. Brittney entered the house and embraced her Mom.

"Hi, Mom," she said softly.

"Is one of these for me, Sir?" Luke asked Joshua politely.

He nodded and held one out to him.

"Thank you, Sir."

"Uh..., Brittney..." he replied with some hesitation.

"Oh, thank you, Mr. Hernando," she said politely, as she took the second cup from him.

"Didn't I say for you to call me, Josh. Anyone else, want some tea?" he asked the room.

"I'm good, Dad," Rita answered coldly.

"No, thank you, Josh," Tim said with a smile.

"No, thanks," Maria said, as she stared at Brittany.

"So, who had text us all to come here now?" Rita

asked with an unpleasant tone in her voice. "I'm kind of busy these days as you all know."

"I did," Kim answered calmly. "I know, I didn't say anything on the way over here. I should have, and I'm sorry."

Rita stared at her now. Maria walked over to the couch and sat down. Joshua watched her.

"What's Dad's sketch pad out here?" Maria asked in a low but calm voice.

"Your Dad did a drawing of me back when he was in the service," Kim answered back. "I wondered if..."

"NO!" exclaimed Maria. "I'm sorry."

"It's okay," said Kim. "I understand."

"Why did you want Tim, Luke and I to be here?" Rita asked, as she folded her arms across her chest now.

"Well, you are writing an article on Vietnam vets. Right, Tim?" Kim asked, as she faced him.

"I was but getting nowhere," Tim answered sadly.

"Who have you talked to so far?" asked Luke.

"My Dad, but no one will tell me anything. I find it strange since your Dad wanted to tell Rita and her siblings about that war," Tim answered, as he faced Maria.

"You haven't talked to anyone from my platoon outside your Dad," Joshua replied a little surprised.

"We wanted to save them for the last," Rita snapped back. "To give it some distance."

"Plus we or I'm having a hard time getting a magazine willing to publish an article about Vietnam," Tim explained sadly.

"You said there's a drawing of you back in Vietnam, Mom. Can I see it?" Brittney asked with some excitement.

Kim nodded and led her daughter over to the couch and Maria. She made eye contact with Maria. Maria held it up to her. Kim dove into it when a piece of paper slipped out. Luke picked it up and read it briefly.

"Maybe you should read it, Sir," Luke said, as he held it out to Joshua.

"Why?"

"It's addressed to Mr. and Mrs. Hernando, and I think, it was from Roger," Luke answered coldly.

Joshua stepped forward and took the piece of paper. He stepped back carefully since he wasn't sure where Bryan was at this point. He felt all eyes were on him now, so he cleared his throat.

"Dear Mr. and Mrs. Hernando," he begun to read out loud. "Mid-November 1963:

My name is Roger, and I'm over here in Vietnam with Joshua or Josh, your son. But you don't know me, but I hope we can meet after this damn war. Your son doesn't talk about his family, but I see pain in his eyes. You see, I'm an artist and have done a lot of drawings all my life or since I was five. So I notice things that others might not see.

I draw your son, and I see it. He's in this war that seems to be not his war to fight. He's sacrificing his life for someone close to his heart and very soul. If he dies over here, I'm sure that he believes that no one will care. I won't be able to change his mind. He convinced his comrades to bury the elderly, women and children."

Joshua paused and glanced around the room. He walked over to his chair to sit down. Bryan climbed up and settled in his lap before he continued.

"I bring this up because a little while ago or back in

August we buried a mother. Your son was with the little girl afterwards. He's so gentle and loving, as he sang to her. She took food and water from only your son. He found her crying beside her dead mother in a hut in one of the abandoned villages we entered. He convinced her the next morning to be shipped out with all the other orphans or misplaced children and elderly of this damn war. But she wanted to be with him and only him.

He'll be a great Dad someday. I hope he will be, and you will see what I see now, as he worked with her. That's if we make it home again. All of us were asked to write our own wills on and off in the months we've been over here. Well, Josh didn't write one to give to the chaplain. I asked your son who was going to get his will. He said he had no one to leave anything to besides; he didn't read and write very well even if he did have someone. I pressed him about you, his parents. He admitted you were still alive live or at his last knowing but wanted me to leave you alone. He walked away from me."

Joshua cleared his throat again. Then he stared into Rita's eyes briefly before he returned to the paper.

"I found a crumbled a piece of paper near where he sat. I read it and knew his problem and was going to help him with his disability. The paper read simply. "Deer Mom +Dad. Sorry to disapoint you. I fite for him so he won't. I lo..." He stopped there. It made me see how what or how I read in his eyes about not being his warm, but who?

I want to make it home to find out. I hope I can get this letter to you State side before anything happens to me or your son. War is hell over here. I'll help him. I promise.

Yours,

Private First Class Roger Daniel Clemens"

Joshua folded up the paper in half again and looked over at Maria, Kim, and Brittney now. Then he glanced over at Luke then Tim and Rita.

"He worked with me every chance we got but never let on he had read that brief letter either. We were laying low because it was nearly Christmas, and it was late August when we met up with Kim and her mother. Two months later, we entered another village," he replied sadly, as he shook his head. "But it's another story."

"I couldn't tell when I was little," Rita said as a little shocked by the news. "You seemed to read and write pretty well back then."

"That's how good of a teacher he was," he replied thoughtfully. "I didn't know he read it until now."

"Did you know about this letter to your parents?" asked Maria.

"No, he went about teaching me to read and write differently than any school teacher I had before," Joshua answered thoughtfully.

"How so?" asked Maria.

"Reading was hard to do but writing was far worse. I'm surprised how anyone was able to figure out what I was writing or trying to say."

"I take it that wasn't your first attempt at writing them," pointed out Luke.

"No, I tried and have to rewrite what I wrote prior to going over there. I guess I wanted them to know what I was feeling in my heart and soul about it all. If that was the only thing I had to leave them it was that one short piece of writing of my thoughts of where I was going."

"What became of it?" Rita asked with tenderness in her voice again.

"Not sure really, baby girl."

"Getting back to reading and writing, how did my Dad help you?" Maria asked with interest.

Joshua cleared his throat the third time and remembered back.

"Hey, man, look at this," Roger said, as he held a mirror next to the written word. "It appears backwards in the mirror. Isn't it interesting, man?"

"Not really. I do it most of the time. My teachers got upset with my papers because I did that," Joshua answered sadly.

"You got to be kidding," Roger stated a little surprised. "How did you get into college?"

"Uh... I didn't."

"I've got an idea. Every time you write a letter cast the mirror near it, so you can see it the other way then trying writing it that way," Roger said with a big grin and thoughtfully.

"How will that help?"

"It can help with the reading process. Words will be facing all the same way and make reading easier, too. Maybe help in your writing, too," explained Roger. "Do you want to at least try, man?"

"Sure why not," Joshua answered with a small smile now. "How do we start?"

"This way, my friend," Roger answered with smile back.

"We spent days or nights before and after Kim was

shipped out. I was beginning to notice a difference. I started to do more on my own. Roger would draw for hours if he could which gave me time to work on my own, too."

"How did he manage to keep this from getting wet? I heard about the rain over there," Maria asked, as she held out her Dad's sketch pad.

"He created a portable dry shelter that covered him outside our two man tent. He was pretty amazing how he did things sometimes," Joshua answered thoughtfully. "But as a soldier, he was careless. He didn't belong there."

"He didn't think you belonged there either," Rita pointed out.

"I know, but I had to go for your Uncle Andrew's sake. They had him enrolled in law school when I enlisted."

"But it wasn't your war, Dad."

"It doesn't matter, baby girl. I kept your Uncle Andrew from possibly being killed over there. You, guys, should talk to Steve. He liked to fight before, during and after the war. He can give you his experience over there."

Tim shook his head. "No, he won't."

"What! Why not?"

"He's in a psycho-ward dealing with his anger issues," Maria answered calmly. "They're trying to keep him out of prison. They're trying to use his Vietnam experience as a result of his temper. I don't know if they can pull it off."

"How long has he been in therapy?"

"Since the end of Alex's trial, so it makes a little over two weeks now. We're in March now," Rita answered coldly. "Tim, I need to get home to my kids..."

"Of course, Rita," he said, as he nodded. "Did you need rides back...Maria...Kim?"

"I'll take them home when they they're ready," answered Luke.

"You might try talking to Scott, too," Joshua replied to Tim.

"Why?" asked Tim.

"He might be able to give you some insight after I headed out and came back. He was the first one I approached after Roger triggered the wire on the platoon which caused the crazy attack," Joshua answered thoughtfully.

"We'll see. Bye, everyone," Tim said with a small grin.

Kim and Brittney were sharing Roger's sketch pad. They seemed very interested in it now. Luke stood by them and stared back at Joshua. Maria sat there quietly next to them.

"Yes, son."

Luke shook his head, no, and headed back outside. Brittney looked up and glanced over at him.

"He loves you, Mr. Hernando," she whispered to him.

"Probably so but if he's like me then he needs time and space. I told you to call me, Josh. Remember."

"I'm sorry," she said with a bright and friendly smile. "Josh."

"What was he like?" asked Maria.

"Who?"

"My Dad before everything changed."

"He was the joker, teacher and a gifted artist."

"I see his art work, and you explained the teacher in him. But I don't remember him ever being funny."

"Cream in our boots while we slept, but I still don't know how he managed to do it since we hardly ever took off our boots except to change our socks," he replied thoughtfully, as he shook his head.

"What else did he do?" she asked, as she leaned forward with interest.

"Tied boot laces together," Kim answered with a small grin.

"That was his favorite one of all," he replied with a big smile. "But how..."

"He did Steve's. It was the morning I was leaving you, all. I thought he was going to kill Roger after he was done untying the laces," she explained with a small grin still. "Steve got up and took a couple steps before landing face first into a puddle of mud."

Everyone laughed, but Joshua glanced over at Luke. His back was to them, as he stared out at the ocean. He knew he had to reach him since it was important to Carly and his sisters. He had a start back in the hospital but regressed some.

Joshua hadn't seen or heard Rita since the trial. It shattered her world. So he was surprised that she even spoke to him today. But Rita was the first of his six children who came to him and witnessed his attacks in recent months, too. She didn't hate him but loved him because would always be her Daddy. So little by little, his family witnessed a change in him. He smiled but felt a little sad, too.

"Josh, hey, Josh," called out Kim.

`"What?"

``You seemed a million miles away right now," answered Kim.

"Lukie is a lot like him, Mom," said Brittney.

"Yes, Honey, but you've always been able to reach Luke where I can't."

"Not everywhere. I know something he doesn't talk about and troubles him deeply," commented Brittney.

"Do you have any clue what it is?" asked Joshua.

"Desert Storm, but he won't talk about it. I know my Dad served in it, too but didn't come home," answered Brittney.

A loud noise had come from the front door.

"Scott, what brings you here?" Joshua asked, as he noticed him march into the house unannounced.

"I can't take it anymore," he answered fixed his eyes on Joshua.

"Easy, Scott," Joshua replied slowly moving to his feet.

Bryan rushed into the kitchen quickly. Luke stood in front of the women now.

"Talk to me, buddy," he continued in a calm and steady voice, as he approached Scott. "Tell me, what's going on?"

"I've tried. God knows, I've tried all these years. I really have tried," Scott said with tears in his eyes now. "I can't get it out of my head. It won't leave me alone. It haunts me, Josh."

"Come over here and sit down," he replied, as he guided him to his favorite chair. "Take a deep breath and let it out slowly. Now do this a few times before you speak again, Scott."

Scott nodded. He became calmer and more relaxed with each inhale and exhale. Then he focused on Joshua.

"I'll get you some water," Kim said, as she stepped away from Luke's protective stance.

Joshua nodded back. He felt trickles of sweat glide down his neck and other parts of his body when Kim returned. He took it and offered it to Scott. His hand shook then steadied, as he held the glass to his lips.

"Better, buddy?" he asked Scott.

"A little thanks," Scott answered, as he stared at the glass. "I need to tell someone, and you were there, Josh. You would understand. You understood Roger. You seem to get it all. I'm not questioning how or why. I only know you do."

Joshua nodded, as he stood near the chair. Meow. He glanced towards the kitchen. Bryan stood there and stared at him.

"Come here, little fella," he replied calmly. "Scott is a friend. He won't hurt you."

"I didn't know you had a cat," commented Scott.

"They found each other shortly after the first of the year," Maria said, as she looked on. "Are you talking about Vietnam?"

Scott nodded, as Bryan walked up closer to them. Scott reached out to pet him when Bryan jumped into his lap. Scott pulled back and stroked Bryan after he put the glass down.

"I had a ring side seat when your Dad tripped over that wire. It would cause metal and rapid gunfire instantly," Scott explained, as he continued to stroke

Bryan.

"Stay calm, buddy, and explain what you're comfortable with," Joshua replied, as he picked up the glass now.

"We were ordered by Lt. Grahams to hold back. You were going ahead of us since Roger spotted an enemy camp about one hundred yards ahead" Scott started to explain slowly.

"Corporal Hernando is going to see how many he can take out before we precede forward," said Lt. Grahams. "No one move until then." He glanced around. "Where the hell is Private Clemens?"

"Probably taking a leak, Sir," answered Steve. "You know, how he get nervous, Sir."

"Yeah, I know. What the hell! Take cover, everyone," barked Lt. Grahams.

Scott scrambled to a nearby rock and tree. He saw flying metal through the air followed by rapid gunfire. He looked ahead where they were going. His heart was racing, as he felt a firm hand on his shoulder. Then he made eye contact with the face. It was Joshua, and he dragged Roger over.

Explosions soon arrived out of nowhere, and Scott looked down at Roger's legs. He had a big chunk of metal in his right leg. It was a made shift tunic at his thigh to stop or slow the bleeding. The screaming wasn't Roger who screamed. His face was pale as snow and in a great deal of pain. Then quiet filled the battlefield of the jungle now.

"I'm going to take the others back to the river. I'll be back for you and Roger. I promise. Oh, crap," Joshua replied, as he glanced ahead. "I need to get Steve back here. Stay low and here. I'll be back. Do you understand?"

Scott nodded.

"I lost track of you when you went after Steve. He had gone mad and was going after them on his own. Then you were there hauling me out," said Scott. "You held us, all, together that day. You were out of breath and very tired when you returned. But you kept your promise."

"I had to carry or pull most of you back to the river that I told you about on my own. Steve was running blindly into their camp. He wouldn't have come out of there alive if I hadn't tackled him when I did. Do you know how hard it is to tackle a man in full gear like we had?" asked Joshua. "And mad as hell like he was."

"But you managed to get him and the rest of us out of there alive," answered Scott.

"I knocked him out with the butt of my gun, and he didn't see it coming."

"You were good at hand and hand combat despite our limited basic training."

"So I've been reminded. How did you know what day it was?"

"You saving us on Christmas, you mean. Well, we heard about Kennedy was killed in Dallas. So I figured it out from there. We owe you, our very lives to see that Christmas and every one after it."

"I didn't know," he replied honestly.

"You took care of all of us despite the scalpel in your own shoulder. None of us helped you that day, but you didn't complain either, as you hauled our sorry butts out. No one was left behind. Just like pact we made with Lt. Grahams."

"Do you remember the mist?" asked Kim.

"Yeah, I thought it was odd since we had a clear, blue sky above us just like the day we came across you. But Josh was in the middle of it all since he rescued us, all," Scott answered thoughtfully. "Then it rained again, as we got shipped out to various hospitals."

"Why different hospitals?" asked Brittney.

"They didn't want to lose whole units in case of attacks. I was with Steve and Trevor. I'm not sure about everyone else," answered Scott. "It's a good thing when he got your Mom out four months earlier."

"Why?"

"It would get nasty, as the war progressed."

"Johnson wanted a victory, but it wasn't possible," added Joshua. "How are you feeling now?"

"Better. I think it helped talking about that day. It changed all of our lives. We didn't see each other again until early '64 when you received your medals and promotion, Joshua."

"But I wanted to get home..." replied Joshua.

"To Grandma Sara. You heard about her stroke followed by slipping in a coma," said Luke.

Joshua nodded. "But how..."

"Rita," Luke interrupted him then walked outside again.

"He never said that before," Brittney said a little surprised by it.

"He does listen and protects people who matter to him," replied Joshua.

"Then he's like you," commented Kim. "I should have known. It was so familiar when he and I first met."

Joshua stared at Kim now. She looked back.

"I'm going to see if he's okay," Brittney said, as she headed outside.

Joshua started to say something then decided not to after all. Kim smiled at him now.

"What?"

"You wanted to say something but decided against it. You want to reach out to him but don't know how. Did fear ever enter your mind over there?" Kim asked.

"Once then it was gone. Scott, I wish Tim and Rita were here to hear your story of that day."

"You heard where Steve is, right?"

"Yeah, maybe they can help him."

"Maybe, thanks for listening. Nice kitty. He seems happy and healthy, but I should be going now."

Bryan jumped off his lap and walked over to the couch. Maria was back staring at her Dad's drawings. Scott walked out quietly. So Joshua and Kim walked over to join Maria there.

"He caused the attack," Maria said painfully. "But no one said anything after all these years."

"He was carless when he was nervous. But we all got out of there alive."

"But at what cost," stated Maria. "Dad lost his leg and possibly his mind at times. Allen lost a partial leg and an arm. Scott suffers from trauma of that day. Allen couldn't follow you out after the hit to the leg, so you had to go back for him. What else do I don't know about?"

"Stop this, Maria," Joshua snapped, as he took her hands into his. "We, all, came home for the most part in one piece and that says a lot for that damn war. We didn't come home like some did in black body bags. Do you hear what I'm saying to you now?"

Maria nodded.

"Mom, you look beat. Let's leave," Brittney said, as she leaned into Luke's chest.

"How old are you, Brittney?" Joshua asked a little curious.

"Just turned twenty, I know, Mom is older than Lukie here. He was eighteen when they met."

"Turned nineteen at the beginning of Desert Storm, but Albert was older than Luke," added Kim.

"I was nineteen when she was born, Sir. I'm thirty-nine, Sir, if you're wondering. I was little older than you when you went to Vietnam."

Joshua only nodded, as Maria closed the sketch pad. She kissed him on the cheek followed by a quick hug. Then Kim hugged him and Bryan, too.

Then they filed out of the house one by one, and Joshua picked up Roger's letter again. He had dropped it when Scott arrived, so he placed it back in the sketch pad before stretching out on the couch. Bryan jumped onto his chest and purred as he settled down.

"It has been a long day, little man," he replied before closing his eyes and let out small sigh.

Meow. Meow.

18

Joshua thought of Luke and Brittney. She knew his son better than he did. She called him, Lukie, but he didn't seem to mind it. She stood and stared out the ocean like they both did. He knew Luke spent a lot of time with her. But why Joshua felt drawn to her, too? Was she a reminder of Kim, her Mom? He shook his head and placed Bryan's dish down. The doorbell rang, and Bryan looked up.

"I wonder who that could be," he replied to the kitty. "Well, let's go find out."

They walked into the living room to front door. He stood face to face with Brittney.

"Hi, Josh," she said with a bright and friendly smile. "Can I come in?"

"Of course," he answered, as he stepped back to let her walk in.

"Thank you," she said politely, "Hi, Bryan."

He closed the door, as she entered deeper into the house. She turned to face him now.

"I bet you're wondering why I'm here," Brittney said trying to act cheerful. "Tim and Rita abandoned the article. I think, they should continue, but they won't listen to me. I have no voice on the matter or so they say. Well, according to Rita anyway."

"That doesn't sound like Rita," he commented thoughtfully.

"She's changed since the trial. Didn't you sense it four months ago in March? I find it hard to realize this is the same woman I met as a little girl. It's like..." said Brittney. "She has been shocked to the very core of who she is, and she had lost something deep within her."

"Yes, she has to find her way again. She's a divorced mother of two small children. I know to keep my distance."

"I noticed that. You seemed surprised how she was actually talking to you. I love the view of the ocean. Lukie has always taken me to the ocean to talk or celebrate something important in my life," she said, as she headed for the deck. "Do you mind?"

"Be my guest," he answered with cheerful smile, too. "Do you mind if I ask you a personal question about something?"

"I'm an open book or so Mom and Lukie tell me often. I'm too trusting and open to people," she answered, as she leaned on the railing.

"Why do you call my son, Lukie?" he asked, as he leaned on the railing near her.

"The funny thing I started out saying cookie then Lukie whenever I saw him," she explained, as her eyes danced with delight. "He always had animal crackers or cookies in his pocket when I was with him. Mom said he was spoiling me. He would smile and laugh then said 'No just well-loved that's all.' Mom would only shake her head and walk away."

"I don't recall his laugh or even his smile for that matter. Does it make me a bad father?"

"No. I would get him to talk about you prior to your divorce. I heard a hint of love for you in his voice, as he talked how you used to paint the house, fix broken things and make things without much effort. Then you helped Roger, but he has been looking up to you his whole life despite the years you two were apart."

"I didn't know this."

"Lukie doesn't let many people into his private thoughts, but you'll get your chance. He'll come to you, and you will know him truly. I know, he puts up this wall to hide something from his past, and I can't get him to share. But I think, he will with you when he's ready," Brittney said thoughtfully.

"So do you go to college?" he asked her.

"No, but Lukie wants me to. But I told him that I'll go if he does."

"What does he say to that?"

"No dice, little bit," she answered seriously. "He calls me that pet name still after all these years. I noticed you do the pet names, too."

"Well, you do call him, Lukie, still, too."

"Yeah, I do," she admitted with a small chuckle. "I love him like a Dad. I never knew my real Dad or my grandparents. It has been Mom, me and Lukie all these years. I was adopted by his siblings when I was growing up. That's why I was hurt by Rita saying that I had no voice on the matter. They're related by extended family."

"I think, your Mom mentioned something about your Dad and grandparents," Joshua replied thoughtfully.

"Dad died in Desert Storm, and my grandparents died in route to the hospital where I was born," she said sadly. "They weren't my biological grandparents, but Mom loved them all the same. You've always carried a special place in her heart. She would never let me have the frog keychain. It's extension of her. She would tell me when I was little what she remembered about you. It's the same peaceful feeling that I feel with Lukie. So I understand her more than most."

"Why didn't she marry another man after your Dad died?"

"I asked her it so often in the past that we don't discuss it anymore. She would get misty eyed, so I had to leave her alone for a few days. Lukie would talk to her. I never knew what he said to her, but it was only a couple days pass," she answered thoughtfully. "I would ask her what they talked about, but she would only hug me. Then she said 'never mind'. He didn't tell me anything either. It was a secret they shared between them."

"So you left it at that," Joshua replied a little surprised.

"Yes. Now we don't talk about it at all. She's happy with her career and life. I don't want to keep rehashing the past. But I think, she's curious about something in Lukie's past, too."

"Why do you say that?"

"Anytime he says something I notice Mom is all ears. She's completely focused on him. It's those times I wish he was my real Dad since he has been there for everything important in my life including my birth. I call him Dad sometimes."

"How does he react or say to that?"

"He gives me a big grin then hugs me briefly followed by a kiss on the forehead," she answered thoughtfully. "Then he walks away and shuts down for awhile. He spends a lot of time on beaches and looks off in the distance a lot. But like I said before, he'll come around."

"I see. Have you eaten?"

"Uh, yes, and I know you're famous for fresh crab and hot clam chowder. It's uncanny how you and Lukie are alike in that and other things. But I would like to walk on the beach to look for sand dollars. That's if you don't mind."

"Of course not, but you might be disappointed though," he added with a big smile.

"I know I missed the low tide. It's the best time to hunt for things like that. But I love the ocean as much as Lukie does. That's why I call him Dad sometimes. We have a lot in common. Shall we go? I'm sorry, I assumed you were coming."

"I don't mind, Brittney. Bryan and I walk the beach daily."

"Great!" she exclaimed, as she clasped her hands together in excitement. "I never walked with a cat on the beach before. Come here, Bryan."

He walked up to her, and she scooped him up into her arms. They headed down to the beach. He wiggled in her arms the closer they got to the ocean.

"He wants to walk," he informed her.

"Oh, sorry, Bryan," she said, as she released him.

Bryan bolted out ahead of them then stopped to look back. Joshua smiled at him. "Go ahead, little boy."

Bryan stepped deeper into the wet sand. Joshua laughed a joyous laugh when Bryan slapped at the wet sand. Then he sprang forward towards the water.

"That's Lukie's laugh," Brittney pointed out. "He's

not going into the ocean. Is he?"

"He smells the fish and goes as far as his belly touching the water. Then he runs back to sit on the sand and licks his self dry on the warm dry sand."

"He's happy and carefree."

"I suppose," replied Joshua. "But when you get older like me, you're a little more cautious because of life experiences taught you to be more careful."

"I guess you're right. Mom says it, too."

Then they both fell silent, as they watched Bryan. It was warm day despite the light breeze. Joshua breathed in the fresh air deep into his lungs. He closed his eyes and was glad to be alive. He stretched out his arms above his head and opened his eyes. Brittney stared at him and shook her head.

"What?"

"Lukie."

He nodded.

"Mom's been trying to get some answers about the mist you guys were possibly exposed to over there," Brittney said, as she stared back at the ocean. "Maria has been trying to help, too since she worked at Veterans of Foreign Wars."

"I thought Joan was going to help me find out more about it on the Internet, but she hasn't done it yet," he replied back. "But I knew Maria worked there prior to nursing school. She wanted to help and understand her Dad more, I think."

Meow. So Brittney reached into her pocket to pull out her cell.

"Hello. Yes. He's here with me. I'll tell him. Bye,"

she said, as she flipped it closed and looked back at him. "That was Mom. She said Steve wants to talk to you and Lukie."

"Are you sure my son, Luke? We did have a Luke in our platoon."

"He said your son specifically. He's in the psycho-ward in Palo Alto. Mom said you knew the hospital. They're meeting us there."

"You're coming."

"He asked for me, and uh... Uncle Andrew, your brother, too. I'll grab Bryan."

"Let me. Why, my brother?"

"I don't know. Neither does, Mom. I think that's why she hesitated to call. She wanted to know more, but she got nowhere."

"So she called you. Another time, baby boy, I promise and longer."

Bryan purred in his arms, as they headed back to the house. He climbed up on the couch and curled up into a medium size ball upon his release on the deck.

"Will he be okay alone?" she asked him.

"Yes, but yours or mine?"

"It doesn't matter to me, but Mom said you know the hospital," she answered with a big smile.

Joshua shook his head then picked up his keys. She petted Bryan before she joined him. She stepped through the open door out to the Blazer. Then they headed down the road.

"You shook your head back there. Can I ask why?"

"Oh, you remind me of me years ago. My brother may call it crazy or I wasn't trying hard enough. But I had never wanted to view life so serious like he and Dad did."

"He can be a stuffy shirt sometimes. I don't know a whole lot about him, but I do remember your Dad."

"You don't see my Dad anymore," Joshua replied back.

"Your Dad died ten years ago, remember? So why do you think Steve wants to see us, all?" Brittney asked, as she stared out the open window.

"Okay, so you don't want to talk about my Dad. I get it, Brittney. He was hard on me the whole time I lived under his roof," he answered, as he focused on the road ahead of them. "I didn't remember that he was gone. I guess things have been left unsaid between us, so we had no closure. I didn't think Steve remembered any of my kids, and I don't know why he wants my big brother Andrew there. It's odd to me."

"I guess we'll find out then together. Your Dad was nice at times but not at other times. I never knew what to think of his moods. I'm sorry. I know, I brought him up then cut you off when you pressed about him. I got scared."

"You thought maybe his moods were your fault."

"Yes," Brittney said honestly.

"You can manage to drive, but you can't do well with the books. You are a strange boy, Joshua," Martin snapped back at him sharply. "Here we're in a war, and Andrew maybe called to serve any day now then there goes our plans in law school for him. We started the process already."

"Why can't I go to law school?" Joshua asked with interest.

"You're stupid. Look at those grades. You'll be

lucky if you finish high school. I was a farmer's son but managed to make school work a top priority in my life outside of, my love for baseball. I wanted a career in it, but your grandfather was right," Martin snapped at him.

"About what?"

"Making a career in baseball," Martin answered with the shake of his head. "You weren't listening to me as usual. Were you, boy?"

"Dad, we all have dreams," he answered painfully. "No one should be allowed to take those away from us ever."

Martin stared at him with anger in his eyes. It sent a chill deep into Joshua's warm and loving heart.

"Get out of here loser! I can't be bothered by you now. I need to see what Andrew's doing right now. So out of my way, boy," Martin said, as he shoved Joshua aside.

"But..."

He pulled into the parking lot of the hospital in Palo Alto. He sat there and stared at it from his parking space. It had been four months since he was here last. He shook his head and got out.

"Are you okay, Josh?" Brittney asked, as she stood tall beside him.

"Memories, so let's go now."

"I have to admit something first," she said when she took his hand into hers.

He stared at her and stood there, "Sounds serious."

"I used to wish you were my grandfather because the way Lukie talked about you and not having any grandparents of my own."

"But what about your Dad's parents?"

"They didn't like the idea of him being involved with Mom, so they split before I was born. I don't blame them really," Brittney answered sadly. "The whole world didn't seem to know who to trust after Vietnam. Men were doing drugs and other stuff like you might have been exposed to. I don't know. But they missed out on knowing me, and me loving and caring about them."

"That's an interesting way to view it all."

"It's one I can accept and live with," she said, as she leaned into his shoulder now. "Do you think less of me now?"

"No. Why because you were rejected by your Dad's parents. No not at all. So you can call me, Grandpa, if you want to," he answered honestly, "Or whatever you want to call me."

"Grandpa sounds nice," she said, as she smiled brightly and cheerful. "Let's go, Grandpa."

"Okay, Princess," he replied with a return big smile back.

"I like that, Princess," she said confidently.

They walked into the hospital and headed for the psycho-ward. She smiled the whole way and glowed with her overall beauty. It warmed his old, tired heart to see how happy this made her. Brittney knew who she was and more confident than he ever been his whole life.

"Someone's happy today," Kim said, as Luke and Andrew stood beside her.

"I am, Mom," Brittney said, as they made eye contact. "What's Steve want with all of us?"

"Still no clue, but his therapist got us all together, and we're meeting in a conference room," Kim answered back. "I'll let him know we're all here now. Please excuse me."

"Sorry this place probably brings back some bad memories of Roger," Andrew whispered to Joshua.

"I'm fine," he replied, as Brittney still held his hand in hers.

Luke leaned against the nearest wall. Joshua glanced over at her.

"He needs you, Princess."

"I think so, Grandpa," she said, as she walked up to him.

Luke stared at her. She smiled at him, but he didn't smile back. She talked to him, as Joshua looked on.

"So she calls you, Grandpa," commented Andrew.

"Yeah, she doesn't have any grandparents. Do you have a problem with it?" he asked, as he stared at his big brother now.

"No, not at all," Andrew answered back.

"Good. You're all here," a man said in a stripped blue and white shirt. "My name is Mark Anthony. I'm Steve's therapist. You must be Josh, and you are his brother Andrew and attorney. Please follow me this way."

He headed back through a door. Kim took Joshua's hand into hers. He noticed Brittney took Luke's. Andrew followed behind them alone. They walked into the conference room while Steve sat quietly in a chair.

His sandy brown hair was longer than usual. His cheeks sank in and dark circles under his eyes. He looked like he had lost ten or more pounds, too.

"Please have a seat everyone," Mark said, as he sat the closest to Steve. "Steve, they're all here as you requested."

Steve blinked his eyes and nodded. Everyone sat down. Joshua watched Steve, as he took his seat. Steve cleared his throat and glanced over at Kim.

"We had come across a lot of villages with no survivors, so we buried a lot of the elderly, women and children in unmarked graves or no names on their headstones. Then we entered what was left of your village, Kim. Death had been all around us since our arrival back in August of '62 before and after you left Vietnam in August of '63," Steve said thoughtfully and calmly. "People didn't know we were first sent over there as peacekeepers, and it changed as we got into it."

He sighed then looked at all the faces of who was there in the room with him. Then he reached for Kim's hand that wasn't holding Joshua's.

"I won't hurt you, Kim, not now and even back then," Steve continued calmly.

So Kim let him take both of her hands into his. He stared deep into her eyes before he spoke again.

"You lost your Mom in our war. You were too young to be without a mother. I'm sorry for your loss. Josh was right about getting you out of the war zone. You deserved a better life than that." He paused for moment and drew in some air. "I can see you've had a better life than would have had there."

"Why am I here?" she asked him.

"I had to tell you this, Kim. I know, you probably were afraid of me back then because I was mean SOB," Steve answered calmly. "I don't blame you. You should have been, but I'm sorry for that, too."

He released her hands and moved on to Brittney. She readjusted herself in her chair. They made eye contact. "I look into your eyes and see the pain that once was in your mother's eyes. We buried your grandmother on her native soil. You would spend your life hoping to find a woman to fill that void," he said to her. "Just when you didn't think it was possible that's when she comes to you with open arms and heart. You'll know it in your very soul. Maybe you already found her. I don't know."

Steve cleared his throat again and focused on Luke. Luke glared at him intently.

"I see your Dad in you, Luke, but only a younger version. You've seen war at its worst actual combat like your Dad and I did in Vietnam. War changed us, and we lost something there that people don't know about. Do they want to listen? I don't know. I can't speak for them but only for myself. I was a mean and angry SOB back then which it brings me to your Uncle Andrew here."

Andrew moved a little in his chair now. He stared back at Steve, so he turned to face him.

"You didn't see how or even know your brother was in basics. When he got those merits for marksmanship and hand in hand combats. I was jealous of him. Then he got the promotion to Corporal before we were shipped out. I couldn't deal with it all," Steve explained thoughtfully and painfully in his voice. "I thought he had nerves of steel and could face anything that came his way. But I saw him face to face with the enemy. They stood eye to eye before Josh pulled the trigger. It happened shortly after we arrived on their soil."

"Steve," Mark said to him.

"It's okay. I want to hear this," said Andrew.

"He changed a little after that," Steve continued, as he blinked his eyes again. "I got angry at him for wanting to bury all those people. They weren't our people, but they were people, too. I only saw it was us and them, not all of us as being human beings. Your brother made me see it despite I didn't want to accept it then and years later."

Steve shifted to Joshua now. Joshua leaned back in his chair.

"Do you know how many we buried over there, Josh?" he asked in a raised voice. "Too many, buddy. I wanted to kill those bastards that day. But I heard your voice saying 'Pull back, pull back, and stop.' I could hear you gaining on me, as I chased those guys back to their camp. A camp we were heading into. You were sent ahead pick off as many you could. It was so unfair."

"What are you saying, Steve?" asked Joshua.

"You got first pickings," answered Steve.

"I was only following orders," replied Joshua.

"And it sucked, man. I don't know what triggered everything to go crazy, but I wanted to fight like no tomorrow."

"So you ignored my call."

"Yes. Then I met the ground and darkness," said Steve. "I woke up to my head feeling like it was split wide open. I felt a bandage on my head then realized I was in the hospital. I had pieces of metal taken out of my leg, side and arm. They weren't life threatening, but they were sending me home. I didn't want to go home, man. I wanted to fight."

"But he saved your life that day. You wouldn't have

come out of there alive if he didn't stop you," Andrew snapped back.

"That's why I started fights and let him finish them. I knew he could and would," Steve snapped back at Andrew. "He was angry over his failed marriage, and I used it to my advantage. I wanted someone to bring him down like he did me in the jungle that day."

"Why?" Joshua asked calmly.

"I was jealous of you. You could have a career in the military, but you walked away from it all," answered Steve.

"Steve," Mark said again.

"I know, I'm getting to it," Steve said, as he nodded his head. "I'm sorry, Josh, for everything over there and here. Are we good, man?"

"You have a lot of nerve to ask that!" Brittney exclaimed, as she got to her feet. "You wouldn't be here if it wasn't for Josh here hauling your sorry ass out of there."

"Easy, Princess," Joshua replied, as he touched the hand on the table.

"How..." she asked in hesitation.

"Let it go, Princess," he replied, as he gazed deep into her eyes now. "I wondered why Steve was angry all these years, and now I have my answer. Now I can let it go. If I can let it go, so must you." He stared back at Steve. "We're good, Steve."

Steve smiled then Joshua smiled, too.

"Is there anything else?" asked Mark.

"Nope, thank you all for coming," Steve answered, as he got to his feet. "Have a good life, man."

Steve walked out of the room. Everyone got to

their feet. Andrew cleared his throat. Mark looked at them all.

"Why did he say that?" asked Andrew.

"Trevor died of a horrible death of Cancer throughout his body. Due to Steve's drug and alcohol use after Vietnam, he's in stage four of his Cancer and AIDS. He's on his way out," answered Mark. "He wanted to make his peace on his own terms."

"But why not with the rest of the platoon?" Josh asked with interest.

"He said you were the closest he had to a true family, so he wanted to see you, Josh."

"But why me, Kim and Luke?" Andrew asked a little confused.

"I guess, he wanted you to know why he was so angry with Josh. Life is short and shouldn't be taken for granted for any reason," answered Mark.

"Is there anything else?" Joshua asked Mark.

"I've kept your number in his file," Mark answered back, "If that's okay with you?"

"It is," he answered with a slight nod. "He can call me anytime day or night. I'm there for him even at the end."

"I'll tell him," Mark said with small smile.

"Thanks. Princess, your car is at my house," he replied reminded her, as he glanced her way. "Do you want to come with me to pick it up?"

"I would like to be with Dad for a little while, Grandpa," she answered back politely.

"Of course."

"You're not driving all the way back alone. Are

you?" asked Kim.

"Yes. I have Bryan waiting for me. See you all later," he answered back.

"But..." Kim started to say.

"Let him go," said Andrew.

"Let him go, Mom."

He walked down the long hallway alone. He saw Roger, Trevor and now Steve in their military combat uniforms. They were young then because it was 1962. They disembarked with all their gear, as they stood on enemy soil. He shook his head and headed home to Bryan. But he remembered what Steve said or remembered of that day. However, it wasn't complete.

"We have to kill every last one of them, Josh," Steve's voice echoed in his brain.

"No, get back here, buddy. Let's get out of here with our lives," he replied back.

"No, man, we came here to fight, and fight is what I'm going to do, man."

"I won't let you; it is suicide, buddy."

"That's the whole truth of what happened between us, Steve, not where you stopped at," Joshua replied, as he got into his Blazer alone and drove home.

19

A couple days had passed since being Steve, and Joshua had thought back farther of the day in question. He also recalled Matt was a hot head, too, but Henry and Scott were silent about that day pretty much. Trevor, Luke, James, Jerrod and Robert didn't say anything about it. He knew Scott, Allen and Steve's view of that day. But he wasn't likely to know Trevor's since he was dead. But maybe the others will come forward or maybe not.

However, Scott had finally broken down about it. What did Matt and Henry remember of Vietnam? He wanted to know, but he had no clue of where or how to start despite he reasoned that they may or may not tell him anything. He dunked his tea bag in and out of his cup, as he stood there and thought at his kitchen sink.

"So you know what Steve and Scott remembered on that day in December of '63," Matt said, as he stood beside him now. "I came in with your son, Luke. He's using the can right now. Kim told me that Brittney had seen Steve, and she had listened to Scott."

"Why were you so angry over there, Matt?" he asked him. "I couldn't figure it out. I know and understand why Steve was. Do you want to share, buddy?"

"I guess, I could tell you after all these years. You were the top marksman of our platoon. Everyone had a purpose in the unit including clumsy Roger as he was. He still had a place in the unit," Matt answered, as he stared at him.

Meow. Matt petted Bryan. Then he left the room.

"Nice cat," Matt continued on. "You were the first and only one in of our unit who got promoted and was barely out of high school no less. We, all, figured you were eighteen and didn't plan to go to college. So you had the option of flee to Canada or serve, but you chose to serve. We knew a lot of men our age who were fleeing to Canada since college wasn't in their future plans. But the rest of us were going to college in the fall or already there when we got drafted. We were nineteen to twenty years old but on the outside you were only eighteen had a maturity we had."

"You're stalling, Matt," he replied with a sigh.

"See that's what I'm talking about, man. You cut to the chase with no bull," said Matt. "I get it. Get to the point. Luke looks a lot like you."

Joshua cleared his throat, as he glared at Matt.

"Okay. I didn't know my purpose," Matt explained finally. "So I followed Steve's lead. He was angry at you, so I followed him in that anger. I probably would be kicked out of college because I barely got through high school anyway."

"But you were going to Julian Art in the fall," he replied a little surprised.

"That was just talk. My music talent wasn't that good. Dad was debating on whether to pay or let me foot the bill. I made it easy for him. I signed up for Vietnam," Matt said sadly.

"So you played an instrument. What one?"

"Two actually banjo and piano," Matt answered, as he turned to the deck. "Can we go out there?"

Joshua nodded, as he picked up his cup. Luke walked but ahead of them and leaned on the railing. Matt scanned the deck and found a chair. Joshua held his cup to his lips but kept a safe distance from Luke and Matt.

"My grandfather taught me the basics of playing the banjo at a very early age. I can't remember how old I was, but Mom taught me how to read sheet music. Mom had a piano and was quite good. She could play for hours at time, and I slowly got interested in it. She had good patience, as she taught me the basics of the piano. Everyone told them that I had natural ear for music, but I was losing interest in both by the time I was sixteen. I never let on to Mom and my grandfather," Matt admitted sadly. "I didn't want to go to college much less a music school. I guess, Dad, must have known something was up."

"But you played the harmonica in basics," pointed out Joshua.

"Self taught. I only picked it up a couple days before I was drafted. I was playing it when Steve and I met outside the bar," Matt said thoughtfully. "He was angry that they wouldn't give him a drink."

"Whiskey was his drink of choice as I recall."

"Yeah, burned like hell going down at first then your throat got numb after that. He and Roger seemed to start a lot of fights after your divorce. You would always step in and didn't seem mind fighting someone else's battle," added Matt.

"You did your fair share of starting them, too, Matt."

"I guess I did. Sorry about that. You remember that one bar in Berkeley with that impersonator of Elvis."

"Why don't you shut up, man? You're off key and don't even sound the King of rock and roll," Matt said, as he snapped another shot of whiskey.

The Elvis impersonator stared at him now from the stage. He had stopped singing "Jailhouse Rock." The audience had gone still, too.

"Make me or show me that you can do any better," the impersonator snapped at Matt.

"Ah, shut up, man," snapped Matt.

"Come on put up or shut up. You're lazy and probably have been since you came home for what war."

"Vietnam."

"That was no damn war."

"You better stop right there, man," warned Matt.

"You probably were probably too high to know the innocent girls you were...."

"We didn't do that over there," Joshua interrupted in anger. "You must have us mixed up with some other vets. Our platoon wasn't like that, buddy."

"Yeah, right," the impersonator said with a chuckle. "Tell me another lie."

"Come on, I'll show you what we did over there. But you will have to throw the first punch though," he replied, as he put his glass of milk aside.

"He tried but missed your Dad," Matt said, as he looked over at Luke. "It was a case when we, all, had to haul your Dad off the guy. You didn't have that anger in the service, but you sure got angry after your divorce. It changed you like something snapped within."

"It did. I lost my wife and kids. But I didn't know how empty I felt inside until I had reached rock bottom and a chance to think about it. Fighting was a temporary fix for that loneliness I felt inside. I was starting to look for them but no success, so I got frustrated too on top of being aware of how I treated Carly that last time."

"But we stayed around those first two years after the divorce," said Matt.

"But you all drifted in and out. Roger stayed close because of his bouts with his flashbacks."

"I never asked you what you did from '64 to '69. I had met up with you that day in late '85 outside a construction site. Scott, Steve and I stayed around the next couple years after that."

"A string of odd jobs to support myself but got steady job in construction after Carly and I married in '68. I raked in some good money by the eighties, but PIs would eat it up fast."

"I think we, all, struggled with work because we were still fighting over there until the early seventies. Johnson might have wanted us, all, over there fighting. He might have gone as far as signing documents to that effect. But we were sent home after our experience in the jungle," said Matt. "We lost a lot of good men over there in that damn war."

"Yes, we did," he replied in agreement. "Have you picked up an instrument since then?"

"I taught kids for awhile, until I got job in a warehouse. I passed the test for forklift operator and made good money there. I retired last year and have a good retirement despite the dives in the stock market in '01, '07 and '08. I stayed conservative and didn't put all my eggs in one basket," Matt answered with a small smile. "I had no clue what I was doing though, but I read the prospective they handed out and went from there. Do you get a good retirement, too?"

"Fair, I guess, four thousand a month plus benefits like life, dental and health insurance," he answered thoughtfully, "Plus some other things, too."

"Wow!" exclaimed Matt. "I have three thousand five hundred plus all that, too. But you worked in construction trade, so they have their own union and pension plans, too, right?"

"Pretty much."

"You're not the same guy I knew in the service and definitely not the same guy after your divorce in the late eighties, either."

Joshua nodded.

"You're more open than before. I can remember those days we, all, sat around to find out where we were going after the war. Roger was drawing, but you were off writing something away from us, all. We whispered about our lives back home including Roger. But not, you, man. You kept everything close to your chest. But you talked to Kim. It's hard to believe how she has grown up from the frightened little girl back in Nam. She told me before Alex's trial that we, all, frightened her except you. She felt safe with you," Matt explained with a small chuckle.

"What's so funny?"

"None of us were Dads back then, but she latched onto you for dear life. You talked to her a lot and shared your rations and water with her," Matt answered thoughtfully. "Then we met up with the soldier alone in the village in October of '63."

"Did you know if anyone who caught his name?" Joshua asked thoughtfully.

"Henry might have. He sat with him until the medic got there."

"He and Scott seemed to be in shock. But I remember Scott's face pale as a ghost when I brought Roger over to him. I asked Henry to get us some help, but he froze while I hauled everyone out," he replied, as he glanced at his son briefly then to Matt. "We, all, reacted to that day differently."

"I guess we did. But I failed to do one thing all these years," Matt said, as he fixed his eyes directly on Joshua.

"What's that?"

"Thank you for saving my sorry ass that day. You know if you ever need or want anything, call me. I owe you my life and will do anything for you or your family, too. Have you heard from Steve? You know he was hot head, too. But wait you already talked to him. I forget things then remember them later. Kim said he's in psycho-ward now. But she didn't say why or how he was doing there."

"He has mellowed in the psycho-ward, and he's dying of Cancer and AIDS," he replied sadly. "I guess he wanted to make his peace with me before..."

"Damn. I better go see him then before..." Matt said but stopped in mid-thought. "Do you think he'll see me?"

"I don't know. I was surprised he wanted to see me," he answered back. "But I know why he was angry back then, and I understand you now, too. Thanks for sharing."

"Your brother looked older than you. Why didn't he go to Nam?"

"I enlisted before he got the chance besides my parents had big plans for him two words called 'Law School.'"

Matt nodded. "You were something back then and now." He walked over to touch Luke's shoulder. "You're a good man, too, just like your Dad. Take care of him. He's a good man, too."

Luke nodded and gave a brief smile. Matt smiled back, as he headed for the front door. Joshua watched Matt leave and left his cup on the railing at a distance from Luke.

"You've heard Steve and Scott's account of that day I pulled their butts out of the jungle. But you haven't said much. I'm sure James, Robert, Henry, Jerrod and Luke will have something to say about it, too. I think it all comes back to that day whether I want to or not since it defined who we were and would become back then."

Luke stared at him. He cleared his throat and blinked his eyes. "What about Trevor and your CO?"

"Trevor is dead, but I'm not sure about my CO. I guess, we'll have to see," he answered honestly. "I never grow tired of this view. What about you, Luke?"

Luke stared at the ocean. His eyes fixed on the view, but he didn't answer back.

"I didn't' always work when you, kids, were growing up. We went places or vacations when it was possible. I loved it here and Tahoe best of all. Do you remember Lake Tahoe, son?"

Luke stared at him but still no word between them.

"We, all, got in that old station wagon your Mom loved so much. I think, she called it Bets or something like that," he pressed on thoughtfully.

"It was Betsy, and it was '64 Chevy two station wagon and was tan in color. It broke down in May of '87. I couldn't fix it. Mom cried, as we left it in Missouri for another car," Luke said coldly.

"That's right, Your Mom had a habit of naming cars," he replied back.

"Oh, a camping we will go," Joshua sang joyfully. "Oh, a camping we will go."

"Daddy's being silly, Mommy," commented Susan.

"Yes, but he's glad to take us camping," Carly said with a big smile.

"First Tahoe then the redwoods and eventually the Grand Canyon," he informed them, as he loaded the roof of station wagon. "I hear its breath taking just like Tahoe and the ocean. Maybe we can stop there on our way home. Would you like that?"

"Joshua, we've only have two weeks. There is always another time," Carly answered seriously.

"I suppose," he replied sadly. "But let's not waste any more time in this driveway. Everyone get in."

"Kids get in, Betsy," Carly said with a big smile.

"It was the last trip we did together as a family. I should have spent more time with you, guys. I'm sorry."

"I've got to go," said Luke.

"You came over here for a reason. Do you mind telling me, son?"

"Henry wants to talk to so do the others. They contacted me through Maria, and they want me to come with you if I have the time."

"Do you?"

"I'll let you know," Luke answered with glance back at the ocean then smile. "Excuse me, Sir."

Joshua nodded and let him leave. He continued to make an effort for the sake of Carly and his daughters. He owed them this and so much more. Joshua walked back into the house and lie down on the couch. Bryan joined him there, as he closed his eyes. His mind drifted back to another time with Roger on a roof top but at a construction site not a hospital.

"What's Clemens doing up there?" a fat man asked, as he looked up.

Joshua glanced up then replied, "Oh, crap." He rushed up the stairs two at a time. "Hey, buddy, it's me, Josh. What's going on?"

Roger stared at him with a drill in his hand. He looked confused then cracked a smile at Joshua.

"Come over and talk to me, buddy," he replied calmly.

"I barely feel my leg. I get sharp pains in it then I discover it doesn't bend well either. What's with that?"

"Step away from the edge of the roof, and we'll talk," he answered back.

"Why, not, here? Aren't we taking on the enemy ahead of us?"

"No, Roger. We're home now. We've been home from Vietnam for six years now," Joshua informed him calmly.

"But I got papers saying that I need to report for basic training. I have to fight for our country," pointed out

Roger. "I need Mom and Dad to be proud of me. I'm not avoiding it by fleeing to Canada like some others."

"Buddy, listen to me. We're home. We served and now have come home. Your parents are proud of you. Now please, come over to me carefully."

Roger shook his head and dropped the drill. Joshua glanced quickly at the crowd forming below. He felt sweat throughout his body, as the sun baked their bodies with super intense heat.

"What the hell is going on up there, Hernando?" the heavy set man asked in anger. "Get your butts down here right now."

Joshua held out his hand but looked back Roger. He didn't want to spook him now. Roger turned his head away from him.

"Roger, come away from the edge. Let's go get some ice cream. Rocky Road your favorite, buddy."

Roger looked at him again with a big grin. Yes, he was getting through to him finally, and it was a little relief but not completely. He still had to get him away from the ledge of the building because they were twelve stories high now.

"Can I have two scoops?" Roger asked with delight.

"Sure two scoops, buddy," Joshua answered back.

Roger slowly walked over to Joshua who wasn't too far from the stairs. Joshua took his arm and guided him towards the stairs. Roger smiled now.

"It's got to be good. Right, Josh?"

"Yes, buddy. Easy does it down the stairs," he answered back. "How did you get up there anyways?"

"That," Roger answered, as he pointed to a crane

beside the building structure. "I could do it again."

"No, let's go this way, buddy."

"Okay."

They reached the bottom, and the man approached them. Joshua knew he had to explain what was going on.

"Sir, we need a small break," he replied quickly. "You can dock us pay, but the heat got to him."

"Fine, I won't dock you just get him taken care of and be back here in a half hour, or you'll be docked pay."

"Thank you, Sir. Roger, let's go get that Rocky Road."

"Oh, goodie," Roger said with excitement. "Two scoops."

"I'm almost done with the wiring, Sir. I'll finish when we get back, Sir."

"Fine, go."

Joshua woke up and walked into the kitchen. He grabbed a cup near the sink and poured some milk in it. Meow.

"You want some, little guy," he replied, as he poured some into Bryan's bowl.

Then he walked into his living room and headed for his easy chair when the phone rang. So he picked it up.

"Hello," he replied on his end.

"Hi, Josh," a male voice said on the other end. "It's me, Jerrod."

"What's up, buddy?" asked Joshua.

"We need to talk."

"I'm meeting with ..."

"I know Henry in a day or two, and you talked to

Scott, Steve and Matt; but I need to see you, too.
It's important," interrupted Jerrod.

"After I talk to Henry, I'll make time for you, man."
"But…"

"I didn't ask to hear from you, guys, so I think, you can back off some. I need to breathe. Bye."

He slammed down the phone and regretted it. But he didn't ask Scott to tell him about the day in the jungle. He also didn't plan on seeing Steve either. These men spent a lot of time away from him, but now Roger was dead. They're back in his life. He shook his head and headed for the couch instead of his chair. He closed his eyes and heard Bryan's purring, as he drifted off to sleep.

A couple days later, Joshua sat in one of his chairs and petted Bryan. He waited for Henry to arrive. Luke sat on the side of the deck and strummed his guitar. Luke didn't sing but strummed out different sounds at various times. Joshua was surprised that Luke brought it with him. It filled the awkward silence between them.

Henry walked in without them realizing it until he stepped out on the deck. Luke glanced over at him. Bryan looked over at him, so Joshua saw his friend standing there. Henry looked tired now.

"Hi, Henry," Joshua replied calmly. "Pull up a chair."

"I'll stand. Thank you," Henry said, as he walked over to the railing. "I've never told anyone about the solider we found in that village for reason. But I guess someone needs to know beside me now."

"You were shocked by what he told you. Weren't you?" asked Joshua.

Henry nodded.

"It was a war that we really didn't understand, and we saw things hard to explain to the people back home," added Joshua.

Again Henry nodded.

"But you want to share it while you still can. You told us about the day I got us, all, out of there, but the solider in the village was your secret from all of us," Joshua replied calmly. "Take your time, buddy. I know and Luke knows it won't be easy."

"I see it so clearly in my mind now," Henry said calmly, as he looked back at them now. "He was our age when it happened."

"We didn't expect the attack, as we entered the village, but there were women and children there, too," the solider told Henry.

"What do you mean?" asked Henry.

"They were in their homes or what we call homes hiding out. We assumed there wasn't anyone there, so we didn't use our normal caution. But something was lingering in the air, but it's gone now or not as thick as before," the solider explained to him.

"What are you saying something came out of the sky?"

"Yes, an orange mist from a clear blue sky. We see a lot of rain over here, so we notice when the sun comes out," the solider continued on.

"What's your name?" Henry asked him.

"Robert," answered the solider. "That's all you need to know. What's yours?"

"Henry," he answered back.

"I think it was our people who dropped an orange mist on the village. We didn't see any bodies like I said, so we didn't do our normal checks."

"What happened?" asked Henry.

"They had us surrounded because we walked down the middle of the village. I had to take a leak, so I stepped away from everyone while they headed in," Robert answered, as he shook his head.

"What did they do?"

"They had women and children run towards us, so it forced them to stop and put down their weapons. They wanted to see if they had any injuries then all hell broke loose."

"They opened fire on their own women and children," Henry said in shock.

"Yes, and my platoon," Robert said, as his voice cracked a little. "It was a sight I want to forget, Henry. We heard about what happened to the Jews in World War Two, and how they were treated. But seeing this first hand isn't easy to stomach. I don't think I have anything left inside me now."

"You mean you did that," Henry said, as he pointed to the several places vomit was sitting.

Robert nodded.

"That's a lot," Henry said, as he offered his canteen. "Drink this slowly."

Robert's hand shook, as he took it to his lips. He looked pale and very weak from his ordeal. Henry stared at him and waited. Robert pulled the canteen from his lips and hand it back to Henry.

"Thank you," Robert said with an unhappy

expression on his face. "I am so cold now."

"That's normal after what you just did," Henry informed him. "Let's get you out of this area now."

"What will happen to my platoon?" Robert asked with concern.

"We'll call it in, and they will collect the bodies. They will be sent home to their families and get a proper funeral," Henry answered calmly.

"But..." Robert started to say.

"I know you should have been among them. There must have been a reason you survived this, Robert. I don't know what that reason is, but I'm sure someday you will know why."

"I have a fiancée back home. I don't know how I will be able to explain this to her or my family. I am sure they will have questions, and so will their families. Do I need to tell them what we came upon here?"

"I can't give you the answers you seek, Robert. But I would like you to keep in touch with me when you get settled State-side."

"But why? Wouldn't you want to forget this war, too? I am sure that you've seen some of the same things I have," Robert asked him painfully.

"We need to be around people who understand what we witness here, and we can be there for each other as moral support."

"I see," Robert said, as he pulled his jacket collar closer to his neck. "What do we do now?"

"Are you strong enough to stand?"

"I will give it a try."

"Let's go, men," barked Lt. Grahams.

"It must been hard for him to walk after vomiting like he did," Luke said, as he brought them all back to the present.

Henry stared at him then nodded. "He was so weak that he leaned on me most of the way. He ate very little, and I worried about him before he was shipped out of there. Then I saw him after I got home."

"You know where he is," Luke said a little surprised.

"Yes."

"Do you think we could see him?" asked Joshua.

"I'm sure I can arrange it," Henry answered back.

"Good and thank you. I know this wasn't easy for you, Henry."

"It's, okay, Joshua. This generation needs to know how Vietnam changed us. We thought we were men going over there, but we really were men when we came home. We were changed forever."

"It was a war that not everyone wants or will understand," Luke added, as he put his guitar down.

"But you can make them understand by what we've told you," Henry said back.

"That's why he's here every time you, guys, talk," replied Joshua.

"But he's seen and witnessed war first hand, too," Henry said back. "Is it fair to add our war mixed with his own?"

"It's okay," Luke answered back. "I'm a lot stronger than you might think, Sir."

"For man who doesn't talk about his experience," Joshua replied, as he sat there in his chair still. "I know it's hard to talk about war, and what we saw. But I learned through Roger and all we went through after he came home. I was wrong to be silent all these years. The generation after us and beyond need to know some of what we experienced over there."

"I understand, but we aren't done. Are we?" asked Luke.

"No, but we are close to the end of it all," Henry answered back. "I'll arrange you to visit Robert and get back to you. Until then I need to go."

"Thank you," Joshua replied politely.

Henry nodded, walked back through the house and out the front door. Luke glanced over at him. They made eye contact now.

"What?"

"That was horrible what that Robert witnessed," Luke answered back. "But why do you want to meet him again?"

"I don't know really, but I guess, I'll know when we are face to face," Joshua answered back.

Luke nodded and nothing more was said between them the rest of their day together.

20

Jerrod started and paced the floor, as Joshua fixed hot green tea in the kitchen. Luke sat at the Oak table and petted Bryan. Clearly, they didn't know what to say to other. Luke had been there when Matt and Henry talked to his Dad just like the others before them. But Joshua started to think of a third person when Jerrod showed up on his front doorstep. James walked in the house now, and he was another buddy from the war.

"How are you feeling today?" Jerrod asked James.

"Tired but you know how the treatments are," James answered back.

"Hey, buddy," Joshua called out from the kitchen.

"Luke, isn't it?" James asked Luke. "Hi, Josh."

"Yes, Sir."

"I suffer from minor exposure to Agent Orange. The doctors linked my cancer growths on my arms and back two years ago. However, the government denies it since being a long time after we were exposed," James explained calmly. "The treatments are eating away at my savings. Your Dad was exposed to it, too. I suspect someday he'll be like most of us then, too."

"That's why I'm so angry. The government should be paying for those treatments not you out your bloody pocket," Jerrod said in anger. "You served your country, man. They owe you not ...."

"Stop, Jerrod," James said calmly. "You'll upset the kitty on his lap. He's a little, guy, right?"

"Do you want some peppermint tea to help your

stomach," Joshua asked, as he stood at the doorway of the kitchen.

"How can you be both so calm about this?" Jerrod asked still angry. "Trev had cancer everywhere you could imagine. He died of a horrible death."

Jerrod walked towards the deck. He shook his head walked out the open sliding glass door.

"That would be nice, Josh. I won't hurt you, little guy. What's his name?"

"Bryan," Joshua answered, as he returned to the kitchen.

"Hey, Bryan," James said, as his voice cracked.

"Here, buddy," he replied, as he held a cup to him.

"Thank you," James said politely, as he sat across the Oak table from Luke.

Bryan hopped onto the table and sat on the table in front of him. James reached up and stroked him. Joshua could hear his purr, as he sat down, too. Jerrod reentered and sat down at the table, too.

"Sorry, guys. It's hard to see this happen to our unit. I know, we went our separate ways pretty much after we got home," Jerrod said calmer now. "But we didn't know the chemical warfare in which we were exposed to for years, Luke. It's not fair to us and our children like you to see us go through this hell. The government needs to take responsibility for us not your generation. We fought for our country proudly despite it didn't start out as a war. Do you understand?"

Luke nodded.

"Jerrod, he served in the Air Force. My guess is maybe Desert Storm," James said, as he sipped his tea.

"Good. Nice kitty."

"So cancer is linked to Agent Orange. What else can you tell us?" Joshua asked him. "That's if you feel strong enough to talk about it, buddy."

"Can I finish this then take a nap first?" James asked politely.

"Of course, buddy. You can use the spare room."

"Thank you," James said, as he tried to steady himself.

But Luke was at his side quickly then threw his arm around James's waist and one arm about his shoulder. They made eye contact.

"Thank you, Luke."

Luke nodded and led him to the spare room. Jerrod only shook his head.

"What? You're thinking about something."

"He's been a medic or something," Jerrod answered back, "To react so quickly. Was James right?"

"About what?"

"Your son being in Desert Storm."

"Yes, but no one can get him to talk about it. I don't even know how to approach it with him, and I'm his Dad."

"Wow! You're not the mouse anymore. You were always so quiet in the war. None of us knew how to reach you, but you talked to that little girl who lost her Mom," Jerrod said surprised back. "But not much to any of us back then."

"I never thought you would speak out against the government. Weren't you going into politics or something like that after the war?" Joshua answered thoughtfully.

"Things change, Joshua. Take a look at yourself now," Jerrod snapped back. "James wants to believe the government has done everything for us Vietnam vets. I don't by it. Look at him."

Jerrod shook his head again. Luke returned with Bryan at his side then took his seat at the table again.

"Thank you, son."

Luke nodded.

"When we came home, he thought he had money in the bank and money dating back to the Civil War to present, but his family drained his savings and sold the money collection not knowing its real value. Then he struggled to build up his savings again through the years. He doesn't have much with all these treatments," Jerrod continued on. "His money collection was worth a fortune since it was consecutive. He still collects them now. We shouldn't have to pay like this. We proudly served our country. It's a matter of time we, all, have effects of that damn mist and anything else they dropped on us over there. They owe us. Damn it!"

"Easy, buddy, we need to let James rest," Joshua replied calmly. "I can see you're opposed to the government. Joan said there's a website about Agent Orange. I haven't seen it yet, but my daughter will help me with it. Now you have to settle down since James is for the government for whatever reasons he has. We are his comrades and brothers and have to respect his belief. We owe him that much, Jerrod."

"Damn it! You're right. Why do you have to be my voice of reason, man," Jerrod said, as he got to his feet again. "I need to take a drive."

"Walk it off, man," suggest Joshua. "There's a long beach out there, and no one will get hurt."

"I get your point, man," Jerrod snapped back. "Fine, I'll walk to only get you off my back."

"Good."

Jerrod headed for the beach. Now Joshua sat in silence with his son Luke. Bryan stared at them both like he didn't know who to go to.

"Hey, little boy, do you want some loving'?" Joshua asked him.

Bryan walked up to him and rubbed his face against Joshua's. Joshua could hear his purr now. He stroked him, as Bryan danced a little on the table. He knew Luke looked on without a word.

"Uh, Joshua," James said in hesitation near easy chair then Luke.

James looked very pale and weak when Luke sprung up and escorted him to the table. James slowly eased into a chair and stared at them again.

"Thank you," James said to Luke.

Luke nodded again.

"Do you need something, buddy?" Joshua asked him unsure what to say or do.

"I'm cold, but I need you to hear this," James answered, as he rubbed his arms.

Luke reached for a blanket on the couch and brought it over. He unfolded it as he placed it over James's shoulders prior to returning his own chair.

"Thank you. It's warm."

Luke nodded again.

"I'm all ears, buddy."

"I believe in our government and the country our early fathers fought for our freedom," James said calmly. "I know Jerrod gets upset with me when I stand up for the government like I do. But he doesn't know why."

"Have you ever tried telling him? He said your family took your savings and money collection when you were in the service. You've been struggling with funds for your treatments."

"Yes, I have. But he doesn't know my family came from a political background. My uncle is a sitting judge back in Sacramento. He came out with us years ago. I have to believe in the system. Yes, I know, everything and everyone has flaws, but nothing can be perfect," James pointed out calmly. "Agent Orange has a website now, so the government is trying to help us. But you have to understand there are a lot of us out here needing help. Not all of it is related to it. We were lucky, Joshua. Our unit and CO weren't into drugs and alcohol like some of the other platoons who served. Those soldiers have come home messed up what they did over there. We, our platoon, was messed up by what we saw and experienced over there besides Agent Orange exposure. Could I have a glass of water? Please."

Luke got up and walked into the kitchen. James sat there, as he collected his thoughts when Luke returned.

"Thank you," James said, as he took a sip. "How can it all be the government's fault? We took in alcohol and drugs into our bodies under our own free will. Yes, the government used chemical warfare like Agent Orange, but what about the Atomic bomb? They, meaning the government, wanted to stop the fighting. Lives were being destroyed, so Truman used it despite not knowing what it would do. But it ended the war."

"You seemed to have given this a lot of thought," replied Joshua.

"I have, Joshua. I have wanted people to know it's not all the government's fault. People like Luke here need to understand these important facts. Hell, they probably don't know a whole lot about our war. How can they learn from our mistakes if we don't tell them our experiences of that war? Don't we owe it to them?"

"Good point, buddy. Roger wanted to tell, my kids about our war, but I wouldn't let him. I guess I wanted to forget it and move on. But it will always be a part of who I am. I can't change this fact. We're doomed to repeat things because we haven't learned from them. You said about an uncle who's a judge."

"Yeah, I did. Judge George Montgomery," said James. "Before you say it, yes, he was the one who sentenced your former son-in-law to prison. He called me after the trial. Your profile and talking to you got him thinking about me. He also thought of senators in the family back east as well. My uncle was deeply troubled how the relatives treated my family because they moved out here. They were cut off from the family fortune, so I understand why they did what they did to me."

"But it wasn't right, buddy," Joshua replied back.

"It comes back to flaws. We are human, and it's a part of our human condition to have those flaws. None of us are perfect, so how can we expect the government to be. Who makes up the government? You and me."

"So you still side with the government despite your

blackouts and other ailments that mist did to your body. You're a bloody fool," Jerrod said, as he stood at the opening of the sliding glass door. "It's a matter of time we, all, are faced with the effects of it. I know I'll want the government to take care of me. I deserve it. I served my country. Its politics and the crap they do to deny what people deserve. This is why I gave up politics, Josh. Look at him. He's dying painfully but won't give up paying for his treatments. James is a biggest fool of all to think it'll be cured. Well, buddy, it won't."

Jerrod walked by the table, so Joshua got to his feet. He stood face to face with Jerrod.

"I thought, I saw hate in Nam as those children walked up with those hand grenades. But I see worse hate in your eyes, man. I looked up to you, all, since I was the youngest and thought these men knew what they were doing," Joshua replied confidently. "But I've begun to see beyond it now in my journey of talking to you, all. Robert and Luke are the last two of our platoon that I'll talk to after that no more. You wanted to know why James believes in the government so much. Well, you should be here, man. You and James owe me nothing for that day back in Nam. I did what I had to do, so move on. I have always wanted to move forward, but one thing kept me in the past. It's not the war, but my ex and children."

Joshua stepped around Jerrod and headed for the ocean. He knew Bryan was at his side when he headed out to the beach.

"It all comes back in an instant without warning," the doctor said to him. "We can't figure it out."

"I know that's why it's so damn hard," Joshua

replied back. "I hate it when he stands on those ledges. He might fall to his death."

"But you always seem to know what to say to bring Roger back every time," said the doctor.

"But what if I'm not here every time; or what if I don't get here in time. Is it my responsibility after I got him out of that damn jungle ten years ago?" asked Joshua.

"I know, it's hard, Josh, but he says you're his best friend. We have him sedated, so go be with your family for a little while. I'll bet the kids are getting really big now," the doctor said with a small smile.

"Susan and Luke just turned year old the other day," Joshua replied proudly. "They're all growing up so fast. It's hard to believe."

"What are their names and ages now?" asked the doctor.

"Patrick will be four, James is two and Susan and Luke are one," he answered thoughtfully. "Same amount Mom had, but she had boy, girl, boy, girl."

"Do twins run in your family or Carly's?"

"I don't think so. Why? But I hope Susan won't be the only girl. She needs a sister. Are you sure about Roger being out for awhile?"

"I'll make sure of it. Now go be with your wife and kids. The rest will do him some good."

"Thank you, doc," Joshua replied, as he headed for automatic doors.

Joshua sat in the sand and stroked Bryan. He stared out at the ocean. He breathed in some of the fresh air into his lungs. It hurt a little on his right side, but he shook it off.

"Penny for your thoughts," a familiar female voice said above them.

He glanced up and saw Carly standing there. She sat down beside him. Bryan walked over to her, and she petted him, too.

"He's turned out to be pretty cat," she said with a small smile. "You take good care of him like you do with all the people you love. Did I tell you how cool you looked up on that witness stand? I don't think I could have been that calm, as Alex brought up about his Mom and brother. You showed your strength to not want to tear him apart because his revenge. I know, Rita took it hard and has kept her distance. But she'll come around. It was a big blow..."

"She loved him. I understand it, and no, you never told me how you felt about me being up there," he interrupted her. "What brings you here?"

She smiled at him. "It's official. I'm finally retired. This is my first day of retirement."

"And you're here with me, why not with our kids?"

"Well, they have their own lives besides we had a promise. Do you remember?"

He stared to shake his head, no, and then remembered, "One picnic lunch or dinner on the beach with sparkling cider."

"Oh, you remembered," she said, as she grabbed him around the neck and still held on.

He wiggled free and kissed her on the cheek. Her face turned a shade of pink. He laughed out loud and got to his feet. He held out his hand to help her up, as he smiled back.

"Some things never change. Do they?" he asked, as

they stared face to face. "You got a little pink that first time I kissed you."

"I…just," she answered in hesitation.

"I know you didn't expect it then and now. You were the only girl I ever kissed then outside Mom. Now I've only kissed my girls, granddaughter and back to you again. Where it all begun."

Carly side stepped him and Bryan and stared out at the ocean. He turned her to face him.

"Why are you crying?" he asked, as he took his thumbs to her cheeks.

"You were the first man I kissed outside of Robert. I wanted more of it that day from you but didn't know how or if I should ask for more," she admitted sadly. "I wonder what happened to him."

"You didn't see him again," Joshua replied a little surprised.

"When I called off our engagement, I headed for the bay area to rebuild my life again," she explained in a low voice. "I didn't want to run into him on the streets of Sacramento. He wasn't the same. Then you walked back into my life, and I hadn't thought of him in long time."

"Maybe your paths will cross again. Ours did again. Let's have a picnic dinner right here. Let's say around five thirty," he replied cheerfully.

"Sure," she said, as she touched his cheek. "We can watch the sunset together like we used." She glanced down at Bryan. He rubbed against their legs. "Bring him along."

He nodded, and she petted Bryan before she left. Joshua and Bryan lingered a little longer before they headed home. He noticed Luke against the railing, and

James had the blanket around him in the chair.

"Couldn't leave him like that," Luke said to him. "Jerrod left an hour ago."

"Can you take me home, Luke?" James asked, as he opened his eyes.

Luke nodded. James started to get up, and Luke was at his side again.

"You're a good man, Joshua. I still owe you despite what you think, man. Take care."

Joshua escorted them to Luke's truck. He watched they drive off before he headed over The Tides to order lobster, clam chowder and side salad for his picnic dinner with Carly. They threw in a crab cocktail and chocolate mousse for free. But he still had to get the sparkling cider and get a picnic basket. This excited him now.

"I'll be back around four to pick it all up," he replied to the manager.

"So we got it all straight now, two side salads with ranch dressing on the side, two crab cocktails, two small clam chowders, two lobsters and two chocolate mousse's," repeated the manager. "Sounds like a romantic dinner for two."

"Nah, my ex retired today, so I'm keeping a promise that I made years ago. I'll see you in a couple hours," he replied, as he smiled. "Let's see where to go now?"

"You're nervous, man," Roger said, as he sat on the edge of the bed. "You're acting like you never dated before."

Joshua stared his reflection in the mirror. He

re-adjusted his collar for the now fourth time and checked his navy blue shirt was tucked into his nice beige slacks. He glanced down at his black boots that shined. He spent the last hour or so polishing them to high shine. Joshua proceeded to part his hair to the right and combed the military crew cut. He was also cleaned shaven, too.

"What's that smell?" asked Roger.

"Old Spice aftershave," he answered back. "How do I look?"

"Fine, but I told you that already, man. Relax or you'll have to...."

"No. She's not that kind of woman," he snapped back to her defense. "I won't have you bad mouthing the mother of my children. A woman might take an interest in you if you cleaned up some."

"Yeah, right, man. What girl or lady will want to be around a man like me with my problems?" Roger asked with a chuckle.

"Give it a chance, buddy. You might find your soul mate out there," Joshua answered with a big smile. "Well, I'm off to meet Carly. You're welcome to come along. She doesn't mind it, you know."

"I'll stay here and watch TV for awhile. Have a good time, man."

"Thanks," he replied, as he slipped on his army jacket. "Goodnight."

"Hey, if you get engaged or married, I'll be your best man, man. Okay?"

"You bet, buddy."

Joshua headed out of the room of their apartment they shared. Now Joshua stood before a mirror again. His body looked pretty much the same as in '66. He still had the military crew cut but a few white hairs appeared at the tips of his bangs now.

Meow. He glanced down on the sink board to see Bryan. Bryan looked up at him. So he smiled and stroked him gently.

"Still nervous, little boy," he replied, as he heard Bryan's purr. "You're coming with us, you know. You seem presentable." He glanced down at his watch 4:20. "I got to get the food. Let's go, boy."

He rushed out of the bathroom and picked up his keys and picnic basket. He was at the door when he stopped dead in his tracks. Carly stood there before him.

"I'm going to pick up dinner. Do you want to come?" he asked, as his caught his breath.

"Okay," she answered back with a smile and picked up Bryan. "Do you have a blanket and light when the sun goes down?"

"In the Blazer," he answered, as he closed the front door. "I'm late in picking up the food."

"Oh, and I'm early."

They headed down to The Tides. He cracked open his window and Bryan cuddled into Carly's lap. He pulled in and grabbed the basket from the backseat before he headed inside.

"You're late," said the manager.

"Sorry. I got a basket."

The manager took it and left. Joshua walked over to the deli and spotted a bouquet of flowers.

"How much?" he asked quickly.

"Five."

He dove into his wallet and slapped down a ten. "Keep the change."

He rushed back to where he saw the manager return with his basket. He smiled.

"Pulling out all the stops," the manager commented, "For this retirement celebration."

"She's special and is the mother of my six kids," he replied back. "When's sunset?"

"Six fifteen, I believe."

"Thanks for everything," he replied, as he headed for the Blazer.

Carly looked beautiful with her hair back loose on her back. The glow of a summer tan touched her face. He could drink in her beauty all day. But they had to get to the beach before sunset.

"For you," he replied, as he held out the flowers.

He slipped the basket in the backseat with the duffel bag that held everything else. He moved quickly and sped down the road.

"Hey, slow down, I'm not going into labor here," she said calmly.

"I've got to beat the sunset. We need to be on the beach when it comes," he replied quickly.

He pulled into his driveway and grabbed the basket and duffel bag. He headed for the beach. Carly was behind him with Bryan at her side and her flowers in hand. Joshua glanced at his watch again 5:55. He stopped at the spot on the beach.

"Do we still have time?" she asked, as she caught her breath.

"Barely," he answered, as he unfolded the blanket

followed by another. "Candlelight, please sit."

Carly and Bryan settled on the blanket. She glanced out at the ocean.

"Josh, stop! It's coming," she said back.

He sat down next to her and pulled the basket and duffel bag closer to him. He glanced at the sun then quick glance over at her. He wanted to kiss her again. But he focused on the sunset again. It turned cold quickly. So he wrapped the second blanket around her.

"That was beautiful," she said with a smile. "So what do we have to eat?"

"A small salad, crab cocktail and chowder to start off," he answered, as he opened the basket. "They put the dressing on the side like you like it."

She leaned in and helped herself to a salad. He smiled at her. She gave a return smile. He laid out the food and gave some crab to Bryan on a plate, too. Carly and Bryan ate, as Joshua opened the cider and poured some in two glasses. He held a glass out to her. She took it.

Then she put her glass down and asked, "What's the main course?"

She took a spoonful of chowder and stared at him.

"Local Lobster with streamed vegs and melted butter," he answered back.

"A woman could get used to this."

"Yeah, I know, but this is only to celebrate your retirement, my lady."

She turned pink again. "I haven't heard that pet name in years."

He stared at her. "I'm sorry. What was it like?"

"What?"

"Those twelve years we were apart," he answered, as he slipped Bryan more crab from his cocktail.

She grabbed containers of steamed vegetables and melted butter. She placed them on their plates. Then she placed the cracked lobster down, too.

"Hard," she said finally. "I was married three times after you. The kids needed..."

"We can talk about them another time," he interrupted her. "I want to focus on you right now. Please."

She had begun to eat her dinner slowly before she spoke again. "I worked a lot of waitress jobs and made good tips for the kids. I know they didn't see me much because I held down two or three jobs just to keep a roof over their heads and basic necessities of life. I had school guidance counselors watching over me since they had been in so many schools. I didn't allow them to have many friends back then."

He ate and listened. Bryan fell asleep on the blanket now.

"This is great. Thank you," she said politely. "None of my husband's after you dined me this way. I tried big cities, small towns and out of the way places, but you were always hot on our tail. I didn't want to face you again. What about you?"

"I had my bouts with anger, Roger's flashbacks and frustration of PI's taking my hard earned money to find you, guys. They said they had a lead and needed more money to check it out. But it always ended up the same way a dead end," he answered honestly. "You were always several steps ahead of me. It was like you had inside information."

"I did. Andrew knew where we were most of the time. I met up with him when Patrick was little .But I told you that already. I would drop him a line here and there during those twelve years then I couldn't run anymore," she said sadly. "Can we talk about something else?"

"Joan and I found you at the library," he answered back. "You wanted to be a librarian."

"You remembered, I told you that on our ...."

"First date," he interrupted her again. "Yes."

"But I didn't finish college, so I could only volunteer," she said back. "I've been easing myself into retirement these last couple years. Rita needed help with Jordan and his special needs."

"You were and still are amazing, Carly," he replied, as he stared at her now.

"Stop that, Joshua," she snapped back, as she stared out at the ocean. "Do you remember the night, oh forget it."

"What?"

She shook her head, no, so he turned her face to look into his. He cleared his throat.

"I was remembering it a little while ago."

"You always listened to me back then and even now," she said with tears in her eyes. "You were remembering the night you proposed on our first date."

He nodded then replied, "But not all of it just before picking you up."

"You didn't even have a ring until the one popped out of the machine."

"It was like God was reminding me of that first time I saw you at Joe's Diner. I told Roger how I wanted to marry you, but he reminded me of the big rock on your finger. To be honest, I really didn't notice it and didn't want to admit it to him."

"Why?" she asked with some curiosity.

"I was caught up in your beauty. It was a first for me because I had to be alert back in Vietnam. I lost all focus when I saw you."

"You're not the same man back then. You're still polite all the time and quiet at times, but I see a change in you. Roger's death has changed you in some ways, too. You're more open about your family and your life. I know, I said this before how our son is a lot like you, but I'm not so sure anymore."

"But he is. I've noticed it when we're together. He's an earlier version of me."

She laughed, as he leaned back onto the blanket. He gazed up at the stars above them. She snuggled close to him and covered him partly with the blanket.

"You aged well," she said sweetly.

"So have you," he replied back, "Some many stars up there. Patrick used to look up at them for hours at night."

"Just like his Dad. I see you so much in the kids. It made it hard when we were on the run. I couldn't completely get away from you because of them. Don't get me wrong, I love our children very much. It was just hard with them doing some things you did like Luke fixing things. He grew up so much without your help, and now I feel, I'll never reach him like I did when he was small."

"I know he said he was almost thirteen when we divorced. It was tough age to be without a Dad around," he replied back. "Again, I'm sorry, Carly."

"He needed his biological father not subs. I begun to realize it after awhile but didn't want to admit it to them or myself. I guess I was being stubborn. But it's okay. Let it go," she said, as she rested her hand on his chest.

He closed his eyes. His mind drifted back to last December.

"Roger, it's me, Josh," he replied, as he stood on the roof top now. "Roger, do you hear me?" He noticed two men in white lab coats. "You two go away, now!"

He continued to stare at them, as one held out a straight jacket. Joshua shook his head no, so they started to back up, He walked up closer to the ledge and Roger. Yes, he had a handgun in his hands. Roger looked worse this time somehow. He wore a hospital gown and socks on.

"I won't give up without a fight, man," Roger snapped back.

"Easy, now, buddy. It's me, Josh," he replied calmly, as he walked towards him. "Come on over here and away from there. Maria is worried about you. She loves her Daddy so very much."

He moistened his lips and walked slowly towards Roger. Roger backed up more to the ledge now.

"Who's Maria?" Roger asked shacking from the cold.

"As I said before, your daughter and only child she's downstairs waiting for us," Joshua answered, as he stepped even closer. "She loves you."

"They're going to have to kill me this time," Roger snapped back.

"What do you mean, buddy?"

"They took my leg. Now they want to finish me," Roger answered back.

"Come inside with me. I got your back. You called me your hero in '64. Well, I don't feel like one now if I can't get you away from there," Joshua replied, as he felt sweat pour out. "Please come over and talk to me. Tell me what's going on, buddy?"

Roger stood very close to the ledge now more than ever before. It made him and the others very uneasy. A helicopter drew in closer on Roger's position, but his footing was slipping. Joshua lunged for him, but he was too late. Roger headed down off the roof with a scream that echoed in Joshua's ears. His once silent right ear knew what had just occurred.

He knelt near the ledge now and cried. He didn't look down but up at the helicopter. It was a news station logo on the side. He stared at it and shook his closed, tight fist at it.

"Damn you, bastards," he yelled at the top of his lungs.

He felt the rain on him now, as he cried. The pilot pulled away. Joshua failed Roger this time. Why did it happen this time? He had been so successful in reaching Roger in the past. Joshua got up and headed downstairs to Maria.

"Josh, wake up," Carly whispered to him.

He stirred and opened his eyes to see Carly's face was in his. She had her hand on his chest and looked worried. She combed back his bangs from his forehead.

"Easy, Babe," she continued on. "It's okay. Bryan and I are here."

He tried to sit up, so she backed away but still stared at him. He noticed Bryan had big, shiny eyes, so he motioned for the kitty to come to him, Bryan walked over easily. He stroked the cat before he spoke.

"I was remembering last December with Roger," he whispered to them.

"I could see whatever it was how it bothered you. I had a hard time bringing you back from it. Has this ever happened before?"

"Not of December of last year but of another time and place," he answered honestly. "I'm sorry if I scared you, both."

"As long as you're okay, I think, that's what matters to us now," she said back. "But I'm glad you told me."

"Me too, I don't want to keep things from you ever again. I promise you here and now that I'll share everything with you good and bad."

"You don't have to go that far, Joshua," Carly said seriously.

"But I do. Things got messed up in the past, and I don't want that to happen again," Joshua replied seriously back.

"Wow! I can see the change in you since his death," she said, as she shook her head. "It's late, and I don't think we want to sleep out here."

"It wouldn't be a bad thing," commented Joshua. "But you're right that we should head back to my place."

"I need to get home. Thanks for everything. You're still my prince, you know, after all these years."

They gathered up their stuff, and she carried Bryan in her arms. He snuggled there, as they got back to his place. She headed for her car and kissed Joshua goodnight on the cheek. He watched her drive off and headed back inside the house.

As he unpacked the basket, he noticed their dessert still there untouched, so he slipped the mousse into the fridge. Then he placed the glasses and the stuff to be washed in the sink. He walked out to his living room to find Bryan asleep on the couch in a loose ball. He smiled and joined him there.

21

"**I** called you and your son Luke over to discuss what happened to me after you pulled my sorry ass out of that jungle in '63," Allen said, as he moved his artificial leg to the edge of his chair. "I hate not being normal."

Joshua sat on the couch of Allen's home. He wore his army jacket still despite the house being fairly warm. Luke sat on the edge of the couch and focused on Allen, too. He unzipped his Air Force jacket but didn't remove it either.

"I woke up in that army hospital to find my leg missing despite I felt it was still there. I would try to stand," Allen said calmly. "That's when I noticed my arm was gone, too."

"It must have been blown off with the explosions, Sir, I mean, Allen," Joshua replied stumbled to say. "It wasn't there when I came back for you."

"I don't remember it," Allen continued thoughtfully. "But I do remember metal and things flying through the jungle. Screams of people I couldn't make out what was being said during all that noise."

"I had a hard time finding you, so you and Roger were the last to get out. You told me that it wasn't bad, but you could follow me," explained Joshua.

"You lead, Corporal. I'll be right behind you."

"Sir, you have pieces of metal in your leg..."

"Are you defying a direct order, Corporal

Hernando?" barked Lt Grahams.

"No, Sir."

"Then lead the way out."

Another explosion exploded by them, and Joshua would readjust Roger across his shoulders with their full gear as well. He couldn't locate Roger's gun, but he had no time to look for it either. They had to get out of there and head back to the river with the other men.

"Sir, we're almost there," he replied back, as he saw the others lying where he left them, "Sir."

Joshua glanced back and didn't see Lt. Grahams anywhere. He placed Roger next to Henry. Scott stared back at him.

"Stay here. I've got to go back one last time for Lt. Grahams, but radio for some help while I'm gone."

"So you found and hauled me out," said Allen.

"Yes. You had cuts on your face now and your arm was missing," replied Joshua. "You were out like a light, so I carried you out like all the rest gear and all."

"Did Scott radio for help?"

"No, I did when I came back with you. He was in shock like Henry. I couldn't be sure, but I had to get us out of there quick."

"And you did. You left no man behind that day," Allen said with a small smile.

"You said you were in a dark place from '64 to '77."

"Yeah, the pieces of metal tore into my flesh. They said the leg couldn't be saved, so they took it. The doctors were so cold by what they did. It caused me to be angry," said Allen. "Why? I didn't know how many of us survived except for whom were with me at the hospital. They didn't give any answers."

Joshua sat there and listened.

"I didn't know what I was going to do when I got home. I had no arm and leg and had no idea how my family mainly my parents would deal with me like this. I was their only child now. I told you about my little brother before Christmas."

"You said something about your wife didn't put with your crap," Joshua replied calmly.

"Yeah, but let's go back to when I came home," Allen said. "The doctors sent me State side and left me to cope with the loss of limbs. But you need to talk to Robert when we came home, too. I was stuck in wheelchair before I ran into Roger at Walter Reid. He told me what you did for all of us. I had brief sense of clarity at that moment, so I acted quickly on what I did for you."

He tapped his fingers on the armrest and seemed to be in deep thought.

"We came home to people protesting the war and us being over there. I started to drink to deal with the loss of limbs and face seeing my parents again," Allen said thoughtfully. "Both were hard to face, Josh. I hadn't seen Mom since I entered the military. Dad left her while I was over there. I still remember the horror on Mom's face when she saw me in the wheelchair."

"Allen Gregory Grahams," she cried out, as color drained from her face. "Is that you?"

"Yeah, Mom, but where's Dad?" Allen asked, as he looked around for him.

"He didn't come with me."

"Is he coming later?"

"I don't know, Allen. You are different, son. You have no leg and arm."

"I know, I'll have to have someone with me all the time until I'm fitted for an artificial arm and leg," Allen said calmly. "But I'm home alive, Mom."

"But not any use to the world," a man said from behind her now.

"Dad, Mom didn't seem..."

"We don't live together anymore. I have a new lady in my life," he said, as he stepped up closer to Allen. "This is Erin. Erin, this shell of man is my oldest and only son surviving son, Allen."

"Nice to meet you," she said politely. "Do they hurt?"

"Loss of limbs, no, because my brain makes me believe they're still there," answered Allen. "How old are you?"

"Eighteen," Erin answered with a bright and cheerful smile. "Your Dad is pretty sexy for an old guy. But he knows his tricks since we've been together a little over two years now. You're going to be a big brother again."

"You're pregnant!" exclaimed Allen.

"Three months along. He's a stud muffin. We've been trying ever since we hooked up."

"No!" a female exclaimed from behind them.

"Yes, we're having a baby. You didn't want me to touch you that way after he died. A man has wants and needs, woman."

"So you hooked up with a sixteen year old," stated Allen.

"What can I say, son. I'm her stud muffin, and I'm

going to be a Dad again. I like…"

"Stop, bastard!" Allen exclaimed in anger. "Can't you see what you're doing to, Mom?"

"She doesn't care. Do you, woman?"

She had tears gliding down her face now. She glanced over at Allen then bolted down the hallway alone.

"She divorced me two months after you left for Vietnam," he said coldly. "Erin and I plan to have more kids after this one. The guys are charged and ready to go up stream right after this one is born."

"Barefoot and pregnant just the way I like it, stud muffin. I can't wait for it to happen again," Erin said, as she focused on his face. "Can you?"

"You know, I can't at this point of your pregnancy maybe in a couple months. Then we can do it until you beg for mercy."

"Oh crap! You two make me sick. You were jail bait when you met up with him. What do you parents think of that?"

"I don't know. I was on the streets a couple days when he offered me a ride," Erin answered with small giggle. "We couldn't wait to get to that motel five blocks away. He turned into the alley and took me right there in the backseat of his car. I knew I didn't want anyone else after we did it a couple more times there. We haven't been apart since."

"You're probably so ripe right now, Honey cakes, that makes me horny as hell. I want to take you here and now."

"Dad!"

"We've done it pretty much everywhere else. This

is one place that we haven't done it in."

"Get out of here. Do you hear me?"

"So did he leave?" Joshua asked with interest.

"Yes, I heard from him once in a while. After my little sister was born, they did it again on Erin's hospital bed, and they agree Benny after Benny Goodman was conceived that night. Dad is slowly down now, but I think, he and Erin have about six kids now."

"Does Erin work?"

"No, or not that I know, of anyways, she told me that Dad has dementia now. She misses the sex acts or tricks. She talks about how sexy their gardener is."

"You think..."

"She might see if he's like Dad. It's possible. It was his relationship with Erin and loss of limbs that I went into a very dark place. I had so much hate in my heart and soul, and Tim's Mom saw through it all. She saw something in me and snapped me out of it because I stopped drinking and hate all right there, as she stood there before me." He paused before he continued on but not before he sighed first.

"What did she say?"

"She loved me but hated my drinking. She looked beyond the missing parts and saw a handsome man who could stand to be loved again. I had no idea she thought that way. She was my caregiver. I was lucky to have her in my life. We didn't waste any more time. We got married, and Tim was born a year later," Allen said sadly. "Mom never got to see him. She...."

"What?" Joshua asked with interest.

"She took her own life that day she left the

hospital. I had to ask him from money to bury her. I guess I carry a degree of guilt in Mom's death, too."

"Why do you say that?"

"I contacted them when I came home from the war. She was shocked by my loss of limbs then Erin being pregnant," said Allen.

"But you needed them."

"What did your family do when you came home, Josh? You never talked about them ever over there, not even once."

"They were angry since Mom slipped into a coma and buried her two days before I got home. I had to stay to receive those medals, merits and promotion before I headed for home. It was the delay would cost me my Dad and siblings to turn their backs on me in anger. It didn't matter what held me up from being there the end of Mom's life."

Allen sighed again and sat back deeper into his chair. "I'm sorry, Josh. I couldn't let what you did the day in the jungle go unrecognized. I was your CO, yet you held us, all, together."

"It's in the past. Is what it is," Joshua replied back. "They're coming around now."

"Yeah, I remember them at Roger's funeral."

"They'll probably be there for Steve's, too," Joshua asked sadly.

"What are you saying?" Allen asked, as he sat up straighter in his chair.

"Steve's in the psycho-ward at where Roger died. He has Cancer. He told us about what he remembers of that day. I think he's looking for closure and peace now."

"So the end must be near," said Allen. "My wife told me about how people know their days are numbered. They gather up the people who matter to them and check off their to-do list. It's like they don't want any regrets or road blocks to their final journey."

"So you did listen after all," a woman said, as she stood at the front door.

"Oh, hi, Honey," Allen said, as he looked that way. "This is Josh Hernando and his son, Luke. Josh pulled my butt out of the jungle. This is my lovely wife, MaryAnn."

"Nice to meet you, MaryAnn," Joshua replied, as he got to his feet.

"Pleasure," Mary Ann said to Luke. "You look a lot like your father."

"Yes, Mrs. Grahams," Luke said politely, as he stood up, too.

"Where's Timmy Button?" MaryAnn asked Allen with a bright and cheerful smile.

"Not sure, Honey."

"He was to stay home until I got back," MaryAnn said back. "Would you, gentleman, care for some tea, water or milk? I don't have alcohol in this house. I don't want to tempt my husband here. He's been sober since '77. I'm so proud of him."

"I'm good," Joshua answered back with a small grin.

"No, thank you, ma'am," Luke said politely.

"So what brings you two here to visit my adorable husband at our humble home?" asked MaryAnn.

"Filling in the blanks of my life of that day and days

leading up to the day you told me how you loved me,"
Allen said with a small smile.

MaryAnn's face turned a bright pink now.

"Honey, it's okay," Allen said with a wink.

"Hi, Dad, oh, hi, Mom," Tim said, as he entered the
room.

"Where were you?" she asked sharply.

"In my room answering Brittney's emails,"
answered Tim. "She's hot that we or I decide to forgo the
article." He glanced at Joshua now. "She said you and her
had gone to see Steve."

"You didn't tell me that, Tim," Allen said a little
surprised.

"It's not relevant, Dad."

"But Steve's dying. Can't you see that, son," Allen
said, as the tone in his voice rose slightly. "When did you
plan to tell me?"

"Dad, don't go dramatic on me now. Me and Rita
have heard a lot from Brittney and Kim," Tim answered
back.

"Kim," Allen said in anger. "Who was all there with
you, Josh?"

"Uh...I believe Brittney, Kim, my older brother
Andrew and myself."

"So he meaning your brother knows Steve's
version of that day," said Allen.

Joshua nodded a little. "Or what he recalls anyway.
There's a piece he left out, and I remembered it later."

"I see."

"Allen," MaryAnn said sharply.

"I'm okay. I'll let it go, Honey. You know how I hate

secrets."

"Yes, I do, but I don't think Josh intended to. You may not have asked, so it wasn't kept from you," pointed out MaryAnn.

"You're right as usual," Allen snapped back. "I'm sorry, Josh. I'm tired now. Will you all excuse me? Oh, thanks for coming over."

He struggled to get to his feet and left the room. Tim's eyes were blood shot, and his shirt was askew.

"What did you say to my daughter?" Luke asked, as he and Tim face to face now.

"I can't get a magazine interested in the article, so I had to let it go. I emailed her calmly and explained it to her. Then she exploded in anger how Rita said she had no say. I've spent the last hour or more emailing her and Rita to smooth things over. I never said it, and Rita regrets to having said it to Brittney. Everything is good now," answered Tim.

"Excuse me," Luke said, as he headed for the front door. "I'm sorry. I meant no disrespect in your home, Mrs. Grahams."

MaryAnn nodded, so Luke walked out the front door.

"Is Allen okay?" Joshua asked her.

"He tires easy these days. His Dad died last week," she answered in low voice.

"I'm sorry. I didn't know."

"I thought they died years ago," commented Tim.

"We thought it was best for you believe that, Tim. Your grandfather married someone after your grandmother..."

"Died," filled in Tim.

"After she took her own life," Joshua replied honestly. "It has been hard on your Dad with your uncle dying in his arms, Vietnam and losing her. Cut him some slack, Tim."

"You're had it tough, too. Nobody gave you a break."

"That's true in some ways," Joshua replied thoughtfully. "I don't recall if I would have accepted distance if it was offered. I was too busy putting one foot in front of the other and determined to make something of myself and get my family back, too."

"So you say you reached success then," said Tim.

"Not really. It's a work in progress. I don't have a real relationship with Luke. I still struggle with him and the others."

"And it hurts Rita isn't close now," pointed out Tim.

Joshua nodded. "I need to go home."

"Will you be talking Robert about his homecoming?" asked MaryAnn.

"I don't know. Why? I know Allen mentioned it, too."

"I think, it'll you help heal and understand you weren't alone in the way you were greeted by family," answered MaryAnn.

"Thank you," Joshua replied, as he walked out the front door, too.

He saw Luke off in the distance, so he headed his way. Luke turned to him with his cell in one his hand. Joshua knew Luke wouldn't tell him who was talking to due to past experience he had with him.

"No one seems to know where Robert is, but Maria said he mentioned poetry after her Dad's funeral," Luke said calmly. "I have one more lead to follow up on."

"Thank you, Luke. I didn't expect..."

Luke nodded before going back to his phone. He texted someone while he headed for The Tides. They parked his truck there to hike up the hill. Joshua was in fairly good shape despite his cough attacks at times.

"Are you hungry, Luke?" Joshua asked him, as they descended down the hill.

He gave slight nod.

"Clam chowder and crab cocktail my treat, son," Joshua replied with a little excitement building inside him.

Luke put his cell in his shirt pocket and produced a credit card. Joshua knew what it meant. Luke wouldn't let him buy anything, and it bothered him. But he was proud of Luke, too, for wanting to pay his own way. So they would order and pay separately, too.

However, Luke brought a half gallon of milk which he poured some into two cups. He placed one in front of Joshua when Luke got to his feet again. He walked over to the deli to pick up their orders clams and fries and crab cocktail when they were ready. So Joshua didn't have to get up again.

"Thank you, Luke."

He nodded, as he made the sign of the cross. It was side of Luke that he hadn't seen before. But they ate in silence and on occasion Luke slipped clams and fries next to Joshua's crab cocktail. It made Joshua smile.

Two days had passed when Luke returned because he located Robert. So they headed off to San Francisco.

They traveled in silence except for the Jazz music on the radio. Then they pulled into a place, and Joshua followed him. It had a stage with a podium and microphone. They took some seats in the back.

"Drinks?" asked a cocktail waitress.

"No, thank you," answered Luke.

So Joshua shook his head, no, too. The lights dimmed, as people sat quietly.

"No one cries for the wounded soldier. No one cries for his broken up body and is now a shell of man. No one cries for the man longing to be held by a woman or someone. No one cries for the man who served his country without complaint. No one cries for a man that many discarded like waste," a man read from the paper in front of him.

The audience roared with applause and cheers he didn't expect. He gazed out into the audience and saw a familiar face. He smiled and turned back to his paper before him on the podium. Silence filled the room again. He cleared his throat and adjusted his reading glasses as he continued.

"I'm not waste but a man who walks the earth just like you. I'm a veteran of a war that generations after the seventies do not understand. I'm not waiting to be held anymore. I'm broken on the inside, and you can't see my scares because they run long, deep within my soul and memory. I'm a man who served my county and would do it again but maybe with more caution then the first time. I'm proud to be an American and what we stand for as a Nation."

He stopped again and looked out into the

audience. He saw the familiar face still there. He smiled again and placed his paper in a book of some kind.

"It's done, my friends, countrymen and comrades. It's done," he said before he left the stage.

The audience applauded and cheered again. But he didn't return to the stage. Luke headed backstage and Joshua followed.

"Hi, Robert," replied Joshua.

"Didn't know you were into poetry," Robert said back. "I see, you have your sidekick."

"I suppose, everyone seems to want him around these days," replied Joshua. "I didn't know you wrote poetry."

"Brittney has caught my readings once in awhile in recent months," Robert said, as he looked over at Luke.

"She's the one who told us where to find you," Luke said back. "No one else seemed to know despite Allen and MaryAnn wanted him to talk to you."

"What about?" Robert asked, as he focused on Joshua's face now.

"Your homecoming," he answered back. "They seemed to think it was important."

"Come to my dressing room," Robert said, as he walked into a short hallway.

They followed him to a room not too far from the stage. Robert put down the black notebook and faced them.

"I didn't want to discuss it out there," Robert said calmly. "So it has come to this now. We try to make the generations after us understand our war. War protesters made us unwelcomed when we arrived home. I pity them all now."

"Why pity?" asked Joshua.

"Because children who were born in the sixties have no real understand of it all. It's a clouded view because no one bothered to give them the facts or the whole truth. So they march around carrying what they were told as to be the whole true."

"It's not a true picture. Is it?" asked Luke.

"No, son, it isn't. So you want to hear about what happened when I came home from the Vietnam War. I didn't come home to hero's welcome as you heard in my poem tonight. It's only a taste of what I would witness at home. Take a seat and get comfortable."

"We don't need war. Stop the killing. Bring our men and women home," yelled protesters outside the airport in unison.

"Step back people," a uniformed officer said, as Robert made his way through the terminal.

"He's a vet coming home," said one of the protesters.

All eyes were on Robert now, as he headed for the waiting taxi to take him home. He felt uneasy by that statement, so he tossed his duffel bag in the cab and hopped in quickly. They attacked the taxi, as they pulled away.

"Where's home, soldier?" asked the cabbie.

"Woodland," Robert answered back.

"Woodland, it is then," the cabbie said, as he sped away from the airport.

Robert leaned back on the seat and closed his eyes. He was home. It had been almost two years since he left for Vietnam or basic training then Vietnam. But he was back on American soil, and it was mixed emotion now, as he remembered those protesters.

"What's the address, soldier?'

"1229 Barely Street," he answered back.

"We'll be there in ten."

"Thank you."

The cabbie grunted. But Robert didn't open his eyes. He thought of his parents, brother and sister that he left behind. The cab stopped, so he opened his eyes. He saw the house before him. It looked the same, so he got out and paid the man. He swung his duffel bag over his right shoulder and headed up the steps.

"Robby," a woman said, as she wore a dirty apron around her waist.

She held back an embrace, so he noticed her salt and pepper hair. She also gained about twenty to thirty pounds, but she was still Mom.

"Mom," he said back, "don't I get a hug."

She glanced back, as a man stepped out of the house. He had stood tall and proud, as he stared down at Robert. Robert stopped at on the mid-step to the porch. His Dad hadn't aged at all and still had his thick black hair.

"Dad," Robert said back. "I'm home."

"I can see that, boy. How many innocent women and children did you kill over there? How many did you rape over there?"

"Uh…" he said in hesitation. "I don't follow you, Dad."

"I know what was like, boy. I served, too. Or have you forgotten how I served in the last year or so in Korea?"

"I haven't forgotten, Dad."

"Why are you here?"

"This is home," Robert answered back. "I didn't rape anyone over there. I helped bury..."

"Liar all of you, boys who have come home from that damn war did that and drugs, too," his Dad snapped back. "I've heard what you, guys, did over there from someone who has come home already. Get out of my sight. Do you hear me, boy?"

"I have nowhere else to go, Dad."

"Well, you're not welcome in this house. Heroes live here not men like you, boy. Go find somewhere else to live."

Robert sat at the make-up table and looked at Joshua and Luke. He shook his head before he continued on.

"I didn't know where else to go. I walked back up to Main Street. I changed in the local gas station out of my dress uniform to jeans and t-shirt. I was tired and hungry," Robert said sadly and thoughtfully. "It wasn't what I expected to happen to me. I wondered where Angie and Cameron were. Did they feel the same way Dad did? Did Mom? I cried, as I managed to get a burger, fries and soda to go. I wanted to a place to lie down and forget what had happened back home."

"Did you find a place?" asked Joshua.

"Yeah, an old abandon barn on the outskirts of town," Robert answered thoughtfully. "I was chased off early the next morning."

"What happened that night?"

"I found paper and a pen in my bag along with my

will. I reread it over and over a couple times, as the light faded. I had to find a match to light the oil lamp I found earlier. I shook my head often and remembered traveling with the platoon. We trudged through almost non-stop rain over there. Didn't we, Joshua?"

"It's, Josh, remember," he answered back. "Yes. It was the oddest times we experienced blue sky above us."

"I didn't think we would ever get home alive. We saw so much death over there. Do you remember that one village Henry had thrown up all the way through it?"

"I didn't think he had anything left in him. He told Luke about it and that one army soldier who survived before we arrived."

"That was something to witness your whole platoon gone, and you're there alone to fend for yourself. It sure made me glad that Lt Grahams told us to leave no man behind. It was our pact with each other, and you would carry that out two months later," Robert said thoughtfully.

"Did you ever get to go home to your parents' house?" Joshua asked him.

"No, I started to write poetry that night in the barn. It was my way of healing from all we went through over there and here State side."

"Did you go back to the house?"

"Yeah after Dad left with my siblings to go somewhere. I didn't follow them. I saw Mom alone. I thought I could find out why Dad felt the way he did."

"Did she help you understand?"

"Yeah, boy did she ever," Robert answered back, as he shook his head. "I got an earful, as I sat on the front porch with her."

"You have to understand the news reports say you boys are raping young girls as young as Angie over there. Then you gun down anyone who stands in your path of getting the job done," explained Mom.

"But we didn't all do that, Mom. I tried to tell Dad that I helped bury elderly men and women, women and children over there. We had a soldier who was with us named Joshua. He wanted to bury as many as we could," Roberts explained painfully. "Yes, there were times we shot them, too when the men used them as human shields. We didn't plan on it. It just happened that way, Mom. You have to believe me. It's case of you being killed or the other. I wanted to live. I wanted to come back to you, Dad, Cameron and Angie. Here is the will we had to update almost on a daily basis. I wanted to come back to tell you how much mean to me, and how much I love you, all."

"You're not the same young man who left here almost two years ago," she said back, as she fought back the tears.

"No, I'm not. I nearly died over there if it wasn't for Joshua. He saved us all from the enemy camp that we were entering. He had enough sense to get us all the hell out of there, so I could stand here before you. Tell you thank you for everything you and Dad ever did for me, but most of all how much I love you, Mom, Dad and my siblings. Please hear me now."

"I can't take you into this house, Robby. Your Dad won't stand for it. You're best to find your own way in life and move on down the road. I'll pray for you daily for the rest of my life, but I can only do that for you now," Mom said sadly.

"But, Mom, I'm your son, too."

"Your belongings are in the attic. I'll leave the spare key where we always kept it when you were a child. So you could come by tomorrow and take them with you as you travel that road alone, Robby. I love and believe you. You're my first born and hold a very special place forever in my heart. Go before your Dad returns and come back tomorrow after eight in the morning. We go to church at nine. Be safe," she said, as she leaned over to kiss his cheek and placed a crucifix and Saint Christopher medal around his neck. "I won't forget you, Robert."

"I left that porch a broken man," Robert said, as he wiped away the tears. "I brought a beat-up old '50 Ford that still ran for twenty bucks from the farmer who chased me out of his abandoned barn. I gathered up everything that was mine from the attic and embarked on a journey which led me here to San Francisco. I've been reading and writing my poetry for the last forty years on and off. I keep hoping to see in the audience Cameron and Angie."

"What about your Mom?" Joshua asked him.

"I subscribed to the Woodland paper and found her death notice there," Robert answered sadly. "I wasn't mentioned just Cameron and Angie. She died of Cancer. It was two years after my homecoming. I didn't go to her funeral because I didn't know if she ever told my Dad of my trip back to the house."

"So what happened to your Dad?"

"Heart attack six months later, I imagine. Cameron and Angie went to live with relatives since they were minors when I left. Cameron was fourteen, I believe. Angie was twelve. I was stranger to them, so I couldn't step in and take care of them like Mom and Dad did."

"I see why Allen and MaryAnn wanted me to know this," Joshua replied back. "It's a side of what people don't know about us, soldiers, coming home to."

"We're only a piece of the puzzle, Josh. There are many of us out in the world that remain silent and trapped with what they experienced over there. We can only give the public a taste of it if they want to believe and understand it."

"That's very true," Joshua replied thoughtfully. "Thanks for sharing it with us."

"I'm grateful that you saved my life back in December in '63. We, all, can't seem to forget it. I know, you have said countless times how you did what you had to do. But can I read you something?"

"Uh..." Joshua replied with hesitation. "I suppose."

Robert held his black notebook and opened it. He searched through it before he stopped and put his reading glasses back on. He cleared his throat again.

"Heroes come in all forms. They may be someone standing next to you in foxhole or at a crosswalk when the light changed so quickly. You didn't have time to think but to react to what was happening. You're called a hero, yet you try to explain it a way. But nothing can change the fact that's there. You're hero, so smile and nod your head then we know you finally have accepted your role."

Robert placed his reading glasses on the top of his head and stared at Joshua. Joshua stared back. They didn't say anything until a knock on the door broke their silence.

"Yes," Robert called out.

"There's a man here to see you with a woman," the voice said from behind the closed door. "They want to speak to the poet."

"Fine, we're done here anyway," Robert said, as he offered his hand out to Joshua. "Thank you for saving my life that day, Josh. I love you, buddy, forever."

Joshua shook his hand and turned to open door. There stood a couple who seemed to be very nervous. He looked over at Luke.

"We should leave him to his fans," he replied back.

"No more like his long lost brother and sister," said the man. "That's if he'll have us back in his life."

"Cameron! Angie!" Robert exclaimed, as his voice started to crack.

They stepped in and embraced Robert, as Luke and Joshua left the dressing room. They headed back to Joshua's place in silence.

22

"You got to be kidding," Patrick said, as he walked up to Joshua. "What does our little sister have to say about it?"

"I don't know," James answered, as he walked up too, "Hi, Dad."

"What's up, boys?" he asked, as he stared at them both.

"James, tell him," answered Patrick. "I still find it hard to believe."

"I planned to," James said calmly. "Alex was killed in prison."

"How? When?" Joshua asked in rapid gunfire at James.

"Another inmate, it was late last night. I have a friend who works in the morgue," James answered, as he remained calm.

Joshua walked over to a chair on his deck and sat down. Bryan climbed up and begun to purr, so he petted him.

"Are you okay, Dad?" Patrick asked, as he knelt before him now.

"It's shocking that's all, son. But I'm fine."

"They haven't told the media as of ten minutes ago. I didn't hear anything on the car radio," James continued on. "It was multiple stab wounds, but one was directly to his heart."

"But don't they check for weapons and lights out at a certain time," Joshua replied thoughtfully.

"I don't know all the details yet, but Dirk plans to text me more, later," said James.

"So Rita and Susan don't know yet," replied Joshua.

"Not that I know of, Dad."

"I wanted the bastard to die but not this way," he replied thoughtfully.

"How far a long is Susan now?" Patrick asked him thoughtfully.

"Seven or eight months, I think. Robyn is surprised how she has carried it this far."

"It's due in mid-September, right?" asked James.

"I believe so, son."

"Now here we are in the middle of summer and barely see the kids and Rita," said James.

"I noticed it, too," commented Patrick.

"She and Tim have been spending a lot time together with Jenny and Jordan," filled in Joshua.

"It was months ago that they started to work together on Tim's article. But most they've been helping the kids deal with their Dad being in prison. This is going to shock them all," Patrick said, as he got to his feet.

"Excuse me," James said, as he checked his cell.

"I wonder if that's Dirk now," Patrick commented to Joshua.

"Turn on the radio or TV. It doesn't matter which one," James said quickly.

"A radio is in the kitchen on the breakfast counter," Joshua replied to Patrick.

Patrick rushed in the kitchen and returned quickly. He had the radio on.

"Just in Alex Walters was stabbed last night. He

was an AP photographer convicted of three counts of rape, attempted murder on his unborn, bastard child and its mother who was one of his victims of rape and two counts of child molestation on two minor children," the announcer said calmly. "Tragedy has struck his family again with his loss. He was an excellent photographer for getting in the middle of the action throughout his career. He was respected..."

"Shut it off," snapped Joshua, "No more, please."

"Sorry, Dad," Patrick said, as he silenced the radio.

"Dad, what are you thinking?" asked James.

"Jenny and Jordan, they don't have a father anymore," he answered, as he looked off into the ocean.

"And my child will never know him either," Susan said, as she stood behind Patrick. "Not like he would ever see this child, but Alex is its father no less."

Meow. Bryan jumped off Joshua's lap and headed to Susan. She glanced down and smiled at him. She struggled to pet him on the head.

"Sit here," Joshua replied, as he got to his feet.

"I'm okay, Daddy," she said, as she walked up to James. "Does Dirk have any details about his death?"

"Well...uh..." James answered in hesitation.

"Tell us what you know, James," Joshua replied, as he walked up to the railing.

James stared at his cell and moistened his lips. "Alex was stabbed several times but the fatal blow was to his heart. His eyes were wide open as if he knew his attacker or attackers. His mouth had redness around it and rope burns on his ankles and wrists." He looked at Susan. "He couldn't defend himself from his attacker or attackers.

He wasn't meant to walk away from it."

"I'll take that chair now, Daddy," Susan said calmly, but her face was pale as paste.

Joshua eased her into the chair, and Bryan jumped into her big lap and barely stayed there. So he moved around then settled for the arm of her chair. She leaned back and stared to pet him. He purred.

"Are you okay, Sis?" Patrick asked, as he knelt beside them.

"Just shocked that's all, Pat," she answered back. "Could I get a glass of water?"

"Of course," Joshua answered, as he headed inside.

"Easy, Sis," Patrick said, as he noticed their Dad leave then return.

"Here, Honey bear," Joshua replied, as he held out a glass.

"Thank you, Daddy," she said, as she sipped it slowly.

"What brings you here?" asked James. "Should you be driving giving how far along you are?"

"It's Daddy's birthday, and I wanted to be with him and Mom. Or did you forget Mom's text?" she answered sharply.

"Joshua...Joshua," Carly called out, as she slammed the front door hard.

He turned and bolted through the sliding glass door to greet her. She had a panic look in her eyes.

"Slow down, I'm here," he replied calmly. "What's wrong?"

"Did you hear about..." Carly answered, as she tried to catch her breath.

"I know about Alex. We just heard...."

"No about Luke but not our Luke. You're army buddy," she said quickly.

"What? No," he answered with confusion.

"He was Alex's roommate in prison. He admitted to torturing Alex before he killed him," she explained, as she stared at him.

"Luke was in prison," Joshua replied thoughtfully. "Why?"

"Bank robbery a couple months ago, he killed a teller and the guard. I thought you knew about it," Carly answered back quickly. "I'm sorry, Babe."

"Well, that's why his phone isn't in service anymore," he replied thoughtfully. "Did he say why he killed Alex?"

"No. He only admitted it and acted alone," she answered calmer now.

He walked back inside, as the phone rang. So he answered it. "Hello."

"Hello. Is this Josh Hernando residence?" a male voice asked on the other end.

"Speaking."

"This is Warden Jacob Colby. Could you come to Folsom Prison as soon as possible?"

"Why?"

"Luke Rogers would like to speak to you, Sir. He won't speak to anyone else. He killed another inmate last night Alex..."

"I know who it was. He was my ex-son-in-law. Tell Luke, I'm on my way," interrupted Joshua.

"Oh, he said to bring your youngest son, too," said

Jacob.

"Why?"

"I don't know."

"Fine, it'll take me awhile since I live outside of Bodega Bay."

"That's over at the coast, right?"

"Yes."

"I can stall the press that long with by checking their credentials," said Jacob. "Thank you."

"Bye."

He walked over to pick up his jacket when Luke walked in with Brittney and Kim. Kim had a wrapped package.

"You and I are being requested by Luke Rogers at Folsom Prison. Do you know how to get there, son?"

Luke nodded and turned towards his truck.

"See you, all, later, I hope," he replied, as he stared back at them. "What a way to start off my birthday?"

He shook his head and headed for Luke's truck. He slipped in and fastened his seatbelt. Luke focused on the road while Jazz music blared from the speaker system. It was a side of his son that he didn't know very much about. He heard the music before and didn't question it or anything else for that matter right now.

Joshua's army buddies wanted Luke present at every discussion they had with him. Luke was the last one of the platoon. They talked or listened to Scott, Steve, Matt, James, Jerrod, Robert and Allen in the last few months. So it explained a lot that Joshua didn't know about Luke Rogers and the bank robbery. He had a lot of his plate besides his buddies from the war.

He wanted to be with Susan and her pregnancy, and they gotten closer because of it. He was a part of Patrick's, James's and Joan's lives, too. Carly popped in and out like she was busy all the time. Luke was around when an army buddy needed Joshua. Rita and her children were absent, and her older brothers noticed it, too.

"We're here, Sir," Luke said, as he stared at him now.

Joshua noticed the media vans and trucks with satellite dishes above them. He gulped down some air and glanced over at Luke.

"This is worse than Uncle Roger on the roof at the Palo Alto hospital."

Luke nodded then stepped out of the truck. Joshua followed his son's lead. They walked through the press and arrived at the main gates. Luke held out a black wallet, and the guard nodded. He looked over at Joshua and ushered him inside the walls of the prison.

"You made good time, Luke," a fat man said dressed in a tan business suit. "This is your Dad, Josh Hernando."

Luke nodded.

"We spoke briefly on the phone. I'm Jacob," he said, as he offered his hand out to Joshua, "Sergeant, impressive."

"How..." Joshua started to ask, as he started to shake his hand.

"Luke Rogers told me since this guy here doesn't say much. He's a man of action not words," Jacob interrupted him. "This way gentleman, I trust no weapons of any kind. We thought maximum security would be best for him right now since whom his victim was. Again, I'm sorry about your son-in-law. In here, gentleman, please."

Joshua saw Luke at a table. He didn't look up, but Joshua saw blood on his clothes as they walked up. Jacob tapped the table, so he looked up.

"I'll leave you, gentlemen alone," Jacob said in a low voice. "You know what do in getting the guards help."

The younger Luke nodded and sat down across from Luke Rogers. Jacob walked away, so Joshua sat down next to his son. He folded his hands in front of him and waited. Older Luke looked harsh and broken, and it wasn't the same man who stood by him at Roger's funeral back in late December.

"We're here, buddy," Joshua replied calmly.

"People don't' understand war," older Luke said, as he stared at Joshua. "They don't understand the impact it has on those who served their country so proudly for. A nation where we can have our freedom to do whatever we want within limits. Men died for such freedoms back in history, yet we haven't learned anything from it. We keep repeating it over and over. The only difference is the name of the war, but the heart of it is all the same."

"You've never talked about our time in Nam," Joshua replied back.

"I don't wish to discuss it now either if you don't mind, Josh. I killed your son-in-law," older Luke said calmly.

"That's what the warden said on the phone. He said you wanted to talk to me and my son, Luke, here," replied Joshua.

"I followed the brief trial. I wanted to be there for

you and your family as moral support. He was someone from your past his older brother. Alex held a grudge and bitterness in his heart and soul. It didn't change when he got here. It only got worse," explained older Luke. "He wouldn't change even if it meant a chance for freedom and was ever granted parole. He was a lost and troubled soul, not even Rita and his children could or would be able to save him."

"So you took his life," Joshua replied back surprised.

"I didn't intend to. In fact, I couldn't believe my dumb luck to share a cell with the jerk," older Luke snapped back.

"What happened?" younger Luke asked older Luke.

"I guess, I should take you back to Easter morning," older Luke answered thoughtfully.

"It's up to you, buddy. No pressure on our part. I'm here for you, buddy."

He nodded and drew in a deep breath before he exhaled.

"I was working in the laundry area when he walked in. He was sporting a tattoo of a tiger. He wanted everyone to know it was new and to keep their distance. I didn't care since I survived Nam."

"Hey, old man, over by the washers," Alex called out. "Aren't you my new roommate?"

Luke nodded and placed more clothes into the washer. Alex walked over. He had a load of clothes in his opposite arm where he had the new tattoo.

"I need these done yesterday, roommate," Alex said in low voice.

"There's a washer over there you can use," Luke pointed out to him, as he added soap to his washer.

"Hey, vet, everything okay over there?" asked another inmate.

"I'm good," Luke answered back.

"You're a war hero," Alex said a little surprised.

"I didn't come home to a heroes' welcome. I'm busy here."

"All soldiers come home to heroes' welcome," Alex said confidently.

"Not the Korean and Vietnam vets. It was before your time, Alex."

"You know me. Which war?" Alex asked, as he stood taller now.

"Vietnam and I don't wish to discuss it with you or anyone else for that matter. Yes, I read about your trial."

"Shh...a lot of these guys don't know how to read, so they don't know why I'm here. Can we keep it between us?"

"Sure why not."

"That doesn't explain why you killed him," Joshua replied with interest now.

"That was our first meeting of many talks," Luke said, as he stared at Joshua. "He wanted to find out how much I knew about him. There's two things inmates hate most are child molesters and former cops gone bad. He was on thin ice if they knew why he was here."

"What do they think he did?" asked Joshua.

"I don't know and didn't care either. I wanted to do my time and ignore or block out what we experienced in Nam. I wanted to forget I ever served."

"But Alex wouldn't let it go, right?"

"Yeah, he got a charge out of it. His eyes danced with excitement then his whole body got into it. Then he bragged about taking on a vet," Luke said, as he glanced away from a moment. "I knew, it was you, Joshua."

"You, Vietnam vets, are precise fighters in hand to hand combat," Alex said in their cell a couple days later before lights out.

"Why do you say that?" Luke asked, as he placed his pencil next to legal pad on his bunk.

"I got into a fight with my father-in-law. I got a black eye, split lip and two badly bruised rib and think he would have broken them if he had more time," Alex explained back. "But I got a few licks in on the old man. He served in Vietnam, too."

"Lights out," yelled the guard. "I said lights out."

"We'll talk more tomorrow," Alex said, as he climbed up to his bunk.

"I didn't say anymore, man. But I knew it was you all right. You were the best of unit in hand to hand combat and marksmanship. It was known to us, all, and to be promoted from private to corporal before we were shipped out to Nam," Luke said calmly. "You could have made a career in the service if you stayed in it and probably done very well. You were calm and level headed that day and every day we marched on. You were in control for almost every situation we encountered."

"Excuse me," a guard said, as he stood at the table.

"Yes," Joshua replied, as he looked over at him.

"There's a gag order on the murder. So you can't discuss it with the media when you leave here," the guard explained to them. "I need to return him to his new cell."

"Can you two come back tomorrow?" older Luke asked, as his eyes stared at Joshua. "Please."

Joshua glanced at him then to Luke, his son. Younger Luke only nodded.

"Sure, man. You take care of yourself."

"I will. Thanks for coming. I'll see you, two tomorrow."

Older Luke got up and walked with the guard peacefully. When he was out of sight, Joshua got to his feet, and Luke guided him outside the prison walls in silence. They drove halfway or better home before Joshua spoke again.

"It surprises me that he's in there for murder and robbery, but he never explained why," Joshua replied thoughtfully. "He talked a lot about Alex. He was never much of a talker back in the service either. Scott, Luke and Henry were quiet and followed the others lead. But I think it's interesting to hear Allen, Matt, Henry, James, Jerrod, and Robert's, too. Steve's view was different, too, but it explains why everyone else, as you sat through the others after. Do you remember them or it is clouded now?"

"I recall them after Steve. What Robert shared about coming home?"

"Yes. That was interesting, too."

"James and Jerrod are the ones to explain what the government has and has not done for the Vietnam Veterans."

"We learned a little about Agent Orange, too," he replied thoughtfully. "Can you bring me back there tomorrow?"

Luke nodded. They headed back to rest of way to Joshua's place in silence. Joshua glanced over at his son now who shut down again. He managed to break through a little by little but knew Luke still held back. But he felt a little hope, as Luke pulled up behind his Blazer.

"Nine tomorrow good for you, son," he replied, as he got out of the truck.

Luke nodded. He watched him pull away. He noticed no cars around just his Blazer. He walked in and was greeted by Bryan, so he fixed him something to eat. Then he fixed himself a crab sandwich and glass of milk.

"Well, little boy, I'm sixty-five today, and everyone left me except you," he whispered Bryan.

Meow, as Bryan looked up at him.

"Hey, Daddy," Susan said, as she stood in the doorway of kitchen. "You didn't think I would forget my Daddy's birthday. Did you?"

"But there aren't any cars out front except mine," he answered back. "I thought you, all, left for the day."

"Now we didn't get everyone here, but we did our best Daddy in the whole wide world," she said in low voice. "But we had to get more food for a man who turned sixty-seven today."

"But ..."

"How could I forget your birthday, Babe," Carly said, as she stood next to Susan. "Come on, we have cake and presents in the living room."

"Oh, we didn't forget the milk, Daddy," Susan added with a smile.

He smiled and carried his crab sandwich and glass out to the living room. He scanned the room to see his siblings, niece, nephews, friends but most of all his family except for Rita, Tim and her children or his only grandchildren. He was so moved by it that he didn't fight back the tears. Meow.

"They remembered, Bryan," he replied, as he smiled at them now.

"Happy birthday to you," they, all, had begun to sing on key.

Then he blew out one candle, and Luke stepped forward to hand him a medium size box. Joshua stared at him briefly before he opened it.

"Thank you," he replied politely.

Luke nodded and stepped back. Susan danced a little, as Joshua opened the box. He saw drawings and handmade items in there.

"Mom found the box of all our birthday presents we made for you those years we were apart," explained Susan.

"I'll look at them all carefully then later," he replied with a small grin. "Do you guys mind if I finish my sandwich?"

"Well, you might have to fight for it," Carly answered, as she pointed down at their feet.

Bryan stared at the sandwich with shinny eyes. Then he glanced up at Joshua. Meow.

"I'll share, little boy," he replied to him.

He took a couple pieces of crab out and gave it to Bryan. Everyone laughed. The rest of the day was busy and onto into the night. Later Joshua stepped out onto the deck before sunset.

"Can I join you, Babe?" Carly asked politely.

"You've always loved the ocean view."

"Of course, and all my life," he answered with a smile back. "Thank you for everything."

"You're welcome. It's one of thing I remember most about you when we divorced. I guess that's why I kept the children away from it when we were on the run. But I know you are missing Rita and the kids. She's busy, you know."

"I know Luke Rogers talked about Alex. They were cellmates at the prison," he replied thoughtfully. "He hasn't told me why he killed Alex yet maybe tomorrow."

"You're going back there tomorrow," she said a little surprised.

"Yeah, Luke and me who seems to know the Warden and the prison, I noticed he showed a black wallet to the guard at the front grates."

"I know I noticed it, too, when I was with him one time," she said thoughtfully. "But he never told me about it when I asked. So I figured to leave it alone. It's coming."

He glanced out at the ocean, as the sun melted into it. It was colorful just like the sunrise. They stood there in silence. Bryan sat on the railing in front of him now.

"Hey, little brother, I've got to go now," Caroline said, as she stepped out onto the deck. "I hope you had a great day."

"I did. Thanks for the flannel shirt, Sis."

"Now you have a whole new wardrobe," she said with a bright smile.

"I love them, all."

"And the clipper ship, too?" asked Andrew.

"Yes. Did you build it?"

Andrew nodded. "I worked on it every chance I got since Christmas. You always wanted one for Christmas, but they could never afford it. Goodnight, little bro. It's nice having you back in our lives again."

"Same here," he replied with a big smile.

People walked out onto the deck to say their goodbyes while Carly and Bryan stayed with him. Luke only nodded and turned to head out. Carly hugged Joshua briefly, as they walked out to her car. He watched her drive away before he returned inside. He noticed the pile of shirts and cords stacked on the Oak table with a box of twelve years of forgotten birthdays. He smiled, as he stretched out on the couch. Bryan joined him. He closed his eyes and drifted off to sleep instantly.

The next morning Joshua watched another colorful sunset and fed Bryan. He wrote some notes on a legal pad that he could only understand. He looked up from the laptop Joan brought and showed him briefly how to use on the Oak table when Luke walked in. Luke looked tired, but he stood before the table without a word.

"We were over there to negotiate in '54, and Ike was afraid they may become communist like Japan and Russia," he informed him. "They started to trade food and other things which we thought possible military weapons or chemical warfare. But the leader was a man of peace and influenced by our revolutionaries like Washington, Franklin and Jefferson. Then it all started to fall apart in mid-'61 probably, my guess. War was there in late '63 when Kennedy wanted to pull us out. Some people believe the CIA and others were behind the murder of Kennedy. Your Grandma Sara followed his career as a Senator."

Luke nodded then tapped his watch. Joshua proceeded to close down the laptop. He kept his notes on getting on and off the computer nearby. They were written on the back of an envelope. He left everything on the table.

Luke headed for the door and waited for him. Joshua walked over to the couch. Bryan opened his eyes, so he petted him.

"Be a good boy now. You have everything you need," he replied to him then at Luke. "Can we play this in your truck?"

Luke nodded, as he took the CD. They headed out. So Luke popped it into the slot in the radio, as they pulled away from the house. It was CD of Jazz music and was a present from Luke. They headed back to Folsom Prison in silence except for the Jazz music. He watched Luke show his black wallet again before they headed in again. They waited for his friend now.

Older Luke walked in and sat down in front of Joshua this time. Older Luke stared at him. He seemed to want to say something, but Joshua had no clue as what it might be. Then Older Luke swallowed then cleared his throat.

"Alex said he got the upper hand on this old Vietnam veteran who was his father-in-law," Older Luke said finally.

"He went to the hospital."

"I know, I figured with his injuries that he did."

"You're lying," Luke said to Alex.

"No, I'm not. This vet fights like a girl I tell you the truth. He took my big brother from me and my Mom years ago," said Alex.

"What are you saying?" asked Luke.

"I tortured him and have destroyed his family. I hit home in the bastards family," Alex answered with excitement, "Despite what he did to me. It still hurts, but I'll get him back for it."

"You're not being very clear, Alex. Slow down and explain yourself."

"I had sex with his ex and his three daughters' one being my wife. Boy did it get him angry when I did that. I had my first taste of revenge and couldn't stop there," Alex explained proudly. "I took the final step and in for the kill."

"What did you do?"

"I went after our children or his grandchildren. They didn't fight it because I'm their Dad, you know. It hurt as I used it on the kids. But I thought of how sweet this revenge was," Alex answered with a big smile now. "I had him destroyed or so I thought. Then my wife or his daughter divorced me while I was heading for trial. I'll get my revenge on him for that. He won't escape it now."

"What do you mean?"

"I had relations with his other two daughters. Well, one of them is pregnant with my child. That's the ultimate torture for him. He'll look at the child and know I had a hand in its being here on this earth," he said squirmed in delight. "I don't care if I had to take six times, but all it takes is one time. This guy knew what and how to do it then."

He held his penis out of his pants for Luke to see him erect, as he spoke about it.

"You raped her," yelled Luke.

"I don't call it rape, man. What you guys might

have done in Vietnam might be but not me. What was it like fucking a woman or young girl from Vietnam? Is it different then woman and girls here?" Alex asked with excitement in his eyes.

"You don't know what torture is, Alex. And I never did a woman much less a girl over there," Luke answered in anger. "Do you want to know how to really torture someone? I can show you. Now put it away."

"That would be great. What do you need me to get for you?"

"I didn't think he would take me up on it," Luke said, as he stared at Joshua.

"Well, what happened next?"

"He got the supplies I suggested we would need. It surprised me how he got a rope, tape and homemade knife sharp enough to slice your finger off with a single swipe," older Luke answered, as he swallowed hard. "I tried putting him off, but he kept at it night and day in our cell. I convinced him to take my bed, and he was ever so eager. Then I couldn't stop after I bound his hands, legs and mouth. I begun to slice him, and he squirmed a little then a lot. I did a quick thrust to his heart, and I said this is for messing with my family. I told him this, as he was dying on the bunk. You saved my life in Nam. I owed you one."

"They said he knew his attacker or attackers," he replied thoughtfully.

"I owed you, Josh for that day in the jungle in December of '63," older Luke said seriously.

"That explains a lot."

"We killed over there to survive," older Luke said in a low but painful tone in his voice, as he spoke of the war.

"We, all, know how much your kids mean to you, man. He had taken great pleasure in how and what he did to Carly, Joan and Susan. He had no remorse of giving Carly and Joan the Date rape drug. He got off screwing them two, no he said three times before the drug started to wear off."

Older Luke breathed hard but continued to focus on Joshua.

"He did Susan six times," pointed out Joshua.

"I know because he didn't like the lifeless body, so he did away with the drug. He applied his home remedy that he used on his wife and dove in hard," older Luke said, as his color from his face went deathly pale. "He said it was the best sex he ever had his whole life and couldn't wait to get out of prison to get her again or maybe all three of them again and torture them somehow with his friend screwed them as many as times he felt like it."

Joshua glanced over at his son. Young Luke was stern, expressionless look on his face, as he sat there. He couldn't read what he was thinking or feeling, so he turned back to his buddy again. "But he went after his kids," pointed out Joshua.

"It was to get rise out of you and destroy his wife that she would be declared mentally unstable to raise their kids..."

"A mental breakdown," Joshua replied, as he tried to understand it.

Older Luke nodded. "Then she would blame you for everything."

"Wow!"

"I had to stop him, Josh. I was already in here for life, and I don't know how he got the supplies I suggested.

But he had to be stopped, Josh. I had to save your family like you saved my sorry ass back in Nam."

He nodded and silence fell on all of them. It had drained older Luke to recount those events, but the truth was out now. His son got to his feet and saluted older Luke, and waited for a return salute. So the older Luke returned, it after he stood face to face with young Luke.

"Goodbye, Joshua. Please don't come see me again," Luke said, as he glanced down at Joshua. "I asked the warden to notify you upon my death, so I could have a military funeral like Roger had. Will you make sure it happens, man?"

Joshua felt a knot in his stomach. He tried to find the words, but they, all, escaped him now.

"I needed the money for my Cancer treatments, so I robbed the bank. I didn't want to fight the government for more money. I'll probably make a month or two at the most. It's getting worse each day. I've seen and felt the changes in my body when it comes to eating lately. You're a great, loyal friend and brother, Joshua," Luke said with a weak smile. "It was an honor to serve with you despite what I said yesterday."

Luke offered his hand out to Joshua when he got to his feet quickly. Joshua hugged older Luke and allowed the tears glide down his cheeks now freely. He didn't care who saw him cry now for it didn't matter Luke was his friend and brother in a war they fought together in side by side.

"It..." Joshua started to say.

"I'm okay with dying, man," older Luke said, as he stared at him. "Cry now but not when I die for I'm going to a peaceful place called home. You know what I mean since you wore the crucifix around your neck with your tags all through Nam."

Older Luke turned and walked away from them. Joshua turned to his son now.

"You're named after him, son."

Luke nodded. Then Joshua headed out of the prison and glanced back at the walls, as they stood at Luke's truck. He shook his head and climbed in. He thought of Trevor, Roger, Steve and now Luke, as he gazed out the closed window.

"I need to explain to the family why he killed Alex," he replied, as he glanced briefly over at his son.

Luke nodded, as he drove Joshua home. He spent time alone with Bryan. Luke had driven off without a word but handed him the CD back. Joshua turned on his handheld radio to find that the prison didn't know who or why Alex Walters was killed.

So he sat on his deck with Bryan in his lap to watch the ocean and hear the sounds around the area all so familiar to him. He found peace in it more than six decades now.

It tamed his restless heart and soul, and it was one of things that had power over him like that. But it was the first, and Carly's singing voice of "Ava Maria". He discovered it, as he followed her into church before they were couple. Joshua needed this calmness now.

23

Henry paced the floor, as Joshua walked up with Carly on his left hand Luke on his right. Joshua noticed Henry's pacing which meant he was nervous about something. But Joshua brought the people he requested without question. He trusted Henry.

"We're here, buddy," Joshua replied back. "Now what's up?"

"Uh...I heard you're into poetry," Henry answered back in hesitation.

"Oh, not another one of Robert's poetry readings," he snapped back. "I make one reference to a favorite poem of my Mom's, and now everyone thinks or believes I'm into poetry."

"Joshua, hear Henry out," Carly said calmly. "He must have his reasons for this."

He shot her a quick look now.

"Please," she said, as she touched his face with her left hand, "For me."

"Okay for you," he replied back. "So why is Robert in a hospital?"

"It's not Robert from our unit," Henry answered honestly.

"I only know of one Robert," he snapped back.

"No, you know, at least two. You and Luke heard me talk about him," Henry corrected him.

"The lone survivor of his unit," pointed out Luke.

"Yes, Luke," Henry said with a small smile. "You

remember how I mentioned him."

Luke nodded.

"Come this way, please hurry. He's about to start," Henry said, as he rushed to a big open room.

They followed him and stopped in the doorway.

"Bobby, you're up," a man said in a white lab coat.

A man had an arm in a sling struggled to walk to the podium, and he wore a black eye patch over his left eye. The first man unfolded Bobby's paper and stood beside him now.

"She was my moon and my stars. She was my sun which shined ever so bright she was. Then one day she had only memories of her and him. I was wiped clean from her memory," Bobby read out loud.

He cleared his throat but didn't look up. Joshua heard Carly gasp next to him. Her mouth was covered, and her eyes were larger than usual.

"Or so I thought was the case. But I saw her and she gave me hope by what she said. So I wanted to stay with her but then he arrived. I fled like a rabbit with my emotions and memories twisted in knots. No one pierced my heart and soul like she has. I'll wait for her to come back to me if I'm meant to be with her. This ache I find in me is so unbearable at times. How could she not know how I feel about her?"

Silence filled the room now. Bobby struggled to fold the paper back up, so the man helped him. Then Bobby returned to his chair.

"Mom, are you okay?" Luke asked in a low voice.

"I'm fine, son. Where's the ladies' room?" she asked Henry.

"Uh...that way," Henry answered, as he pointed behind them, "On your left."

"Thank you," she said politely. "Please, excuse me."

She headed in that direction. Joshua turned to Henry.

"What?" Henry asked him.

"Who is this guy? I know you said he was the lone survivor of his platoon. I get it, but there's more to it. Tell us now."

"He came from a wealthy family. He married shortly after he coming home but not to the same girl he left behind," Henry started to explain.

"Who was she?" asked Luke.

"His high school sweetheart," Henry answered, as he focused on him now.

"She was me years ago before I met your Dad. I loved him, and I was so happy to be with him. But then he came back six months after your Dad from Vietnam," Carly said sadly. "He changed over there and wasn't the same man I loved. I broke off the engagement and moved on with my life. Dad said he married and had family years later. I didn't want to know more. I had your Dad and your kids. I was happy. What happened to him, Henry?"

"Exposure to Agent Orange in the worse possible way, Trev was like him in a lot of ways. It's how it affects people," Henry answered thoughtfully.

"Why did you bring us here?" asked Joshua.

"I've been in touch with him on and off for decades. I know his son Richie's godfather and I were talking to Bobby of our talk about Vietnam. He said how he would like to see you again," Henry answered, as he stared at them all especially Carly now.

"But why did I have to be here?" asked Carly.

"That's the interesting part," answered Henry. "He pulled out photos of his kids and grandkids then he showed me another photo."

"Of, who?" she asked in her eagerness.

"You, he said you were the one who got away, the great and true love of his life. Yes, he married, but he didn't love Sabrina like he loved you, Carly. He's dying."

Carly had tears in her eyes now. She stared at Joshua then Luke then back into the room.

"Go to him, Carly," whispered Joshua.

She glanced up at him. He nodded, so she started to walk in but reached out for his hand. He followed her, as she took his hand. Her hand was moist in his, and she squeezed it harder when they reached Bobby. Bobby sat there with his head down now.

"Robert," Carly said, as her voice begun to crack slightly.

His head shot up and gazed into her eyes. Joshua felt like a third wheel and tried to leave. But Carly held tightly to his hand.

"My love, my sweet love," Bobby said, as his eye danced with excitement.

"It's been a very long time," she said, as she regained control again.

"How did..." Bobby tried to ask in his hesitation.

"I asked her to come, Bobby," Henry said, as he stood next to them with Luke at his side. "Well, I asked Joshua to bring her after you showed me that photo."

"You mean this one," Bobby said, as he pulled a photo out of his sling.

He held it out to them. Joshua noticed Carly's brown eyes and long brown hair which graced her shoulders and the smile that took his breath away years ago.

"Mom...you," Luke said a little surprised.

"It's my senior year photo. I hadn't looked like that in decades," she said back.

"You're still beautiful, Carly. You've aged gracefully unlike me. I'm falling apart," said Bobby.

"You lost your eye to...." Joshua replied in hesitation.

"Yes. It's one of many things from that damn thing did. Do you want to hear more?"

Joshua nodded.

"Let's go outside. Young man, fetch my wheelchair over there with the American flag on it. Please. Yes, I'm still a proud American despite what was done to me over there and experienced."

Luke walked over to the row of wheelchairs and walkers. He returned with the one with a flag. Henry and Luke helped Bobby into it.

"Out there, young man," Bobby said, as he pointed to the glass doors.

"Yes, Sir," Luke said politely.

They, all, followed them out into the mid-day sun. He motioned them to sit at a table with chairs and an umbrella. Luke locked the wheels and stood near his Mom now.

"He looks a lot like you, Joshua, but I also see Carly

in him, too," Bobby said, as he cleared his throat. "Take this son along with this." He reached into his sling again and held out the two photos. "It's of us before I was shipped out to Vietnam. Remember the purple streak you had in your hair."

Bobby stared at Carly now. She nodded and still held Joshua's hand in hers.

"I didn't see it at the diner but at church. I followed you to church one Sunday morning," Joshua replied. "I couldn't believe my eyes or ears, as you did your solo."

"It took your breath away when she sang "Ava Maria,"" commented Bobby.

Joshua nodded. "But I also felt a calmness I hadn't felt in awhile. I noticed the streak as I listened."

"I didn't know," Carly said, as she stared at Joshua now. "You never said anything. I was protesting the war to bring our troops home plus the women nurses over there. Dad was angry about the streak. It was one of two times I stood up against him."

"But you didn't say that you didn't want me to go," pointed out Bobby.

"I cried hard when you left. I missed you so much that I knew I would. So I did the purple streak against the war not you, guys, over there and him," Carly explained seriously.

"You said it was the first time. What was the second time?" asked Henry.

"When I was falling in love with this guy here, Dad and Harry, my big brother, didn't like his silence," she answered, as she squeezed Joshua's hand. "They didn't know much about him only he served in Vietnam and loved the ocean. Mom liked him from the start since she loved milk and me."

"So you were different than me," Bobby said to Joshua. "You won her heart, and I lost the best thing to ever happen to me. You're lucky to have her."

"I have to admit something to you, Robert," Carly said, as she repositioned herself in her chair.

"Sounds important," Bobby said with interest and focused on her now.

"You scared me when you came home. You weren't the same man in the photo, but you were mean and rude. I feared for my very life."

"That's why you called off the engagement. I was angry you did that to me, but I had time to realize what a SOB I was to you. You had every right to leave me. I'm sorry, truly, sorry, Carly," Bobby said, as he cleared his throat again. "I noticed you weren't the same girl I left behind that day at the bus station. I had lost you to something or someone. I felt it in my gut. I hid it in my anger."

"So the poem was written for my Mom," Luke said in a soft voice, as he held the photos.

"Yes. When I didn't see her again, I had to move on too, but I thought of you often. I didn't think I would see you again," he said, as he glanced quickly at Luke then Carly.

"What did she say to give you hope?" Luke asked him.

"If I ever got passed whatever this meaning, what I was going through, and we can sit down and talk like we used to," answered Bobby. "Now here we are four plus decades later."

"Talking like we used to do as teenagers and beginning of our adult life," added Carly. "I still care about you, but I had no idea you two had crossed paths."

"A fork in the road," replied Joshua.

"Who knew in Vietnam would bring us together," Bobby said, as he reached into his sling again. "Could you open this for me, young man?"

Bobby held out a bottle to Luke. Luke tucked the photos in his pocket and opened the bottle.

"Do you need water?" asked Henry.

"Got it," Bobby answered, as he grabbed a sports bottle attached to his chair. "I've got pancreatic cancer. This helps the pain a little. It's been a series of meds through the years. It's hard when your immune system is shot to hell. Thanks, young man."

Luke nodded.

"It's two of several things wrong with me. It's the change in drugs that has kept me alive this long. My body is breaking down slowly and painfully at times. Yes, I'm dying, sweet cookie. I'm sorry to tell you this way."

"You've always been blunt when it came to uncomfortable situations, or you were like that in the past. But you know, somehow I think, you're back to the man I once knew before the war," Carly said thoughtfully.

"Excuse me," the man said, as he stood next to the table.

"Yes, Randy," Bobby said back.

"Did you take your meds?" asked Randy.

"Yes, and I would like to stay with them longer."

"No can do, man," Randy said back. "Sorry, guys, you need to come back later."

"Damn I knew shouldn't have taken it," Bobby said in frustration.

"You know what's coming up, man," commented Randy.

"Oh crap! I forgot."

Randy rushed over and unlocked his brakes quickly then rushed him by them. They were moving pretty fast. Joshua got to his feet and so did Carly. She looked concern and still held his hand in hers. Bobby and Randy headed into a room across the hall. Another man walked in with a nurse.

Carly clung to Joshua and her face was colorless now. He knew she was worried. He held her close, too. He glanced over at Henry and Luke. They stood like statues and locked on the closed door.

"What do you mean I can't see him now?" a man dressed in a three piece suit asked a nurse at the front desk. "He's my Dad."

Henry walked over to him now and placed his hand on the man's shoulder. The man stared at Henry then back at the nurse.

"I'm sorry," the man apologized to her.

Henry guided him away from the desk and over to rest of them. The man stared at Carly, but she didn't look at him. Joshua felt tightness around his ribs and lower back now.

"Everyone, this is Richie, Robert's son," Henry introduced him. "Joshua, here..."

"Served with Henry and my Dad," Richie

interrupted him. "You must be Carly who broke his heart years ago." He glanced over at Luke. "And you must be her son."

Luke nodded.

"My parents have been divorced roughly forty years but remained friends since," Richie said coldly.

"I have to say this," Carly said, as she loosened her hold on Joshua, "Except for white hair at the temples, you look like your..."

"Dad," Richie interrupted her. "I know my grandfather had the white at the temples. I know firsthand how William and Harry must have felt in their parent's marriage. Mom knew she wasn't you. Does Dad still have those photos?"

Richie turned to Henry now. Randy walked out of the room. He looked sheepish now, but he walked up to Richie.

"Oh, crap, not again!" Richie exclaimed back. "How long did this one last?"

"A couple days, we thought at first it was the heat, but we don't think so now," explained Randy. "He's tired now, but you can see him."

"Get these people out of here," Richie snapped back coldly, "Now."

Richie headed for the room. Randy stared at Carly, Joshua, Luke and Henry.

"I'm sorry that I have to ask you to leave," Randy said in a low voice. "I'll call you later, Henry. You know how he gets. My hands are tied."

"I understand, Randy," Henry said calmly. "Let him know we'll be back soon."

"Will do," Randy said with a small smile. "Richie is a brat spoiled brat."

"But he loves his Dad," pointed out Carly.

"Bobby didn't show signs or symptoms until about twenty years ago. Doctors didn't link it to his time over there," said Randy.

"What did they think it was?" asked Joshua.

"His lifestyle," Randy answered calmly. "Please, excuse me."

Joshua nodded. Luke stood at attention, as Randy left. Henry walked down to the room.

"I think we should go now," he replied to her.

She nodded and headed out. Luke followed in beside her. So Joshua followed them. They stepped out into the warm air.

"Uh...Josh," Carly said in hesitation. "I know, Henry told you and Luke about Robert being alone in that village. I would like to know about it."

"Of course," he replied back.

"Could Luke drive us back to your place?" asked Carly.

"Sure," Joshua answered back. "Maybe we can stop at The Tides."

"I don't think I can eat anything," she said sadly. "But if you and Luke want to stop, I'll watch you two guys eat."

"Luke, you'll need these and decide whether you want to stop or not. No pressure, son," he replied, as he held out his keys.

"Fuzzy," Carly cried out. "You still have him after all these years."

"I found him in some stuff I had in my hall closet."

She slipped the bear off the key ring and handed the rest to Luke. Then she slipped into the backseat. She kept the door open.

"Come sit with me, Josh."

He slid in next to her, as she still held Fuzzy. She managed to squeeze him, as he reached to close the door.

Luke slide behind the wheel and pulled out.

"I gave Fuzzy to your Dad when I found out I was pregnant with Patrick," she explained a little happier now. "I didn't know the sex of the baby nor did I care. But I wanted to tell your Dad but didn't know how. So I put Fuzzy on his dinner plate."

"You said there were two bears but not anymore," Joshua replied back. "It took me by surprise, but it was always happy with each announcement of you, kids."

She snuggled up closer to Joshua, as Luke drove on. Luke slipped a CD into the player, so Jazz filled the car now. Carly closed her eyes and held Joshua's hand loosely into hers with Fuzzy. They stopped at The Tides for a pint of clam chowder each before they headed back to his place. He fed Bryan, as Luke kissed his Mom bye then left in his truck.

Carly managed to find an appetite again. So Joshua was glad that they had pint of clam chowder each. She smiled again. He felt warmness deep in his heart now. She wanted to rest a little while before she headed home.

So Joshua took the couch and let Carly have his room. He didn't want to her or himself use the guest room. She kept staring at Fuzzy. He didn't have the heart to ask for it back. She held the bear close to her face, as she drifted off to sleep. He stretched out on the couch and fell into a comfortable sleep.

A couple days later, they were back with Bobby or Robert. Luke walked up to the nurse. Joshua and Carly waited in the hallway. Carly held his hand, as she looked down the hall impatiently.

"What are you thinking, Carly?" he asked in a low voice.

"I broke two men's hearts," she answered back thoughtfully. "First Robert's then yours. Now I'm face to face with you both again. Why?"

"Why, what Mom?" Luke asked, as he rejoined them.

"Later, Honey. Can we see him?" she asked, as she stared at him.

"He's on new meds and is now bedridden. His room is down this way," Luke answered calmly. "Randy is with him. But he can't keep solids down, so he looks worse than the last time you saw him, Mom."

"Thank you," she said, as she kissed him on the cheek. "Let's go see him."

Luke nodded and took her free hand into his. They, all, walked side by side down the hall. They stopped at his room. Luke knocked on the open door. Randy turned to face them.

"It's Carly," Randy said to him. "She's not alone."

"Get out!" Bobby yelled in a weak voice. "I don't want her to remember me this way."

Carly drew in a deep breath and exhaled. She had let go of their hands now, as she marched deeper into the room.

"I'm not going anywhere, Robert James Parker," she said firmly and confidently. "You're going to hear me out, so shut up and listen to me good. I'm not going to repeat it."

She stared at the bed. Then she looked back at Luke and Joshua as if trying to find strength from them or something. Joshua wasn't sure.

"Well, get your butts in here, gentleman. I don't have all day," she snapped at them.

They walked in, and Carly stepped towards the window then turned around to face the bed again.

"I had a hand in breaking your heart Robert years ago. But you came back from Vietnam different. I saw no love in those eyes of yours only hate and mistrust. You told me how I must have been unfaithful to you when you were over there fighting for our country. I denied it, but you didn't listen to reason. So if I broke your heart, I'm sorry, but you broke mine with what you accused me of. I've grown up a lot since August of '64. Many of you didn't come home. You and Josh were the lucky ones." She paused for a time, as she was collecting her thoughts then plugged back in. "Life has changed me and a lot of things have happened around me and to me since last year, too. I don't like how it all came about, but everything happens for a reason. Maybe you and I can find closure or final closure. I'm not going to be blamed for your failed marriage either. Richie, can go to hell. I'm no Camellia Parker Bowles. Set him straight on that fact, Robert. You owe me this much. I asked why to that man over there why I broke two men's hearts. I think I know my answer now."

She faced the window again. Joshua stared at her,

as she folded her arms in front of her.

"You were my young love, Robert," she said, as she faced him again. "I don't think it was meant to last. Why else would I walk on a beach with a man I hardly know? A man who made me felt valued but most of all cherished. A man I stood up against Harry and Dad for. I would break his heart, too, by betrayal. I slipped up that one time, and I've regretted ever since. I ran like a wild jack rabbit with his children not waiting to see if he had calmed down. This man has stood by his family and my side through all our hell and only wants to know why I ran with his kids. I can honestly say I know, this man despite he had only said he wanted a wife and family on a beach. It was enough for me. You wanted to buy me a big house in the Hamptons away from our families and friends. You brought me expansive things including my engagement ring a two carat diamond ring. Was it necessary? That man didn't have an engagement ring to give me the night he proposed. He didn't have a string quartet either. We dropped a nickel in a candy machine and a small ring appeared at the hole. I was happy with that until he slipped a small diamond ring on my finger a couple days later."

She stopped to catch her breath and dove back in. "I understand his anger now, but I didn't at first. But we talked it out. But you had no cause for your feelings, bucko. I'm done. I'm out of here, Robert."

She headed toward Joshua and Luke.

"Carly, wait," Bobby said in a weak voice.

She faced him now with a serious look on her face now. But she was also drained, too, and Joshua could read it on her face. He knew not to stand in the way of this. This was her moment, and he had respected it because he still loved her.

"I'm sorry, too. I can make all kinds of excuses for what I said to you, but none would be the whole truth. I didn't trust you. You were right about what I did when I brought you expansive things. I wanted to win you over with all that because that's how my Dad was with my Mom. I thought all women wanted that," Robert said in a hoarse voice. "But you didn't. You didn't complain about it either really. You only said it was too expensive, and I would tell you that you were worth every penny of it. But it wasn't my money but my family's money that got you those expansive things. You came from working class, and I was forcing you to live in my world. I didn't belong in your world despite we had gone to same schools. My Mom wanted me to mix with other kids not rich like us. That's how we met. Remember? I wish, I could change the past, but I can't do it now. It's done like you said. You're right our marriage wouldn't have lasted a year. I can see it now."

Robert stared a Joshua now. Joshua glanced back at him. Robert looked like he was about to die. Joshua knew a dead man's face before over there. Now he saw it in Robert. Death was coming quickly for the man. He had only this chance to say what he wanted to say before he never got to ever say it again. Joshua knew this for sure. War taught him this fact. Joshua let out a small sigh.

"You won her true heart, man. I thought I knew her. But I think I only saw the things I could change in her. Thank you for bringing her back, man. Go now and don't come back," Robert said to him. "Take good care of her. She's a remarkable woman that I don't even know."

Carly walked out of Robert's room, and Luke and Joshua followed close behind her without a word. They reached outside before she crashed into Joshua's chest and cried.

"Here I thought you didn't know why, but you found it within yourself," he whispered to her.

"I couldn't have done it without you," she said, as she looked up at him. "You know me better than any man I've ever known. I meant every word I said about you in there. This family doesn't realize how lucky we are to have you in our lives. Your family doesn't realize it either. But you bet they will find out soon enough if they haven't already begun to see what I see in you."

"Your Mom is pretty special woman, Luke," Joshua replied, as he glanced over at their son.

Luke stood there and watched them exchange words and embrace. She glanced over at him.

"Does this surprise you, Luke?" she asked him.

Luke gave no reply back. She walked over to him and took him aside. He shoved his hands in his pockets, as he listened. Joshua couldn't make out what she was saying to him, so he walked away.

"Have you ever been in love before?" Carly asked him, as they walked on the beach.

He shook his head, no.

"What do you want out of life?" she asked him.

"A wife and a family," he answered, as he stopped to stare at the crashing waves. "What do you want out of life? What does Carly want out of this life?"

"Pretty much the same as you with a devoted and loving husband and at least four kids since I come from a family of two, kids. How about your family? What do they expect from you?"

"My family isn't important. Yours is and you," he answered back. "Do you want a college education or career?"

"My... no one ever asked what I wanted like that," she answered in surprise. "You're someone special Joshua Hernando, and I would like to get to know you if you'll let me."

"I want to know more about what you want and believe in, Carly," he replied back. "I'm not important here. You are."

"But..."

"I mean it," he interrupted her. "Isn't this breath taking and so peaceful which makes you want to stay right here forever?"

"Do you want to?"

"Want to what?"

"Live here at the ocean," she answered back.

"It would be nice."

"Hey, where you are at, Joshua?" Carly asked, as she brought him back into the present. "You seemed so far way there."

"Just remembering things and how they used to be," he replied with a small grin. "I suppose you, guys, are ready to go home now."

"Yeah, he has some work to do. He won't tell me what, so I have to leave it at that," she said with a smile back.

They headed back to his Blazer. She climbed in and stared at him.

"Like what?" she asked him.

"Our first date on the beach," he answered back. "I was getting to the part where I was going to ask what your career goal was."

"We know what I said to that, right?"

"Librarian, you told me on our first date then again on the beach when we celebrated your first night of retirement."

She nodded and smiled at him.

24

"How can you stand it?" Luke asked in a harsh but demanding voice, as he stared at Joshua now.

"What, Luke?" he asked calmly back, as he placed Bryan's bowl on the floor.

"Stare death in the face and not be changed by it," Luke answered, as he fixed his gaze on him.

"Is that what you faced in your war, son?" he asked, as he gave Luke his full attention now. "You only reveal the depths of your heart and soul through your music because it's safe."

Luke blinked his eyes but held his deep gaze no less. "I lost something over there. I can't get it back ever again."

"Your innocence," replied Joshua.

"How...di..." Luke said in hesitation.

"Your song that you sang in my hospital room, you said it was dedicated to me and my fellow Vietnam vets. But I think, it was also for you, son. You don't talk about your war either," he interrupted him. "Can I tell something, Luke?"

Luke nodded.

"I didn't know it was missing in me, too. I went through years of not knowing until one day it hit me. It hit me smack damn in my heart and soul. I heard your song Luke, and it touched me like nothing before. After Alex's trial, I found I was remembering part of your song admitting loss of innocence. Your sister Rita had lost hers that day in the courtroom. I couldn't help her because I lost mine in back Nam," he explained. "I take it that you lost yours in Desert Storm after you got shot down."

Luke nodded again.

"Do you want to talk about it, son?"

"Tell me about yours first," Luke answered, in a soft voice now but on the verge of cracking at any second.

"Let's go outside on the deck then," he replied, as he left the kitchen.

Luke headed out and walked up to the railing. Joshua glanced back at the bathroom. Kim stood there in silence. He put his finger to his lips before he headed out. She nodded. So he cleared his throat before he joined Luke there on the deck. Luke glanced at him.

"I guess it left me shortly after I got there. I could hear fighting off in the distance, and my platoon had to replace another platoon's position in the battlefield. It rained a lot of the days, weeks and months ahead. We didn't know it then," he explained, as he stared back at Luke then out at the ocean. "I was good at distance shooting, so I was known as the sniper of the platoon."

"That's why you were out ahead when your unit was attacked."

"Yes, but that's stepping ahead of what we faced in the beginning."

"Sorry, Sir."

"It's, okay, Luke. I'm not good at explaining things. Sometimes I guess I shut down emotionally a lot after your Grandma Sara gave up on me. Then I struggled with your Mom and you, kids, all because of what I experienced over there."

"War isn't pretty or glamorous like some people are led to believe especially World War Two and your war for that matter possible Korea as well," added Luke.

"Exactly and definitely not like Hollywood's versions of war, they don't show the public through the eyes of a true soldier, as he stands face to face with someone else."

Luke nodded in agreement. Joshua caught out of the corner of his eye, so he pressed on.

"You have a split second decision to live or die. Will you be the lucky one to see another sunrise, another ocean or another colorful sunset?"

"Or see someone you care about and maybe even love? The possibility of never telling them what you should have said instead of what you did say."

"Yes, then a sound rings out, and you believe you're going to die with all those things running rapidly through your mind. It's all unclear since it's so fast. But then you see him go down before you and realize it was him not you who got shot. You're standing there with your finger on the trigger of your assault weapon. You made it through this time, but you wonder how long will your luck will last. So you bury innocent victims like the elderly, women and children in hopes to change what you've done. In hopes to make it right and maybe among the dead will be one who can or will survive. You saved one life for the one you took who was a son maybe a brother maybe even a father or all, three. But you don't know for sure."

"Is that what happened to you, Sir?" Luke asked him.

"Yes, and now what about you, Luke? You were in the air."

"I was shipped out after Brittney was born. Albert went ahead to fight and planned to marry Kim when he got home," Luke answered calmly, as he faced Joshua now. "I convinced my CO to let me stay State side long enough to see my baby born. If I died over there, I know I hadn't died in vein because I would know I had seen him or her at least once."

"But Kim...."

"We were both virgins and just came off a horrible twelve hour shift. I would like to believe in that brief moment Kim and I created Brittney. We never told Albert about it, so Kim announced she was pregnant. I hesitated, and he stepped up to the plate. He admitted to having sex with her more than once around the same time."

"So you backed down, and let him take Kim and possibility your child away from you forever."

"Not forever, Sir," Luke continued on. "I didn't think we would ever be in a true war. Albert wanted to go to college and study computers, so he signed up and was ready and willing to serve. He believed Hollywood's version of war. As Kim got bigger, I had to tell my story to my CO, so I was held back. But when I got over there, saw and talked to Albert. I even showed him an early photo of Brittney."

Luke stared back at the ocean and shook his head. Meow. Bryan stood before them on the railing. So Luke stroked him briefly before he clasped his hands before him.

"He had seen combat already. He had a look in his eyes and written over all face I didn't know or recognize him at first. But then he went crazy with anger and jealousy I never saw in him before. I told him how he was no friend of mine then he hit me hard on the back for no real damn reason."

Luke paused, as he played with hands now and seemed to be in deep thought.

"What happened next?"

"I hit him back then boarded my plane and left. The last words I said to him were "You are no friend of mine." He wasn't the same guy I knew. I didn't understand it until I got shot down behind enemy lines. I was the only one who survived the crash. I crawled out since I injured my leg on impact. When I was able to stand, I stood face to face with the enemy, and I only had a knife and a handgun on my waist. Then it's like you said in a rapid motion everything goes before your eyes at alarming rate. I thought of Albert, and what I said to him that last time we were together," Luke answered sadly. "I haven't told Kim that I saw him over there. I don't want her to remember him that way. She needs to hold onto the fun, caring and loving man that we both knew before war entered our lives."

"But how did you know about loss of innocence?" Joshua asked with a deep interest now.

"I saw my reflection in the mirror at the camp I was in. I looked like he did that last time saw him just before he attacked me."

"But you said..."

"Yeah, I killed the man in front of me which caused more of them to surround me. They were checking for any and all survivors of the down plane. I was outnumbered by five to one. It wasn't good odds at all. Then I thought of you when I was boy. I surrendered peacefully. But I got to the camp and couldn't forget you since you had seen combat, too just like us. Suddenly, I understood what had happened to Albert, too. Then I had remorse of what I had said to him that last time. So I decided to break out and risk getting captured again or being killed this time. But I had to back to our side and find him again. He was and is my best friend. We connected that first day we met. I know Mom didn't want us to make friends while we were running from you. But she stopped when he and I became friends."

"Did you?"

"I barely got out with my injured leg. Then I was captured again since I was dressed in clothes of the enemy."

"What did you do?"

"I had to show my tags and was lucky someone had recognized me or the name. So they sent me to the nearest hospital. There I asked for the chaplain to help me locate him, but I was a week too late. He was killed in combat, and his body or remains were being shipped State side," Luke said with tears in his eyes now. "I never had a chance to take it all back. I loved him like a brother. So I've kept it to myself ever since. I gave up being an EMT because I couldn't help him. So how could I help others?"

Joshua placed his hand on Luke's shoulder, but Luke didn't pull away this time.

"You find something deep inside yourself that gives you what you need to do. I did it that day in Nam, and people hail me as a hero," commented Joshua.

"But you have always said you did what you had to do."

"Yes, I have."

"I think I'm beginning to really understand you, now. I saw a distant man as a boy. I turned thirteen when you and Mom divorced, and I thought of how you could do a lot of different things. You were pretty amazing in my eyes. Then I started to do the same thing, but I found I could help people in medicine."

"So you studied to become an EMT."

"Exactly, Sir."

"Then things changed, but you have to listen to me now, son. I spent twelve long, hard years to get to be a part of your guy's lives again. I was angry in the beginning but learned to control it in time. But I realized something along the way and just recently as well, too. You're in charge of your own destiny so when you turn your back on your true calling then you're truly lost. You're losing who you are meant to be."

"Were you always this open as a child?"

"No. As a matter of fact, I can't recall ever saying I love you to my Dad, my whole life. I could say it to my Mom. But it was different with my Dad."

"Did he ever say it to you?"

"No. I don't think so. He spent more time with your Uncle Andrew than me. I learned a lot by watching them at a distance. I kept trying things until I mastered it with a degree of success. It wasn't always easy to do on my own. But I never gave up."

"I have to go now," Luke said, as he glanced at his watch. "But I'm glad we really talked about you know what."

"Me too, Luke," he replied with a big smile. "The

door will always be open anytime day or night for you."

Luke nodded and headed back inside and out the front door before Kim stepped onto the deck. She had Bryan in her arms now, and she had been crying.

"I had no idea," she whispered. "Did you?"

"About his experience in the war or with his friend Albert or your fiancé?"

"All of it."

"Carly said so did his twin how he changed after he came home. He was or is a lot like me. I guess my wife or my ex-wife and children need to know what I experienced over there. Roger wanted to tell the kids at various times, but I wouldn't let him. I guess I wrong to do that."

"I remember the ground being wet and muddy but not the day you found me in the abandon village," Kim recalled thoughtfully. "It was a break in what seemed to be endless rain, sometimes. I can't remember why or how my mother died. At times I can't even remember what she even looked like."

"What about your biological father?"

"I can't even remember him at all. You were right to get me out of there, Joshua," Kim answered with a small smile. "I have a life because of you. I can't imagine what my life could have been if I stayed there. Thank you doesn't seem to be enough."

His face felt warm, and Kim stepped even closer to him. She released Bryan from her arms, as she touched Joshua's face. He hadn't let many women touch his face in his life. It was a small handful when he thought about it.

"You had seen death all around you, yet you also battled with something deep within your very heart and soul, too. But you reached out to me, and I looked into your eyes and wasn't scared anymore."

He stared at her before he spoke again. "You held my hand until you drifted off to sleep. You wouldn't leave me, so I gave up Frogger. I had him ever I was five until that day."

"You said Frogger would chase away the devil. I believed you then," said Kim.

"It has been a long day."

"We need to check that spot on your right lung," Kim pointed out.

"Another time, Kim," he replied back. "Please."

"Let's not wait too long. Okay?"

Joshua nodded and stepped away from her. He headed back inside and knew Bryan was at his side. Then he walked into his dark bedroom and went straight to his bed but sensed someone else in the room.

"Did you get anywhere with the government?"

"No, not yet," Kim answered back. "But I hope soon. I'm worried about you and others, you know."

"I know please see yourself out, Kim."

"I will. Thanks for letting me hear Luke. It helps me understand him a little better now. It's like when we heard his song. But I'll be touch. I know you're tired."

Joshua didn't reply back but heard her close the door. Then Bryan's purr filled the once noisy room now.

"Hush, little boy," he replied, as he stroked the cat's long but lean body now.

Bryan had grown considerably since they found each other. It was now mid-September, and Susan's baby was due any day now. She managed to bring the baby along this far without much problem. He pictured Carly in his mind now and smiled. So he drifted off to sleep now but thought of the following things.

Alex was no longer a threat to his family. Luke had come to him about his Desert Storm experience. He had shared with Luke his experience of Vietnam. Things were not the best in his world because Steve passed away in late August. Luke Rogers was dying alone in prison. He had talked to Jacob and wanted to know how he was doing.

It was a couple days ago when the warden finally told him that the end was near. So Kim coming over today was not the best time to harp on the spot on his lung. How can he worry about himself when one of his army buddies was facing death?

The other had gone in his sleep or so they said. He had his doubts. It wasn't Steve's way, but then he had to remember he was a lot calmer than he ever been that last time he saw him. So it was possible. He shook his head and drifted into a deeper sleep now.

25

"Dad wanted you to have them," Andrew said, as he held out two envelopes and a wooden box. "I couldn't bring myself to give them to you after Roger died. But a promise is a promise, so I pass on what Mom gave Dad to pass onto you on her death bed before the coma and his as well.

"What's in them?" Joshua asked him with a little interest.

"I know, they each wrote you a letter, but I didn't read them. It's between you and them. The box is Grandpa Adam's pocket watch which was a gift for his faithful service to Southern Pacific," Andrew explained carefully. "I have Dad's hunting knife. I leave you with those things now."

Andrew walked out of Joshua's front door. He heard the engine start and pull away. So he walked out onto his deck with Bryan at his feet when he opened the box. There a gold watch stared back at him. He lifted it up briefly before he returned it to the box. He placed his Mom's letter under it.

Yes, he noticed the difference in their handwriting. Dad's handwriting was in all caps to make his point or statement where Mom's handwriting had conveyed warmth, everyday life and less harsh. He opened his Dad's letter first and prepared for a lecture like he always remembered. But these first words hit him hard, so he read them again:

My son Joshua,

I have lived without your mother since early 1964. Now less than forty years have passed by, and you're home from a war I still don't understand. I haven't made any effort to ask you what you experienced over there either. But it was a different war then the one I fought in or took part in, son.

I have had opportunities to make my peace with you, but i still can't bring myself to do it. I was hard on you more than Andrew because I knew you were better than us both combined. Andrew and I needed to be pushed into making something of ourselves. I had to give up my dream and didn't know what to do. But you didn't need this push because you found your own way or path early on.

I followed your life from the first day you returned home. I heard about your marriage to Carly and my grandchildren Patrick, James, Susan, Luke, Joan and Rita. You worked in construction, putting up fences, a brick layer and laid carpet, but you were also a best friend, too. I saw your marriage end and the fights that followed it.

Yet, you managed to hold your friend's life together while you searched for your family. You wanted them back because they are your anchor, Josh. You drifted in and out of jobs to help your friend while you searched for them. You needed them to feel whole and sane despite the craziness your friend added to your life.

Your Mom was my anchor. I didn't want to admit to her or to you or anyone else in this whole wide world. She was stronger than me mentally. You watched me work with Andrew and learned from it. But you had the mental and physical strength very early on. I saw it when you were only a small baby. You had something I lacked in me, Josh.

I'm proud of the man you have become. You're everything I wanted to be, but I was too damn scared to take a chance. But not you weren't afraid to take chances since you always jumped in with both feet sort of speak. I hope, you will be your anchor again, son. I know, I didn't say it to you, but I will say it now. It's been long overdue, son, and I'm truly sorry for that. I can't reverse the damage I caused you by not saying it. I love you, Josh, with all my heart and soul. Please forgive me in your heart, son.

Love,

Dad

Joshua folded it up and placed it back into its proper envelope. He wiped away the tears from his eyes. He glanced out at the ocean and breathed in the fresh, clean and cool air deep into his weak lungs now. He still didn't have that spot on his right lung checked out, yet. He kept putting it off, so Kim stopped bothering him about it. But he noticed a change in his body since he had been told about that spot. Luke Rogers was gone, too now, but Rita was back in his life again.

"Dad, are you home?" Rita asked, as she walked into the house, "Dad."

He turned to face her and smiled. She walked up closer to him. He held out his arms to her. They embraced a lot now since she had come back into his life.

"I love you, Rita, with all my heart and soul and don't you ever forget it either," he whispered into her ear.

"You've been crying, Dad. Why?" she asked, as she examined his face closer now.

"Your Grandpa Martin loved me and was proud of me," he answered with a small smile. "Your Uncle Andrew gave me letters they wrote to me. I haven't read hers yet, but I just finished his when you arrived."

"Do you want me to read hers to you?" she asked with some interest.

"No, maybe later, but let me show you something. I used to admire it on your Grandma Sara's dresser as a kid. It belonged to your Great-Grandpa Adam. He worked the SP Railroad when times were hard and prior the great Depression," he answered, as he reached out for the box. He tucked his mother's letter into his pocket. "This."

"It's gorgeous, Dad," she said, as she stared at the gold watch.

She touched it lightly then smiled. His heart beat faster against his chest now. He couldn't believe how happy he was at this moment in his life. She cleared her throat before she spoke again. He gazed into her face now.

"We need to go, Dad. They'll be worried," she said rather calmly.

"Are you up to it?"

"Yes, I am, Dad."

"Then let's go, baby girl."

She nodded.

"Oh, baby girl, I have to say this," he replied, as they climbed into her minivan.

Rita stared back at him, as she slipped the car into reverse. "What's that, Dad?"

"I'm so proud of you with all what you had to face in this last year," he answered with a big smile.

"You mean with Alex, and what he did to my sisters, Mom and his own kids."

He nodded.

"You said I'm like Grandma Sara. It's not Susan's fault that Alex couldn't keep his zipper shut. Plus it's not yours either, Dad. You told the truth years ago of what his Brother did. But I still don't know how to deal with Martin as their half brother sometimes. But Jenny and Jordan adore him now, and I'll have to explain it to them someday. We'll cross that bridge when the time comes. We have to get to his baptism now."

He nodded again and pulled out his Mom's letter out of his pocket. He glanced over at Rita and smiled. Then he opened it. He readjusted his eyes and body in his seat, as he begun to read her letter. It went something like this:
My dearest youngest son,

I heard today that Kennedy was struck down in the prime of his life. Leaving behind a very young wife and two small children, I think, of you my dearest son, Joshua. You enlisted in a war that we don't understand, so your big brother could stay home and stay in law school.

You are sacrificing your life for your big brother. I lay awake at night and wonder if I had drove you into this damn war. I turned my back on you when you probably needed me the most. I said I wouldn't do that but I did. Lord knows I knew deep down you were trying to do your very best in school.

I did notice your grades picked up some, but I didn't tell you that I knew or how I noticed it, son. I was so proud of what you were doing, Joshua. You were standing firmly on your own two feet. You struggled with self-confidence right up to the day I turned my back on you. But you must have become self-confident as days, weeks and months and years after I did that to you. You are a better man than

Andrew could ever be. I know, he wouldn't want to hear that, but you do need to know this truth, my son.

I saw my Dad in you slowly emerge and knew you would be okay. You have his name as part of who you are, and what he stood for is in you, my dear son. I sense something is taking my body from me, your Dad, your brother and sisters but mostly you, Joshua. I can't explain it. So I've put it to pen and paper in hopes if I'm not here upon your return home that you will know how I feel about, my dear son.

I was wrong to say how disappointed I was in you. No parent should ever say or tell that to their child ever. I had no damn right to do that to you, Joshua Matthew Adam. I'm so very sorry my dear youngest son. I love you so damn much. It troubles me now to know what or how it will affect your life now and in the future.

I know, you will have a troubled life because of what I did to you, but you will also have a strong sense of what is right and wrong and a very big heart for family and friendships. It's who you are because like I said before. You are a lot like my Dad Adam. When you breath your last breathe know, I'll be waiting for you in heaven with open arms. You will have made a difference in this world far in this world far better than I ever did. This is your journey, my dearest, most cherished and loved son, Joshua Matthew Adam. I will always love you.

Love always,

Mom

"Dad, we're here," Rita said, as she leaned into the van now.

He folded it back up and tucked it back into his

pocket. He joined her and the rest of the family who gathered in the church. Carly looked even more beautiful each time he had seen or been with her in the last year. Susan looked a lot like her now.

"Grandpa," called out Jenny.

She rushed down the aisle to his open arms. He carried her up to the baptism font with a big smile.

"You seemed in very deep thought back there," Carly said with a bright, warm and friendly smile.

It warmed his heart, as he nodded back. "My parents loved me. So I have to ask you something rather important." He didn't wait for answer. "Do you still love me?"

"I never stopped but you know that," she answered quickly. "We can talk later."

"Dad, we decided to baptism him Martin Roger," said Susan.

"Why Roger?"

"He was your best friend," she answered with a small smile.

"Then add another name, too," Andrew said, as he stared at Joshua now.

"What?" Susan and Rita asked echoed each other.

"Adam," Carly and Andrew said calmly. "His great-great Grandpa and one of Josh are of two middle names."

"He looks like you when you were a baby," added Andrew. "So he deserves one of them at least."

"But..."

"Just nod your head and we'll talk later," Carly said calmly.

He nodded. Joshua didn't remember much after

that. He could only see and hear Carly. He knew what he had to do despite what this day was meant to be for, so he cleared his throat at the conclusion of the ceremony. He felt all eyes fixed on him now.

"Are we done here?" he asked politely.

"Yes, Joshua. What's on your mind, my son?"asked the priest.

"I know, I don't have the formal papers, but I can get them in a day or two," he explained, as he turned to Carly. "You and I spent years apart, yet we still love each other. I don't want to spend time sending you flowers and notes since I've been there and done it. Will you marry me again, Carly?"

"Yes," she answered with tears in her eyes.

"Father O'Brian, could you do the honors today?" he asked, as he gazed deeply into Carly's eyes. "I don't want to live another day without her."

"Yes, my son."

"But you don't have rings to exchange," Rita pointed out.

"Mine's here with my tags, baby girl," he replied back.

"And mine are here with the crucifix your Dad gave me years ago," Carly said, as she revealed them.

"The morning Patrick was born," added Joshua.

"I've been wearing it and the rings through all this. You told me to put my trust and faith in the Lord, and he will guide and help me. You were so wise back then and now, Babe."

"Let me get the book," said Father O'Brian.

"Can we speak our own vows this time?" she asked

him.

"Sounds good to me," answered Joshua.

"Whenever you're ready," said O'Brian.

"I do take you as my husband again. I will spend the rest of our lives loving and caring for you, Joshua Mathew Adam. No man ever held a candle to you either, my love. I love you, Joshua always," Carly said clearly.

"I do take you as my wife again forever. I love you, Carly Ann Peterson-Hernando always," he replied with a big smile.

Andrew took Carly's rings and handed them to Joshua. Luke slipped his Dad's ring over to Susan, so she and their sisters could hand Carly their Dad's ring.

"A family affair," he commented with a small chuckle.

"You marry us, all, Dad," Luke said with a small smile. "Not just Mom this time."

"And you marry into my family minus my parents," he replied, as he stared at his big brother, Andrew. "You, all, should have been there the first time, but you're here now."

"We were fools back then," said Elizabeth.

"But we are here now," Caroline said with a big smile, too.

"We have a much bigger celebration now," James said in delight.

They did party long and hard that night. Joshua held Carly in his embrace, as they watched colorful sunset together from the deck. Everyone seemed happy and at peace now.

EPILOGUE

A month later November of 2011, Rita filed the necessary paper work about Joshua's true age. She said it been a typo error that they only discovered recently. So they didn't question it because of who she was. The family learned Joshua had a learning disability, and Roger helped him secretly master reading and writing. He had gotten his high school diploma two years after coming home, but didn't tell anyone not even Carly or Roger.

Now six months later Carly is at Joshua's bedside. The oxygen mask covered his face, and his eyes were closed. But he knew she was there like she had been the last seven months.

"Carly," he replied, as he spoke through the mask.

"Yes, I'm here, Babe. Stay quiet," she said, as she combed back his bangs from his forehead.

He opened his eyes to gaze into hers and pulled the mask down. "I love you with all my heart and soul," he replied back.

"I know, and I love you, Joshua. Please take in the oxygen," she said, as her hand touched his with the mask.

"Are they, all, here?"

"Yes, but you need to rest, Babe. Please."

"Send them, all; in one by one in the order I listed. I want Rita and Luke to be second to last because the last is you, my love."

"Joshua."

"Please, my love."

"All right for you, Babe."

She left the room. He breathed in the oxygen, as he would talk to his brother and sisters. They were followed in by his children except Rita and Luke and his three grandchildren with his niece and nephews. All of them left with tears in their eyes. Rita walked in slowly and sat down next to him.

"You were first of my children to come see me," he replied, as he breathed in more oxygen.

"Dad, don't do this," she pleaded with him, as she fought back the tears.

"I have to go, baby girl," he replied back. "You will be stronger from this day forward because you will have me with you always. I'll be a part of you, my baby girl."

"Daddy."

"I love you. Now go get, Luke. Please," he replied, as he kissed her on the cheek gently.

She kissed and hugged him back one final time. She glanced back at him, as she walked out of the bedroom. He stared at the door when he saw Luke emerge there. Luke walked slowly over to the bed. Then Luke sat down tall and proud.

"My dearest son, Luke," he replied calmly. "You and I fought in wars that we never shared with people. There we have been united despite we haven't discussed it in detail like we should have, son." He drew in more oxygen. "No one tells you what you will face when you are face to face with someone on the battlefield. For a split second is all it takes to know your fate life or death, as you pull that trigger. You hope you did it before you feel the burning sensation in your entire body. Are you alive or dying?"

Luke blinked his eyes.

"In the drawer there is box, it was your Great-Grandpa's on your grandma's side. He worked hard for the SP as a plumber and was well respected," Joshua explained, as he took in more oxygen.

Luke opened the drawer and held the box before he opened it. He had a stern look on his face then glanced over at Joshua.

"I can't tell you much about my side of the family except Grandpa Martin served in World War Two and loved baseball. He wanted to make it a career but didn't. But by when Korean War came your Uncle Andrew and I were too young for war. So by the time Vietnam War came your uncle was old enough to fight, but I took his place as you well known. I sacrificed my life for his," he replied, as he drew in more oxygen.

"You had a forged birth certificate that said you were two years older than you were," Luke spoke calmly, "But why?"

Joshua nodded then pulled down the mask. "I thought I was a big disappointment to my parents then things changed."

"How?"

"Their letters, they're in the drawer, too. I want you to share them with the whole family. Will you do that for me, son?"

"Yes, Dad, but I have a letter of my own. I carried it with me all this time. Can I read it to you? It's from Roger days before he died," Luke said to him.

Joshua nodded, so Luke took out the paper and

cleared his throat.

"Dear Luke," he begun to read out loud. "You asked me why I call your Dad, my hero. He had not only saved me but our platoon." He paused for a moment or two before he continued on. "He's a modest man who has great strength, character and wisdom. I'm lucky to have him as a friend or my best friend. He has helped me countless times on the various roof tops through the years. You, your siblings and Mom had to deal with that. For that Luke, I'm truly sorry. You guys deserved to know and love him like I have during and after the war. He knows war, and what war does to a person. Talk to him, Luke. He does understand and wants to be a part of your life. Let him in Luke before it's too late."

Luke stopped and looked at him before he cleared his throat one more time.

"Yours truly Roger Clemens," Luke finished the letter. "No amount of training can prepare you for what you find on the battlefield."

"No, you walk away changed forever. You can't explain it to anyone who hasn't experienced it," Joshua replied back. "Find peace, Luke, and work through it but not alone. Promise me that."

"I promise, Dad. Dad, I love you. I never stopped all these years, and I wanted to tell you that ever since the day we talked about our wars. But I also held out hope you and Mom would get back together sooner or later," Luke said sadly. "But now..."

"I know, I'm blessed to have her, you kids and my siblings back in my life," he interrupted him. "No regrets or disappointments just love, forgiveness and understanding."

"And peace," added Luke.

Joshua nodded. The rest of the family filed in, as Joshua struggled harder to breathe. Carly went to his other side once again. Bryan had come up on the bed with a purr at his side, too.

"Remember me with a smile and know I love you, all, ever so very much," he replied, as he glanced around the crowded room. "This has been a decent life that I lead, and you're all a part of it."

He closed his eyes after that, and silence except for Bryan's purr was heard in the room besides the faint breathing of all who were there now. This was what he wrote years earlier, as he entered the Vietnam War which his son Luke found among his father's belongings after his death.

I don't enter this war to become a hero, but a man much like the fathers before us. I fight for the land I hold so dear to my very being to achieve freedom, peace and happiness. It doesn't matter if I have volunteered or was drafted into this war. I would do my duty for love of my country.

If I stand face to face with what they call the enemy, it will be our choice of who will live and who will die because you are not standing in our shoes at this moment in time. I ask you to not judge me for my actions I must make. I'm not a hero but just a simple man who answered the call to serve his country like so many other men had done before and after me will be asked to defend it. We may not speak of what we experienced in the war because some of us are just little boys inside a big body trying to make sense of it all. Nothing can or will prepare you for the day you will stand face to face with the other person. Your sweaty hand on your assault weapon and for a split second how all it can be lost forever along with your innocence of small child.

Joshua M. A. Hernando
August 14, 1962